Tony qualified in Law and practiced as a solicitor in his country of birth, South Africa before emigrating to Israel in 1961. Since then, after a stint on a kibbutz, he lectured at the Tel Aviv University and opened a chain of fast food restaurants and established a travel company specializing in incentive travel. The company won several international awards. For the last 34 years, as a highly respected trainer, he has conducted seminars in personal development and self-awareness in Israel, Turkey, the United Kingdom and around the world with his wife, Orit Josefi Wiseman in their company, Outlook. He has also been a coach and mentor, often dealing with issues pertaining to intimate relationships, which formed the basis of the book, Relationships I.Q., written together with Orit and published by Austin Macauley.

This book is dedicated to Orit Josefi Wiseman, my wife, my best friend and the person who has to put up with my idiosyncrasies. She has the patience of an angel. As a child therapist, she is the model for Dana, the child therapist in the novel, who also loves children, the fragile flowers of the future and has the knack of earning and keeping their trust.

Tony Wiseman

# BETWEEN HEAVEN AND EARTH

# AUSTIN MACAULEY PUBLISHERS™

LONDON * CAMBRIDGE * NEW YORK * SHARJAH

Copyright © Tony Wiseman 2023

The right of Tony Wiseman to be identified as author of this work has been asserted by the author in accordance with sections 77 and 78 of the Copyright, Designs and Patents Act 1988.

All rights reserved. No part of this publication may be reproduced, stored in a retrieval system, or transmitted in any form or by any means, electronic, mechanical, photocopying, recording, or otherwise, without the prior permission of the publishers.

Any person who commits any unauthorised act in relation to this publication may be liable to criminal prosecution and civil claims for damages.

This is a work of fiction. Names, characters, businesses, places, events, locales, and incidents are either the products of the author's imagination or used in a fictitious manner. Any resemblance to actual persons, living or dead, or actual events is purely coincidental.

A CIP catalogue record for this title is available from the British Library.

ISBN 9781035802814 (Paperback)
ISBN 9781035802821 (ePub e-book)

www.austinmacauley.com

First Published 2023
Austin Macauley Publishers Ltd®
1 Canada Square
Canary Wharf
London
E14 5AA

I am indebted to the many people who read the manuscript during the long process of writing. They provided invaluable feedback. The list is too long to include all of them. However, there are several who warrant a special word of thanks.

First and foremost, is my harshest critic and the greatest source of encouragement with multiple suggestions and endless patience, my precious wife, Orit. Without her, this work would never have seen the light of day.

Jeff Wolfin supported me by reading the book and because of his excitement insisted on composing the outstanding synopsis.

Philippa Donovan of Smart Quill set me on the right track to writing fiction. She was consistent in utilising her professional expertise to make certain I never veered off the path.

Robin Wiseman, my brother has always been there for me throughout the long years of our sibling relationship. He has never flinched from telling me the truth. He honoured that commitment to our connection throughout by giving me honest feedback and offering priceless ideas.

Kevin Smith of Austin Macauley succeeded in keeping my spirits up whenever they were flagging. I truly appreciate his support.

Finally, I want to acknowledge and say thank you to the thousands of people I have met in the course of my life. Many of them were willing to share with me the joys and successes as well as the trials and tribulations of their lives. They provided the foundation on which Between Heaven and Earth is based.

# Table of Contents

| | |
|---|---:|
| Prologue | 11 |
| Chapter 1 | 15 |
| Chapter 2 | 20 |
| Chapter 3 | 23 |
| Chapter 4 | 31 |
| Chapter 5 | 38 |
| Chapter 6 | 43 |
| Chapter 7 | 52 |
| Chapter 8 | 57 |
| Chapter 9 | 66 |
| Chapter 10 | 75 |
| Chapter 11 | 85 |
| Chapter 12 | 90 |
| Chapter 13 | 93 |
| Chapter 14 | 97 |
| Chapter 15 | 100 |
| Chapter 16 | 104 |
| Chapter 17 | 108 |
| Chapter 18 | 122 |
| Chapter 19 | 126 |

| | |
|---|---|
| Chapter 20 | 136 |
| Chapter 21 | 142 |
| Chapter 22 | 150 |
| Chapter 23 | 158 |
| Chapter 24 | 165 |
| Chapter 25 | 177 |
| Chapter 26 | 183 |
| Chapter 27 | 191 |
| Chapter 28 | 199 |
| Chapter 29 | 202 |
| Chapter 30 | 205 |
| Chapter 31 | 213 |
| Chapter 32 | 220 |
| Chapter 33 | 223 |
| Chapter 34 | 227 |
| Chapter 35 | 235 |
| Chapter 36 | 242 |
| Chapter 37 | 245 |
| Chapter 38 | 250 |
| Chapter 39 | 256 |
| Chapter 40 | 261 |
| Chapter 41 | 270 |
| Chapter 42 | 276 |
| Chapter 43 | 284 |
| Epilogue | 294 |

# Prologue

Ecstasy! He was floating, free, with a lightness he had never experienced before. Or had he? His head spun. He was being sucked into a vortex, imperceptibly gaining momentum, swirling deeper. Suddenly, he found himself in a vast, open space. Even if one could not see the boundaries, there was always finiteness. Here, though, there was just shimmering endlessness. With a slow, sweeping gaze, he took in the scene that greeted him.

*"Where on earth am I? Everything is strange but it looks familiar. It is like coming back to a place you left a long time ago."*

Surprised, he heard his name and turned to face the direction from which the sound had emanated. He was blinded by a figure, completely enveloped in a glowing light. The spirit addressed him in a quiet voice, more of a whisper.

"Welcome home. I am your celestial messenger." He stared at the apparition in amazement, dazzled by the radiance.

*"Home? What do you mean, home? I don't understand. Where am I?"*

"You are where you are," said the celestial messenger. "Here, we do not measure physical space as you do in human life."

*"Really? So, I suppose this must be Heaven, then."*

"It is, if you want it to be.*"*

*"Well, what did you mean when you said 'welcome home'?"*

"This is home. It always was. You simply forgot. Everyone begins and ends life's journey here."

*"Who are they, the 'everyone' you refer to?"* he said, with a trace of sarcasm. *"I don't see a living soul."*

"Beings exist on a different plane where we are. As I said, we do not occupy physical space so there is no encroachment," the voice explained.

*"Now, I am more confused than ever,"* he countered. *"Anyway, what the hell is a celestial messenger?"*

"As a recent-arrival, my responsibility is to accompany you until you refamiliarize yourself with your environment and the way things are here."

*Why? Do you think I can't fend for myself and I need you to show me the ropes? What a nerve,* he thought with an air of superiority.

"Here, you are free. You need nothing," said the celestial messenger, reading his thoughts. "And what's more, there is nothing to show you. I am simply on call until you acclimatise to the fact that you are in 'the afterlife'. This is just another stage of enlightenment, a new level."

*"Oh! So then, you must be an angel, a teacher,"* he said, mockingly.

The spirit explained, patiently. "We are all angels. Nor am I here to teach you anything because you already know. You simply do not know that you know. In the beginning, newcomers tend to continue to be 'human'. Of course, that is not the natural state of things here at home."

He sneered. *"Not much of a welcome home is it?"*

Unperturbed, the celestial messenger took no offence. "Human life is just one step in the endless voyage towards full awareness. There are more. Until you are properly re-orientated, it may take a while. I am with you for your journey through eternity until you cut your ties to the 'other world'. I assure you everyone adapts, eventually."

He was at a total loss to understand almost everything the spirit had conveyed. Even the gender of the celestial messenger was not apparent. It could easily have been male or female. Strangely, it was neither. To his surprise, though, he trusted it as there was an honesty and an absence of any egotism, just kindness in the tone of voice of his new acquaintance. His attitude mellowed slightly.

*"Alright, but what about those we left behind and the anguish they must be suffering?"*

The celestial messenger answered in a sympathetic tone. "It is understandable that you still think this way. You will re-discover that 'moving on' is a part of living. The purpose of life is to grow, including dealing with such abysmal pain, as that occasioned by the departure of a dear one."

*"Fair enough, but how do THEY deal with the pain?"* he pleaded.

"All things have a beginning and an end. You and they will discover that everything is for the best even though it may not appear so at the time. Remember, there is always a lesson to be learned. Just wait!"

*"Do you mean we grow stronger through pain? Is that what you are saying?"*

"Is steel not tempered by the furnace?" the light said, enigmatically.

He smiled at the wisdom of the celestial messenger.

It continued. "When I arrived here, I was conscious of the grief I left behind, just like you. My own awareness is still an ongoing process."

*"I am sorry. Whom did you leave behind?"*

"Like you, precious ones."

*"I suppose they pine for you as she probably does for me?"*

"Yes, but children do not hold on to the past as adults are wont to do. They heal, the pain passes, life continues."

*"That may very well be, but we had no children."*

*"I know."*

*"You seem to know a lot about us. Do you know how special our love for one another is...or was?"* he corrected. *"She must be utterly heartbroken."*

"True, but it will not be so, forever. Although she is no longer with you, you will always be with her. Fortunately for them, they believe that their time heals all wounds. Her pain will pass, too."

*"I hope so. How long have you been here?"*

"Again, for us, there is no such thing as time like there is for mortals. I arrived not long before you did."

He shook his head to clear his confusion, which was greater than it had been before this weird conversation began. He considered the possibility that he had not understood the language in which they had conversed. On reflection, they had not 'spoken' in a corporeal sense at all. Wherever he was, communication occurred at a different level making words superfluous.

Without warning, his celestial messenger faded away into nothingness. He had not even asked its name.

# Chapter 1

The first time Mona felt a lump in her breast, she was not sure if there really was one or if it was her imagination playing tricks on her. Although she was consumed with worry, she did not mention it to Teddy, partly due to her uncertainty but also because she knew how he was likely to react.

When, eventually, she did tell him, not unexpectedly, he was a nervous wreck and fussed over her as though she was an invalid. Fortunately though, after undergoing a mammogram and various other tests, to their great relief, it proved to be a benign cyst and she received the all clear from Dr Barnett, their family physician.

It is an almost incontestable contention that when trust is compromised, it is virtually impossible to fully restore it. Consequently, because the ogre, as she named it, was firmly lodged in her mind, Mona would constantly check herself, praying that it had disappeared for good. But when she prodded and palpitated the area, she could detect the lump quite clearly. This time, however, she was even positive that it was growing larger. Unable to bear the burden alone, she decided to confide in Teddy.

In bed, before switching off the lights, she gently took his hand. As usual, she hated having to inflict pain on this kind and sensitive man. For that reason, she always put his feelings above her own. How much she loved him.

Looking deeply into his eyes, she said quietly, "Teddy, I am sorry to worry you, but I think the ogre is back."

"No, Mona, are you sure? Oh my God, it can't be," he said in a panic. He too, had been praying that it was behind them and now, this. He could feel the mounting desperation flooding over him. "When did you discover it, my darling?"

"I have been checking regularly. I first felt it a couple of weeks ago but now, I am pretty certain."

"We must have it examined, immediately, Mo. We can't wait," he said, his voice wracked with concern.

"I know, Teddy-Bear. I have already made an appointment to see Dr Barnett. He knows how serious it is so he booked us in for tomorrow morning. Please don't worry, though. I'm sure it will be the same as last time," she reassured him with blatant vain-hope.

They were very apprehensive prior to the pending examination since neither of them had recovered from the previous trauma. The fear had always lurked in the background like a scavenger waiting to pounce on the unsuspecting quarry. Although he was beside himself with worry, he did his best to keep up her spirits and allay her fears. They maintained an artificially, cheery atmosphere and studiously avoided talking about the subject but the matter loomed over them like a dark storm-cloud.

The doctor's receptionist ushered them into Dr Barnett's surgery immediately on their arrival. He was a big burly man with a greying beard and kind eyes. Despite his size, he exuded a gentleness, which was never more important than at that moment.

"Hello, Mona, Teddy, it is good to see you after such a long time," he greeted them warmly. "How is Guy? He is growing up into a strapping young fellow, isn't he?" But he quickly detected their tension and immediately reverted to his more serious and professional demeanour.

His physical examination proved inconclusive but he informed them that indeed, there was a growth.

"It is fairly large already. However, as before, it may well be due to a variety of different things, especially after the experience of the previous occasion," he said, unsuccessfully trying to reassure them. "Again, only further tests will enable us to diagnose the true situation, so I have arranged for an immediate mammogram and some other tests. You remember the last occasion, I am sure, Mona. When we get the results, we can talk about it further. Meanwhile, keep your chins up."

The doctor's injunction proved to be an impossible undertaking. The results were expected within a day or two but nothing provided any respite from their gnawing terror.

When the results arrived, they were horrified at the news. Their worst fears were confirmed. Mona turned pale and she began to tremble, uncontrollably. Teddy's blood seemed to freeze in his veins.

Dr Barnett explained the findings with a serious expression. "The tumour is indeed malignant and unfortunately, it has already metastasised into the lymph nodes," he said, looking from one to the other. They were aghast.

"I am going to refer you to one of the leading oncologists specialising in breast-cancer. She will recommend the most effective treatment. The situation is urgent, so there is no time to waste. We must start chemotherapy immediately and once they ascertain how you respond, they will decide on further treatment, whether radiation or a partial or full mastectomy is advisable," he said, solemnly.

They stared at him, thunderstruck. "Mona, Teddy, sorry to be the bearer of such bad tidings but it is my responsibility to let you know the full extent of the situation. Of course, you know my door is always open. If there is anything you need, please do not hesitate to ask."

Teddy took Mona's hand. She looked at him, sheer disbelief registered on her face. He squeezed her fingers as though telling her, "I am here with you."

Doctor Barnett continued, "It will be a difficult time for both of you and I recommend that you find some outside help with the daily chores, housework, Guy and so on. Even work may be a problem," he told them. "Mona, you are going to need all your strength in the next few months, so we can get you well again." He gave them a few moments to digest the import of what he was saying.

"Naturally, this will put a heavy burden on you, Teddy. Mona needs to devote herself exclusively to her recovery. That is the only thing that matters."

Neither of them said anything. They were too shocked to respond, each struggling to cope with their personal emotions.

"I hate sounding so business-like. I can imagine how you are feeling but all is not lost. We will make sure you receive the best possible treatment, I promise you, Mona," the doctor said, kindly.

They nodded in unison, thunderstruck by the news. In a few minutes, their world had come crashing down around them. They were completely distraught by the shocking news. On the way home, Mona burst into tears. She had suppressed her roiling emotions in the doctor's surgery but in the privacy of the car, the floodgates opened. She sobbed uncontrollably and Teddy had to stop the car to comfort her. He held her in his arms and stroked her hair lovingly.

"It cannot be happening to us," she cried. "This sort of thing only happens to other people. How can it be true? Perhaps the doctors are wrong."

He knew that after the discovery of cancer, frequently, the first reaction was often denial. He had secretly read up on the subject as much as possible on the previous occasion. He was aware that it was futile to indulge in such a charade.

They were facing an enormous challenge and there was no certainty that at the end of it, there would be a positive outcome.

Eventually, shaken as she was, Mona composed herself and took a few deep breaths until she felt calmer.

"That's it, Teddy-Bear, enough is enough. We are not going to give in to the ogre," she said, firmly. "We need to fight it with all our strength, together. We are not going to let it beat us."

Teddy smiled with pride at his beloved Mona. She was always more sanguine than he was. He could sense her resolve as she girded herself for the coming battle. Gently, he dried her tears with a tissue and kissed her on her still warm forehead.

"Not bad for a woman in my position, right, Teddy-Bear?" she said as she examined her reflection in the mirror behind the sun-visor.

She touched up her make-up, patted away the black streaks her mascara had sketched down her cheeks and combed her fingers through her hair.

"We have a responsibility to Guy, my darling. For his sake, we have to prevent this 'ogre' affecting him. …for as long as we can," she added, ruefully. "I know it will be difficult, but we have to make sure that everything goes on as normal. We cannot allow this to disrupt our daily lives any more than is necessary."

He nodded and grinned at her. He was far from certain he had her courage and fortitude.

The next evening, Guy sat on Teddy's lap in the sitting-room. Mona perched on an easy-chair facing them. In order not to alarm the child, she spoke in a matter-of-fact voice as much as she was able.

"Guychick, we went to see Doctor Barnett, yesterday because I have not been feeling well for a while. He did some tests and told us I have an illness, which needs to be treated. So I will be busy quite often going to see doctors and perhaps even having to stay in the hospital sometimes."

"Will you have to take horrible medicine or have injections, Mummy?"

"I am not sure but I may need to. Don't worry, I know the doctors will do whatever they need to make me better. We just want you to know because I may not be able to play with you and do some of the things we love doing together, at least not until I am well again. Daddy will make sure you are not affected too much."

It was clear that an almost four-year old would not fully appreciate the seriousness of the situation and Guy took a few moments before he responded.

"I will be a good boy and eat all my food, Mummy. I also won't make a noise or bother you. Will that help you get better, Mummy?"

"Thank you, Guy but that is not necessary. You just continue to be the boy you always are. We love you very much and all we want for you is to be happy. Just don't worry if there are changes taking place at home for a while. Okay?"

"Alright, Mummy. Will it take long until you get better?" Guy asked.

"It will probably take quite a long time but Daddy and I will be here with you all the time," Mona said, recognising the first signs of concern in the expression on the small boy's face. He looked like he was about to burst into tears and was struggling to hold them back.

Mona leaned forward and took Guy in her arms to comfort him. She did not want him to see the tears in her own eyes. Teddy embraced them both, wondering what lay ahead for his beloved family. How many more opportunities would they have in the future to hug each other as they were doing at that moment.

They answered Guy's questions about her illness with the honesty a child of his tender age could understand. They did not consider it advisable to hide the truth from him. Mona insisted that it was important for him to understand why she would no longer be able to play with him as before. She was even convinced that if she were to die without him being aware of her illness, he might resent it later on.

"Trust is not only for good times when things are easy but more so, when there are things we don't like. At least, out of this nightmare, I can leave our son that legacy," she told Teddy, bitterly. He was so distressed he could not find any words to comfort her.

"You remember, I told you all those happy years ago that for me, trust is the cornerstone of any relationship? I want Guy to know he can trust us, no matter what. We agreed always to tell each other the truth, right, darling?"

"Right, my love." he echoed, with little conviction.

# Chapter 2

Dana Gould shuffled her papers as she wrote up the notes of the previous session in her neat, even script. For her, it was the least enjoyable aspect of her profession as a child therapist. Although inundated with work, in fact too much so, her deep sense of compassion and love of children, in her words, the fragile flowers of the future, compelled her to accept the pleas of distressed parents, who appealed to her to treat their offspring.

Her concentration was interrupted by the sound of children's laughter, the ringtone of her mobile telephone. She saw it was Sally Campbell, her best friend.

"Hello Dan," Sally trilled in her customarily bright fashion.

"Hi Sal. Lovely to hear from you. How are you?"

"I am so excited. I can hardly concentrate," she bubbled.

"Wow, I can hear," Dana said, with a smile.

"I just had a call from someone I met at a dinner-party which Myrna arranged. You remember Myrna?"

"Yes, of course. I haven't spoken to her for ages, though. How is she? How was the dinner?"

"Wonderful, she is an outstanding hostess. You can't imagine what an impressive banquet she provided, as usual."

"As usual," echoed Dana.

"Most of the other guests were couples so I was seated next to Peter Broome. He is also single and a lawyer. We just hit it off," swooned Sally.

"Sounds great," Dana said, anxious to get back to her work.

"It was but I must admit though, I was very disappointed when he never asked for my phone number at the end of the evening."

"Impossible," said Dana, sarcastically. "You always succeed in ensnaring any man you like. It's about time you took the trouble to teach the art to your best friend."

"I love your flattery, madam, but this time, it didn't work. I assumed that he was less impressed with me than I was with him."

"I don't believe it. After you hit it off, he never called?"

"No, but here is the surprise," she giggled, girlishly. "Can you imagine the shock when I heard his voice on the phone this morning?"

"That is wonderful. I am so pleased for you. He probably got your number from Myrna."

"You sound a little sarcastic to me."

"No, no, I just wish I had the same talent as you."

"It will happen for you, sooner or later, Dan. You have everything. It is just a matter of luck before you find the right person."

"Never mind the right person, any person will do. I have my fingers crossed for luck, and toes, as well. I hope I am not too old by the time he shows up, if he ever does."

"Oh please Dan, don't lose hope. Talking about luck, I think I have hit the jackpot with Peter. Wait until you meet him, good-looking, smart, charming, and a thorough gentleman."

"He sounds Mr Perfect, doesn't he?" Dana gave an exaggerated sigh.

Undaunted, Sally gushed on without waiting for a response. "He called to ask me out. He wants me to come with him to a concert at the Arturo Toscanini Auditorium. It is a gala-event in aid of Children in Need."

"Wonderful, Sally, it sounds perfect."

"Thanks, Dan, it definitely is. And he has four tickets!"

"Four? Why four?" said Dana, suspiciously.

"Yes, he has four! They cost a fortune. His best friend, Michael Weston and he are on the organising-committee. Peter is actually going to be Master of Ceremonies. He will be busy in his official capacity on the evening. He feels awful that on our first date, he will not have as much time for me as he would like."

"Oh. I get it," exclaimed Dana as the alarm bells started ringing. "You want to set me up on another of those blind dates as Michael's partner. Correct?" she said, angrily.

"Oh Dan, please, pretty please, are you busy next week? We thought if you could come as Michael's escort, I would not be left alone with him while Peter is busy. Then, both he and I would be more relaxed. I would feel less abandoned and Michael would not need to babysit me. It would be win/win for all."

"That sort of a win/win is only for you! Good lord, how many times have I asked you to stop your machinations and here you go again? When will it end? Finding me a life's partner need not be your main purpose in life."

"OK, Dan, you are right. I am sorry. I promise to hold off in future, but I so want you to meet that special someone. You deserve it."

"Enough is enough, Sally. It is tiring. And you know that I am not very good with romantic relationships."

"You are right, Dan, about my attitude, that is," she said, apologetically, "but not about you not being good with romantic relationships," she explained in order to set the record straight. "But this time, I am asking you for my sake. It really is for me. I admit it, I need your support. I have a feeling this could be it. I am begging you, Dana. Please say yes. I would be so grateful. Would you do this huge, huge favour for me?"

She smiled at Sally's incorrigible wiliness. After all, she was her best friend.

"Peter assures me, Michael is a real sweetie. He is also a lawyer. And by the way, they are playing Beethoven's Sixth, the Pastoral, your favourite," added Sally, to sweeten the pill.

"Oh darn! It's pointless arguing with you, woman. In the end, you always get your way. Alright! I will come with you," Dana conceded, with irritation, "against my better judgment," she added.

"Thank you, Dan. Thank you, so much. I cannot tell you how grateful I am."

"At least the music should make up for my sacrifice. I read about the concert in the papers. If I am not mistaken, the conductor is that young South American sensation. He is being courted by the world's leading orchestras, isn't he?"

"Yes, he is. It should be a fantastic evening. I am sure you will love Michael. He and Peter have been friends, forever."

"Oh! Come on. Don't think for a moment I am not aware of your underlying motive. These blind dates never work out, especially this one when I will be the fifth wheel."

"No, you won't," Sally assured her. "I have a feeling this may be a turning point for both of us."

"Bye, I doubt if that is very likely," Dana said, curtly, shaking her head as she ended the call.

She knew Sally well enough. Her latest catch was just another notch in a long list. Within a month or two, she would be just as excited about her latest Mr Perfect and Peter would be stale news.

# Chapter 3

Teddy woke up at sunrise while Mona was still sleeping. Lying next to her, he rested his head on his arm and gazed in wonder at his wife, while gently stroking her hair, tumbling on to the pillow. He reflected on their lives together, especially the past three and a half years since Guy's birth. His most treasured recollections were indelibly etched in his memory; how much pleasure he had experienced from watching Mona cradling the infant in her arms, while he suckled; the first time Guy smiled had lit up their lives, a milestone to cherish; how they whooped with joy and clapped hands when he took his first baby-steps, falling into their waiting arms.

Lying there, he realised how blessed he was and he luxuriated in the memories. That early morning calm, when the home was quiet was his favourite time of the day. But, now, he was tormented with worry at the diagnosis they had just received. He refused to consider the likelihood of her succumbing to the cancer. He would not be able to deal with such a loss. He was not even willing to entertain such a possibility.

He had known Mona since their youth. They had both loved music and joined the school-choir at the prompting of Mr Bach, the school music-teacher. He smiled when he thought back to the first time he had ever spoken to her. Mr Bach had excused the children after a lengthy lesson during which, they had practiced some of the choral sections of Handel's Messiah, which the choir was going to sing at the year-end school graduation.

"Well done, boys and girls," he boomed, "I am very pleased with all of you. These are difficult pieces and you should be proud of yourselves. Your timing and the quality of your harmony were excellent. Next week, we will resume our work. No doubt, at the ceremony, the audience will be most impressed."

As the pupils left, Mona Stewart slung her satchel over her shoulder and walked out of the music-room together with some of her friends. She noticed Teddy Goodson standing alone.

"He is such a snob," said one of the girls, with a toss of her curls. "He never talks to anybody."

Mona shook her head. "He is probably just shy, that's all."

"Do you really think so? Go on, then, Mo, you are always a sport to take risks. I dare you to talk to him," she said.

Mona weighed up the situation. She could not refuse such a challenge and then have to endure the endless ribbing of her schoolmates. But, she had to admit to herself, she was quite attracted to the quiet youth, who seemed to be on his own most of the time. She took a deep breath, swallowed and went up to him. "Hello, Teddy," she said, bashfully.

"Hello," he replied, with downcast eyes, unsure how to deal with such an unfamiliar and somewhat threatening situation. She smiled at him, warmly as the other girls, tittered, watching the interaction.

"My name is Mona. I wanted to introduce myself to you a month ago after we joined the choir, but I thought you might be embarrassed."

"I am glad you finally decided to do it in the end," he said, surprising himself at his uncharacteristic brashness.

"I must admit I was a bit shy, today, as well, but I finally made up my mind to speak to you. I hope you don't mind." She gave a quick glance in the direction of her friends, who were watching the unfolding scenario with great amusement.

"Of course, I don't mind," he replied, turning a deep shade of red. Noticing his awkwardness, she said, "I love your voice. When I hear you sing, I really enjoy it."

"Thank you," he mumbled, self-consciously.

"You really like music, don't you?"

"Yes," he answered, mono-syllabically.

"What is your favourite sort of music?"

"I like most kinds but mainly classics and jazz. I also like popular stuff, sometimes. It depends on my mood."

"Hey! We have nearly the same taste. Those are my favourites, too. I go to concerts and festivals as often as I can. Do you, Teddy?"

"Not much. It is not much fun going on my own. I don't have that many friends."

"Then let's be friends. We can go together."

"I would like that," he said.

"Cool! Do you live far from school?" she asked.

"No, about fifteen minutes from here. We live near the church, although we never go," he answered, guiltily.

"It is on my way home. Do you mind if I walk with you?"

"Of course not. I would like that," he said.

Mona's friends giggled, and gave her a thumbs-up sign as they waved goodbye.

He found himself actually enjoying the company of this very forward girl as they walked home. For the first time, he had no problem carrying on an interesting conversation with her. His customary embarrassment, which usually led him to becoming badly 'tongue-tied', seemed to have evaporated into thin air.

"There is a concert in a couple of weeks. I am planning to go. Would you like to come with me?" she asked.

"I would love to," he replied, smiling to himself as he realised he had not even asked what sort of concert it would to be or who else was going with Mona.

"Fantastic," she said. "I'm sure you will enjoy the music. I know I will."

"Thank you for asking me," he said, more relaxed than he had ever felt before in the company of a girl.

They became firm friends and went to many concerts, together. As they got to know each other better, besides simply enjoying each other's company, they discovered they had many common interests, aside from music. They enjoyed reading and often discussed and exchanged books, which they had enjoyed. Cryptic crosswords, too, intrigued them and frequently, they would work on a puzzle, jointly.

"What can be the eight-letter word for four down?" he asked after they had spent time on a particularly difficult puzzle.

"Is that the clue about 'Tea without sugar or milk for a Minister'? Do we have any letters, yet?" she asked.

"Something 'h', something, something, something 'a' something, 'n'," he answered.

"Maybe it is one of the different kinds of tea? What sorts of teas are there?" she mused.

He scratched his head. "There is Chinese tea or English tea, for instance."

She gave him an impish grin.

"What exactly is the difference between Chinese and English tea?" she said, with a makeshift la-de-dah smirk.

He answered with a faux upper-class accent. "The Chinese, and most people drink their tea black, without milk," he said. "But, you know the British. We have to make our tea in a particular way. You must brew it, no tea-bags, of course. Then, we drink it from special tea-cups, but only after putting the milk into the cup, first. Then, we pour the tea. Otherwise it is not proper tea, is it?"

"At least, that is what I was taught, too," she said in a similar 'put-on' aristocratic accent, mocking her traditional upbringing. "Well there are all kinds of herbal teas or tea could even be 'cha', 'chai' or 'char'."

"Yes, that's it, Mona," he whooped. "Plain tea has no milk or sugar. So, it is 'cha, tea, plain', no milk or sugar, chaplain, Minister." Triumphantly, they gave each other a high five.

"What a combination!" said Mona, casting a meaningful look at him as he smiled with pleasure at their success but more so at the innuendo in her remark.

Due to their interest in art and culture, they would frequently prowl through museums and art galleries or just browse in bookshops and music stores. However, they loved the outdoors most. One of their favourite pastimes was spending time in nature, hiking or visiting places off the beaten track. They often lay on their backs under the stars in their camp-site, gazing up at the inky-black, night sky searching for shooting stars or satellites or pointing out the various galaxies.

Mona perfected the knack of putting the shy young boy at ease and it did not take long before she succeeding in getting him to open up to her. Unlike the other pupils, she identified his reserve as anything but snobbishness.

"Why do you never invite me to your home especially when you have been to mine so many times?" she said. "My parents have started prying, asking me who the mystery man in my life really is."

"I would like you to meet my parents, too, but they are quite old and they are very finicky with tidiness and rules. I am not sure you would feel comfortable."

"Don't be silly, Teddy. I am sure I would feel alright."

"I don't think so. I have no brothers or sisters and there aren't even any cousins. They had no one else so they molly-coddled me, instead."

"Did that affect you, Teddy?"

"Well, I was never allowed to do things on my own." They believed that they always needed to protect me so they did everything for me. All I have heard my whole life is "Careful, Theodore, I wouldn't do that if I were you" or "Children should be seen and not heard," he said, bitterly.

"Maybe so, but you do very well in your studies. You are one of the top students in your class and you excel at sports as well…and singing," she added, with a chuckle. "Don't they appreciate it sometimes and compliment you, just occasionally?"

"It makes no difference, Mona. My mother is old-fashioned, Victorian in her outlook, actually, and my father is strict and extremely conservative. They always say, "You can do better, Teddy. Why only ninety-five percent in mathematics, Teddy? Why don't you try harder, young man?"

"I suppose it must be very depressing for you."

"I tried as hard as I could but in the end, I just gave up. That's all. I lost all my confidence. No, actually, I can't remember having any."

"So that's why you prefer to remain in the shadows and do your utmost to avoid the spotlight," she said, sympathetically.

"Yes, because I always feel an outsider no matter where I am," he said, wistfully.

"Oh! Teddy, I am so sorry. Now, on top of all that, you are worried I may not like to come to your home? I can see why it isn't easy for you."

"I got used to it although it still bugs me. I don't want them to judge you. If they meet you, they will always check with me to find out what is happening between us."

"That's all right, my Teddy-Bear. At least, now I know a little more about you. That is what matters most to me."

As time passed, even though they spent most of their time together, she was never truly sure how he really felt about her. She suspected he had a special affection for her but because he was so reserved, he hesitated to open up to her and never said anything. He, for his part, could not contemplate that she had anything more than a platonic interest in him.

Towards the end of their final school year, on an outing strolling through a forest in one of their favourite locations, she decided to broach the subject head-on.

"Do you think when boys or girls meet the right person, they would be willing to share their secrets with each other?" she said, taking the bull by the horns.

"Why? What do you mean?" he asked.

"Well, because they would trust each other. Don't you think so? I think trust and total commitment are the cornerstones of any relationship," she said. "Just look at us. We have known each other for over five years. We trust each other completely, don't we?"

"Of course, we do."

"That is what I mean by 'total commitment'. You have always been there for me and I will be there for you, too, no matter what. So, we do have that special commitment, don't we?"

"Aha! I see what you mean. Yes, we have," he said, with a nod.

"OK, so, when you meet the right girl, will you share all your secrets with her, Mr Goodson?"

"I suppose so," he said, hesitantly, anticipating an impending trap.

"I doubt it," she teased. "If you had met the girl of your dreams, you would already have told her she was the one."

Floundering, he squirmed as she waited for an answer but he never took up the challenge. She said no more as they strolled in the shade of the trees. Stewing with embarrassment, he realised he was on the spot.

Finally, because he realised that she was waiting for some form of response, and would not let him off the hook, he blurted out, "I already have."

He was looking everywhere but at her.

"You have what, already?"

"Met the girl of my dreams," he said.

"And?"

"And, what?"

"And so, who is she?"

"I. Ah. I suppose…she is…" he stuttered, silently pleading for her to change the subject.

"Who is she?" she pressed. "I am not going to let you escape this time, young man. Who is the lucky girl?" She quite enjoyed tantalising the uncomfortable Teddy and waited for him to declare his fondness for her at last.

"Well, who is she, Teddy?" She did not take her eyes off him. "Do I know her? I think I knew all your girlfriends, right?"

"Yes, you do know her. Well, um, not exactly."

"What do you mean, not exactly? Either I do, or I don't. Come on, speak up." In the end, realising she would not relent, he muttered, quietly, "You!"

She stopped and turned to face him.

"Oh! Teddy do you really mean it?" she whispered as she looked deeply, into his eyes.

"I do mean it, Mona. I hope it is alright."

"Of course it is, you fool. It is very alright."

"That's good because I think about you all the time," he admitted.

"Then, why have you waited so long?"

"I didn't dare tell you because I never thought you liked me that way."

"I can't believe you never realised it. I thought I had made it clear enough to you. I have wanted to say something to you for so long, but I never knew how you would react," she sighed. "Thank goodness you plucked up the courage to admit it at last."

"You know I am not very good at this sort of thing. That's why I never said a word about it."

"But, it isn't as though you never went out with other girls."

"It's true I went out with a few, but nothing ever came of any of those dates. You know that."

"Of course, I know. I have followed your love life, carefully."

"I never really understood why they lost interest in me so quickly," he said, more of a question than a statement . She giggled and hugged him.

"You blind darling. Even at the beginning, your girl-friends saw the special connection between us. They knew they never stood a chance. That is why they gave up."

"Honestly?" he said, with surprise.

"Yes, honestly! They knew you were a one-girl-man and I was that girl."

"I always knew you cared about me, but I thought we were just very good friends," he said. "Lucky for both of us then that I didn't find a proper girl-friend."

"Really, Teddy Goodson, do you think I would have allowed you to escape my clutches or let some other hussy steal you away? Don't forget, I set my sights on you very early." She pouted, pulling a wry face and gave him a playful tap on the shoulder. "I was always a one-man-woman and you were the man."

She stroked his face, tenderly, a loving smile on her lips. His pulse was racing and his skin was tingling. To him, even the breeze, rustling the leafy foliage, sounded like music.

Teddy was afraid he would faint when she moved closer to him. He could feel her lithe figure pressed against him as her arms encircled him and she stroked the back of his neck. He felt her breath on his face and the aroma of her intoxicated him. She held his gaze and looked, lovingly, into his eyes. His body was trembling, uncontrollably.

To calm the quivering youth, she said, "Don't worry, Teddy, what you are feeling is quite natural and special, and so is this."

She lifted her face, their lips met and the first, innocent kiss sealed their love.

# Chapter 4

When Mike called for her on the evening of the function, Dana realised that it was not going to be a complete waste of time. He was everything that Sally had described, tall, ruggedly good-looking and, to her surprise, his quiet confidence and charm put her at ease. The initial niceties on the drive to the venue passed off comfortably.

"I understand you and Peter are old friends."

"Yes. We go back even before Law-School. We began our studies together about twelve years ago. Since then, we have become brothers in law," he said, accentuating the phrase. She laughed.

"And what about you and Sally, does she always ask you to come to her rescue?"

"No. Not really. It is the other way around. She thinks she needs to rescue me."

"What do you mean? You seem quite capable of looking after yourself."

"I am. But my dear friend has ulterior motives."

"Do you mean that she tried to organise an invitation to the concert for you?"

"No. It is more surreptitious than that." She laughed, shyly.

"I don't understand," he said, with a shrug. "When Peter invited Sally to this evening's function, he asked me to come along and take care of her while he was busy. I agreed. Why not? Later, he suggested to her she bring a friend. She mentioned you and here we all are. Voila! You came to her rescue. The prosecution rests."

"Yes and no. Is it the chance for the defence to plead, yet?"

"Go ahead. You have two minutes, my learned friend."

"She thinks her mission in life is to find me a partner," she explained.

"What! To me, you seem quite capable of finding your own partner," Mike said with surprise.

"Maybe so, maybe not, but she thinks I am not focused enough on that objective, at least, not as much as she is. That is why she inveigled Peter into organising this invitation." She smiled, shyly. "And, I may be letting the cat out of the bag when I tell you that Sally was smitten by Peter at Myrna's dinner party," she said, skilfully changing the subject.

"She may be your very good friend, but I imagine you would not have much trouble with her stated objective…even without her help, Mike said. "And I am not letting the cat out of the bag either, when I tell you that the reverse is also true, Peter was smitten by Sally." They both laughed at their friends' nascent relationship.

"I was told that you are a lecturer in the Law Faculty and that you are due to become a professor. Isn't it very young to be a professor? she asked, primly, anxious to get away from such a touchy subject."

"Twenty-eight but it isn't the record," he said, modestly. "The present Dean was a professor at twenty-seven, although that was many years ago."

"Still, it is quite impressive. From what I was told, you have acquired quite a reputation. In your career, I mean," she added quickly, as she realised the possible double entendre of her comment.

This time, he laughed. "Yes, I am about to become a law-professor in a few months, but my academic reputation is over-flattering," he said, with unbecoming modesty. "Anyway, we have spoken about me most of the time and we only have a few minutes until we get to the concert hall. Tell me about you. Tell me who Dana is. Peter told me you are a child therapist."

"There really isn't that much to know, just the usual, boring things except for the fact that I am proud of myself because I chose my career against my parents' wishes."

He was puzzled. "Didn't they want you to be a child therapist?" he asked.

"They wanted me to continue the family tradition and be a doctor like both of them and my paternal grandfather but I refused. Thank heavens, I never caved in."

"I told you that you seem like a woman, who can look after herself."

"Never judge a book by its cover," she warned, wondering if she may have sounded a little helpless.

At the auditorium, Sally and Peter were waiting and greeted them warmly. She and Dana excused themselves to go to the ladies' room to powder their noses. As soon as they were on their own, Sally began her cross examination.

"Well, what do you think of Mike? He seems a darling. And you got on well, didn't you? I could see it as soon as you arrived."

"Yes, you are right. I enjoyed meeting him. I just hope I don't mess it all up." She saw the grimace on Sally's face at her erstwhile remark.

"Alright, Sal, I will try not to. At the same time, Peter is obviously charmed by you, too. I hope you don't mess this one up, either. He looks perfect for you."

"So, let us make sure we don't mess up anything, OK? Now, let's go and wow them," Sally said, as she flounced off.

For the first half-hour, both Peter and Mike were busy attending to their duties and had little time to spend with them. Dana found herself more of an observer as she took in the elitist, socialite ambience from a safe distance. Sally, on the other hand, enjoyed the heady atmosphere and revelled in her 'privileged' status.

The hall was crowded with elegantly dressed men and women and the hum of conversation, occasionally interrupted by an outburst of laughter, was not the ideal environment as far as Dana was concerned. She felt like a fish out of water.

There were frequent flashes of cameras as the photographers went about their job of taking pictures of the numerous VIPs at the function. In no way, did she see herself as a part of the crowd, a 'celeb'.

When they were not busy, Sally carried on an incessant conversation with Peter and Mike. Dana was grudgingly grateful as she really felt out of place. Sally did her utmost to involve her in the conversation but most of the time, she was ill at ease.

Nonetheless, she did enjoy the concert. The music both thrilled and soothed her. She allowed the Pastoral Symphony by Beethoven, her favourite piece of music, to envelop her and take her on flights of fancy to the countryside.

The lilting first movement of the symphony conjured up the rolling fields, the never-ending sky and the aroma of new-mown hay. It was as though she could even smell the dank earth, sodden after a light summer rain.

In the following movements of the symphony, Beethoven's genius created a gurgling brook meandering, slowly, through fertile fields, followed by a storm, with booming thunderclaps and a torrential downpour.

In the melodic strains of the final movement, the composer paid tribute to nature and the reawakening and celebration of the cycle of life, the storm having passed, the earth refreshed and ready to give forth its limitless bounty.

She was enraptured. The audience gave the conductor and the orchestra a five-minute standing ovation until the conductor, with a modest bow and a flourish of his hand in the direction of the orchestra, mounted his podium and treated them to an encore, Brahms' Academic Festival Overture.

Once again, the audience applauded till Peter climbed the steps leading up to the platform. When silence had descended on the auditorium, Peter acknowledged the performers briefly. before thanking the members of the audience.

"I do not want to spoil the incredible musical celebration we have all experienced by making a long speech. However, I think it is appropriate to say thank you to the Maestro and the orchestra for a brilliant evening. We have been privileged to enjoy beautiful music performed at the highest level." The audience stood up, again and applauded loudly. Peter signalled for them to sit and when the audience was settled, he said, "A very special thanks to you, the people who have graced us by attending this evening and making the event not only an outstanding musical occasion but also an immense financial achievement. Many children-in-need will benefit from your generosity."

After the concert, the conductor and specially invited guests attended a private cocktail reception at which Peter welcomed everyone in a short speech.

"Thanks to all of you, who have worked so hard to make this evening an outstanding artistic and social achievement as well as such a brilliant financial success. Thank you, Maestro Miguel Santos, for having given of your time and genius for the sake of the children, who will be the ultimate beneficiaries. It has been a pleasure and a privilege to have been involved with you in this inspiring venture."

Miguel Santos replied with modesty and great sincerity. "In the country where I was born, I have seen with my own eyes, how children often pay the heaviest price in society. Whenever I am able, I am glad to play a small part in doing something to improve the lot of young people."

After the formal speeches, Miguel, Mike and Peter began drifting around the banquet-hall, speaking to the special guests.

"Just look at them," said Sally. "They are so graceful at massaging the egos of the 'vips and donors', aren't they?"

"I imagine it is all part of the necessary format. There seem to be some very big hitters here tonight. They probably expect it, Sally," Dana replied.

They watched as their partners for the evening, accompanied by the young conductor, moved around the reception-room, shaking hands. Every so often, there would be a burst of laughter and back-slapping, as the trio went from person to person, group to group. Eventually, they reached Sally and Dana. They were introduced to Miguel Santos and Sally was taken aback at his youthfulness. She made sure that she was her charming best.

"We loved the concert, didn't we, Dana? The Pastoral is Dana's favourite so it was a perfect evening," she crooned.

"I am glad you enjoyed it. I certainly did," answered the Maestro, smiling at Dana, who blushed at the gesture. Peter took his elbow to direct him to the next group.

"He cannot be more than twenty-five or twenty-six, a baby," she said, after they had moved on.

"Yes. And, he is so modest, probably due to his humble beginnings," Dana agreed. "I loved it when he mentioned how he welcomes invitations such as this from Children's Aid. Obviously, he is not a man who has allowed his international success to go to his head."

"These celebrities are so shallow, though. They will say anything they think you want to hear," Sally said, caustically.

"I am not so sure," Dana countered. "I had the feeling he was really very sincere. From what I have read about him, he comes from the slums of Rio de Janeiro or from some other South American country, maybe Venezuela. I think he is genuine. That was my impression."

Sally tossed her head, dismissively but Peter, who had joined them, agreed with Dana.

"I was also very impressed by the man's sincerity," he said. "Despite his exalted position, I noticed that even the theatre-staff, including the cleaners respect him because he does not look down on them. Isn't it interesting that so much fame has not spoilt him?"

"Not yet!" Sally huffed.

Suddenly, Dana found Mike in front of her with two glasses of white wine. He smiled as he offered her one.

"Thank you," she said. "How do you know I like white wine? Did Sally tell you any other secrets of mine?" she asked, coyly.

"No, she didn't. In fact, as you must have noticed, I have hardly had a second to spare to exchange a word of conversation with her, or you for that matter, since we got here, let alone the time to coax any of your secrets out of her," he laughed.

"So, then how did you know that I liked white wine?"

"I saw you took a glass a little earlier and I assumed you are fond of it. Was I wrong?"

"No, you were not wrong, but I am surprised that you noticed and remembered. Do you always pay particular attention to detail?"

"Well, I am a lawyer and one of the most important requirements of a lawyer is to pay careful attention to detail."

"Most impressive, I must say."

"I suppose I should admit, though, when we arrived, I overheard you ask one of the stewards for a glass of white wine. So, you see, I am not that observant."

"Thank you for your honesty," she said.

"I am also trying to correct the impression I may have given, that I may be a trifle arrogant. I hope I am being even moderately successful. You are not very impressed by hubris, are you?"

She was surprised at his confession. "No, of course I am not impressed by hubris," she said. "And yes, you are being more than moderately successful in creating a favourable impression. And I suppose it is time we joined Sally and Peter."

"Just look at them," he chuckled. "Since we arrived here, they have been wrapped up with each other. They certainly look to me as though they do not need our help." She glanced in Sally's direction. She and Peter were oblivious to their surroundings, their faces close together, engrossed in conversation.

"May I tell you the unvarnished truth?" Mike asked.

"Go ahead. I hope I am ready for this," she replied, swallowing.

"OK. When Sally suggested to Peter that she would like to invite a friend called Dana as my partner, he first asked me if I agreed. I told him I would do him the favour although he knows I never go on blind dates. The last thing I expected was to find that I would be the one to benefit from this so-called favour. I have really enjoyed our evening. I hope you have enjoyed it, too."

She never answered. Her head was spinning. She knew exactly how she wanted to respond but her insecurity held her back.

"Why would he be interested in me? Aside from the drive here and the last twenty minutes or so, we have barely exchanged a dozen sentences all night. As soon as he gets to know me better, he will probably be bored. Obviously, he is well versed in the art of romantic relationships and I most certainly am not."

*I can hardly believe it, though*, she thought. *This is the first time I have ever felt any genuine interest in a man. Grow up, girl. Say something!*

He noticed the bewildered look on her face. After a slight hesitation, he asked. "Is everything alright, Dana?"

Fortunately, her good sense prevailed. She took a deep breath.

"So have I. I enjoyed being with you, too, Mike, really," she said, finally, blushing a deep shade of crimson. She stared at the floor. He gently placed his finger-tips under her chin and lifted her head.

"Dana, I know very little about you, but I want to see you, again, soon, if possible," he said, staring into her eyes.

"I would like that, too," she whispered.

# Chapter 5

As Teddy and Mona left the innocence of childhood and entered the realm of young adulthood, their relationship strengthened even more. They became inseparable.

"Don't you think it is time we moved in together?" Mona suggested.

"I would like that but I am not sure my parents would accept the idea," Teddy said.

"We would save a lot of money. It is crazy that we are both paying rent for separate accommodation," she reasoned. "Wouldn't that be an important consideration for them, Teddy?"

"I am not sure but I don't feel like arguing with my parents, again."

"Why would you need to argue with them, Teddy? This is a new age in which people who are in love do that sort of thing. You told me your parents are old-fashioned. We don't need to be as well."

"I also told you they are Victorian in their ways. They would really frown on such a step."

"Come on, Teddy. Tell them it is because we want to save the money. And anyway, are you telling me we are not in love?" she taunted him.

"No, I am not saying that. We do love each other. We will definitely live together one day."

"So, let's do it, now, instead. It will be fun."

Eventually, they made the decision to move in together, ostensibly 'to save money' but in truth because Teddy wanted it as much as Mona did.

At university, she studied Music while he specialised in computer science. They both received their degrees cum laude. After his graduation ceremony, Teddy took Mona to dinner at their favourite, local bistro.

"Is something worrying you, tonight, Teddy?" she asked. "You have been uneasy all evening, wrapped up in your own thoughts."

"No. Everything is fine," he said.

"Then, why are you so quiet? You seem on edge. Come on, out with it. No secrets. Remember?"

"I wanted to ask you…"

"Ask me what? Any chance that you so nervous because this a 'dear John evening, now that you are a fully-fledged professional? All the women will be in hot pursuit." She feigned alarm, teasing him.

"Of course not," he said, staring at her in shock. "It is nothing like that."

"Don't worry, I was only joking. Then, what is it?"

His face was a deep shade of red. Suddenly, what he wanted to say dawned on her.

"Are you by any chance planning to propose to me?" she yelled. "Well, even if you aren't, yes, yes!" she shrieked with excitement. She threw her arms around his neck and kissed him, passionately to the amusement of the other patrons, who began applauding the young couple.

Neither of them had much family, so they married in a simple ceremony.

Although both were keen to start a family, Mona was more impatient than Teddy, who was the circumspect party. She could not wait to meet their child.

"Yes. It will be wonderful," he acknowledged, as the issue cropped up for the umpteenth time. "You do realise though, that with the birth of the baby, not only will we be hard pressed, financially but your career will certainly be severely restricted, at least in the beginning?"

"True, but I think we are ready for this step. That same reasoning applies no matter how long we wait."

"I am not so sure. I agree that sooner or later we need to decide. Yes, we both want a family, but I think we should delay it until later when we are on our feet, financially and perhaps able to afford some outside help if we should need it."

"I don't believe that delaying will solve anything. So, why not go ahead, now?"

"Because you know how much pleasure you get from your work," he said. "And satisfaction," he added. "Are you willing to sacrifice all that?"

"I don't see it as a sacrifice. To me, it is exactly the opposite, a gift. I would have no regrets, I assure you, darling. Anyway, you know that women are good at multi-tasking. And don't forget, the process of conception might be quite pleasurable for you. And for me," she insinuated with a giggle.

They were ecstatic when Guy was born just over a year and a half later.

The birth changed the tenor of their lives, drastically. It placed a heavy responsibility on Mona's slender shoulders. From being a couple with only their own needs to satisfy, they were suddenly burdened with a colicky infant, who did not take into account that his parents had a life of their own. To sit down together for a meal, occasionally and just talk to each other would have been a very welcome interlude to the never-ending chores, tending to Guy, which included waking up several times at night, shopping, doing the housework and mountains of washing, preparing meals no matter how basic and at the same time, trying to attend to their respective careers.

"It is incredible how rarely you are irritable," he said, apologetically, after an argument on the recurring theme. "I admit from time to time, I get ratty, more than you do. I am sorry. How do you manage it?"

She nodded in agreement.

"My darling, I don't have to get up every morning or venture out into the world to bring home the wherewithal to support our little family."

"But I have begged you to rest. Why not take advantage of the time when Guy sleeps during the day and sleep yourself?"

"Honestly, Teddy, I don't feel the least bit tired during the day."

"I think you are running on empty. You usually get up to breast-feed a couple of times at night. During the day, you never stop for a moment, either. You are exhausted. That is why we bicker and it is taking a toll on both of us."

The conversation always ended with the standard reply. "I am tired, but I am fine. As soon as Guy settles down to a routine, we will both feel better."

The baby grew into a bright and inquisitive child, with a placid disposition, coupled with limitless energy and curiosity. He constantly bombarded them with a never-ending variety of questions.

"Why is water wet, Daddy?" he asked Teddy, who reported the conversation to Mona.

I had no idea how to explain. Just as I was about to say something, he follows up with, "Who puts water in the taps?" She laughed at his frustration.

"Don't worry, he wanted to know why cows like grass? He thinks we should eat it, too?" Teddy gasped.

"I am afraid if he does not get a satisfactory answer, he may start eating it to test the taste and nutritional value," she said, pretending to look worried.

"He loves animals and chicken fingers. At supper, he asked me where they come from. Do we disillusion him so young? He did not accept my explanation that we buy them in the supermarket. He thought it was too facile an answer."

On his chubby fingers, Guy would count off the time till his first day at nursery school. To their surprise, when they reached the kindergarten, he said goodbye to them, immediately and ran to join some children playing in the yard.

A fortnight later, as Teddy was about to leave after bringing Guy to nursery, Edna, the head teacher, said to him, "Guy has adapted, perfectly and we all love him. He is a beautiful child and the entire staff is so pleased to have him with us."

"Thank you, Edna. He is very happy to be here. H always tells us about his day in great detail when he comes home."

"You told us some of his questions, which have trumped you," she said, with a chuckle.

"Yes and he never stops, always insisting on getting an answer that is to his satisfaction," he said.

"It is the same with us. His inquisitive mind keeps us on our toes, and highly amused, I can tell you. He wanted to know how many children of his own God has because he was told we are all God's children."

"He certainly did not get that from us," Teddy assured her.

"What is surprising is that he was worried that it couldn't be easy being God's child as he would have to be good all the time because of who his Father is. Now, where does that comes from?"

"Again, not from us, I promise you," he said with a broad grin.

"He participates in everything including in some of the more impish activities with the other boys, but a raised eye-brow is enough for him to know he has crossed an unspoken line," she said proudly, as though she was describing her own child.

When he related to Mona everything Edna had told him, she giggled. "It is obvious that she has a soft spot for him."

"Can you blame her?"

"Don't think he can't be a little monster, too, at times," said Mona.

"Luckily, not often," he said.

Beaming with pleasure, she pulled a face in mock irritation.

"Do you remember you said I would miss work?" His face fell but she continued. "I did, a little, in the beginning, but now, there are absolutely no regrets. I assure you. We have waited for Guy all our lives. Just think how lucky we are. Can you imagine a gift more precious than him?"

He smiled with relief and took her in his arms.

"You are right but I am even luckier. I have waited my whole life for two precious gifts. They are much more than any person could wish for," he whispered, softly into her sweet-smelling hair.

They kissed passionately and launched themselves at each other to take advantage of their rare opportunity, until duty called again, as it was sure to do.

# Chapter 6

Dana finished a session with one of her young clients and noticed that Sally had phoned three times during the hour she had been busy but left no message. She decided to return the calls as she suspected it may have been something serious. When Sally answered, Dana was relieved that it was simply to report on the progress in her relationship with Peter. As usual, she was effusive in her language.

"It is better than anything I have ever known, Dan. I am over the moon. Perhaps, at last, this is the real thing" she said, breathlessly. "I had a feeling about it. Remember, I told you so and…"

"I am really happy for you, Sal but I can't talk at the moment," Dana interjected. "I am expecting a child in fifteen minutes and I need to look at my notes before she arrives."

Sensing her peevishness, Sally asked, "What about you, darling? Has Mike been in touch? Peter told me he was enchanted by you."

"The truth is that I have not heard a word since we met almost a week ago. I must say I was disappointed."

"Don't worry, he'll call," said Sally. "I can tell you he is quite a catch according to Peter. Women are after him all the time but he is very particular. The fact that he was so taken with you is fantastic. You must be excited."

Dana considered the idea. "Excited? No!" she decided. "I liked him, and I thought he liked me, too. In fact, he even told me so, but I suppose he has had second thoughts."

"Don't sound so downhearted," Sally said in an attempt to perk up the spirits of her dejected friend.

"He is probably too experienced for me, anyway. I imagine I was not sophisticated enough for him," Dana said. "Oh! And please do not ask Peter to speak to him. If he ever decides to ring me, well and good and if not, it is just too bad. I am used to it." Sally promised faithfully.

An hour later, Mike phoned. Clearly, Sally had not kept her promise and had either spoken to Mike, directly, or at least to Peter. Dana did her best to sound polite and a trifle off-hand, as though she was not in the least bit perturbed at Mike's not calling, when in fact, he had constantly been in her thoughts.

"Hello, Dana. How are you?" he asked, hesitantly.

"Fine, thank you. Busy."

"I am sorry I never phoned you earlier. It was wrong of me."

"That's alright. I imagine you have been busy, too."

"I have been busy but my behaviour is quite out of order," he insisted. "Please forgive me. I apologise."

"Apology accepted."

"I must admit, I have thought about that wonderful evening, over and over. I meant to call you several times but quite unlike my usual self, I did not know what to say. So, I kept on procrastinating."

"I cannot imagine you being at a loss for words."

"It was not that I was at a loss for words," he explained. "I really enjoyed our evening together. I told you that."

"Yes, you did, very explicitly," Dana said, pointedly. She firmly believed that her friend, Sally, had been up to her old tricks, again. *Why let him get off so lightly for leading me up the garden path*, she thought.

Mike ignored the dig and continued, "The problem is that I was confused at what I felt during and even after our 'date', if that is what you want to call it. I am still trying to sort out my thoughts. I know one thing for certain, though. I want to see you again, if you are still willing to see me."

She was reluctant to let her guard down or build up her hopes and trust the tremor of excitement she felt running up and down her spine. It might just loosen her tongue too much, so she chose her words carefully.

"Whenever you have a spare evening, give me a call and we will see if we can arrange to meet. There is no need to be formal, I would prefer it if we could be spontaneous," she said, coolly.

"But can we see each other, soon?"

"Yes, I would like that," She recalled that those were the very words with which their first date had ended. She hoped she would not experience the same crushing disappointment, again.

As Mike walked along the path leading to the front door, he admired the well-tended garden, with colourful flower-beds carved out of the lush lawn. Two magnolia trees provided a shady bower in one corner. He noticed the mosaic plaque on the pillar alongside the gate with Dana's name and a figure of a cuddly teddy-bear.

She opened the door, immediately. There was an awkward silence as though neither of them knew what to say. Then, she threw the door wide-open and with a curtsy and an exaggerated flourish said, "Come in, sir. Welcome to my humble abode."

He was struck by how tidy the house was and she recognised the expression on his face, immediately.

"I work from home, you see. I have my clinic here, so I need to make sure that it doesn't become too messy. Clients arrive at all times of the day."

"I see but still, it is exceptionally neat," he said.

"I must admit, I did clear up earlier after we arranged for you to visit," she confessed, guiltily.

"Are you normally this orderly, though?"

"Well, yes, I suppose I am. But after my children leave, sometimes it looks like a bomb has exploded." she explained.

"Your children?" he said, with some confusion.

She laughed. "I call the children I treat, my children. I love them, so it just seems natural to call them mine." She saw the relief on his face and realised what he had thought. "I have never been married," she stammered.

This time it was Mike's turn to laugh. "At least, you are not married, now. That would be devastating, before I even get to know you, properly." He handed her a bottle of wine, which he had been holding.

"White, I remember. Correct?"

"Thank you. I love white wine. I will need to find out the things you like, too. So far, you have been the one with all the attention to detail."

"I hope that you are impressed by more than just my attention to detail." She blushed at his inference.

"OK, then. Where are we going on our second date?" he inquired.

"This is actually our first date," she corrected. "Remember, the concert was our first undate."

"Funny, I did not think of it as a date, either, although from my point of view, it was a great success. But this feels more like the first time we are seeing each other because we both want to. So, where should we go?"

"Unless you prefer to go out, I would be quite happy if we stayed home," she said. "We already have the wine and I can make something to eat."

"OK. Suits me if it suits you."

"Good, then, just relax and I will prepare something. Any preferences?" she asked.

"No way, madam, I am a whiz in the kitchen. Why don't you lay the table and I will whip up one of my fortes, if you have the necessary ingredients?"

"Which are…?" she prompted.

"Are you a fish-lover, vin blanc and all, mademoiselle?" he said with a poor imitation of a French accent.

"Mmmm," purred Dana. "I have a cut of salmon, if it suits out three-forks, cordon bleu chef?"

"Perfect," he said, tying on an apron on the front of which was a photograph of The Last Supper by da Vinci except that, in the picture, all the Disciples were slumped on the table, drunk and semi-conscious.

"I hope our first supper is more of a success than that," he said, pointing to the apron.

"It had better be," she laughed. "And what else will monsieur conjure up for this memorable meal?"

"A cream-sauce, created wiz mois unique recipe goes ideally with the salmon," he said, persisting with an unimproved Gallic accent. "If I make a vegetable and green salad with dressing, ala vinaigrette, it will sweep madame off her feet."

"It sounds heavenly. While I get all the necessary ingredients ready, you put on some music."

He went over to the well-stacked rack of compact discs and immediately noticed the set of Beethoven Symphonies. He chose the Pastoral and as the first strains began to float, merrily in the room, she turned to him and smiled. He grinned back at her.

"I thought it appropriate," he said. "I know you love it, a reminder of our official undate."

He busied himself in the kitchen while she laid the table with her finest tablecloth and cutlery. A pair of Crystal candlesticks completed the perfect décor. She realised that this was the first time she had ever entertained a man in her home. It felt strange, yet she enjoyed how natural and relaxed she felt with him.

The conversation flowed effortlessly. She had already told him a little about her childhood and career as a Child Play Therapist and he plied her with questions.

"I want to know more about this woman, who devotes herself to children. What were her reasons for choosing such a profession? How do the sessions work? You are the first Play Therapist I have ever met."

"Well, I love children. I always have. That is the main thing. They are the fragile flowers of the future as one of my teachers who I really admire calls them. The definition stuck in my memory."

"Fine, that is a beautiful description, but what do you do as a Child Play Therapist. Why did you choose it?"

"Actually, it chose me. I had loving parents, but my own childhood was not a happy one. My parents come from the old school where a child should remember his or her place. They were stern disciplinarians with strict rules."

"Do you think of them as bad parents?"

"Of course, they never did anything 'bad' but they seldom asked me what I wanted."

"Did you really know what you wanted as a child?"

"I knew I didn't want to be a doctor. But that is what they wanted, and their expectations created huge pressure. I was always afraid to disappoint them, so I usually did whatever they expected."

"It must have been very difficult. How did it affect you?"

"I never had a voice as a child with the result that I never developed much self-confidence. I want to protect children from having to go through their own lives like that, with low self-esteem."

He shook his head. "I must admit, you seem to have adequate confidence and your self-esteem looks fine to me but I am beginning to get a clearer picture of the woman behind the mask and the incredible contribution she makes in the lives of so many children."

She smiled. "I see Sally has been talking to you."

"No." he said. "It was Peter who told me about you. He was very impressed with all that he learned about you from Sally. He said you achieve amazing results, over and over. Apparently, you have succeeded with all sorts of complicated cases."

"That sounds typical of Sally, to overstate the situation. But, I still love her."

"You are really very close aren't you?"

"Yes, we are. We have been friends ever since child hood. In fact, we met at nursery-school. We would do anything for each other."

"Soul-sisters, right? But tell me more about your work."

She smiled with embarrassment. "Naturally, in life, when children undergo some of the traumatic things that happen, often, they don't know how to cope with these negative experiences."

"I'd imagine they would probably be major events to have a real influence on their self-image."

"Not necessarily. There are serious cases like bullying or abuse, for instance. But it could be trivial such as the birth of a new sibling or being laughed at in class for not knowing something simple that has a profound impact."

"Wow! What a huge responsibility we have as parents."

"Never a truer word spoken, Mike!"

"It sounds as though it is more important to teach parents. Is it enough if you treat just the child?"

She nodded, vigorously. "You are absolutely correct. There really are few bad children. Unfortunately, many parents have neither the time, energy nor the inclination to learn. Whenever possible, I try to involve the parents in my work with their children."

"You must have witnessed some satisfying results, then?"

"I love it, especially when I see kids rediscovering themselves, healed in spirit."

"It sounds fascinating, Dana but can you earn enough from the work? It must be very demanding on you, emotionally. Also, from what you have told me, it does not appear that parents are always willing or able to pay for your services, especially if therapy extends over a long period of time."

"Again, you are right. It is taxing for me, emotionally at least, in the beginning, when I meet my 'patients' and witness the sadness in the lives of many of these young people."

"Dana, to me you seem like an angel in disguise."

"No, I am not," she said, modestly. "I enjoy my play time with them and the joy and satisfaction I experience when the therapy is successful is more than ample reward, far in excess of any financial consideration."

He was amazed at the depth of Dana's passion and love for 'her' children. "What you do is truly sacred."

"It is nice to know you are appreciated," she said. "Now tell me more about you. All I really know is that you lecture in the Law Faculty."

"Well, it is really a stepping stone for me. My ambition is to become Dean of the Law Faculty."

"Do you want to remain in the world of academe?"

"I prefer it to the hassle of the legal practice where you usually get your hands dirty. It is not for me."

"I thought you would enjoy the rough and tumble."

"Not really. My interest is more in the legal theory. That is why I am also writing a book on Constitutional Law. Believe it or not, I am considered an authority on the subject."

"Very impressive, I must say."

"I have had articles published in prestigious legal journals and I have even been consulted by official bodies, such as the government or municipal councils, which require clarity on obtuse points of constitutional law. Incredible, isn't it?" She stared at him in awe.

"I suppose there are those who say I am arrogant and perhaps they are correct. I have succeeded in most things I have done so I prefer proud instead of arrogant."

"You should be," she said with admiration.

"Thank you. I come from a background where we had very little and I have had to work hard to achieve what I have."

She paid careful attention to everything he was saying but there was a burning question she had wanted to ask all evening. When she felt the moment opportune, she took a deep breath.

"Mike, did you really mean what you said on the phone yesterday?"

"I said a lot, Dana, and I meant every word."

"It is just that I am relatively inexperienced in matters of the heart, as you can probably discern. I am very afraid of being hurt, which is why I have showered my love on children instead of investing it in romantic relationships. But you seem the exact opposite."

"Perhaps, that is why my romantic relationships have never lasted," he said. "I get bored and start to lose interest or else the woman loses interest in me because she senses my lack of commitment."

"Why will this be any different?"

"I sincerely meant it when I told you I have never felt this way before. I realise we hardly know each other and we only really met a couple of weeks ago, but I am amazed at how you have been in my thoughts ever since. It has never happened to me before."

"Really, we have spent so little time together. This is only the second time we are seeing each other."

"True, but I love your disarming openness and innocence. Perhaps it is the inexperience you referred to. I don't know. Yes, I have been in lust or madly attracted to someone before but what I feel about you is different."

When he noticed Dana's eyes shining, he took her hand.

"Dani. I wanted to be sure of myself before speaking to you. That is why I never phoned. I decided it was best to wait before I called you. I just could not wait any longer. I was dying to see you."

"You didn't phone because Sally asked you to?"

"Of course not, why would you think that?"

She smiled self-consciously. "I know her only too well. I thought she asked you to phone."

"No, I never spoke to her. The reason I rang is because of the things I just explained."

"I am sorry I even doubted you for a second, Mike," she said.

"I was never one who believed in love at first sight but I think I may have disproved one of my basic beliefs. And it feels wonderful." He hesitated for a moment.

"I hope I have not scared you off with my rattling on like this. I can't believe that I just said all that I did."

"You have done exactly the opposite," she said, gazing into his eyes.

He took a pace towards her. His arms enfolded her and he held her tightly. He kissed her forehead and she felt her head swimming while she nestled in his arms.

They remained tenderly holding each other, neither of them wanting this moment of bliss to end. She felt his hot breath on her neck as he bent to kiss her eyes, her cheeks, her ears. She was dizzy with abandon, no longer the Dana from before. She pulled him closer and pressed her body against his. He felt her fingers digging into his back as she began to writhe in his arms. Suddenly, after a few moments, Mike pulled away and stood opposite her, staring lovingly into her eyes, which were brimming with tears of passion.

"My darling, I don't want our first time together to be like this," he whispered, "I would love to stay here with you, forever, Dani, but I want us to have all the time in the world. I am afraid I must go."

She was bitterly disappointed, suspecting he had changed his mind after all. Probably, the time they had spent together during the past few hours was just another fling on his part. He saw the expression on her face.

"Dana, please don't be upset. I have a very early-morning faculty meeting. That is why I must leave, now. We have our whole lives ahead of us."

She wanted him to stay but her customary reserve held her back. "Yes, our whole lives," she murmured, instead.

# Chapter 7

Dana and Mike became like Siamese twins, spending every moment of their leisure time together. At a concert in the University Auditorium, she got a glimpse of the esteem in which he was held both by the academic staff as well as by the student body.

"They relate to you with such awe," she told him. "Students, I can understand. But your colleagues! It must be difficult to live up to that standard and constantly prove yourself. How do you manage it?" He casually brushed aside her observation.

"It is nothing, really. I am used to it. They think I know more than I actually do." But she recognised his pride and satisfaction at her observation.

At a comedy-club they rolled in the aisles. He invariably held his own with the best of the stand-up comedians. When they chose him to be involved in their banter with the audience, he was a match for them.

"How can it be that a woman as beautiful as your partner agreed to come with you, tonight? Were all her other boyfriends busy?" one of the performers threw at him.

"No! She was just curious. I told her I wanted her to see the worst stand-up comedian in town." Mike shot back to the applause of the audience.

They spoke to each other on the telephone several times a day, the first call in the early morning when they awoke and the last, late at night, before going to sleep. Neither of them ever wanted to be the one to end these conversations.
 "Good night, Dani."

"Good night, Mike."

"One, two, three. Good night."

Pause…"Why didn't you ring off?"

"I thought you would, so I waited for you."

"OK. Again. One, two, three." They disconnected at the same time. One of them always phoned back, immediately.

"I forgot to tell you, I love you."

"I love you back. Good night, sleep tight, mind the bugs don't bite."

They found themselves saying the same thing at exactly the same time. Whenever that happened, he would ask her, "OK! What am I thinking now, you witch?"

"Probably law, football or sex, in that order, Michael Weston?"

"You have the topics right but the wrong order," he said with a wicked leer.

They ate leisurely-paced dinners at fine restaurants or occasionally enjoyed breakfasts at some 'greasy-spoon' places, which he had discovered in his student days. During week-ends they went for long drives into the countryside, listening to their favourite music on Mike's top-of-the-range stereo-system. They hiked on forest trails through woodland and swam in mountain pools or gently flowing rivers. Often, when they were tired after a hard day's work, they stayed at home, either at his apartment or in her house. After a light snack, they watched television or read while music played in the background. Conversation was irrelevant. They were completely relaxed in each other's company.

"This must be the most perfect relationship possible," Mike said. "I never dreamt it could be like this. I always imagined it would take so much effort and here we are, just being ourselves."

"I think that is the beauty of our relationship," she pointed out. "We have fallen in love with each other and not with the put-on act or falseness that people usually present in new love affairs."

"You are so right, except, a few months is not so new, anymore, is it, Dani?"

She hugged him and kissed him on the forehead. "Yes, old man, not so new, anymore."

When they parted, they went to their own homes as though there was a subliminal understanding that they would not permit their sexual passion to affect the unique relationship that was blossoming between them. He was afraid that from past experience, his previous relationships had suffered a fatal blow when sex took place too soon.

He swore to her that theirs' was so important that he did not want to risk spoiling it and he preferred to wait. She accepted his reticence although she found it increasingly frustrating because, to her, he was the knight in shining armour she had dreamed would one day come riding into her life.

After a few weeks, they went to see the musical, Carousel, by Rodgers and Hammerstein. During the scene when the heroine, Julie, cries at the death of her beloved husband, the barker, Billy Bigelow, he noticed a tear trickling down Dana's cheek. At home after the play, he asked. "What brought on the tears, my darling? Why were you so overwhelmed?"

"I know I may be overly sentimental, but I really identified with Julie. My heart was breaking for her. I could not bear losing you, Mike."

"Don't worry your pretty little head, my angel. We will be together for a long time." She smiled, weakly but said nothing.

"The only thing I think about these days is you. I told you how it was in my previous relationships. I waited to be certain that what I felt with you was not just a superficial or sexual attraction. Now, I know."

"Thank heavens for that," she sighed, overly dramatically, pretending to swoon.

"Very good, Greta Garbo but I am in love with you, Dani," he said, tenderly.

"Oh! Mike," she cried, reverting to being her usual self. "I love you, too. I think about you all the time."

He cupped her face in his hands and she looked into his eyes with tears glistening on her lashes. He wiped them, gently with his finger tips and tasted them.

"Now I have a part of you inside me, my darling," he said.

"It isn't fair. Why should you be the only one with something inside of him, Mr Selfish," she said, quite unlike the demure Dana. He laughed at her bawdy comment.

"Come here, you."

He pulled her closer. She threw her arms around his neck and nestled against his chest. She could feel the pounding of his heart and the heat emanating from him aroused her even more. He stroked her body, from the back of her neck to her buttocks. His touch electrified her. She began to tremble and moan. He kissed her closed eyes and moved his lips sensuously down her face until they met hers. Their mouths locked together. She could taste him.

She surrendered herself to the tsunami raging in every cell of her body. As he caressed her and ran his fingers roughly through her hair, she shivered with ecstasy and writhed in his arms. Her body was tingling under his fingertips. She groaned and wept at the same time, abandoning herself to the emotional tumult overwhelming her. She had waited all her life to give herself to someone with such complete abandon.

His musky aroma intoxicated her. She wanted him inside her, needed him inside her, to feel she had swallowed him. He, too, groaned with a deep, husky voice, turning the normally tame Dana, into a wild animal, free, unfettered. They began to claw at each other, ripping off their clothing as their passion reached a crescendo.

When they were spent, they lay on the floor, panting, their bodies still intertwined.

He cradled her in his arms, his chest still heaving, as the raging emotions he had felt, began to subside. She lay with her eyes closed but the smile on her lips said more than any words could do.

"I am so glad we never rushed, my love. This is the moment we have waited for all our lives. It was heaven," he whispered.

"Yes, my darling, heaven."


A few weeks later, an envelope with the official emblem of the University emblazoned on it dropped through her letter box. She opened it and discovered an invitation to the induction ceremony at the University at which doctorates and professorships were to be bestowed on the laureates. She immediately rang him.

"Darling, I just received the invitation in the mail. At last! How exciting."

"I was asked who I wanted at the investiture. Obviously, you were at the top of the list. For me, you are the only person who matters to me. You must be there."

"It would take a team of wild horses to keep me away," she assured him. "I am so proud of you. In my entire life, I have never been as happy as I am today."

"The feeling is mutual, Dani. We are very good for each other and after so many months, it is safe to say, we fit together."

"Isn't it amazing how a chance arrangement brought us to this? Our friends Peter and Sally did us such a favour and they thought we were doing them the favour."

"That's what friends are for," he said.

Although she had received her degree at such an event, there was an atmosphere of pomp she never remembered from her own graduation. When 'her' Mike was capped, she nearly burst with pride as he strode onto the stage, his robe flowing behind him, his mortar board perched precariously on his head. She was filled with love for the wonderful man, who had become such an integral part of her existence.

After the ceremony, a reception was held for the graduates and staff and he introduced her to everybody as his 'partner'. He gave her a confidential wink and smiled, knowingly. She was intrigued.

Later, sipping cups of hot tea at her kitchen table, she said, "I am not sure how all those people are going to regard us in future. Was I your partner just for the evening or was there more to it?" He looked at her tenderly.

"Dana, my darling, the last months for me have been the happiest of my entire life. I wonder if you remember our conversation, when I phoned after our first 'undate'."

"Of course I do. How could I ever forget it? It is only seven months, but it feels like forever."

"It seems like that for me, too, Dani. Isn't it time we made the decision to live together?"

"We almost have or are?" she said. Soon afterwards they had or were.

# Chapter 8

The jingle on his cell-phone woke Mike. "Please, Michael, we must meet, urgently. I have something I need to talk about with you."

"For heaven's sake, it is Sunday morning, Pete. Do you know what the time is?"

"Yes, I know and it is urgent enough for me to insist, my friend."

"But, I have arranged to spend the day with Dana. Can't it wait for tomorrow?"

"Definitely not, it has to be this morning."

"Come on, Pete. We are going on a picnic to our special hideaway and the weather is beautiful."

"Sorry, old boy. I know the place. It is great, but I assure you what I want to discuss is even more important than a day out with a beautiful woman and such perfect weather."

He was so insistent that Mike could not refuse. Dana reluctantly agreed to postpone their arrangement.

"I have been looking forward to our day together, all week but you cannot let Peter down."

"I know, so have I but when he called, he sounded very mysterious. That is why I never told him to jump in the lake."

"I wonder what could be that urgent," she mused.

"He refused to give me even the slightest hint. He is my best friend, so I could not very well say no, could I?"

"I suppose not but I wonder what could be so pressing. I hope it is not something negative to do with his relationship with Sally."

"I doubt it. More than likely, it is to tell me that she is pregnant, if I know them. Well, we will find out soon enough. We have arranged to meet for coffee in an hour. I will come straight back. We won't miss out on our picnic, my darling."

Mike and Peter sat at their regular table in the usual coffee-shop drinking the customary cappuccino. Mike got straight to the point.

"OK, what is so pressing that it has necessitated this Sunday morning rendezvous?" Peter was smiling like a Cheshire-cat. It was uncharacteristic of him to behave this way. He took a sip of coffee and inhaled deeply while Mike stared at his friend with a look of amusement.

"Sally and I have been an item for over seven months, now. You and Dana have also been seeing each other for roughly the same length of time, haven't you? Since that famous concert, is it not?" he said with a conspiratorial nod.

"Yes, m'Lud," Mike said in response to Peter's grammar.

He continued as Mike stared at him, intrigued. "We love each other, and we are certain that we were meant to be together. At dinner last night, we spoke about the future for the first time, seriously. We feel that we know one another well enough so it is foolish to delay taking the step that we know is right for us." He stopped speaking and looked at Mike, waiting for some sort of reaction.

"Are you telling me that you have decided to get engaged?" Mike asked, incredulously.

"Exactly," said Peter. "I proposed to her last night on bended knee. Well, not quite bended. But, I asked her to marry me and she accepted. We want to have the wedding in about three months' time and, of course I want you to be my best man. What do you say, old boy?"

Mike jumped out of his chair and grabbed Peter in a bear-hug, while the other guests in the coffee-shop looked on in amazement as they stood, slapping each other on the back.

"That is the best news I have heard for ages," said Mike. "No wonder you could not wait until tomorrow to tell me. We knew it was serious between you and Sally, but you have still managed to surprise me. Dana will be over the moon when I tell her, if Sally doesn't beat me to the draw. Congratulations, Pete. Wonderful." They sat down.

"So, what is happening between you and Dana? You have been seeing each other exclusively and Sally told me you moved in together." Mike just smiled.

"I must admit, I have never seen you as dedicated as this to any woman and certainly, not for this length of time. It must be serious, my friend," Peter said.

"Yes, Pete, it is. We have spoken about it before, so you know how I feel about Dana. However, I have hesitated to make any irrefutable declaration in case there was not genuine reciprocation on Dana's part…"

"Whoa, m'Lud, spoken like a true lawyer, my learned friend!" said Peter, stopping Mike in mid-flow. "I am YOUR best friend, remember, not a trial court judge. It is very simple. In plain English, sir, you are in love with each other and from what Sally and I know about both of you, it is really a match made in heaven."

Mike sat quietly for a long time. Finally, as though he had reached some conclusion, he confessed to his best friend, "I think I knew from the first second I saw Dana that I would marry her. Of course, at the time, I never acknowledged the fact, even to myself."

"Now, isn't that just typical of you?" He ignored Peter's remark.

"We have been friends forever. You know me better than anyone else. I loved Dana from the first moment I clapped eyes on her even if I found it impossible to accept it, at first."

"Again, so typical of you, Professor Weston," said Peter.

Mike nodded in acknowledgement. "As the months have passed and we have grown to know each other more, the love between us has grown. It has matured. We can sit together, sometimes and not say a word to each other, both of us busy with our own thing. And yet, we still feel the connection. It is uncanny, a sort of spiritual contact."

"I told you, a match made in heaven," Peter repeated.

"Until fairly recently, I was still not sure. My legal training, my background, my past history, everything kept on warning me that perhaps it was not the real thing and it would pass."

"I can't believe it, the real thing. Really, Mike! Are you serious?" Peter said, mockingly.

"Actually, I didn't really know what the real thing was. Now, after more than seven months, the connection between us is much deeper than I could ever have imagined. Do you understand what I mean, Pete?"

"I certainly do," he answered.

"So? What do you think?"

"What do I think? I keep asking myself why you have waited all this time. We have done so much together, would a double wedding be out of the question?" he said, floating the possibility.

"I have already confessed to Dana that I am head over heels but that is out of the question. No!" he replied.

"NO?" yelled Peter.

"No, only because we should never do anything to spoil what is probably the most important day in a woman's life, her wedding."

"I doubt if a double wedding would spoil it for either of our future life's-partners. I think it is just the opposite, really. They are so close," said Peter, trying his best to persuade his friend.

Mike insisted. "Sally and Dana have looked forward to being brides all their lives. There is only room for one bride at one wedding."

Peter shrugged, his disappointment clearly registered on his face.

"Here, I should be the one showering congratulations on you for your big news. Instead, we seem to have been focusing on me. Sorry. If it is any consolation, Pete, you have helped me to reach clarity, for which I thank you from the bottom of my heart," said Mike.

"That's what friends are for. And, by the way, how much longer are you going to continue calling me Pete? You are the only person who calls me that. You know I prefer, Peter."

"Perhaps now that you have finally grown up, I will start but it won't be easy," said Mike, grinning broadly.


Dana listened to Sally, breathlessly describing ever minute detail of Peter's proposal and her acceptance as though it was the first time in history that anyone had ever become engaged.

"I am so happy for you...and Peter," she said when Sally finished talking.

"I know you are, Dana. I will be just as happy for you and Mike when you make the big announcement, too. Funnily enough, I had a feeling it would work out for you the moment I saw you together the first time at that famous concert." Dana laughed.

"What about you and Mike? When do you think he might pop the question?" Dana thought for a long time before answering.

"I am not sure. We know that we are going to share our lives together. No doubt about that. We have even spoken about it."

"Sooo!" cooed Sally.

"Mike is being typically Mike, super-responsible and anxious to make certain that he will be able to provide the standard of living to which he thinks I am accustomed."

"Men are funny, aren't they?" said Sally. "They think so differently from us women. They are mostly head and little heart."

"No. Mike is not like that at all. He is sentimental and very sensitive," she explained, "It is just that he thinks he needs to provide me with a lifestyle, that I really don't need and certainly, have never had."

"I imagine that together you earn enough to do very nicely, don't you?"

"Of course we do but he could earn much more if he were to leave the university and accept any of the numerous offers he receives regularly from some of the most prestigious law firms in the country."

"But, of course, Mike wants to make his mark as a lecturer in the academic world and as an author. So, I suppose he turns them all down, right?" Sally opined.

"Yes, I keep telling him that I don't care what he chooses. I will support him in any decision he makes. Anyway, when the time comes, I am sure we will take that step."

"He adores you, Dan."

"I love him very much, too and I will always be grateful to you for introducing me to him that night. My life has changed beyond belief."

"Mike is a lucky man. Sorry, bye. I have to go. The caterers want to speak to me." She abruptly, ended the conversation. She would always be Sally, a heart of gold and the sensitivity of a rhinoceros.

Their wedding was a gala affair, ideally suited to Sally's taste. It was a memorable day, despite the rain; the smiling faces of the three hundred guests, the cake and the lavishly decorated reception room were evidence of that. Mike and Dana, smiling, arm in arm, made an impressive couple. And, of course, Mike caused gales of laughter as he toasted the bride and groom in his speech as best-man.

Each and every event was meticulously preserved for posterity through the countless photographs and DVD's filmed and recorded by the technicians who stage-managed the function.

The four friends met to view the DVD of the wedding when the happy couple returned from their honeymoon. They split their sides laughing at the clip of Sally, snapped in mid-pose, throwing her bouquet directly at Dana, after carefully taking aim and missing, as it landed in the hands of one of the other bridesmaids. The look of disappointment on Sally's face spoke volumes.

Five months later, Mike was appointed vice-dean in the law faculty. He decided the time was ripe to propose and Dana was overjoyed. They decided on a small, intimate wedding. Even Dana's parents, who had been impressed by Mike when Dana had introduced him to them for the first time, beamed with pleasure on the occasion. No doubt, in their heart of hearts, they were relieved that their daughter had managed to land what they considered a rather big fish.

The wedding was the exact opposite of the function of their best friends and only forty-five of their closest friends and family attended on a glorious sunny day, which augured well for the future.

Sally and Peter had gone to Thailand for their honeymoon and tried to persuade them to do the same. However, they had made up their minds to spend theirs at the Hillside Beach Club Resort on the Aegean coast of Turkey.

After being appointed vice Dean of the Law faculty, Mike completed his first book and its publication was eagerly awaited by the legal community. The draft manuscript was read by some of the leading lights in the field and they showered him with compliments on his work.

Dana continued building a list of highly satisfied clients, who sang her praises and constantly referred cases to her. She even had several articles printed in leading, professional journals.

Their wedding too, was chronicled in photographs which they often looked at together. Two bulky albums captured many of the happiest moments of their life.

Harmony existed between them, despite occasional arguments, most of which were won by Mike, due to his debating prowess. She was realistic enough to accept that it really mattered little. The openness and patent expressions of love for each other and their similar taste in most things brought a perfect sereneness to their relationship.

He frequently sprung surprises on her and she delighted in his zany imagination and never-ending creativity. He would often leave gifts on her pillow, which she would discover when she was about to go to bed at night. For her birthday or wedding-anniversary, he would write her love poems, which she hoarded in an ornately-carved wooden box. She would take them out, occasionally, and reread them at her leisure.

She vividly recalled the time Mike had arranged to take Peter to the airport.

"Pete is going to Spain on a business trip in a few days," Mike told her.

"I see habit dies hard," she said. "How long will it take to get you to call him Peter, which is the name you know he prefers?"

"He will always be Pete to me. Anyway, he would like us to take him to the airport in his car, so we can drive it back. He wants to leave it at home for Sally to use while he is away. Of course, I agreed. Do you want to come with us?"

"It depends whether I have a treatment at my clinic. If not, it would be lovely."

At the appointed time, Peter called to pick up Mike and Dana, who was free and had decided to go with them to the airport. When they reached the terminal, Peter got out with his bulky suitcase and asked Mike to park the car.

"Why?" Mike asked. "We are going straight home."

To their amusement he insisted on their accompanying him to the check-in desk. Despite their vociferous objection, they finally agreed. Dana and he waited for Mike outside the Departures entrance until he returned a few minutes later. Peter walked with Dana while Mike trundled behind them, wheeling Peter's heavy suitcase.

"This is when you can tell a true friend," Peter said to her, carrying just a light bag as Mike struggled with Peter's suitcase.

"That's what true friends are for," Mike said, sarcastically.

They embraced warmly at the check in area and Peter turned to her. "Enjoy your trip," he said, giving her a bear-hug.

"What do you mean, enjoy the trip?" she said. "We will be home in twenty minutes. No time to enjoy the journey, not to mention the traffic and Mike cursing all the idiots on the road."

"You are not going home, and it takes a lot longer than twenty minutes to fly to Barcelona."

"Barcelona! What has Barcelona got to do with all of this? I thought you were going to Spain on a business trip," she said, confused.

"No. I am going home. You and Michael are the ones going to Barcelona."

For a moment, she was not sure what Peter meant, before the realisation dawned on her. She glanced at Mike, who was grinning like a Cheshire-cat.

"What a pair of conniving devils! Both of you!" she screamed. "You are the most devious men I have ever known, and I love you," First she hugged Peter and then threw her arms around Mike's neck in a passionate embrace.

"Not a bad start," Peter said to Mike with a lecherous leer. "I hope you can get her to maintain this kind of attitude in the hotel in Barcelona but make sure you do some sightseeing as well."

They strolled around, gaping, open-mouthed at the magnificence of the city, drinking in the atmosphere, pointing out places of interest to each other. They were especially fascinated by Gaudi's imprint on the city, which had made Barcelona synonymous with his name. They strolled along the Ramblas, intrigued by the never-ending panoply of merchandise and street-entertainment. They visited vaulted cathedrals, the footsteps of visitors echoing in the cavernous silence. They tasted typical Catalonian dishes in ethnic restaurants or enjoyed tapas in the street, while listening to authentic music provided by locals, enthusiastically encouraging the onlookers to show their appreciation in monetary terms. The Sagrada Familia Cathedral took their breath away. They stood gaping at the vastness of the structure, with its huge, tapering towers soaring upwards to the sky, hundreds of feet above the heads of the spellbound onlookers in the street, below. They were fascinated by the ornate gothic facades and colourful stained glass windows and spent hours exploring the Cathedral and other buildings, designed by Gaudi.

On a cool morning, a ramshackle old bus drove them through the mist up a precipitous, winding road. As they emerged from the fog into the bright sunlight, high above the clouds, they saw the remote monastery of Monserrat, perched on the mountain peak. Inside, a boys' choir, angelically sang the Ave Maria. It turned out to be one of the highlights of an unforgettable trip.

She was not sure, but she had a strong suspicion that the most enjoyable part of their visit for Mike was when they went to the Camp Nou soccer stadium to watch Barcelona play against Real Madrid, arch football rivals, in their legendary Classico encounter. She saw another facet to Mike, who screamed and cheered like a banshee.

Yet, despite almost seven years of unbridled joy, the only regret in their marriage was her inability to become pregnant. They had all the tests and, finally, it was established that the problem lay in Mike's low sperm count. They tried various treatments and even experimented with new, cutting-edge technology as 'guinea pigs', but none proved successful. Month after month, as disappointment followed disappointment, they realised that the solution lay in adoption. They resolved to investigate adoption procedures after she returned from the convention, which she was due to attend a few weeks later.

She had been invited to deliver an address at the meeting and she was highly flattered although she was extremely nervous.

"I know it won't help to say so, but try to relax," said Mike, who was extremely proud of her. "There is nothing to worry about. You will be a huge success and don't forget, after you get home we have important business to attend to."

"Thank you for making me even more nervous due to your high expectations," she said.

"You're welcome and I need to start getting used to missing you already," he replied.

# Chapter 9

Mona and Teddy had done their utmost to maintain their commitment not to allow Mona's illness to intrude into the idyllic life they had established but as one piece of bad news followed another, their spirits sank lower and lower. The particularly virulent strain of cancer had spread to other organs and the various chemotherapy sessions never had the beneficial effects hoped for. A radical mastectomy and radiation also proved ineffective. Mona lost all her hair and Guy could not fail to notice the physical changes taking place with his mother. Yet, even though she was obviously growing weaker, she kept on smiling bravely, through the pain and fear.

They never explained to Guy the nature of his mother's condition but he knew she was very sick. Instead of recovering, she was getting worse. She lay dozing in her darkened room, hardly ever coming into the rest of the house. The fun and lightness that once was an intrinsic part of the Goodson household no longer existed. People spoke in hushed tones. Sometimes, when he entered a room, the conversation stopped, as though they did not want him to overhear what was being discussed.

His father spent most of the time taking care of his mother. Teddy did his best to explain the situation to him, but he never sounded very convincing.

"Guy, Mummy is very sick and sometimes she needs to go to the hospital, so they can make her better. I know it is already a long time since she got ill, and it may take even longer for her to be well, again. You miss her and so do I but we need to be patient and pray that it doesn't take too much longer."

"Why can't Dr Barnett make her better? I want her to do all the things she used to. It isn't fair," sobbed the child.

Teddy cradled him, not sure what to say to pacify him. He, himself was close to breaking point.

"I want Mummy back. Dr Barnett has to make her better," he howled, inconsolably.

"The doctors are doing all they can. It is not easy. Even the specialists don't know what to do, anymore" he said, trying to console the child, achieving precisely the opposite result.

"Whenever Dr Barnett comes to see Mummy, he leaves me a treat, but I don't want his treats. I want Mummy."

Teddy felt helpless and alone. For many months, Mona had not been able to cope with the things she had always done and he handled most of them as best he could. He even gave Guy his evening-bath and he would smother him in the soft, Winnie the Pooh bath-towel he adored, as he dried and sometimes tickled him, but nothing made up for the absence of Mona in his life.

She had not been able to pick him up any more or play with him. The effort was too much for her. He had loved the feel of her smooth hands, caressing him and he longed for her soft touch as she tucked him into bed. Most of all, he missed her soothing voice as she sang to him.

She had even ceased telling him his bedtime story. He used to laugh happily at the way she would put on various facial expressions and use strange voices and accents to suit the different characters. Each evening, he looked forward to the latest episode, delivered in her inimitable style. No bedtime was ever complete without it.

Teddy tried to fill in for her but he was no match. Even when he tried to imitate her funny voices, it was not the same. Guy missed his mother.

Occasionally, she went into hospital and, as the periods there grew longer, he felt her absence more. Teddy tried to be both mother and father to him but because he was totally preoccupied with Mona, he was no longer the smiling easy-going father he had been.

"We love you more than anything else in the world and as soon as Mummy is well again, things will return to normal," he assured the boy.

But, he waited in vain. As his mother's condition continued to deteriorate, five years old Guy was bright enough to realise, not only that his mother was never going to be better, but that his father too, was struggling to deal with the enormity of the situation. When he thought no one noticed, Teddy would quietly weep but Guy saw it.

"Why are you crying, Daddy?" he asked with disarming innocence. Teddy quickly pulled himself together.

"I am sad because of the pain and discomfort Mummy has to suffer."

"When I was sick, you never cried like this. You remember, I had mumps and I had to stay in bed for a long time. Is Mummy sicker than I was?"

"Yes, I am sorry to say that she is, much sicker."

"Is she going to get better, Daddy? Eric, at nursery school, told me his father was very sick for a long time and then he died. Is Mummy going to die?" Mike had not wanted to confront that possibility himself and he had deliberately avoided considering the likelihood as though that would provide Mona with a continued link to life. Suddenly Guy's blunt question brought his vain hope into sharp focus and he realised the futility of it all.

"I don't know, my darling. She is sick with a grown-up illness. It is not always possible for the doctors to help someone as ill as Mummy. We just need to pray for her and show her how much we love her."

Guy weighed up his next remark before he spoke. "When I feel sorry for Mummy, is it alright if I cry, too?" Teddy picked up his son and held him tightly, as though he was afraid he might lose him as well.

The boy grew accustomed to creeping around the house, doing his best not to disturb his now, invalid mother. She never left her bed, anymore. On rare occasions, he would come into her room, where she lay motionless, usually sedated. He sat on the edge of her bed and stroked her bald head, the dark curls he loved long gone and when he took her hand, through her parched skin he could feel the bones. Her voice was very soft, and he could barely hear what she was saying on the rare occasions she spoke. His whole world had been turned upside down.

From a happy and well-balanced child, he became introvert and angry. For the slightest reason, he would throw a tantrum and cry for a long time. He no longer took part in all the activities at nursery school and even when he did participate, he did so without his old gusto.

Edna, his nursery-school teacher, knew of Mona's illness. Teddy invariably apprised her of the latest situation.

"There has been a constant deterioration in her condition," he told her. "Although the doctors are not saying anything, I think they have given up hope. It is ghastly, Edna."

The nursery school teacher was shocked. "It must be terrible for all of you. Please, let me know if there is anything you need."

"I appreciate that. At the moment, there is nothing anyone can do but I am worried and shocked at the effect it is having on Guy."

"True. At nursery, we have noticed that he is less enthusiastic than before and occasionally plays by himself. He is also quite moody and has the occasional temper-tantrum. It is not surprising. If I detect any more serious changes, I will let you know," said Edna.

"I am grateful to you. I know how fond of Guy you are and vice versa. It makes a big difference."

"He is a lovely child. Sad as he is, he still comes out with the occasional pearl. Just the other day, during play circle, he told his friends that his father's name was not Teddy but actually, Theodore. He said we call him Teddy because his mother once told him that she thinks his daddy is as cute as a teddy-bear." Teddy laughed, weakly.

"Another time, one of the boys accused a little girl of being a 'moaner'. His older brother had called him a moaner and he liked the word. Not all the children understood the meaning of the word, so I explained to them that a 'moaner' was a person, who complained a lot. Guy promptly informed the group, proudly, that not everyone who was called a 'moaner' was a moaner because his mother was Mona and she never complained."

"How ironic that is," said Teddy, bitterly.

Mona's steadily advancing illness was having a progressively deleterious impact on Guy's moods and affected his behaviour more and more. Not only was he more aggressive and moody but worst of all, it seemed a spark had been extinguished in him.

He was seldom involved in the play with other children as before. Now, mostly, he would just be an observer, declining to participate in nearly all the activities. Edna and the teachers saw it and were worried.

One morning, Edna drew Teddy aside to talk to him, privately. "We have all noticed changes in little Guy in the last year but especially more recently. We are very concerned," she said. "This often occurs when children lose the foundation of the security they require in their lives."

"He is a bit clingy and unhappy when I leave," Teddy confirmed.

"Yes. That is why he wants you to stay with him longer when you bring him to nursery. He is fearful whenever you go."

"He never did that before."

"No. It only started recently. You have even seen him cry so you don't 'abandon' him. That is now his greatest fear."

"The poor child, it is not fair," he said, angrily.

"Only yesterday, he snatched some blocks from one of the girls and when she tried to take it back, he threw them at her, drawing blood. When that happened, he started screaming and cried for over an hour. It was impossible to pacify him."

"That is terrible. I am so sorry. What you are saying breaks my heart. Mona is clinging to life and little Guy is the one most affected by it."

"True, it is not fair but there is nothing more you can do, is there?" she said.

"Nobody should endure the pain she is suffering, and we don't have any idea for how much longer. The specialists will not commit themselves, other than to tell us that all they are able to do at this stage is to try and keep her as comfortable as possible. She is being given quite massive doses of morphine."

"Isn't that addictive, Teddy?" Edna said with a worried expression on her face.

"At this stage, it makes no difference, Edna," Teddy replied with a shrug. "Honestly don't know what else to do."

"You have been a pillar of strength for both Mona and Guy," she said. "You have our sympathy and admiration. It is a huge burden resting on your shoulders, Teddy."

The misery that registered on his face was patently clear and she continued. "Please, do not think I am being presumptuous, but in the light of everything you and Guy have to contend with, perhaps it would be a good idea for him to see a child therapist, who could help him at this very difficult time. I am positive it would be a relief for you, too."

"Yes, I am sorry, but I spend my days and nights taking care of Mona and he is definitely feeling neglected," he said.

"How is she now?"

Teddy choked on the lump in his throat. "She is not responding to the treatment and the doctors have warned us to prepare for the worst. Obviously, they never give prognoses or time limits, but I am afraid it may not be very long now."

"They never do," she said.

"Oh God, Mona is a shadow of her former self and she is getting weaker by the hour. I don't know how I am going to be able to handle the situation after she…" his voice tailed off. "Not only me, Guy too."

"Perhaps, that is another reason to consult a professional, someone who can prepare Guy for the worst, if and whenever it comes," she said kindly, doing her utmost not to be too business-like.

"Do you know anybody suitable?" he asked, acknowledging the sound sense in her recommendation. "I have been worrying about it for some time, myself," he said, miserably.

She replied with great sympathy. "There is a woman who has an excellent reputation. She has a lot of experience, although she is relatively young. Personally, I know of cases where she has performed miracles. She is extremely busy, but she hardly ever turns anybody down. If you like, I will talk to her and find out her availability."

"Thank you so much. Guy never wants to leave the house any more. Nursery-school is about the only place he is willing to go to. And heaven knows, being at home, is no pleasure for him, either."

She cautioned. "We need to prepare him for any eventuality. He is six soon and starts school next year. I just hope Dana can accommodate him. Dana Weston. That is her name, by the way. I will get back to you as soon as I have spoken to her."

"I hope so, too. The situation is drastic, and I am not sure how much time we have," he said.

He drove home slowly, reflecting on his discussion. It struck him that when Edna had mentioned the need to prepare Guy for any eventuality she may well have been referring to him, as well.

Next day, Guy sat in silence on their way to nursery school. He seemed to be wrapped up in his own thoughts.

"What are you thinking, Guy?" asked Teddy.

"When I finish kindergarten, will Mummy be better so she will be able to take me to big school?"

"How do you tell a child, who is nearly six years old, that his mother is not going to able to see him go to school, let alone, take him there?

At the same time, how much of the truth do you disclose or conceal from him? Is he not entitled to be prepared for the loss of the most essential person in his young life? Even more so, should he not be spared the harrowing experience of the sudden disappearance of his precious mother, without any prior warning?"

These thoughts flashed through his head before he answered. Guy was not a child to be fobbed off with superficial answers and he had learnt that his questions demanded a proper response.

"You see how sick Mummy is. It is taking a very long time for her to get better. We need to be patient and when the time comes, we hope she will be strong enough." Then, to divert Guy's attention, he said, "Wow, soon, you are going to big school. Can you believe it?"

"I hope my teacher is as nice as Edna. Will I be able to visit Edna after I leave nursery-school?"

"Of course, you can. I am sure she will always be pleased to see you."

"Is Mummy going to die? I heard children at nursery talking. They said Mummy was so sick that she was going to die. Is she, Daddy?"

He had dreaded hearing Guy ask this question, again. He hardly dared face the reality and it shocked him to hear it expressed with such candour by his young son. He knew he had not given a satisfactory answer on the previous occasion. Obviously, it was still preying on Guy's mind.

"I hope not, son but we really don't know. She is fighting hard. She really wants to see you on your first day at school."

"I miss Mummy. Do you, too, Daddy?"

"Sure, I do. She also misses us. She is looking forward to seeing you in your school uniform, her big son, all ready for first grade."

Fortunately, they had arrived at nursery school and he was spared any further awkward questions. Edna welcomed Guy and nodded to Teddy, indicating that she wanted a private word with him. The child, as usual, was reluctant for him to leave and so he spent extra time with him until he became involved on his own, in the art corner, listlessly doodling on random pieces of paper. Once again, he had refused to play with any of the other children.

When Edna had taken Teddy aside, she said to him, "I have spoken to Dana, the therapist I mentioned. Fortunately, she is willing to handle Guy's case."

"Wonderful!" Teddy exclaimed.

"She seems the ideal person for him. I have given her the bare bones but, no doubt, she will want you to fill in the relevant details."

She handed him a neatly written note. He knew, with overpowering sadness, that Edna was preparing them for the inevitable that was now imminent.

"Again, thank you for everything. From the bottom of my heart," he whispered.

On the way home, he reflected on the questions Guy had posed. It was obvious that he knew more than either Mona or Teddy thought. It troubled him to think that the little boy was living in the dark and uncertain world thrust on him by the terrible turn of events. The urgency of starting therapy before the damage became irreversible was clear, if indeed, it was not too late, already.

When he got back to the house, Mona was asleep, so he decided to use the opportunity to call Dana. The children's laughter of her phone's ring tone continued for an inordinately lengthy time before the answering machine picked up.

"Sorry, I can't answer right now as I am engaged in a session. Please leave all your details and I will return your call as soon as possible." He hesitated for a moment before he left his name and telephone number in case she phoned back when he was not able to talk freely.

The voice on the recorded message was mellow and soothing and he tried to picture the woman to whom the voice belonged. She sounded friendly and warm and created a sense of trust and reliability. She was professional but not officious. He was relieved that he had not procrastinated and he waited anxiously for her return call.

Meanwhile, a flood of questions was racing through his mind. Will she and Guy find the appropriate chemistry? Does she have the necessary experience to deal with a case as sensitive as this? Have we left the matter for too long, already?

Fifteen minutes later, the phone rang and he saw Dana's number appear on the screen of his mobile-phone. He felt the tension in his shoulders as he considered what he would say to her.

"Hello," he stuttered. "Teddy Goodson speaking," he said, unnecessarily.

"Good morning. This is Dana Weston."

"Thank you for calling, Ms Weston."

"Please call me Dana. I think we should be as informal as possible, Teddy."

"Certainly," he said, still not completely relaxed. "I appreciate your ringing back so soon."

"Is it convenient for you to talk, now?"

"Certainly," he answered, again, realising, with increasing embarrassment, that he probably sounded robotic.

"Edna gave me some information about Guy and your situation. I am truly sorry. I can just imagine how difficult it must be for you. How is your wife?"

"I am sorry to say she is in a terrible state. She has been ill for over a year and a half now and the doctors have told us not to hold out too much hope. Her condition is deteriorating daily."

"Yes, Edna mentioned it. How awful it must be for you."

"I can't begin to tell you how heart-breaking it is," he said, miserably.

"No doubt, Guy too, has been affected by it all. We will see what we can do to help him through this very difficult time. The first thing is to meet so you can fill me in with some details and then I want to meet Guy."

"Whenever you like is fine. Soon, I hope," he said and then, he added, "If necessary, Edna can tell you a lot about the changes in Guy's attitude and behaviour."

"She already told me a little. She adores him."

"The feeling is mutual. He adores her, too. She has been there for us through thick and thin. We appreciate her more than I can say. When would you want to meet?"

"I am leaving for a conference in a few days so the sooner, the better. How would tomorrow morning do? At about ten, if that is good for you. I will text you my address and directions to get here."

"Fine," said Teddy. "I'll see you tomorrow at ten. Should I bring anything with me?"

"No. Just set aside about an hour or two for the normal intake. Is that possible?"

"This is so important that I will move heaven and earth to find the time," he said.

# Chapter 10

Teddy arrived well before the appointed time. He wanted to make absolutely certain that he would not be late. He hurried to the front gate, where he noticed the welcome sign bearing the names, Dana and Mike Weston.

The area was fairly affluent with the homes surrounded by well-tended gardens and freshly painted exteriors, which spoke of house-proud owners. After a brief ring, the gate clicked open and he walked to the front door where Dana was waiting.

"Hello, I saw you in your car, so I came out to greet you. Come in," she said and extended her hand. He shook it and unnecessarily, introduced himself, as they went inside.

He found himself in a small entrance-hall. He admired the indoor patio-garden with verdant plants and ferns opposite the entrance.

"The garden is lovely and unusual," he said.

"Thank you, Teddy. It is open to the sky so when it rains, it is enchanting. My husband and I love nature and this brings the outdoors, indoors. If you like, we can sit in the lounge and chat. Later I will show you my playroom. It is also very unusual as you will see."

"Whatever you say," he answered, feeling overawed and tongue-tied. Dana had turned out to be nothing like he had imagined. He had expected her to be older although Edna had mentioned that she was still young. Actually, they were of a similar age. More importantly, she appeared very self-assured, something he never felt. She succeeded in putting him at ease with her knack of being professional, but at the same time, informal and easy-going.

He welcomed her offer of a cup of tea and she went to the adjoining kitchen to prepare the refreshments. While she was busy, he looked around the room, which was tastefully furnished in light pastel colours. On the wall, over the couch was a large painting, which she found him examining when she came back with the tray of drinks and biscuits.

"It may look like an original, but it is not. My husband, Mike and I couldn't resist that painting by Gustav Klimt but of course, we could never afford the original. Mike was recently appointed Dean of the Law faculty when his predecessor and mentor retired. It is common knowledge that salaries in academe leave a lot to be desired."

"It is very lovely. And so is your house" he said, again.

"Thank you, Teddy. Edna gave me a brief outline of the situation. Your wife has been ill for a long time and because she is now very weak, she has not been able to devote attention to your son, Guy, as she used to do. She told me they were very close and all this has had a profound impact on the boy, who is nearly six."

He nodded his assent and she continued. "Edna feels it would be beneficial if he had some therapy in order to help him cope with the trauma. If there is anything else of importance you want to add, please feel free to do so or would you prefer if I simply ask the relevant questions?"

"I think that would be best," he replied, unsure what else might be important.

"I can imagine how difficult this must be for you. My heart goes out to you and Guy. Of course to your wife as well, her name is Mona, isn't it?" she said. Again, he just nodded. He was obviously very distraught, a broken man.

"Shall I explain to you how I work?" she asked, kindly.

"Yes please. Would you," he mumbled.

"Young children express themselves through play rather than in words. Often, children, especially those as young as Guy, do not have the language to express their feelings or their thoughts. So, I employ a technique known as non-directive play therapy. The child leads the way in play and I follow, allowing him to express himself, without my intervention. It is a technique which was started in America and has spread to many other developed countries with great success."

"I have not heard of it, but Edna recommended you very highly," he said.

"I have a clinic, here, a play-room with all sorts of toys from miniatures to dolls and doll-houses, an art corner and musical instruments, costumes, a sandpit, books, all things that children enjoy. In the play room, I participate with them, if they wish or I simply act as an accepting observer, when they don't. It is fascinating seeing the imagination and creativity of children when given free rein."

"It sounds as though children would never want to leave the play-room."

"Yes, but there is a set of rules which is designed to support rather than to inhibit them."

His eyebrows rose in surprise.

"Children need to be aware of the boundaries so they can feel more secure in their play, as in life, by the way. Boundaries are important, and children need to know exactly what they are."

"As long as the boundaries are not inhibiting, I suppose\," Teddy said, memories of his own childhood, suddenly conjured up in sharp relief.

"Quite so, I assure you, Teddy," Dana said, surmising that he was speaking from personal, unhappy experience.

"That is a relief. My own childhood was extremely limited by endless rules."

"I have come across that phenomenon time and time again, but my approach is completely different. I believe it is of primary importance to make sure the child has sufficient freedom to express himself, fully, within the framework clearly defined at the start," Dana said, her suspicion having proven correct.

"I think I have given Guy unlimited rope, too much, perhaps, due to Mona's illness to make up for the time I devote to her at his expense," he said, guiltily.

"We will deal with all that in the therapy. Anyway, through play, the child expresses his feelings and innermost thoughts. I hope I am not being too technical. Am I?" she asked. He smiled, weakly.

"No, you have explained it clearly," he replied. "Guy does his best to cope on his own because he sees how sick Mona is and he knows how worried I am. He is just a child. He should not have to accept that kind of responsibility. He must have many emotions locked up inside him. This might be a perfect opportunity for him to release them."

"Please take into consideration that it may seem that no progress is being made, especially in the beginning of the treatment. Sometimes, there might even appear to be a slight regression. Once we overcome that phase, the benefits become apparent. So much so, that often, one can consider reducing the frequency of the treatment or even ending it." An expression of relief flashed in his eyes.

"Some of the things I need to ask you may seem unimportant at this stage but for me, as a therapist, they have a great bearing on the behaviour or attitude of the child. For example, were there any difficulties or complications during Guy's birth?"

"No," he answered. "Actually, it was an easy delivery. Is that really relevant?"

"It could be but fortunately, it won't matter here because you say there were no problems. Sometimes though, during the actual birth, when there is difficulty during delivery, it can have an impact on the baby, which only shows up later. So, it is important to know this information."

He answered many more questions put to him, always couched by her in sympathetic and compassionate terms. When there was nothing further that she needed to know, he seemed to relax for the first time.

"Honestly, Dana, I have no experience in this area. He was always a happy, open boy. Now, he has lost the spark he used to have. He is far more tentative and insecure. He does not want to leave the house."

"Does he object to going to kindergarten?"

"Not really, although previously, no sooner did we arrive than he was off with his friends. He hardly had time to say goodbye. Now, it is exactly the opposite. He does not want me to leave him."

"How was he with his friends in the past, compared to how he is now? Have you noticed any significant change in his participation in the different activities? Edna mentioned to me that there has been.."

"He used to be one of the gang and loved being involved in games, play-acting, music, everything. Now, Edna says he often sits by himself and does not take part much. She says he is a very sad little boy."

"It is not unusual in such circumstances," Dana reassured him.

He smiled for the first time since he had arrived.

"That is a relief but he is also aggressive, on occasions. When one of the children tries to take something from him, he becomes very possessive and angry. He even injured a little girl, once. Sometimes, he throws a tantrum and cries and it takes a while for him to calm down."

He paused before continuing, his grief clearly etched on his face.

"I am desperate. He misses his mother. I know he does. You were right. They were very close. Recently, he has been worried about the possibility of her dying. He even said so even though it has never been mentioned in his presence."

She watched him with compassion but said nothing. She did not want to intrude while he was pouring out his heartfelt pain.

"I am trying to fill the void, but I am not coping. Honestly, I probably need help as much as he does, maybe more. I am at the end of my tether."

"Forgive me for asking, but have the doctors given any prognosis?"

"They have told us there is nothing further to be done, so we are just waiting for the end, whenever that may be. It could happen at any moment. It is not fair that she should suffer so much. Our beautiful family has…" He stopped speaking in mid-sentence, words beyond him at that moment.

"I think I can help Guy cope with this terrible situation. In all probability, it will also ease the burden, which you are carrying alone at the moment," Dana said with compassion.

"I hope so."

"I want to meet Guy. I will call round to see him whenever it is convenient for you. When would suit you, the sooner, the better from my point of view?"

"Is tomorrow alright for you, then?" he asked.

"As I said, I am due to attend a convention, shortly, so yes, tomorrow would be just perfect."

"How do I put the idea of therapy to him?"

"Just say I am a lady who has a room full of toys in her house. When children come to the playroom, they often feel better about things that may be worrying them."

"Tomorrow sounds ideal, then. I will speak to him tonight as you suggest," he promised.

"Well, I think that is it for now," she said. "Let me show you my playroom before you leave. It will be easier for you to describe to Guy, afterwards."

He was hugely impressed by her clinic and the huge variety of possibilities for creative play it offered children. "I am sure Guy will love being here with you. Thank you for agreeing to treat him."

"Thank you for coming to see me. I am looking forward to meeting Guy," she said. "I am sure we will get on very well."

He was not sure whether she was referring to Guy or to himself. Perhaps he did need her more than Guy did.

That evening, Teddy sat watching Guy in the bath. His little boy had grown and was no longer the baby he had once cuddled in his arms. Although he was listless and reserved, he was still able to do some things with greater agility and stamina than his father had. Guy's endless energy, dexterity and willingness to take risks scared him His physical growth astounded him, too, but his mental development did even more so. His mind was like a sponge, absorbing information and facts.

The trouble was that he was no longer that same child he had been before.

Mona's illness had taken its heavy toll. Although nobody had explained the details to him, he knew more than they imagined because he had a sensitivity that picked up even the most insignificant vibrations, like a well-tuned radio-receiver.

Guy had retreated into himself, into a private place where he could bury his pain. His demands were few and he resigned himself to the fact that, because his mother was very sick and his father preoccupied with taking care of her, he had far less time to spare for him.

He was a shadow of his former self and Teddy recognised the fact with blinding clarity as he looked at his son, listlessly, playing with his bath-toys. Because he had accepted that his mother would never get better, he was bright enough to know that neither would his personal situation. Teddy decided it was an appropriate opportunity to introduce the subject of therapy.

"Edna told me about a lovely lady she knows, and she said I should meet her because we know how worried you are and this lady could help you feel better. I went to meet her today. Her name is Dana."

Guy paid little attention to what he was saying and continued playing with the toys in the bathtub.

He went on. "She lives in a beautiful house and she has a special play-room, in which there are all kinds of toys and games for children, everything you can imagine. Parents bring their children to Dana's house to meet her and play in that special room." He paused, carefully watching the boy for any sign of interest but there was none.

He continued, a little disillusioned at Guy's lack of reaction.

"She explained to me that, if there has been anything worrying those children, who come to see her, after they spend time in the playroom, they usually leave feeling better. Edna told me how you love playing with the different toys at nursery and how you like to paint and dress up in fancy costumes. Dana has all these things and more, books, musical instruments and a special corner for art work, everything. She even has a sand-box. Can you believe it? She built a sandpit, inside her house!"

For the first time, the boy looked at him. Encouraged by Guy's attentiveness, he said, "I asked her if she would agree to you coming to her house to check it out so that you can decide whether you would like to go there to play sometimes. I told her about you and how much you like games and art and she said she would love to meet you. She even told me that she was willing to come to our house and invite you, personally."

"Would you stay with me at her house while I play, there. I don't want it be like nursery school, where you leave me behind and go away?"

"Of course, I will be there. Anyway, it will be different from nursery, Guy. You stay at school for a long time and parents are not supposed to stay. At Dana's house, you would only be there for about an hour each time. That way, you would always be able to go back and enjoy yourself, if you feel like it. I will stay there with you, too, don't worry." At last Guy smiled.

"I asked Dana to come and see you tomorrow, when you get home from nursery, so you can meet her and ask any questions you like. Is that alright?"

"OK, Daddy, we can see her tomorrow if you like."

Suddenly he asked, "Is Mummy getting better, Daddy? She has been sick for so long. Does she really want to get better?"

"I want Mummy to get well but as I explained before, she has a very serious grown-up sickness and the doctors are doing everything they can to help her. Sometimes, they don't know what else to do. I hope it will all be fine in the end," he said, his voice, tinged with a trace of abandonment of any hope.

He phoned Dana to explain that he had spoken to Guy, who was not averse to meeting her and coming to her clinic to play in her special room.

"You were quite right," he acknowledged, with admiration. "I followed your instructions and explained to Guy exactly as you suggested. He seemed quite pleased with the idea."

"Great. That will make matters easier," she said. "He may still be a little hesitant at the beginning, a strange environment, etcetera, but I am fairly certain that when he gets used to it, we will be able to start the real work. With a bit of luck, he will progress quickly enough to be able to continue without me. That is always my aim."

He was relieved to see Dana, again, when she arrived at their house next day. He already regarded her as an ally, a life-saver rescuing a drowning man.

"Thank you for coming so soon. I know how busy you are and I, we," he corrected, "appreciate your taking the time to visit us," he said, embarrassed.

"Not at all," she replied. "Is Guy here?"

"He is in his room where he spends most of his time. I will call him."

"No, don't do that. The first time we meet, I would prefer to see him in his room, on his home turf, as it were. He might be more comfortable. If he is happier in his own room, then that is where we will meet and chat. Just tell him I am here and ask for his permission for me to come to see him."

He recognised the wisdom and sensitivity of her observation. She gave him an encouraging smile.

While he left to talk to Guy, Dana inspected the living room. It had the potential to be warm and comfortable but it was obvious that the room was seldom used. It was tidy, too much so. Clearly, nobody ventured into the space.

There was a general atmosphere of gloom that pervaded everything. She reflected on this for a few seconds, wondering whether her knowledge of the circumstances was responsible for this feeling or because something in the surroundings caused it. She never had long to ponder as Teddy reappeared and advised her that Guy was waiting for her in his room.

Guy's bedroom was bright and colourful, with posters of Disney characters on the walls and an array of soft, fluffy toys scattered around. The room was also overly-tidy, as though its occupant was more concerned about the state of the room than about living in it, not at all typical of an almost six-year-old. There were many books, mostly, well-fingered and she assumed that Guy enjoyed stories and books.

*I wonder who reads to him with all that is going on in the lives of the Goodson family?* she thought.

"Hello, Guy," she said as she extended her hand, which Guy shook, shyly.

"My name is Dana. I met your daddy who told me a lot about you. I am so pleased you agreed to meet me."

"He also told me nice things about you. He was happy when he came home from your house, yesterday." Teddy blushed and looked guilty at Guy's naïve confession, like a child caught sucking a sweet, taken without permission. She noted his lack of ease and changed the subject.

"You have a lovely room. Gosh! There are so many books. Do you like stories?"

Guy nodded. "Yes. And I love it when Daddy reads to me at night before I go to sleep. Mummy used to read to me as well but because she is sick, she can't any more. Now, just Daddy does," he said, sadly. "I can read a little already but soon when I am six I am going to big school and then I will be able to read stories myself."

"Who taught you to read, Guy?" she asked.

"Daddy did, mostly," he replied. "When I saw that he never had time, I asked him to start teaching me. He told me what sound each letter has and I keep on practicing, so I can get better. Daddy helps me sometimes. Mummy also used to show me some words, but she can't do it anymore."

Teddy was surprised at Guy's garrulousness when he had been so uncommunicative for the past few months. He looked at Dana with growing faith.

"You must be very unhappy that your mummy is sick. I am sure it is not easy for you."

"It is not easy for Daddy, too. He looks after Mummy and he is very busy with everything else he has to do as well. Have you come to see if you can help me feel better?" he asked, bluntly.

"I meet a lot of children. I thought perhaps we could spend some time together and get to know each other. I spend time with children, who have things that worry them and who have not been happy. I help them feel better when we play in a special way" He looked at her with interest.

"Sometimes I feel like those children. I hope you can help me, too."

"I am sad you feel like those children but I am pleased you agreed to meet me, Guy. I am sure you will also feel better when you see my play-room."

"I hope so. I have felt lonely for a long time." Dana's heart melted at the child's plight.

"I want you to come to my house very soon. I am sure you will love coming to visit. I will arrange with your daddy to bring you to my house. I suppose he told you about my playroom, didn't he?"

"Yes, he did, and I would like to play there, if you let me."

"Of course, you may. I want you to see where I live and then when you visit me, we can spend a full hour together each time. How does that sound?"

"Good, thank you," he said, politely. "I will ask Daddy to bring me even though he is so busy. OK, Daddy?" he asked, turning to his father.

Teddy blushed. "Don't you worry. I will make the time."

Dana suggested that, as Teddy was very busy, it was quite in order for him to leave her with Guy.

"You will take care of me, won't you, Guy?"

"Yes. I can look after Dana, Daddy. I will show her some of my toys and books. She might like them like I do."

Teddy realised she wanted to spend time alone with Guy to find out to what extent she had gained his trust. Her suggestion had been a test of his reaction.

She had noted how much Guy was concerned about Teddy and his feelings and had kept referring to the need to take his father's situation into consideration, sometimes, putting his needs aside.

Teddy left them and they spent the next hour becoming acquainted with each other. Occasionally, he heard them, laughing out loud, something that had not been heard for a long time in the Goodson home. He was impressed at the speed with which she seemed to have won the boy over and he acknowledged to himself, the aptness of Edna's recommendation.

When she said goodbye at the front door, it was clear that he had found a worthy ally to share the responsibility for Guy's well-being and judging by the impression she had already made on his son, she was someone on whom he could rely. For the first time in many months, he felt easier. When she returned from her congress, the therapy would begin.

# Chapter 11

Mike drove Dana to the railway station, her last major responsibility behind her. Having met Teddy Goodson and afterwards, Guy, at their home, she had seen to what extent the young boy had been affected by his mother's illness. Ever since, her mind had been preoccupied with the terrible predicament in which they were trapped. She was filled with sympathy for them and had reflected on what relief she could provide. At least, it helped her forget the nervousness she felt at her forthcoming lecture.

"I already miss you and I haven't even left yet, my darling."

"By the time you get there, you will be so busy that you won't even have time to think about me," he said. "I know how much you have waited for this meeting. You said the keynote speaker is one of the world's leading lights in the field of Child Play Therapy. She was one of your lecturers at university, wasn't she?"

"Yes, she was. I am looking forward to seeing her again. We have so much to talk about."

"Make sure you enjoy the conference and forget everything else for a few days, Dani."

"I intend to but I have been so busy lately, what with preparing my address and seeing my children that I may have neglected you a little, Mike. I will remedy that when I get back, I promise you. I assure you, no matter how busy I am, you are always in my thoughts."

"So, I interfere with you that much, do I?" he said. She pulled a wry face.

"OK, seriously, what is happening with the case you checked out, the one with the young boy whose mother is very ill?" he asked.

"I plan to start therapy with him. He is a lovely, intelligent child. My heart goes out to him. We just need to coordinate the days and times. I will speak to his father as soon as I get back."

"I will hold the fort while you are away," he promised. "In any case, I need to prepare a lecture for my final-year students and with my inflated reputation, they expect something special. Sometimes, I wish they were less impressed with what they perceive as my razor-sharp intellect and legal knowledge."

"Well dear, that is the price of fame. And it is not just your reputation that is inflated. So is your ego."

"Don't be cruel, Dani. They are constantly consulting me with complicated legal conundrums, which I suspect are designed to deliberately trip me up. Fortunately, until now, I have never failed them but unfortunately, they keep raising the bar. Oops! Pardon the double entendre."

"Very droll, Mr Lawyer. We both know you really enjoy the challenge."

"I do but it is time consuming and I do not really have time to spare. I suppose that is one of the burdens of being the Dean, so I should not complain."

Dana grinned at him. "Knowing how you work I imagine you will do a lot of research on your lecture. This will be a perfect opportunity for you to knuckle down and get it done. Just make sure we talk on the phone every day."

"Don't worry. As soon as you have checked in, let me know so I can call." They hugged for a long time and kissed passionately before Dana wheeled her suitcase into the railway terminal and Mike drove off.

After she had settled in to her room, she sent him a text. A few minutes later the phone rang.

As he usually did, he crooned, "I just called to say I love you." Tradition dies hard.

"Hello, darling, how was the journey?"

"It was short and comfortable with just enough time to revise my presentation. I actually feel a little less nervous now."

"Great. You will wow them all. You know the subject inside out and you have a very convincing delivery style. I would hate to be the person to speak after you."

"As usual, you just succeeded in applying more pressure, you devil," she said with feigned peevishness. "What about your lecture? Have you managed to do anything about it, yet?"

"I started researching the topic at the law library but when I got home, I discovered we have no ink in the printer. I plan to go round to the stationer tomorrow morning to buy a refill cartridge."

"At least, now, you will be able to watch football on the television without a guilty conscience," she said.

"The season ended two weeks ago. There is no more football, so I will watch blue movies instead," he replied.

After a few more minutes of banter, as was their custom, neither wanted to be the first to ring off. At the count of three, they blew each other kisses and ended the call at the same time, laughing.

She adored the way he never tired of delighting her by incorporating funny idiosyncrasies into their daily lives. He constantly amazed her with his fertile and zany imagination.

Most of all, she treasured the poems he wrote for her on special occasions. The newest one was on the card he gave her when she left for the conference. As usual, she had found it propped up against her pillow the night before she left for the conference. She had brought it with her.

On the front, was a picture of a small girl, with pursed lips and a caption which said, 'Sent with love and sealed with a kiss.' When the card was opened, there was the sound of a prolonged, slurpy kiss. "How typical of him," she chuckled. Missing him, she read the poem for the umpteenth time.

My love, it is in no way bound,
Like nature's bounty, tis all around.
And, though the hours slip fast away,
Our love is like t'was on that day
So many precious years gone by
When first I saw you, first, felt I
You were a vision in my dreams,
A gift the spirits sent, it seems.
A voice, the cooing of a dove,
An angel sent by God above.
Dark eyes, smooth skin, soft lips to kiss,
An inner light of radiant bliss.
Caressing hands, Madonna's face,
Majestic poise, with beauty, grace.
And in the gentle lapse of time,
We've built, as one, our lives sublime.
Again today, my darling wife,
You bring such joy into my life.
I waited for you every day

I've spent on earth. Now, I can say,
I give undying thanks, my sweet,
The fates gave us the chance to meet
So, I could spend my life with you.
I pledge my love, eternal, true.

They had been married for over six years and she scoffed at the idea of the possible seven-year itch, which would have no currency in their perfect relationship. She knew she was a woman blessed with an adoring and considerate husband, who filled her days to overflowing. With his weird sense of fun, he never failed to surprise her.

She lay on the bed, daydreaming about her life with Mike, how much it had changed since she had been that prim, young woman, who had believed that love and marriage were not to be her lot.

She reflected on how she loved floating back to consciousness in the morning and the first thing she would see was his crooked smile. He would bend over her, kiss her once on her eyes, closed in semi-slumber, once on the tip of her nose and once, tenderly on her lips, as he intoned the morning mantra, "one for you, one for me, one for us."

Every morning, he brought her a cup of coffee in bed. She could hear the clinking of the teaspoon as he feverishly stirred the cup in time to the melody of the first movement of Beethoven's sixth symphony. She loved that playful tweak of her cheek every morning, as he gently whispered, "Rise and shine, my Dani."

Even when they slept, spent, after making love, it was always the same ritual, the tweak, the whispered endearments, his special kiss, the impishness she so loved.

In the midst of her musing, Sally phoned. After a few minutes of idle chat, Dana said, "Do you recall that I told you about the poems Mike writes for me on my birthday or our wedding-anniversary?"

"Of course, I remember. You often tell me about his surprises. Peter always talks about the time you went to Barcelona."

"It was such a surprise. What a pair? The two of them took me in completely, I was so gullible. I know it is hard to believe our marriage could be so perfect but truly, it is."

"I am sure you are exaggerating, aren't you? Even a little. Admit it, Dan."

"No, Sal. That is exactly how it is. Even I cannot believe it sometimes. We fit like a hand in a perfectly matched glove. We hardly argue and when we do, we sort it out, quickly. We decided never to go to sleep with an unresolved disagreement. It works. Really, it does. You and Peter should try it."

"Don't forget, we have two small boys and that adds a lot of pressure to any marriage," Sally reminded her.

Sally heard the sharp intake of breath her untoward remark had elicited in Dana.

"Sorry Dana. I am such a cow, sometimes. It was totally thoughtless of me."

"Forget it, Sal. I know it was not intentional. We are going to explore the subject of adoption on my return so don't worry."

"Even so, I am still envious of you. Peter is also a darling but he is not in Mike's league."

"In that case, I don't know if I should read you the poem Mike wrote me to wish me a successful conference?"

"Go ahead, Dan. Make me more jealous."

"Okay. If you insist," Dana conceded.

She read the poem to Sally, who listened quietly. When she finished, Sally was silent for a few seconds. Then, with a catch in her voice, she said, "You are married to an angel, Dana."

"Funny, that is what I often call him, my angel."

"I am not surprised that you do. I imagine there are not that many angels traipsing around on earth."

# Chapter 12

Dr Barnett was a source of great support for the Goodson household. He kept Teddy fully apprised of Mona's condition, always taking his sensitivity into consideration, difficult as it was for him to hear.

"Teddy, I am truly sorry, but I am afraid that there is not much time left. I recommend that Mona be hospitalised or go into a hostel. It will be easier to keep her comfortable and it will also be better for you," he advised.

The distress and pain registered clearly on Teddy's face and his shoulders sagged. He could no longer bear the weight of the calamity he had endured throughout the twenty months of Mona's illness.

"I know you are right, but she insists on staying at home." His voice betrayed his desolation because he realised the end was very near. "I will talk to her again although I am sure she will not change her mind."

"I suppose not but the burden on you is huge, Teddy. It has even affected your ability to devote time and attention to young Guy. Perhaps, it would be easier if I spoke to her?"

"I don't think so, Dr Barnett. She has told me many times that she plans to leave this life, knowing that the last sounds she will hear, the last sights she will see and even the last smells she will enjoy will be those of her own home with the two people she loves the most. It means more to her than anything else in the world," he said, heartbroken.

She lay motionless, barely awake due to the soporific effect of her severely emaciated state as well as the morphine, that was intended to dull any pain she might suffer.

Teddy remembered the doctors had told them, "It is dangerous to give Mona such large doses of the drug because it is highly addictive."

"Only when it is used for a prolonged period," Doctor Barnett had reassured him.

The doctor's reply was intended to abate Teddy's fears but instead, he realised that the subtext was actually that Mona was coming very close to the end. He was devastated.

Mona could hear familiar sounds in the house, but they seemed far away. She felt no pain, rather just discomfort, as she drifted in and out of consciousness. Nor did she have any fear. An aura of calm had settled over her, an acceptance of her destiny. There was no resistance to what lay ahead. She was serene and peaceful.

She opened her hooded eyes for an instant and saw her beloved husband, sitting at her bedside. He had maintained his vigil, day in and day out, during the last few months. As usual, he was holding her hand and stroking her fingers gently as he watched her sleeping and waking intermittently. She smiled at him, weakly. He squeezed her hand in acknowledgement. He felt closer to her than ever before. No words were adequate to describe the depth of emotion he was experiencing. He could not trust himself to speak in case he broke down.

Suddenly, her lips moved slightly and he had to lean forward to hear what she was saying. He was careful not to touch the infusion lines flowing into her shrivelled veins. He never let go of her hand, even for a second. As he bent over her, she opened her glazed eyes and looked at him.

With a weariness that filled his heart with pain and longing, she mumbled, slowly, "You had a visitor yesterday?"

He nodded. "Edna suggested we arrange for Guy to have a few sessions with a child therapist to help him cope with the trauma he is experiencing." A tear trickled down her parched cheek. He dabbed it away, tenderly.

"How typical of this angel" he said, more to himself than to anybody else. "She has not shed a tear for herself and here she is, at death's door, and she cries for Guy." He watched her, trying his utmost to keep back his own tears.

"She recommended a woman called Dana Weston, who has a wonderful way with children and tons of experience. She came to meet Guy, yesterday."

"How did you reach her?" she asked, softly.

"Edna recommended her. She inspired great confidence when I met her a couple of days ago. She very quickly won Guy over, too."

"I like her," whispered Mona.

He was surprised at her comment because her lucid moments had become fewer and fewer. He could not understand how she could have reached that conclusion. The effort to speak, though, had sapped her strength.

Struggling to breathe, and with the familiar pauses, she murmured, "I know how all this has affected little Guy. He is not so little any more, is he? Soon, he will be starting school."

Again, she was quiet, a weary smile on her wrinkled lips. Teddy was afraid to take his eyes off her even for an instant.

"How I dreamt about that day. I only wish I could have seen him growing up." Again, she stopped, gathering her flagging strength.

"I am so sorry for what you have had to endure. At least now, I am free. I do not need to worry about my precious Teddy bear and Guychick. You will both be alright, now."

"I love you so much, my darling," he said softly.

Almost inaudibly, still holding his hand, she said, "Same, me too. So tired. Going to sleep. Good bye, my love."

Her eyes closed, and she slipped into unconsciousness, her frail chest rising and falling with shallow breaths. He watched, fearful, angry at God.

"It isn't fair that she still has to suffer so close to the end." He cursed fate for what it had done to his beloved Mona. To him, his precious wife was still the most beautiful woman in the world although she was wasted and her skin as wrinkled and dry as parchment.

He remained at her bedside, knowing it was almost over. He fought to hold back the deluge of tears inside him.

He could not comprehend his life without her; he did not want his life without her. Had it not been for Guy, he was not sure what he might have done, watching her slipping away from him, little by little. He had never loved her more than he did at that moment.

*If only we appreciated the gifts we receive while we still have them*, he thought, bitterly, knowing he was about to lose the most precious gift he had ever received, those many years ago.

All night, he sat holding the hands he loved. Soon, he would not be able to hold them nor would they ever touch him or their son, again. He was wracked with longing for her. He already missed her more than he had ever thought possible. He realised he had subconsciously begun to mourn her passing.

Suddenly, the blanket covering her was still and she was gone. He stared at her peaceful face through the tears that stung his eyes. His heart ached for her. All that remained was the lifeless vessel containing the woman he had adored, all his life. The finality, the loss was overwhelming.

He was bereft.

# Chapter 13

There were so many arrangements to make that Teddy did not absorb the full reality of Mona's death. He had lived with the anticipation for such a long time and now that his most dreaded fear had come to pass, his mind could not grasp the enormity of the situation. Friends and neighbours rallied round, bringing food and offering to do washing, shopping and any other chores, which would release him to grieve.

He anticipated that telling Guy of Mona's passing would be one of the most difficult things he would ever have to do. As he held the young child on his lap and stroked his hair, the boy looked up into his face, waiting for his father to speak. Teddy found it impossible to talk due to his churning emotions.

Eventually, he said, "You remember I told you that Mummy was very sick, and the doctors never knew how to make her better?"

Guy nodded. "Well" continued Teddy, haltingly, "she never got better and…" He was unable to continue.

"Did Mommy die, Daddy?" asked Guy, with disarming innocence. Teddy's voice quavered and tears trickled down his cheeks.

"How do I tell this child that the person he loves more than anyone in the world has gone forever? I just cannot say the words."

The boy watched his father, patiently. Unable to contain the desolation that engulfed him, any longer, Teddy burst into tears. Guy, too, wept with him, father and son, together, grieving for Mona.

Suddenly, Guy took Teddy's hand. "It's alright, Daddy. It's alright if we cry when we are hurt. You told me that when I fell off my scooter and scraped my knee. You said it is good to cry sometimes. It lets you feel better, afterwards."

Teddy wiped his eyes, blew his nose and kissed Guy on his forehead as he slowly regained his composure.

Only after he saw that his father was calmer, did Guy continue. "One of my friends, whose mother died, told me she had gone to Heaven to be with God. I am sure Mummy has also gone to see God. Heaven is a nice place, isn't it, Daddy?"

"Yes, son, it is a lovely place. Mummy will not be sick, there. She will be happy although I am sure she will miss us."

"That's good. We will miss her, too, won't we?"

"We already do," he said, as he held him on his lap and hugged him, tightly.

Suddenly, Guy asked, "Will I still be able to go and play in Dana's special play-room?"

"We may have to put it off for a while, Guychick," he answered. "I will talk to her as soon as I can and make new arrangements. I saw how much she likes you."

"I like her too, Daddy," he said.

Since Guy failed to turn up at nursery, Edna enquired from some of the parents whether they knew of anything untoward regarding the Goodson household. But nobody did. After the last child had left, she decided to call Teddy. The telephone continued ringing without an answer, so she decided to call round at their home because, not unexpectedly, she had a premonition that there was something serious amiss.

Standing in front of the house, she noticed that the curtains were drawn, and an eerie stillness pervaded the premises. She pressed the doorbell. After a few moments, the door opened and a stranger greeted her.

"Good afternoon," he said, quietly. "I am Dr Barnett, the Goodson family physician. Please come in."

She saw a few people sitting in the living room. Teddy was seated on a low chair opposite them, looking exhausted. His eyes were red, and he was unshaven, a stubbly growth covering his sunken cheeks. When he saw her, he got up. She walked up to him and embraced him.

"I had intended calling you today but somehow I forgot, and time just flew past so I never got round to it," he apologised.

"Don't worry," Edna consoled him. "When Guy never turned up at nursery-school, I assumed that something must have happened. That is why I decided to drop by. I want you to know that I am here for you and Guy. If there is anything I can do for you at this very difficult time, please let me know?"

"I have already spoken to Guy and told him about Mona. He was very brave although I am not sure he fully understands what has happened, yet. The funeral is tomorrow afternoon. Perhaps, afterwards, when he realises that his mother is not here," he said, "and never will be," he added, with great difficulty, "maybe then he will."

"I take it he will not attend the funeral?" she said.

"No. I think he is a little too young for that," he replied.

"If you like, I can look after him, while you are away. I think he would feel better with me at a time like this, rather than in the care of someone else who is more of a stranger. I believe neither you nor Mona has much family."

"We have just the odd cousin and an ancient aunt. Otherwise, there is nobody."

"Did you have time to speak to Dana Weston?"

"Yes, I did. I met her at her home. I was very impressed with her. I wanted to tell you but with everything that has been happening in these last few days, you can well imagine. I need to let her know what has happened."

"Leave it to me. I will talk to her and explain the situation. When things settle down a little, you can re-establish contact and make new arrangements."

"I would appreciate that, Edna," he said.

"Actually, I would like to talk to her anyway. There are a few matters I want to discuss with her. It will be one less thing for you to worry about."

"As usual, thank you, Edna. You have always been there for us."

"There are many people there for you, Teddy, if you just give them half a chance. Can I say hello to Guy before I leave?"

"Of course, he will be glad to see you." He led her to Guy's room.

"Hello, Guy," she greeted him, warmly. "We missed you at nursery. All the children send you their love. They are looking forward to your coming back to school whenever you are ready."

He smiled at her. "I am ready, but I have to stay at home until Daddy feels better. As soon as he does, he will bring me to nursery."


The funeral was only attended by a handful of people, mainly a small number of friends and colleagues. When Teddy witnessed the sparse attendance at the graveside, he realised the limited extent to which their social life had shrunk. The funeral was the most difficult event Teddy had ever experienced in his life. Somehow, it was even more so than Mona's passing because it signified the end of her presence in his and Guy's lives, the extinction of her very existence. Their future without her stretched endlessly before him and he was numb with grief.

Next day, Edna phoned Dana to tell her about Mona. Her husband, Mike, answered.

"Hello Mr Weston. My name is Edna. I am calling on Teddy Goodson's behalf."

"Oh, hello, Edna," he said. "Please call me Mike. Dana is away, attending a conference on Child Play Therapy. I am at home being her secretary and taking messages."

"I must say, you seem to be a very efficient secretary."

"I could be better but the pay is very low," he said. "She is due to deliver an address at the meeting today," he told her proudly.

"I am sure she will be outstanding. I have heard so many complimentary things about her."

"Thank you, Edna, she will be very pleased to hear that."

"Anyway, I am Guy Goodson's nursery-school teacher. Dana was due to start therapy with Guy," she explained. "I know they met before she left for the conference."

"Yes, she mentioned it on the way to the station. That is why I recognised your name when you called."

"Unfortunately, Teddy's wife, Mona passed away last night."

"Oh, how awful! Dana will be terribly upset. Although, from the little I know, it is probably a welcome release for the poor woman. Perhaps her family will be able to get on with their lives, when the shock and grief have passed."

"I hope so, but it will not be easy," said Edna.

"I am about to go to the stationers to buy a refill for the printer. When I get back, I will call Dana and give her the message. She will probably return your call on her return from the conference, tomorrow."

"Thank you, I look forward to hearing from her. Nice talking to you," said Edna, as she rang-off.

# Chapter 14

Dana thoroughly enjoyed the meeting and her reunion with her lecturer was the cherry on the top. At the conclusion of her presentation, she received a standing ovation. She was besieged by delegates vying with each other to compliment her and shake her hand.

To her great relief, the lecture behind her, she could not wait to tell Mike. She called him but her excitement was dampened when he did not answer. She was dying to be able to speak to him and share her achievement. She decided to leave a message instead.

*He may have gone out for a few minutes. If I don't hear from him by the end of the lunch break, I will phone him, again*, she thought.

He never called, nor did he answer when she tried again, before returning to the conference for the afternoon sessions. Her concentration was affected and frequently, she found herself thinking about him.

"What is he up to? What is he brewing this time? Is there no end to his devilry?" she wondered.

At the end of the day, when there was still no message from him and there was no reply to the voice or text messages she had left, the first germ of concern began to worm its way into her consciousness.

"Where can he be? This is so out of character. He has never been 'incommunicado' for this long."

About an hour later, Sally Broome called.

"Why, hello there, Sal. How are you?" Dana asked, cheerfully.

"Peter and I are in the lobby," replied Sally.

"How lovely, what are you doing here, so far from home?" she asked, surprised at their sudden and unexpected appearance at her hotel.

"You never mentioned that you were planning to be in the neighbourhood, so far from home. I'll come down to meet you."

After a short intake of breath, Sally insisted, "No, we will come up to your room."

A few minutes later, there was a brief knock. She opened the door and the solemn expression on their faces caused a shiver to run down her spine. Sally burst into tears on seeing her and Peter was struggling to maintain his composure.

"What is it? Why are you her? What has happened?" she asked with alarm.

As they broke the shattering news, she barely heard the details, her mind incapable of absorbing the immensity of what they were telling her. But, she digested enough to know that nothing could have been worse than what they were saying; there had been an accident; a drunken driver; his car mounting the sidewalk, outside the stationers, where Mike had gone to buy ink for the printer; he had not known anything; it had all happened so suddenly, so fast. The driver, too, had been killed and, no, there had been no pain. The terrible words rang in her ears and numbed her to the very core.

"There has to be a mistake," she said, although she knew in her heart of hearts that there was no mistake. Mistakes like that never happen..

She felt the ground beneath her feet disappearing as though her legs could not support her. For a moment, she thought she was going to faint as her world disintegrated around her. She could not catch her breath and she felt she was choking. And then she collapsed on the bed in a deluge of tears, incapable of bearing the ghastliness of the fact.

"But I spoke to him only this morning. We never said goodbye to each other, properly. How can a thing like this be happening?" she cried, stubbornly denying the fact but she knew the truth and she wept, inconsolably. Sally and Peter stood by helplessly. What could anyone do in the face of such a catastrophe?

Her Mike was gone, forever. She had never fully comprehended the true meaning of the word 'forever'. Up to that moment, 'forever' had just meant a very long period of time. She always took for granted, as most people do, that eventually, whatever one might have looked forward to (or dreaded), would happen or pass and life would go on, as before.

But she did grasp its full meaning, then. The real import of the word and the tragedy hit her like a blow to the face. It decimated her. The greatest love, her only true love was over, and life without Mike stretched into oblivion.

The immensity of the shock overwhelmed her. She was living in an impenetrable mist. She longed to see Mike again, just once more, for the last time.

"At least, I want to be the one to identify his body," she insisted, although

Sally and Peter and even her mother tried to dissuade her. She was adamant, and, in retrospect, she was glad that she had insisted. At the same time, she did regret that the last memory she had of her beloved Mike, the one she would carry with her "forever" was his mangled body and almost unrecognisable face.

# Chapter 15

Mike thought back to the moment when he was knocked down. He recalled that literally, he never knew what hit him. He cartwheeled through the air, in slow motion, propelled from behind with such force that his body arched in a graceful curve before landing in a heap in the gutter.

Prior to losing consciousness, all he remembered was hearing the roar of a car engine and the shriek of brakes. It was immediately followed by the screaming of people and then, a colossal bang. The vehicle had skidded along the pavement and uprooted a street sign, before coming to a halt. The car ended up on its side, a smouldering wreck, acrid smoke pouring from the jangled pile of metal. He witnessed the scene, like one of the horrified bystanders, gaping in disbelief but he was no bystander.

He saw a crumpled body on the side of the road. It was twisted grotesquely, its arms thrown out to the side, the legs contorted beneath him at an acute angle. The head was lolling on its shoulders and blood gushed from open wounds on the legs and torso. The face was unrecognisable. People rushed over to the unfortunate victim. They were staring at him in disbelief. With shock, he realised that it was his own mangled body, lying lifeless, in the street.

His transition had not been easy. Despite what he had been told at his first meeting with his celestial messenger, he stubbornly continued to resist because, being typically Mike, he refused to capitulate. The more he did so, the greater his discomfort and he found himself frustrated and sometimes, very angry.

The main bone of contention was his desire to see Dana again. He had submitted numerous requests for an audience with the leading celestial messenger but each time, he had been given short shrift by his guardian angel.

*"When do I get the opportunity to speak to the decision-maker?"*

"Gabriel is very busy," he was told. "The troubles of the world rest on its shoulders. Gabriel bears the ultimate responsibility for deciding which matters should be referred to the Eternal One.

Before bringing it to the Source's attention, the matter must be assessed and considered by Gabriel. If there is merit, the issue is forwarded to the All-knowing and It decides what action should be taken, if any," added his celestial messenger, pointedly.

He was bewildered not only by his surroundings but also by the strange terminology.

*"You keep on referring to the Eternal One, the Source, the All-knowing and similar terms. Is that God?"*

"God, as you define the Supreme Spirit, has more than seventy-nine names. The ones you quoted are just some. You also know words like Allah, Elohim, Yahweh, the Lord, the Almighty, etc. but there are many more. Some people have even ascribed gender to the Source. You recognise the terms Heavenly Father, Father Time or Mother Nature. Many people even refer to Jesus, the Son of God as the so-called God. We prefer to limit ourselves to just a few. It is more convenient."

*"I take that as a yes,"* he said with undisguised sarcasm.

"We realise that you have not yet adjusted to the local conditions or to the time clock, as it applies here. In earth terms, you have been here for over a year. As I have explained to you over and over, in our time frame, there is no passage of time by which mortals live. Here, there is only now, the present. You are still in the process of adapting. Sometimes, it takes newcomers time to acclimatise although usually far less time that it is taking you."

*"Acclimatise,"* he shot back. *"Are you trying to tell me that it takes that length of time to make decisions here? All I want is a chance to see Dana, again, even if she cannot see me. I am a spirit, for heaven sakes. It is not as though I am asking for anything for myself."*

"We appreciate your altruistic motives but, for the time being, in a manner of speaking, you will need to be a little patient. Remember, you have all of eternity at your disposal. There is really no need to hurry, is there?"

*"Very droll, Bureaucracy here is worse than there,"* he snarled.

"You may not yet realise it because you are still relatively new, but what will be, what you refer to as the future, is already as it is supposed to be. Nothing needs to be done to make it that way. It is already what it is."

The exchange left him irate. *Blast,* he thought. *It is like an eternity since I first made the acquaintance of my celestial messenger and we have met on numerous occasions, since. It always turns up whenever I need something, but I still don't understand most of the concepts it explains.*

He was surprised his celestial messenger always knew when to appear. This accounted for his growing confidence as he began to comprehend the true meaning behind some of the familiar human clichés, including the expression, 'guardian angel'.

"I am pleased to see that since our last conversation, although you are stubbornly resisting what is, you are gradually getting used to conditions here, despite your attitude. You appear to be discovering that resistance to any situation only prolongs the discomfort. The sooner one accepts what is, what you on earth refer to as reality or the present, the quicker you adapt to what you resisted in the first place. Often, we find that when we do so, the original difficulty proves to be far less of problem than it seemed to be at first, or, sometimes even turns out to have been no problem at all."

Once again, he was addled by this inverted logic but since he had arrived, many things he had taken for granted in his life as being cast in stone, had turned out to be fiction and the controversial ideas he was learning were actually truths.

"I have been instructed to inform you that Gabriel has agreed to consider your request and interview you," it said, with the glimmer of a non-smile in its non-voice.

*"I am very pleased that, at last, compassion has overridden formality,"* he said, with an air of self-satisfaction, *"though, I don't quite fathom why you had to put me through the ringer before telling me that."*

"I need to remind you that there is an ongoing observation of events on earth to ensure that everything occurs in accordance with predetermined fate, as ordained by the Eternal One. It never permits anything to take place or to be out of alignment with its ultimate will. Whenever It observes something that demands intervention, the wheels are put into motion to correct the aberration.

Of course, only the Eternal One really knows what Its true intention is, which normally, is beyond the comprehension of others. However, the Eternal One, what you call 'God', is solely focused on the ultimate benefit to mankind."

*"Are you saying that 'God' is watching what is happening on earth to make sure that it all turns out as He has planned in advance?"* he recapped to ensure he had understood correctly.

"Precisely, except it is an It, and not a He," corrected the celestial spirit.

He had always believed that when a person left the mortal plane, there would be an instantaneous all-knowingness. Slowly, he was learning that it was not so. It was a gradual process of awareness. There was an unveiling of precepts that took place at a pace in tune with the "growth" of the student.

Perhaps, it took an 'eternity' to become fully enlightened and 'Judgment Day' was not what mankind had always assumed, a time of accountability, with consequent punishment or reward for one's acts during mortal life. Rather, it was a stage to judge whether the individual had reached a sufficient degree of awareness, enlightenment, so it could progress further, to the next level, as it were. Of course, since time, in the accepted sense, did not exist, Judgment Day for each, was at a different time and not at the end of it.

He still had many questions, but it was obvious that his guardian angel was anxious to end the debate. He, though, was encouraged that Gabriel had agreed to meet him because he expected to have his request granted.

*I had better play by their rules, for the time being, at least*, he thought. *I hope that they are not just trying to wear me down.*

"No, they are not," said his guardian angel, again reading his thoughts. "Your request could have been refused, quite easily. But Gabriel is willing to give it due consideration. Nevertheless, you must contain yourself. Patience is a virtue. When the time is right, everything will be revealed."

# Chapter 16

Family and friends rallied around. They took care of the funeral arrangements, death notices, everything. Dana was cosseted, loved and protected. She was never left on her own for a second. There was always somebody with her to ensure that she felt cared for and supported.

Sally moved in to the spare room in the house, where she stayed with her for the first couple of weeks, so she could help her deal with the void created by Mike's untimely death.

The trouble was that when Dana went back to her empty bed at night, alone, aching for him, smelling his masculine aroma that evoked such powerful emotion in her, everything simply accentuated the 'foreverness' of his absence.

She really wanted to be alone, to grieve for him, privately. She never had the heart to tell her loyal and loving friends that, much as she appreciated their presence and their kindness, she found the pity, cloying and the sympathy they tried so hard to conceal, suffocating.

Finally, though, after most people returned to the routine of their own personal lives and the house emptied of the guests and well-wishers, who kept phoning or dropping in to offer their condolences or food, then and only then, did she appreciate the full impact of Mike's absence.

She spent the long hours of the day, aimlessly moping about at home and, except for her best friend, Sally and occasionally, her mother, she spoke to nobody.

"I really can't face the idea of working, yet, Sally. Please, would you talk to my clients and explain that I am temporarily indisposed and I will not be able to continue therapy for a while."

"Anything you want, Dan. I am sure they will understand."

"No! Don't go into details. Simply explain that suddenly, a major crisis has arisen."

"OK. OK. I will do whatever you like. I think it would be better to tell them the reason but if you prefer not to, that is fine, as well."

"Sorry I was so abrupt, Sal. I am not myself as you can see."

"That's alright, Dana, I understand."

"I will give you a list of recommended therapists, whom they can approach, instead. Under the circumstances, that is the minimum I consider appropriate. When things settle down, I will resume therapy. Unfortunately, at the present moment it feels like it may be some time before I do. I know I probably need therapy myself."

"I hope it doesn't take too long, Dana. There are a lot of children, who depend on you."

"Yes, I know. I have included Teddy Goodson in the list. He expects me to start treating Guy, but now…" She left the sentence, unfinished.

Most of the clients did understand and, though many preferred to wait for her, their wait turned out to be in vain. She found it impossible to read or even to watch television. Nothing held her interest for more than a few minutes. All she could think about was Mike. With his death, she had lost all interest in life.

As the days became weeks and the weeks stretched into months, she could feel herself slipping deeper into a bottomless pit of depression. However, she never had the strength nor inclination to take a firm grip on herself and start the long climb back.

At the end of each lonely day, she crawled into her bed and switched off the light. To her, it was symbolic. Mike's death had been like the extinguishing of the light in her life. During every passing moment, she felt his absence more, as though she was missing an essential part of her own body. "Time heals all wounds," they glibly reassured her. However, if anything, the pain and longing only became more acute with each passing day.

It had been the same for almost a year. Ever since the accident, she had not been able to fall asleep at night and after hours of tossing and turning, sheer exhaustion would bring the welcome relief of oblivion. Except, that even then, her mind was not at rest but raced ceaselessly. Nightmares played havoc with her head.

Her dreams were always a variety of the same theme, a car rushing towards her at breakneck speed, the radiator grill snarling at her, through what looked like bared fangs.

She wanted to run but her feet were rooted to the ground and prevented her from moving. The vehicle loomed ever closer, with no sound, all in slow motion.

She could see the driver, unsuccessfully wrestling to regain control of the car.

But the inevitable always happened in the same way. Sound would return. The screech of metal on the road and the roar of the engine, deafened her. The car, catapulting through the air like a lethal missile, left the terrified woman, helpless.

Then, she would see Mike lying prostrate in the gutter, his legs and arms akimbo, what had once been his body, a mangled corpse, its face, missing.

She slept fitfully. She was always awake as the first pale rays of the morning light crept into her bedroom and slowly began to illuminate the dimness. She could sense it through her still closed eye-lids.

Her thoughts would start running riot immediately, as though controlled by a time switch, over which she had no control. She never felt rested. In the early morning semi-light, all she wanted was a few minutes of being neither awake nor asleep before she had to face another day without him.

She normally woke, exhausted, anyway, but relieved that the scenes, that had tormented her during the restlessness of darkness, were over for the time being. She knew it was all just a dream, but it left her breathless and trembling. In the morning, her sheets and nightgown were drenched with perspiration. She dreaded going to bed at night knowing she would have to face the demons that pursued her relentlessly in the shadows.

In the morning, by not opening her eyes, immediately, it helped keep at bay, the pain that gnawed away at her. It was always there, to remind her that he was gone, like an evil spirit, lurking in the dawn light filtering through the curtains. She was desperate and inexplicably began suffering panic attacks, which left her confused and shaking with fear.

Lying in bed, she calculated it had been over a year since she had ceased living. *My God, how time has passed, so fast and yet so slowly*, she thought, shocked.

She had lost complete track of time. She was well aware that her life had spiralled dangerously out of control, into a maelstrom of misery and despair. She hated being the victim she had become, yet felt powerless to do anything to change it.

Most of her friends stopped calling. She declined requests from people wanting to see her or refused invitations from others to come to dinner or just to join them at a social gathering. How often could you turn people down, explaining you were not yet up to it, that you needed a little more time?

Naturally, they were sympathetic and understanding but there was a limit to even the most faithful and loyal person's patience and compassion.

Eventually, she found herself completely alone and isolated. She justified her behaviour by reasoning that she preferred solitude to her putting on an artificial, smiling face.

Her life was over. She still yearned for Mike so much that, as far as she was concerned, there really was no point in going on. She realised she was acting irrationally, quite out of character but the yawning vacuum due to his untimely death had sapped her will to live. She had even considered the idea of committing suicide and had it not been for her fear of the pain involved in the process of killing herself coupled with her terror of death itself, she might have carried it out.

"What is the point if there is nothing to live for?" she told herself with resignation that only buried her deeper into the psychological tomb she had created and allowed to envelop her.

# Chapter 17

"Good morning, Guy. Hello, Teddy."

"Good morning, Edna," said Guy, who kissed his father and went off to find his friends.

"What is going on, Teddy? Guy is late quite often, these days. Is everything alright?" she asked.

"Sorry. For the last few weeks, he has been very reluctant to get up in the morning. It has become a war of wills and he normally wins. I decided to give him more leeway until he settles down."

She nodded with relief. "I am pleased to hear that that is all it is. He is less moody than he was, and he participates more, as you saw this morning but recently, he has shown a few unusual behavioural traits."

"What do you mean? When I think back over the period of Mona's illness and how clingy he became, he seems to have made great strides," he said, suddenly less sure of himself.

"He has but he still does not mix with the other children as freely as he did before," she said. "Also, he has the occasional tantrum, usually, over nothing. For example, yesterday, one of the children refused to give him a book he wanted. He tried to snatch it away and when he never got it, he screamed for close to an hour."

"I remember you told me once before, he behaved that way."

"Yes, that's true. But now, he can be quite aggressive. He tends to use his fists more and he even bit another child. Fortunately, it was just once. It is quite unlike the Guy we know. I wondered if you had seen anything at home."

He raised his eyebrows in surprise "I am shocked. I have noticed that he wants to spend more and more time, alone in his room. He doesn't even want to come to nursery school. I suppose he feels more secure there."

"You are probably right. He lost a lot of confidence during that difficult period in your lives."

He grimaced. "We both did. He has just started twisting the corners of his pillow and picking out the feathers."

"Don't worry. It is quite normal. Don't make an issue of it. It will pass in time."

"I hope it does. He is so unhappy." She waited for him to continue. Finally, he shook his head.

"It seems like yesterday when he was born. I still remember his first smile and how I loved listening to Mona reading him his bedtime story. She made it sound like a Hollywood production. But that has all gone," he said, bitterly.

"Fortunately, though, he is a very bright child, isn't he," said Edna with a smile of encouragement.

"Yes, he is. He has managed to learn most of the letters of the alphabet, already. When I read to him, he often points out letters and even a few words. He has mastered the basics of simple arithmetic, too, and he will only be six in a few weeks."

"That should make it easier when he begins school. Can you believe he is about to start first grade?" she said.

"He often refers to it. He is looking forward to his 'graduation' with great anticipation although he told me he will miss you."

"I will miss him, too."

She hesitated for a moment before continuing. "May I tell you what he told me?"

"Please do," he said. "I want to know. He is growing up so quickly. I feel we missed out on so much during the twenty months of Mona's illness. I hope we can catch up."

"There is plenty of time to 'catch up', as you say. The big thing is that he misses his mother. He accepts that he won't see her again. He longs to hear her voice the way he did when she told him those stories."

When she saw the look on his face, she hesitated. "I am sorry, Teddy. These are the reasons I feel that he would benefit from a few sessions of therapy to assist him after such a difficult time, particularly, so early in his life."

"You are probably right, as usual. His precious mother passed away more than six months ago. Since then, I have tried my best to assume the role of both parents."

"I don't envy you, Teddy, with all you need to handle. I think you have done exceptionally well. I admire you."

"Thank you. Fortunately, I have been able to fill this dual role, but unfortunately, not as well as I would like."

"Don't berate yourself so much. You did as much, even more than anyone could expect."

"It is considerably longer because, as you know, Mona was severely incapacitated well before the end. The demands on me were just too excessive. Had it not been for your support, I would never have managed. You have been a tower of strength, Edna, my Rock of Gibraltar. Thank you from the bottom of my heart."

"I will be there whenever you need me, but for now, we need to concentrate on the important thing, to find a therapist for Guy. I wonder if Dana Weston is available, yet."

They both tried to contact her but to no avail. Messages left for her elicited no response. Over and over, they tried to reach her but always with the same result, a dead-end.

"I don't understand," said Teddy with barely concealed frustration. "She seemed so sympathetic and professional when we met. Then, suddenly, she vanishes without a word of explanation for her disappearance. Now, not even any replies to our messages. What has come over the woman?"

"I don't know. Perhaps, we should speak to the other therapists recommended by her."

According to the list Sally had provided on Dana's instructions, a variety of child psychologists and therapists were consulted but Guy never took to any of them.

Eventually, they abandoned the idea of therapy as Guy was vehemently opposed to anyone other than Dana, the lady with the special play-room. And, anyway, even though he was not the same Guy he had been before, the child's behaviour had improved, considerably. He had been doing better at nursery in the past few months. Edna confirmed the fact to Teddy.

The first day of the school year was a welcome respite from the ongoing struggle. Guy had been very excited and for weeks he constantly talked about big school. He busied himself with preparations for the momentous occasion.

"Please Daddy, make sure my exercise books are properly covered and write my name on the front."

"I already did them all, son."

"I need a pencil-box with pencils and a pencil-sharpener, an eraser, and a ruler with centimetres and inches," Guy instructed.

"We have them, too. Look." Teddy showed him. Guy examined his father's work, carefully.

The matter of his school uniform, too, had all the trappings of a fashion parade. It required several visits to the local supplier until Guy was satisfied that it fitted him perfectly. It had to comply with the strictest requirements of his school's sartorial code.

On the first day, Teddy walked him to school, which was close to their home. Guy exhibited the customary nervousness but it was overshadowed by his enthusiasm and pride at becoming a schoolboy and leaving behind his 'childhood'.

Teddy had expected Guy to insist on his remaining with him until the last minute, especially in the light of his behaviour at nursery during the previous year. To his surprise, he dismissed him as soon as he met his teacher, Ms Commins, who welcomed the children with friendliness, coupled with an appropriate soupcon of discipline, fitting their initiation into the ranks of school-pupils rather than kindergarten children.

Most of the previous signs of trauma had disappeared as Guy acclimatised to the new phase in his life, especially where school was concerned.

Teddy was overjoyed to see his son beginning to shed the effects of Mona's protracted illness and death and he began to resemble the open, sociable child he had once been. He made friends more easily and he participated fully in the class-room lessons and schoolyard activities with his customary zeal.

Thirsting for knowledge, he absorbed information, ravenously. Teddy loved watching him poring over his exercise-books, his little tongue poking out to the side, as he practiced writing the letters he had learned that day.

He was fascinated by Guy, silently, mouthing the words he was reading from his new primer. When he read him his bed-time story, he could already identify sentences, as he followed the text of the story.

"Daddy, that is an 'a' and this is a 'c'."

"Well done. Can you find the letter, 't'?" He studied the page Teddy was reading to him until he identified the 't' and pointed it out, triumphantly.

"What word do those three letters make, Guy?"

The child's brow furrowed for a few moments before he yelped, "Cat!" Teddy clapped his hands and the lad swelled with pride.

After school, he would sometimes go to the homes of his new friends. When

Teddy fetched him at the appointed hour, he was gushing and related to him all the details of his school-day and afternoon visit.

At a Parent-Teacher meeting, Ms Commins told him, "Guy's academic progress is excellent. He is amongst the top pupils in almost every subject. He is well liked by the children and staff and participates in all activities with gusto. It is a pleasure to have such an outstanding child in class. I am pleased to say he seems to have put the tragedy behind him."

Despite the obvious improvement in the boy's behaviour and attitude, there were still a few lingering traces from the past, such as Guy's preoccupation with Teddy's welfare. He decided to seek Edna's advice as he was still concerned.

"What should I do? He is far too concerned about my feelings and is not allowing himself to be a child."

"Although you do your utmost to hide your true emotions from him, he senses your sadness," she said.

"It is difficult for me. I try my best to be cheerful in his presence, but people can't be 'happy' all the time, can they?"

"No, but he knows that you are still grieving. It shows, clearly, Teddy. And so as not to upset you, he is restrained and displays little 'childishness' in his play."

"So, what do I do?"

"The only advice I can offer is that you talk to him about the situation, openly. I honestly think it is about time you followed the example of your son and snapped out of this misery."

Despite the surprise on his face, she continued. "Sorry for my frankness, Teddy, but you did ask and I want to be honest with you. You know I only have Guy's and your best interests at heart."

"No need to explain, Edna. You have proven that over and over without question."

She smiled, shyly. "Don't forget, there is a special bond between the Goodson family and me that goes right back to the time Guy started at nursery school."

"Thank you for your honesty. I know it is not easy to say the things I need to hear. Most people simply mouth platitudes."

"Yes, it is very difficult, as you say, Teddy. You have gone through an impossibly trying experience, but don't you think it is time to move on as Guy has done? You are still a young man with a full life ahead of you. It is your responsibility to set an example to Guy and not the other way around. It often seems that he is the adult and you, the child."

He nodded, flushed with embarrassment. "When you speak to him, be honest. Ask him what he would like sometimes." she counselled.

He knew she was right. To his great relief, Guy had put Mona's death behind him more and more and the father in him envied this ability. If only he had been able to do the same. Guy had moved on and here he was, still bogged down in the past with little prospect of there being any appreciable change in his attitude.

The last two and a half years had been the most difficult time of his life. For the year and a half while she had been sick, there was nothing he could do. He simply stood by, watching the ghastly drama unfolding, powerless to do anything. Now, for the last year, it had all been in his hands and yet here he was, paralyzed, catatonic, still mired in grief.

He forced himself through the day, the hours dragging by and he found great difficulty in concentrating for very long. He was like a heavy-weight boxer, who had absorbed a merciless battering for fifteen punishing rounds and now, having reached the end of his tether, was ready to throw in the towel.

His life was empty and pointless. Even his responsibility for Guy's wellbeing had been neglected and he was ashamed that he had allowed that to happen. He did not want to go on any longer without his beloved Mona but he knew it was forbidden to even consider giving up because of Guy.

He recognised that the child had embarked on this fresh chapter in his short life. He also accepted the fact that, by design or unwittingly, Guy had chosen to get on with living and bury the past where it belonged, behind him. He admired his attitude but he realised how difficult and yet, at the same time how essential it was.

One morning when he delivered the boy to nursery school, he confided in Edna. "You were right. Guy told me that it does not mean that he has forgotten Mona or that he loves her less. It simply means that he has come to the conclusion that life is for living. Naturally, he never couched it in those terms but his meaning was clear," he admitted.

"Of course," she agreed. "And it will not mean that you have forgotten her, either. It is time to get on with your lives, to set an example for Guy."

He desperately wanted to do what she had suggested and become the example to his young son, but he found himself justifying to himself his reluctance to do so.

"Is a year adequate time to mourn? Should I continue for longer? Will Guy imagine that I love his mother less and I did not wait an 'appropriate' length of time? What would Mona feel if she were to witness what might be considered a relatively brief period?" He had no answers to the conundrums his restless mind kept on conjuring up and nor did she when he rationalised his situation with her. Edna listened, patiently.

"Perhaps other people might also consider it a lack of genuine love or respect for Mona," he suggested.

"I doubt if anyone would think so," she said, when he stopped speaking. "And even if they did, so what? Whose life is it, yours or theirs?" He shook his head in confusion as he wavered.

"After so much misery, is it not time to start again? Guy has simply chosen to get on with things instead of grovelling in self-pity. Have you seen anyone who thinks it is not appropriate? You should do so, too," Edna stated.

He decided to accept her advice except he was not sure he had the necessary conviction to follow through with his decision.

Next evening, he sat on the toilet seat, watching Guy in the bath. "Is there anything you would like, anything at all you want, son?" he asked.

"Not really, Daddy, I have everything I want except for Mummy. I still think about her a lot."

"I do as well, Guy."

"I wish I had a mother like other children, but I am glad you are my father. We are going to stay together, aren't we, Daddy?"

"I will always be with you, I promise, Guy. You can rely on me."

"What do you want, though, Daddy?" he asked, throwing the ball back into his father's court. Teddy was taken aback and thought for a moment.

"I want you to be happy even though sometimes, I know I make you sad. When I am feeling low, I do not behave as I should, and this affects you, doesn't it?" Guy fidgeted, uncomfortably.

Nonetheless, Teddy made up his mind to press on. "Whenever you see me like that, tell me and I will try my best to snap out of it and change the way I act. Will you?"

"I suppose that sometimes I am unhappy when I see you like that. But I thought you would only be sadder if I told you. It is not your fault, Daddy."

"No, son, I would prefer it if you did remind me each time I forget."

"Is it because you miss Mummy?"

"Yes. I miss her very much."

"I do, too, Dad. The trouble is I can't remember her face any more. I can't remember exactly what she looked like," he said, guiltily.

"I know, Guy. Don't worry about it. I am sure you remember other things, right?"

"She was very pretty. Do you still remember what she looks like, Daddy?"

"Yes, I do, but sometimes the picture is not clear with me, either." Guy smiled, relieved.

"She loved you so much. She never wanted to leave us. It is just that sometimes bad things happen and all we can do is to accept it" Teddy explained.

"Daddy, it seems that sometimes you don't accept it. Mummy went to meet God in heaven. I am sure she is sad when she sees us unhappy. She never wanted to hurt us, so we have to make sure she does not see us sad, otherwise she may feel she did something wrong."

"Who taught you all these clever things you have been telling me?" he asked.

"Nobody taught me, Daddy. I just remember Mummy told me she would never do anything to hurt us because she loved us so much. I believe her."

"Yes, Guy, you are right," he said as he lifted him from the bath, wrapped him in a huge, fluffy bath towel and held him, tightly, in his arms.

Afterwards, he read him a story, frequently interrupted as Guy proudly pointed out words and sometimes even sentences. When he tucked him into bed, kissed him on the forehead and was about to switch off the light, Guy asked, "Why am I right, Daddy?"

"You said I am sad because I don't accept that Mummy is in heaven and she does not want to see us unhappy."

"I hope you are not angry because I said it."

"Of course, I am not angry, son, just the opposite."

"That is good."

"So, I have made a decision," he said to the boy, firmly. "At least, once a week, we will go somewhere, just to have fun. We need to spend more 'quality time, together."

"I don't know what quality time is. What do you mean?"

"A person has fun when they do things they enjoy, like celebrating a birthday or Christmas. Quality time is being together and doing those sorts of things without distractions," said Teddy. Guy clapped his hands, excitedly and Teddy beamed with pleasure at his reaction.

"That will be great, Daddy. We will both be happy."

As a result, Teddy allowed himself to be absorbed into Guy's life more and more, smoothly bridging the chasm that had developed between them. He became more optimistic and forward-looking.

He re-established some of his old friendships and even his career took off at a sharp upward-trajectory. New clients approached him and the consequent financial advantages permitted him more opportunity to indulge them in their new adventures.

They went to a circus, one of Guy's main wishes. The boy especially loved the clowns and acrobats. At the local cinema, they saw an animated full-length feature film. Guy devoured the pop-corn at interval and a pizza, afterwards, although a small blister in his mouth was troubling him.

Guy was also anxious to learn to swim. He begged his father to take him to the local pool at least twice a week, where his persistence paid off, handsomely. After three lessons, Guy had mastered the basics and he was able to splash his way across the pool with relative safely.

Teddy also taught him to ride a bicycle, running alongside and holding the cycle upright. In the beginning, Guy was wobbly but Teddy kept on encouraging him.

"You are doing very well, Guy, but slow down a bit. I am exhausted. Let's take a rest," he said puffing heavily and short of breath. He did not want his remarks to curb or dampen Guy's commitment to master the art of riding a two-wheeler. Before long, the boy succeeded in keeping his balance and left Teddy behind as he picked up speed and self-confidence. Soon, his growing dare-devil attitude took control and Teddy had no option but to rein in the boy's enthusiasm.

He also wanted to play a musical instrument and he chose the flute. Teddy approached Mr Horne, the music master at school, who recommended a teacher. Teddy arranged for Guy to have weekly lessons.

As usual, the boy applied himself diligently and progressed rapidly. It required great patience on Teddy's part as the discordant squeaks and repetitive 'musical' phrases, which Guy practiced in the beginning set his teeth on edge. Fairly quickly though, he reached the point where Teddy enjoyed listening to his son playing some simple tunes.

One day, Guy came home from school and told Teddy, "Mr Horne has started a youth orchestra. He wants me to join."

"That is fantastic."

"He told me that way, I will be able to learn about classical music."

"He must be quite impressed with your progress, Guy."

"Í think so. He said that when I am ready, I will be able to join the orchestra as a fully-fledged member. Does that mean I will be a proper flute player in the orchestra?" he asked.

Teddy laughed. "Yes, son, that is what 'fully-fledged' means. I am very proud of you."

On the way home from school a few days later, Guy was bubbling with excitement. Mr Horne had advised the pupils that a Christmas concert was going to be held in the city's main concert-hall, the Arturo Toscanini Auditorium. "He gave us a flyer with all the details."

He rummaged in his school satchel until he found the crumpled pamphlet, which he handed to Teddy, who read it carefully.

"This is wonderful. The conductor is very famous. He leads the orchestra in a series of concerts in this auditorium every year. He has agreed to conduct a special concert with music that would appeal to children. The highlight of the programme is Prokofiev's Peter and the Wolf. Children from all the schools in the city will be able to attend, free of charge."

He listened to Teddy's explanation, carefully and his excitement knew no bounds. "Mr Horne said that all children must be accompanied by their parents. Will you come with me, Daddy?" he pleaded.

"Of course, I will. I wouldn't miss it for anything. I know Peter and the Wolf. I loved the music as a child and I still do. I am certain you will like it, too. You can tell Mr Horne we will be there. It will be a lovely new experience for you, us," he corrected.

Guy was awed by the vastness of the auditorium at the concert venue and paid special note of everything, which had been specially arranged to put the youngsters at ease.

Instead of the serious atmosphere normally prevailing at a classical concert, there were big balloons floating high above, bouncing against the vaulted ceiling. When they entered the hall, the children were greeted by people in fancy-dress costumes, like the characters in Prokofiev's musical drama.

The musicians in the orchestra wore casual clothing instead of their customary formal wear and the stage was adorned with huge displays of flowers. Behind the orchestra, welcoming the audience, hung a colossal banner, with a picture of laughing children. Even the conductor's podium was bedecked with colourful ribbons, suspended from the railings around the raised dais.

The conductor was greeted by an enthusiastic ovation from the audience. He entered the concert hall, threading his way through the array of musicians applauding him, tapping on the music stands in front of them. He bowed to the audience and then, towards the orchestra-members.

He turned back to the audience. "Hello children, ladies and gentlemen, welcome to you all. The orchestra and I are thrilled to see so many young people, who have come to hear the beautiful music," he said.

"The first piece is 'A Young Person's Guide to the Orchestra'. The composer, Benjamin Britten, wanted children to learn about the different instruments in the classical music orchestra and demonstrate how so large a group of musicians can cooperate and create music of such beauty. Each player contributes his or her part, big or small, to attain the end-result. No one is more important than anyone else." The message was not lost on the children.

"As you can see, there are many kinds of instruments, varying in shapes and sizes and the sounds each one produces are very different," he explained. The conductor pointed out the various instruments and introduced the musicians by having them stand, en-bloc, the string section with violins, violas, cellos and double basses.

Then, he pointed out the woodwinds, oboes, clarinets and bassoons and the brass and the tympani, as well as the harp, celesta, an ancient relative of the piano and finally, other instruments like the harp, xylophone, triangle and the strange looking and sounding glockenspiel. Each time he mentioned a different instrument, the relevant musicians playing them, stood and received an enthusiastic hand from the excited children.

The audience thoroughly enjoyed the performance. As he led the large orchestra through the complicated and intricate musical score, Guy was enraptured by the melodies and did not take his eyes off the conductor, He was fascinated by his arm-movements. They applauded loudly at the end and the musicians smiled with pleasure at their excitement.

As the ovation died down, the audience readied itself for the main item, Peter and the Wolf. The conductor reminded the audience of the layout and function of the different sections of the orchestra because of the combination of the narrative of the story and the music.

"The composer, Prokofiev, chose different musical instrument to represent each character in the tale. You will hear how appropriate his choices are. I won't spoil the story for you because a well-known radio announcer, who comperes her own classical music programme is going to narrate the inspiring symphonic fairy tale."

"But listen carefully as there are many different characters in this story. There is Peter, of course, the hero, represented by the string section, a duck, played by the oboe, a cat by the clarinet, the bird by the flute, Peter's stern grandfather by the bassoon and the dangerous and hungry wolf, played by three ominous French horns. You will even hear the rifle shots of the hunters so don't catch a fright." The audience laughed.

The conductor applauded the narrator as she made her way onto the stage. She shook hands with him and bowed to the audience and orchestra. When silence had settled over the hall, the music began.

Again, Guy sat wide-eyed, transfixed by the drama and bewitched by each instrument in the story, the lilting Peter, the menacing wolf, the brave marching hunters, the slinking cat, the stern grandfather, the waddling duck and bird arguing with each other about what sort of bird was a real bird if one could not swim and the other could not fly.

Guy was introduced into a new world, the domain of classical music and he listened, enthralled. When the music ended, the conductor made several curtain-calls, in response to raucous applause. Guy was an enthusiastic participant, clapping his little hands, his face glowing. Teddy looked at Guy and smiled with pleasure to see how the boy was revelling in his new-found experience.

The conductor bowed and signalled for the orchestra to stand as the applause continued, unabated.

With a broad smile, he again mounted the podium. Turning to the audience, he announced that as an encore, they would play music from Tchaikovsky's Nutcracker Suite. He told the audience, briefly, the story of the fairy tale, a ballet when the heroine's toys come to life and fight a battle to overcome the evil Mouse King.

As the music filled the auditorium, the audience was swept up by its beauty and began swaying in time to the familiar melodies.

Suddenly, Guy, impressed by the conductor's flamboyant style began to imitate him, at first, conducting from his seat. Then, carried away, he stood up, emulating the conductor on the podium. After a few moments, other children noticed him and began to do the same. Within a few seconds, most of the children in the auditorium were on their feet, waving their imaginary batons in time to the music, as Guy had been doing.

The entire orchestra was smiling, and the conductor, sensing that something was happening behind him, turned to see why they were grinning. When he saw the children on their feet, he remained facing the audience, his back to the orchestra and continued conducting the music, together with the children.

As the last notes faded away, the orchestra-members began to cheer the audience, the conductor leading the ovation. The clapping and whistling went on for many minutes. Guy's spontaneity had ignited the extraordinary occurrence, a chain reaction that had moved the entire audience as well as the orchestra, unaccustomed to witnessing such an event at any classical concert.

While the audience filed out of the hall, he could barely contain himself. "When can we come to another concert, Daddy?" Teddy tousled the boy's head.

"As soon as I find a concert which you would enjoy, I will book tickets. I promise."

On the drive home, Guy bombarded him with questions about music and the orchestra. The experience had opened a valve in him. It was impossible to quench his thirst for information.

"I really loved the concert, Daddy. How can I hear more classical music?"

"It is not always possible to go to concerts but there are recordings of all kinds of music on compact discs, DVDs and even on computers or old-fashioned vinyl gramophone records. Instead of having to go to concerts to hear music, a person can buy these recordings and enjoy them at home, whenever one feels like it."

"Do we have a compact disc player or a gramophone with records?" asked Guy.

"Yes, we do," he replied, anticipating the next question.

"Why do we never play any music at home?" Guy enquired. "Don't you like it? You once told me you did. I loved it when Mummy used to sing to me. Did Mummy not like music, Daddy? Is that why we never heard music in our house?"

"No. No. Mummy loved music. It was just that while she was ill, we did not want to disturb her, so we tried to be as quiet as possible. That's all." Guy was not satisfied with the explanation.

"I am sure if Mummy had heard music when she was sick, even quietly so we would not disturb her, she would have felt better. I felt better when I heard the music at the concert."

"Perhaps you did. From now on, we will have music in our home all the time.

I am sorry we did not play it before, but we will make up for it now."

"Do they have compact discs in heaven, so Mummy can hear music, too, Daddy?" asked the boy.

He laughed. "I don't know but I am sure Mommy would be pleased when she knows how much you enjoy the same kind of music she loved."

"I think anyone who hears that music would like it. I think it is just that they never hear it, so they don't know. I am glad you took me, Daddy."

With that, he nodded off and, unusually fell asleep, before they got home. Teddy watched his son, sleeping with a contented smile on his lips, his little chest gently rising and falling in rhythm with his breathing. He was usually charged with energy, a human dynamo so this was an unusual occurrence, to say the least.

*He must have been really exhausted for him to doze off like this. And he does seem to be a little pale*, he thought.

He reflected on how much Guy resembled his mother and his enjoyment of classical music reminded him of his beloved Mona. He missed her more than ever, but he was proud that his son had inherited so many of her traits. He remembered her as she had been. He was grateful for what she had brought to his life and the gifts he had received from her, especially their son. His heart overflowed with love for her and the boy.

He had travelled a long and tortuous road and had it not been for Guy, he might still have been bogged down in misery.

He mused on the fickleness of life; how the old could learn from the young. Still, from past experience, he suspected that life lulled you into a false sense of security. It waited for you to be contented and then, suddenly, it would introduce an unexpected quirk, which left you powerless and frustrated.

Thank goodness, he and Guy had each other and the bond between them was growing ever stronger with every passing day.

# Chapter 18

Dana was often reluctant to get up in the morning. She would stay in bed, propped up by her pillows and take out the box of photographs, cards and poems, which chronicled their life together. Each picture or poem triggered more longing in its wake. All the memories were there, in the box, those precious years with Mike, that had flashed past without her recognising just how quickly time disappeared.

She had always assumed that there would be a tomorrow until the bitter realisation that life was fleeting and her dreams and plans meant naught in the face of whatever controlled man's destiny. The only photographs missing were those of their unborn children, the sole blot on an otherwise fairy tale marriage.

She would not answer the phone unless she saw that the identity of the caller was either Sally or her mother. They rang frequently to check on her wellbeing but even with them, she often chose not to answer.

This time, whoever was phoning was very persistent and refused to give up even though she never replied. Finally, just to stop the irritating jangling sound, she checked. Not surprisingly, it was indeed, Sally, who she knew would to try and shake her out of her apathy as usual.

She vacillated for a few moments longer before deciding to answer.

"Hello, Sally," she said, curtly.

"Hello, Dan. How are we, today?" Sally said and continued before she had a chance to respond, as though anticipating a listless response. "I met someone who knows you and she asked me to give you warmest regards."

"Who was it?" she asked, suspecting that Sally was simply using this as a pretext to phone and pester her again, the way she had done countless times in the past months.

"Do you remember Edna, the nursery school teacher?"

"The name is familiar," she replied, as she scanned her memory.

"She was Guy Goodson's nursery-school teacher, remember? You asked me to phone her to tell her that you would not be continuing with his therapy," Sally reminded her.

"Oh, yes, she was the person who arranged the connection with the Goodson family in the first place."

"Well, I met her this morning. I needed to talk to her about my little Peter," said Sally.

"From my recollection, she has an excellent reputation. She is extremely professional and really cares about the children," Dana acknowledged.

"I assure you, she is everything you heard and more. She has expanded the nursery-school so that she now has enough children to run two separate streams. She does not accept too many children in either, so the little darlings receive excellent care and attention and her results speak for themselves."

"I am not in the least bit surprised that she has been so successful."

"I wanted to talk to her about little Peter who goes to her school. Can you believe that my young son is already at nursery-school?"

"Time flies by so quickly, doesn't it? One scarcely notices it unless you miss someone," Dana said.

"Well, I still cannot get used to the idea. Peter and I have been married now for almost eight years."

When she heard the catch in Dana's voice, she realised how thoughtless she had been. Dana's grief was still raw, despite the lapse of time and Sally's indiscretion had stung her, deeply.

"Oh Dana, I am so sorry. I was not thinking. Please forgive me. I am such a bull in a china shop, sometimes. I could kick myself for what I just said."

Dana knew her friend well enough to know that she had not meant to upset her and she dismissed it again as an unfortunate slip of the tongue, certainly not the first and probably not the last.

"Really, Sally, it's alright and I do remember Edna well, by the way."

Sally was relieved to have been let off the hook so lightly.

"So sorry, again, Dan. After we finished discussing our business, she wanted to know if, by any chance, my friend, Dana Weston was working, again. Can you imagine my surprise? Out of the blue, like that."

"It is not so surprising. I imagine she remembered our connection," Dana said.

"Perhaps she did. Anyway, she asked me to give you her best wishes."

"Thank you."

"She mentioned that you met the young child and his father, who seemed to need counselling as much as the child did. At least, that is what Edna emphasised, by the way."

"Perhaps, even more so," Dana said.

"Well, both father and son were very impressed with you and they were very disappointed that the arrangement for the lad's therapy never came to fruition."

"Yes, it was a terrible situation," Dana said. "They were a tightly knit family and the mother's illness was devastating both for of them."

"You may not know but the boy's mother died right after they met you."

"How awful!" gasped Dana. "Poor Guy, losing his mother so young. I am sure Teddy must have been cut up beyond belief."

"He was and as far as I know, he has not really managed to get over it. Edna suggested that it might be a good idea for you to speak to him to put the final touches to unfinished business. Perhaps you could even speak to her first. It may make a call to him easier."

"I do remember them, clearly. He was so distressed about his wife that he was barely capable of functioning."

"Edna thinks it would make a huge difference to both of them if you were willing to start therapy with Guy, even now. I think she intends phoning and asking you to ring Teddy," Sally said.

"When I met the child, he was lovely. He was very bright and I enjoyed talking to him. I have thought about him from time to time. I am terribly sorry that in the end, things panned out for them as they did," she said. "And for myself," she added, ruefully.

"We all were, Dan." said Sally.

"I felt a very strong connection to them. It seems the tragedy in both our lives occurred almost simultaneously. I may just speak to him if I can pluck up the courage…and willpower."

"I really hope you will. I am sure it would do both of you the world of good. There are so many children out there, who could use your talent and expertise. Don't let that ability go to waste, Dan."

"Thank you for calling, Sal. Good luck with both big and little Peter, by the way. With two sons now, you really are a family. I envy you."

"Just one more thing," added Sally. "I told Edna the reason for your decision to stop working. I hope that is in order. When I spoke to her originally, I never gave her any details, as you insisted. I felt it was appropriate to let her know

now."

"That is OK, Sal. Bye."

She sat thinking about their conversation. She was fully aware how imperative it may have been to accept Sally's recommendation to call Teddy but her resolve was not strong enough and she put off the decision for another time. Procrastination, as usual was her easiest course of action.

# Chapter 19

For the first time in more than two years, Guy slipped quietly into his father's bed. Teddy could feel his warm body next to his and he held him, lightly, not wanting to waken him.

It cast him back to the times when Guy would regularly appear in his and Mona's bed. Once again, he felt the familiar pangs of sadness at their loss. *At least, we are putting that behind us, thanks to Guy*, he thought.

An hour later, when it was time to wake Guy, he kissed him tenderly on the cheek and whispered, "Rise and shine, big boy, time to get up for school."

Guy rubbed his eyes and smiled at him as he orientated himself. He stretched, arching his back like a kitten.

He went to dress and Teddy began laying the breakfast table with cereals, vegetables, cheeses, yoghurt, fruit and honey. He poured each of them a glass of orange juice before he went in search of the boy, who was still in the bathroom, washing his face and brushing his teeth.

Guy, nearly seven years of age, had matured appreciably and Teddy was struck by his physical growth.

*He is certainly no longer my baby*, he thought to himself with pride.

He noticed a large bruise on Guy's lower back and another on his left thigh and he was slightly perturbed by them but said nothing. At breakfast, Guy ate very little.

"Is something wrong?" Teddy asked, surprised. "It is not like you to eat so little at breakfast. Are you sure you don't want a slice of bread and honey or some yoghurt?"

"No thank you, Daddy. I am just not hungry."

Teddy began to feel uneasy. "Where did you get those bruises on your back and thigh I noticed when you were in the bathroom? Were you in a fight with someone?"

"Of course, I wasn't, Dad."

"Did you bump into something or hurt yourself somewhere? They look quite serious."

"I don't remember hurting myself. I didn't even know I had them. And please don't worry, I am fine. I am just not hungry, that's all."

"I hope so," said Teddy, not entirely convinced. "What is happening with your music lessons by the way?" he asked in the hope that through conversation, Guy might shed some light on the cause of the bruises.

"I am enjoying learning to play my flute very much. Mr Horne told me that if I keep improving, I will soon be admitted to the youth orchestra. I just need to keep practicing."

"Well done. Whenever I hear you playing, I am really impressed," he said, tousling Guy's hair as the boy pulled a sour face and patted his hair back into place.

At school, Guy gave Teddy a cursory hug and dashed off to find his friends. He disappeared in the throng of children playing in the school yard. He was again, as before, a keen participant, cavorting with the other boys. They were extremely boisterous and sometimes, quite rough.

Before leaving, he decided to find Guy's class-teacher and speak to her, as he was concerned that Guy may have been involved in a tussle with one of the other children. Perhaps he had been uncomfortable talking about the incident. If so, Teddy thought it important to deal with the matter before it escalated any further.

When he reached Guy's classroom, he found Ms Commins at her desk, examining a sheaf of papers spread out in front of her. He tapped twice, politely awaiting her response.

She looked up and noticed him at the door. With a warm smile, she walked towards him, with her hand outstretched in welcome.

"Hello, Mr Goodson. It is so nice to see you, again. Is there anything I can do for you?"

"Good morning, Ms Commins. I just wanted to talk to you and find out whether you have noticed anything unusual in Guy's behaviour, recently."

"The school bell is going to ring in a few minutes and then the horde will descend on me. So, we don't have much time. Why do you ask?"

"I noticed a couple of bruises on his back and thigh this morning. When I questioned him about them, he told me he did not know where they came from. I suspect he may have been involved in a fracas with someone or he might have had a small accident."

"I have seen no sign of conflict with anyone at school. He is very popular and well-liked by his peers, and the staff, I may add. He loves the lessons in which he excels. All his teachers say the same thing, the perfect pupil. He is a teacher's dream."

"What about the possibility of an accident, then? Normally, he is extremely active although he has not been his usual, energetic self, lately."

"Whether he fell or hurt himself, playing or had an accident, I cannot say. I have not noticed anything, and he has not complained to me, so I don't think there is anything to be concerned about. I will pay particular attention, now that you have brought it to my notice. If I discover something, I will let you know, but I doubt it."

"Acceptable!" he said. "I know I am being ultra-sensitive and I may be seeing demons where none exist."

"Not at all, Mr Goodson, it is quite understandable. I know what happened, before so I well understand your sensitivity," she said with a sympathetic smile.

"I really appreciate your interest in Guy. His progress is in no small degree, due to you."

"Why, thank you, kind sir," she said. "It is a pleasure having a child as bright and polite as young Guy in my class. I can see now, where he learnt it. I wish there were more children like him."

"Thank YOU, Ms Commins," he said, shyly, stressing the 'you' as he brushed aside the compliment. "He is very fond of you."

"The feeling is mutual, I assure you."

"I felt it important to find out if anything happened. I hope I am not being overprotective," he said, guiltily.

"Don't you worry about it. Should you ever need to speak to me, please do not hesitate to call on my cell-phone. I have it with me all the time. If I cannot answer, I may be in class, for example, you can leave a message on my voicemail and I will get back to you."

All the way home, he had an uneasy feeling in the pit of his stomach. "It is probably nothing," he muttered to himself, but the worry persisted.

After saying goodbye to his father, Guy joined a group of his friends playing a game of soccer in a section of the school playground. They were kicking around a tin can in place of an unavailable football.

Yelling with ebullience and urging each other on, as though the result of this makeshift match was the equivalent of a World Cup final, the boys surged from one end of the 'pitch' to the other.

In his excitement at the prospect of scoring the winning goal, one of them hooked his foot in the open end of the tin-can and with a flick, sent it flying. The jagged end made contact with Guy's face, a quarter of an inch above his left eye and opened a deep wound. Blood flowed down his face and onto his shirt. In shock, the boys rushed over to him.

Guy was doing his utmost not to cry although he was in pain and alarmed at the amount of blood pouring from the injury. He was nursing the wide gash above his eye-brow with a blood-stained handkerchief. Teddy ensured he always had a clean one in his pocket every morning.

He was rushed to the school nurse, Mrs Dunfort, who took one look at the cut and decided that with her limited facilities, it was too serious to attend to herself.

She cleaned and dressed the wound and, temporarily, managing to stanch the flow of blood. She arranged for him to be taken to the casualty department at the nearby hospital so that he could be properly treated. There, he could have the wound stitched, if necessary, and be given an anti-tetanus injection.

When Guy was missing at morning assembly, Ms Commins enquired whether anyone had seen him and learned what had transpired. She promptly notified Teddy, who was at the hospital, having already received an emergency call from the school nurse. He was informed by the doctor on duty in the Casualty Department that he had sterilised and stitched the wound.

"We have given Guy an anti-tetanus injection, which is standard practice. I have also sent a sample of his blood for testing to ensure there is no infection, before prescribing an antibiotic. Fortunately for him, had the injury been a quarter of an inch lower, he might have lost the eye itself and that would be a far more serious matter."

He grimaced at the information but was relieved and grateful for the boy's reprieve.

Guy emerged from the emergency department looking like a war casualty with a large bandage tied around his head. He gave Teddy a wan, little smile and for the first time allowed himself the luxury of a tear. Teddy's heart melted. He took Guy into his arms, as the child released the pent-up emotion he had stifled since sustaining the injury.

"Would you like to go home?" asked Teddy. He knew full well that Guy was quite likely to choose to go back to school because of his industriousness and highly developed work ethic.

To his great relief, Guy whimpered, "Let's go home, Dad. My head hurts and my eye is closed. I can't see properly. Even my legs are hurting. I just want to lie down."

"Of course, you can come home, trooper," he answered. "At least there, you can get over the shock. Perhaps, on the way home, we can buy French vanilla ice-cream?"

"I don't feel like ice-cream or anything, Dad. Can we go straight home?"

Teddy was surprised but they hurried home.

After a quarter of an hour, he went to check on Guy. He found him lying on his bed, tears streaming down his cheeks. He sat next to him and cradled his son in his arms, as he carefully wiped his eyes with his handkerchief.

"Does it hurt, Guy?"

"Yes, it is very sore, and I can't see properly. Do you think I am going to die, Daddy?" he whimpered.

"No, Guy, you are definitely not going to die!" he reassured the boy. "You got a serious gash from that tin-can and the cut was deeper than we thought. But now, you are all patched up and when the swelling goes down in a day or two, you will be as right as rain."

"I hope I don't die," Guy said.

"Please don't worry, son. Everything will be fine, you will see. I think a day at home will do you the world of good. I will talk to Ms Commins and tell her you will not be coming to class today."

He felt Guy's small body had gone limp in his arms. He had dozed off while he was speaking. Very gingerly, he laid him down and covered him with the blanket. He left the bedroom door slightly ajar, so he could hear him when he woke up. Then he went into the kitchen to make himself a cup of coffee.

Guy's question echoed in his ears as he waited for the kettle to boil. He was shocked that Guy had raised the issue of dying.

*I was sure he had buried the trauma of Mona's illness and passing but apparently, he still has not worked through it. To discover that the seeds are still so deeply embedded is very alarming,* he thought.

"The therapy we tried to arrange over a year ago with Dana Weston is now more urgent than ever." He resolved to talk about it to Edna.

He checked to make sure Guy was still sleeping so he could use the opportunity to speak to Edna and Ms Commins. He first rang Edna, who was very pleased to hear from him.

"How is Guy? I am sure he is doing very well at school," she said. He gave her a brief run-down on Guy's progress.

"I had no doubt he would be an outstanding pupil," she said, proudly. "Now then, to what can I attribute the honour of this sudden phone-call?"

He told her about the accident at school.

"Oh, my goodness, it sounds terrible. I hope it is not too serious," Edna said.

"It looks awful, what with the swelling and the bandages, but the doctor has stitched it up and now it is just a matter of waiting till the swelling goes down and he can see properly again. It should not take long."

"That is good, but you must have been very concerned?"

"Yes, but that is not why I called you," he explained. "He was feeling very poorly so I brought him home to rest. A few minutes ago, I found him crying in his bed and he asked me if he was going to die."

"Good heavens, the poor boy," said Edna, taken aback.

"After all this time, you can well imagine my shock. I really thought he had put it all behind him. Now, suddenly, to have him raise that possibility, again. It is really upsetting."

"I think that it is time we followed up on the idea of therapy. I am sure you feel the same, don't you?" said Edna.

"Yes," he said. "That is exactly what I thought. I wanted to find out if there is any possibility of engaging Dana Weston's services."

"Leave it to me. I will see if I can make contact with her. Perhaps, she will be available, this time."

"Thank you, Edna, I hope she will be."

"Anything I can do to help would be my pleasure. Have there been any signs that his teachers may have noticed?"

"I have already spoken about it to his class teacher, Ms Commins. If you would like to talk to her, please feel free to do so."

"Alright, tell her I will ring her later, after school, perhaps, when we are both free."

"I am planning to call her when we finish our conversation to tell her that Guy will not be attending school today as he is still not himself. A day at home is probably advisable. I will give her permission to report to you fully."

"Fine and give my love to Guy. Wish him well from his old nursery school teacher. Bye, Teddy" she said, warmly.

He rang Ms Commins on her personal cell-phone, as she had told him to do. After a single ring, she answered. "I saw you were the caller so I answered even though I was about to go to class. I assume you are telephoning about Guy. How is the young man?"

"He is a bit under the weather so he will not be attending lessons today. I hope he will be well enough to come to school tomorrow. Will he be able to catch up having missed almost a full day?" he asked.

"I would not worry about that, at all," she reassured him with a laugh. "He is amongst the top pupils in the class and he can easily manage anything he might miss."

"Thank goodness for that," he said, relieved.

"Incidentally, Mrs Dunfort told me she wants to speak to you when you bring Guy to school. Ring her now, since Guy will not be at school today. Or would you prefer if I ask her to call you?"

"No, you have more than enough to deal with. I spoke to her when she rang to tell me about Guy's accident. I will call her myself."

"Ring her personal mobile-phone. I think it is quite urgent."

She gave him the telephone number.

"By the way, I spoke to Edna, his ex-nursery-school teacher and she will be calling you, later to talk about Guy. She is going to try and set up some meetings for Guy with a very capable therapist we met before Mona passed away. Her name is Dana Weston. Obviously, you are free to tell her anything at all."

"Fine, Teddy, I look forward to speaking to Edna. Give my fondest regards to Guy and wish him well from me."

He dialled the school nurse a few minutes later, after having checked up on Guy, who was still sound asleep. Mrs Dunfort was far more formal and business-like than Ms Commins had been. She asked about Guy and he gave her the latest information.

"When will you be at school, next? I want to talk to you about Guy and it is really not appropriate to discuss the matter on the telephone. It would be far more suitable if we could meet, face to face," she said. "And it is urgent," she added, to give weight to her statement.

"Guy is still not feeling very well. I decided to give him time at home. I will only be able to see you tomorrow morning. Can it wait until then?" he asked.

"If there is no possibility of our meeting today, then tomorrow will have to do," she said. "Come what may though, we must meet tomorrow."

"Alright, that suits me," said Teddy.

"As it happens, it is quite convenient for me, too. I am waiting for some further information, which I expect later today or tomorrow. After that, I will be in a better position to apprise you of the full situation."

He was alarmed and unduly perplexed by Mrs Dunfort's manner.

"What is it? What do you want to tell me?"

"I already told you, Mr Goodson, there is nothing pertinent I can add at this moment," she snapped.

The more she stonewalled, the more worried he became and the more he insisted on clarification, the more she became cagey and tight-lipped. Finally, completely out of character, he exploded and took the bull by the horns.

"For God's sake, you can't leave me hanging in mid-air like this. What is it?" he demanded. She relented under his pressure.

"Yesterday, when they examined the blood sample taken from Guy in order to establish whether there was any infection, the laboratory, turned up some anomalous findings and…"

"What sort of findings?" he interrupted.

"I can't tell you exactly, but I think it is urgent enough to warrant immediate attention," replied Mrs Dunfort.

The knot in the pit of his stomach began to tighten at the feeling of deja vu.

"How serious is it? Is it blood-poisoning?" he demanded. "I have a right to know what the problem is. I cannot wait until tomorrow to find out what those anomalous findings are," he cried.

"Please, Mr Goodson, I assure you I have told you all I know. I will tell you whatever else I learn when we see each other, tomorrow" the nurse answered, sympathetically, with a noticeable change of attitude. "It is best not to jump to any rash conclusions. I am sorry I cannot be more helpful at this stage. Tomorrow, please come directly to the infirmary and I will make myself available, immediately."

Try as he might, he could not stop thinking about Mrs Dunfort's evasiveness. It had been as though she did not want to tell him something she already knew. *Perhaps an infection? Tetanus!* he thought.

Guy's injury had not been that serious, a deep gash, nothing more. What could be so difficult for her to tell him, he wondered? The nurse had been very uncomfortable and, in her attempt to allay his fears, she had only succeeded in exacerbating them.

He tossed and turned in bed, realising that it was pointless to try and find the answer to the puzzle. But it was also impossible to prevent the mind-games the conversation with the school-nurse had initiated. Finally, in the early hours of the morning, he fell asleep.

He was woken by Guy, who had crept into his bed, again. As he held the sleeping child, he noticed how pale he had become. He also thought that he had a slight temperature as his body felt warm.

"He may have contracted an infection, but I hope it is nothing serious." In his frantic state, he decided he would take Guy to see Dr Barnett the following day, just to make absolutely certain that there was nothing untoward.

In the morning, Guy felt a little better, although the cut was still quite painful but the fever had disappeared. He wanted to go to school and Teddy agreed on the condition that, after calling Dr Barnett to arrange an appointment, he would come to school to pick him up so they could drive to the doctor's clinic.

Once again, Guy was not hungry and ate very little breakfast, which was only an added concern as far as Teddy was concerned.

His friends welcomed Guy back as a conquering hero. His bandaged head only added to the mystique. He was surrounded by his mates, who plied him with questions, which he answered with due modesty.

Teddy said goodbye to Guy with a hug and headed for the infirmary to meet Nurse Dunfort to get some answers to the questions that had been plaguing him. The nurse ushered him in to her office, shut the door and after offering him a cup of tea, addressed him, firmly.

"The hospital wanted me to let you know that the laboratory results of Guy's blood sample showed an extraordinarily high white cell count. It was checked twice to ensure there was no error. For that reason, the doctors would like to carry out some further tests to establish exactly what the cause might be."

Teddy looked at her in horror.

"Just calm down, Mr Goodson, there could be any number of reasons for the situation. It is advisable not to make any diagnoses without further information," she said, noticing his reaction.

"The only thing I was told in addition to this information is that it is not something one should delay. Hence, it is advisable that you organise for Guy to see your family doctor as soon as possible so he can make all the necessary arrangements."

He was thunderstruck.

"Are you saying what I think you are saying?"

"I am not saying anything," she answered. "However, I am saying that only after all the test results are back can an accurate diagnosis be made. Until then, it is futile to hypothesise. I know it all sounds terribly frightening but please, Mr Goodson, don't panic. It is quite likely that there is a far less serious explanation for Guy's symptoms."

Mrs Dunfort's efforts to calm his fears had no effect. He informed her that all along, it had been his intention to let Dr Barnett, their family physician, examine Guy that very morning.

"As soon as the appointment is set, I will collect Guy from school."

"I think that is a wise decision. Mr Goodson," said the nurse.

# Chapter 20

Dana sat in bed, her feet tucked under her. She reflected on how lonely and isolated she had become.

Day-time television had no appeal to her and had long since ceased having the soporific effect she had sought at the time. Her concentration span had shrunk to such short dimensions, that she could scarcely comprehend how someone, as capable as she had once been, had allowed herself to degenerate and sink to the depths she had plumbed.

Her telephone hardly rang any more. Except for Sally, all her friends had long since stopped calling to try to lighten her prevailing mood and cheer her up. Their good intentions had had the precise, opposite effect and she sensed their ill-disguised disappointment and frustration.

In the midst of her daydreaming, the ringing of her house-telephone shook her out of her reverie. Eventually, it stopped as the answering service clicked in. "Hello, Dana. This is Edna, Guy's ex-nursery school teacher. Recently, I met a friend of yours, Sally Broome. I wondered if it was possible for us to talk about a very pressing matter concerning Teddy and Guy Goodson. I would appreciate it if you could call me at your convenience, hopefully, soon. Thank you."

She weighed up calling Edna back and, as usual, decided to leave it for a while.

*I know it is not very professional of me, but I don't feel mentally strong enough to handle whatever she wants,* she thought, still sorry for herself and wallowing in her misery. The following morning, there was another message from Edna along the same lines, except that this time, it sounded far more pressing.

"In a sense, it may be a matter of life and death. Teddy Goodson has no knowledge of your situation, although I am aware of your personal tragedy. I learned about it from Sally Broome who swore me to secrecy. You have my sincere condolences. In the circumstances, I believe you, above others, will appreciate the need to support Teddy and Guy at a time like this.

Although lightning is not supposed to strike twice in the same place, regrettably, in the case of the Goodson family, it has done. They desperately need help and from the little I know, you are the person, who could best provide it. I await your call. It is burningly urgent."

She stared at the phone, in two minds whether to call back but the fetters holding her tightly, as they had done for so long, still inhibited her and she vacillated. She remembered the little boy, who had borne his pain so valiantly, who had been more concerned about his father than he had been about himself. The child who had subjugated his own needs for the benefit of the adult!

His intelligence and inherent goodness were still indelibly imprinted in her memory and she could not get the desperation and anguish of Teddy out of her head, either. He had been devoted to his son and his dying wife with unquestionable love, a love similar to her own for Mike.

Something stirred, deep inside her, as though a smouldering ember had ignited a tiny spark. Suddenly, there was a minute flame, but a flame, it was. There was no doubt about it.

She was stunned and excited at the same time. This was the first occasion since Mike's death that she felt any emotion other than sadness and self-pity. Almost physically, she could feel the glow of compassion, which was slowly spreading through her body, moving from cell to cell and growing in intensity. It began to replace the gloom and depression, that had taken over her very being for such a long time.

True, it was still not very strong, but its mere presence brought her back to the time, when, as a young woman, she had chosen the path she would tread for the rest of her professional life. She had a jolting reminder of the reasons why she had chosen her vocation, to work with young children, their need for love and care to guide them back to health and security, back to childhood, their rightful inheritance. She was almost delirious with the reawakening.

Her mother called about ten minutes later. "Is everything alright, darling?" she enquired.

"Yes, it is, Mum. I am fine."

"You sound different, Dana. Has something happened?"

"Not really, Mum. Why do you think so?" She was surprised by her mother's observation and more at her own reaction, not her customary impatience at maternal prying.

After a slight hesitation, her mother answered, tentatively, as though wary of saying something which might be construed by Dana in the wrong way, again.

"I may be imagining it but it seems your voice has some of the old lilt, which I have not heard for ages. I don't want to sound presumptuous, darling. We know what you have been through, but…" she tailed off, expecting the customary angry impatience in her daughter's reply.

Instead, in a soft voice, Dana said, "I don't know, Mum. I had a message this morning from a woman I met over a year ago. She wants to talk to me about something that has just come up with a young boy and his father, both of whom might need my intervention. They have gone through a very difficult time. The case appears to be particularly interesting and I am considering accepting the child as a patient."

"That is wonderful, Dana. I am sure you know what we all think of you. You are respected and admired for what you do and how you do it. The results you have achieved speak for themselves."

"I haven't made up my mind yet, Mum but I probably will," she said, a little curtly, immediately regretting it. Her mother reverted to her usual defensive posture as she recognised Dana's sharp response.

"Sorry, darling but I am certain the child will benefit greatly from the treatment he receives with you and no doubt, so will you. You often told me that therapy works in both directions. Not only will you be giving a gift to this child and his father, but you will also be healing yourself."

She enjoyed the compliment from her mother, which had been so sorely lacking in her life. "Thank you, Mum. I appreciate what you just said."

"Bless you. We have all been waiting for you to come back and it seems the time may almost be here. I am so happy. I know you will rise to the occasion. You always have done."

She felt her pride metamorphosing into satisfaction, which in turn blossomed into resolve, growing ever stronger. How times had changed. From a mother who had once virulently opposed her choice of profession and who, like her father had seldom, if ever, paid her a compliment, the way she had spoken in her last conversation was the final spur. She decided to return Edna's call. If necessary, she might even accept young Guy as a patient if he was in dire need of her services.

She picked up the receiver and pressed the call-return button. Edna answered immediately.

Dana felt awkward because it had been so long since she had spoken to anyone about any matter of importance. She did not know how to continue. Edna, on the other hand, after greeting her warmly, took the initiative.

"I am really pleased you called back. I know it may have been very presumptuous of me to speak as I did, when I left you that message. I imagine that when you know the facts, you will understand, and you will forgive me."

"No need for apologies. I admire your concern for Teddy and Guy Goodson," she said.

"Sometimes, when circumstances warrant, more precipitate action is required than one is normally accustomed to. Occasionally, a person may have to go beyond conventional borders," Edna replied.

"What do you need from me?" Dana asked.

"Firstly, I would like to express my sincerest condolences. I was told you lost your husband in very tragic circumstances. You have my deepest sympathy."

"Thank you, Edna," she said, softly.

"Also, you may not know that Mona Goodson died within a few days of your meeting Teddy and Guy. Naturally, there was great heartache and anguish for both father and son. It has taken all this time for them to regain some normality in their lives. I am not sure that even now they have fully recovered from the trauma they both experienced."

"True. Getting over the death of a dear one can often take a very long time," she confessed. The inference was not lost on Edna.

"Unfortunately, they may be facing a similar tragedy with Guy's health, this time. He is now at school. I just spoke to his teacher, Ms Commins and found out that there is a strong possibility that he may be very, very ill."

"What is it, exactly?"

"I cannot say more at this stage except that it is extremely serious."

"It sounds terrible," said Dana, aghast.

"I am not sure Teddy will be able to cope with facing this new calamity, not to mention the fear and suffering young Guy may endure, if indeed, the suspicions are verified."

"I remember that Teddy Goodson could hardly function during his wife's illness. For the duration of the illness, he devoted himself to her, exclusively," Dana said.

"Yes, but even after she passed away, had it not been for Guy, I doubt whether he would have pulled himself together."

"It is a terrible ordeal, losing a life's partner," said Dana. "I don't know how anyone can get over it, alone."

"That is an additional reason why I am extremely worried about them both. They have very little family. Most of their friendships have dried up. In fact, they have nobody," Edna said.

"I am really sorry to hear that," Dana said, sadly.

"If your support was needed by them, then, it is far more pressing now. That is the reason I thought it a matter of life and death. Perhaps a little unfairly, I took it upon myself to phone and enlist your support."

Dana felt her heart racing. She was fully aware of the devastating effect Mike's death had caused in her own life and to imagine having to face a similar, ghastly experience was inconceivable.

She could still picture Guy with such an innocent and gentle nature. His having to deal with what lay ahead of him, both physically and emotionally, caused her to recoil in shock.

Her mind was in a whirl. It was clear that for Teddy, having lost his precious wife and now faced with the prospect of losing his child as well, it might be more than he could bear. How does a man contend with a fate as cruel as that? Such a situation could break a superman, let alone a man as sensitive and fragile as Teddy Goodson.

Dana was so overcome with emotion that she could not speak. The horror of Guy's and Teddy's situation filled her with the same pain she had felt at the conference when Sally and Peter had brought her the devastating news of Mike's death.

Her body convulsed. She could not stop the trembling. She felt an overpowering sadness for them, but she was relieved that, after so long, the compassion and pain was for Guy and Teddy and not for herself.

Her head spun while she juggled the options facing her.

It was as though there were two Danas, one the re-awakening professional therapist with all her talent and experience and the other, the doleful woman, drowning in self-pity, who could not come to terms with having lost the love of her life, the woman who chose to be bogged down in gloom and mourning, a true victim.

Suddenly, into her head popped the thought of what her beloved Mike had often said to her. He had been so proud of her.

"God gave you a gift. And not only did he bestow on you outstanding skill in dealing with children, he also gave you the biggest heart possible, a heart filled with unlimited love and compassion. Nobody exudes that more than you do, Dani," he would repeat, incessantly.

What would Mike think of her now if she were to betray his faith in her at such a critical time?

The last vestiges of the effects of her personal grief began to drain away and she felt she was being released from her self-inflicted prison. Her body and spirit filled with strength and commitment. It was an epiphany. The shaking slowly subsided and she knew beyond doubt what was demanded of her.

"I am desperately needed by two people in a far worse position than I am. I need to choose."

She smiled as she realised how often she had said the same sort of thing to her patients and urged them to do what was so obvious to her but not to them? There was clarity in the path she should take and the choice she should make. She resolved to act accordingly.

Dana was back.

# Chapter 21

Mike's celestial messenger had been to see him less frequently and he assumed that his growing acceptance of and his expanding acclimatising to local conditions were probably the reasons. Thus, he was surprised when his celestial messenger suddenly appeared.

He was certain the spirit was smiling, except it had no face with which to smile, just the incandescent light, which enveloped it. Nonetheless, he 'knew' it was smiling because he 'sensed' it was the bearer of glad tidings.

His guardian angel began speaking.

"I have been asked by Gabriel to inform you that after he forwarded your rather extraordinary request to the Council of Sages, the members deliberated and considered all the implications. They will refer their recommendations and those of the Council to the Eternal One.

Naturally, all final decision rest in Its power. However, with infinite wisdom and compassion, It normally waits for the appropriate moment to effect Its will. It seems that moment is rapidly approaching."

*"What do you mean when you say the moment is rapidly approaching? I have been waiting to appear before Gabriel or the Council. Are you telling me that all was already known and it was simply a waste of precious time? Am I not going to plead my case?"* asked Mike, with irritation.

The spirit answered him, patiently. "Firstly, it is not possible to waste time. By now, I thought you would know that. Humans tend to waste their lives or opportunities and then speak about wasting time.

It should be patently clear to you already that whatever happens is meant to be. It is completely unnecessary for you to appear before the Council. You have already been assured by me that they already know every idea or thought anyone has, including yours."

*"So, there is no need to appear before the Council of Sages or Gabriel?"*

"Well done!" said the guardian angel, a little sarcastically. "The Eternal One, being omnipotent will provide a fitting solution and implement it. For that reason, you have been summoned to the council-chamber where Gabriel is ready for you."

Mike waited in the anteroom, which was not an enclosed hall or chamber but rather an unrestricted space. Like everything else, it was as though things were real, physical and, at the same time, ephemeral.

The colonnade of pillars leading to the Council Chamber stretched up into infinity and the passage was so long, it disappeared into nothingness. The ceiling, which, to him, was more like the sky, was so high that he could not see it. Again, his impression was one of endlessness but not of emptiness.

And yet, a soothing and tranquil ambience permeated everything. Wherever he looked, he saw familiar works of art, paintings, sculptures and ornaments, classic and modern, famous and unknown, by artist of repute such as Michelangelo, Da Vinci, Cezanne, Goya, Botticelli, Picasso and others. Many though, were completely unfamiliar. There were even pictures, obviously done by children.

There were billions on display, each created in gigantic dimensions. Mike realised that the pictures were not on the walls but were the walls.

He heard unobtrusive, background music that had been present ever since his arrival, except he had paid no attention to it. Now that he listened, he recognised that it was Beethoven's sixth symphony.

*Have I been sent a personal message? They are intent on persuading me that there is only the present, this moment in time, which they keep on referring to as 'the now'.*

*If it is so, then all the art ever created and all the music that was ever composed, always existed. Perhaps earthly inspiration is simply the Eternal One searching for a human being through whom spiritual creativity can be physically channelled in order to bring works of art into the world,* he thought.

In the midst of his musings, he was ushered into the presence of Gabriel where the same tranquil atmosphere pervaded everything, and his nervousness disappeared.

He moved down a Cardo-style passageway before he reached an elevated dais behind which, he saw Gabriel, the most dazzling spirit-light he had yet encountered. He was blinded by its brilliance and was forced to avert his gaze.

*"I often heard in earthly life that it was forbidden to look at God. At least, that was what the Jews believed. Seeing the blinding brilliance of Gabriel's light, I can well understand it, now. If this is the power of Gabriel's light, what must the Almighty radiate. It would probably render one blind for life...or for eternity."*

He laughed at himself when he reflected on his addition of the word, 'eternity'.

*"Apparently, something must be rubbing off on me."*

As Mike had become aware during his sojourn here, although Gabriel never communicated in the physical sense, he spoke in a warm, soothing voice.

"Welcome, Michael. As you know, in truth, it was not necessary for you to address us as we are fully cognisant of your wishes." He looked up at Gabriel deferentially, humbled by its exalted status.

"The question we have considered is not the merit but rather the mechanism to put into effect your request.

The end of physical human-life like that of everything on earth is part of a cycle, a natural occurrence. It is merely a stage in the growth of the spirit or what you refer to as the soul. There has never been an incident of a person, who has departed human life and returned to an earthy existence, as this would deny the laws of nature. Even in the case of your beloved Dana, it would not be right, as you well understand." His hopes sank.

Recognising Mike's disappointment, Gabriel continued, quickly. "Your true and enduring love for each other is highly commendable and uplifting but it is unprecedented to authorise any individual to return to corporeal life, even if it is for the most altruistic and unselfish of reasons."

For the first time since his arrival, he was not inclined to interrupt as he normally did, so struck with awe at Gabriel's magnificence, was he.

The 'super-spirit' continued, "As you well know, the All Knowing performs Its miracles in ways that are beyond the comprehension of man. Sometimes, when It decides the circumstances warrant, things occur that appear to be natural but are actually due to Its merciful intervention.

Miracles occur, not because they do so, but rather when they do so. It is a kind and loving Spirit, so do not give up hope. It has arranged a solution to your situation in a way that is very different from anything you could conceive."

Even though he was totally overcome by the solemnity of the occasion and, despite the fact that he never really did, he said, *"I understand. I do believe that our love is everlasting. I am willing to accept any conditions the Eternal One imposes if it would allow me to be with Dana, even for one second."*

"Much time has passed in earthly terms, but, as you have been told over and over, time does not exist. The human mind tries to put everything into a framework which it understands. It cannot grasp the concept that we exist in eternity, in perpetuity. It is the natural or spiritual way of being. We do not question it or need to. Here, time is not of the essence. Quite the contrary, our Essence is timeless."

Without giving Mike an opportunity to say something, Gabriel continued, "On earth, humans live for tomorrow, instead of accepting that there is no tomorrow. Consequently, their pursuit of tomorrow instead of being present today, robs them of the experience of the present.

They live their lives as though, only in the 'future', when they have attained or satisfied their ever-expanding desires will they be truly happy. It is the dog-chasing-its-tail syndrome."

Mike listened without daring to ask any questions or offer any comments.

Gabriel continued, "Here, in the now, it is not so. There is nothing to want. All have whatever they need, although not everything they want. When one knows that what is, is simply what is and nothing can be different in this moment of now, the spirit accepts that there are no expectations.

Thus, there is no disappointment or pleasure, both purely transient feelings.

Have faith that everything happens for the best, even though at times, it may not appear to do so. Remember, here, nothing is physical; one does not live anywhere, at any 'fixed address'. The spirit simply exists, not in a euphoric state, as you were led to believe, but rather in a state so natural that no effort is involved in simply 'being' present.

The soul needs nothing. One does not enjoy satisfaction when attaining something nor is there disappointment, if not and anyway, there is nothing to attain. With the elimination of one's expectations and needs, a person is free. By now, you should have learned that. Simply trust!"

*"I understand, I think,"* he replied with hesitation. *"But my celestial messenger told me that you wanted to see me because the moment is rapidly*

*approaching. Which moment and why is it so? What has happened?"*

"You, Mike, have not experienced the passage of time while Dana, on the other hand, has endured her pain and loss through many earthly months, pining and grieving for you because of her typically human attitude."

*"Then what has changed, if I may be so bold as to ask?"* Gabriel looked at him with the compassion of a father addressing an immature child.

"Dana is on the verge of a new stage in her life. Soon, she will emerge from her cocoon of gloom and misery. It may very well turn out to be a test of your love for her, as you will discover. The All Knowing could erase her pain quite easily but until now has chosen not to do so for reasons known only to It."

*"But what is this new stage?"* he pressed, when Gabriel appeared to have ended his monologue.

"The Source has other plans, which will become patent in due course, as we will find out. In Its infinite wisdom and compassion, It has decided to deal with the matter in Its own way."

*"That's it?"* said Mike. *"Nothing further you have to tell me?"*

"She has been selected to heal and be healed. When the appropriate time arrives, all will be made known. If your love for her is true, you will be satisfied with the solution ordained." Gabriel smiled angelically.

"Be at peace. Michael. All is well. There is a loving hand guiding everything."

Without warning, the dazzling light faded and vanished into nothingness.

He reflected on his meeting, confused. He still loved Dana with all his 'heart', as it were. Yet, the metaphysical that existed in this afterlife was as natural as the corporeal had been back on earth. He realised that his awareness had become clearer with no effort on his part.

Here, in 'paradise', finally having understood the true meaning of the term, 'now', it was obvious to him that whatever a person 'had' in that instant was all that was needed, nothing more.

During his lifetime, he had never realised the immutable connection between the moment of now and his physical existence in it. Being alive meant being alive in that moment and all that was needed had already been provided. Being alive was the very evidence of the fact.

During his earthly existence, he had always been concerned about the future, as was the wont of most humans, who lived their lives with a fear of insufficiency, always of something missing. Here, his realisation that there was no future, just as there was no past, had freed him from needing anything more, as it eventually did all human beings, releasing him to simply 'be' in paradise, for eternity.

*"Incredible!"* he gasped at the insight. *"Death is not the end but rather the end of the beginning. The end of human life is the beginning of the afterlife or a stage on the path of eternity. And it is also just a mile-stone, a way-point for the continuation of the existence of the spirit in its growth to complete awareness, beyond the strictures of man's mind, an opportunity to explore endless new horizons without the ever-encumbering fear of survival. In fact, everything in life is simply preparation for this stage, the path to spiritual enlightenment."*

Suddenly, his celestial messenger appeared. "I bring greetings from Gabriel, whom you just met. It is a great honour to have been given such an audience. It sent a message, which It requested I deliver personally."

*"Wonderful!"* he said. *"I have thought about our meeting and I find now, there are more unanswered questions than before. I have no idea where I go from here."*

His guardian angel replied. "Perhaps the news I bring will obviate the need to be concerned about that. You have received permission to return to earth and to be involved in Dana's life." Mike started with amazement.

*"I cannot believe it,"* he said. *"That is the most incredible news."*

"Yes, it truly is. However, Dana will not be able to see or hear you and, in truth, will never know of your presence," explained his guardian angel.

*"Then how am I to be involved in her life?"* he cried with frustration.

"That, you will figure out when the moment arrives," said the spirit, enigmatically.

"You will be at liberty to remain for as long as you wish but the instant you are instructed or choose to return, you will do so, immediately. The Source has deigned to permit you this grace, not only to assist Dana in her healing but also to test your love for her. It may also have other motives but only in 'time' will they become apparent. Are these conditions acceptable to you?" asked the guardian angel.

*"Yes, yes, I agree to all the terms. I will do whatever is asked of me. Just tell me what needs to happen. What should I do? What else do I need to know? When do I leave? How will I know what to do or where to go?"* he answered excitedly.

"Nothing needs to be done. You will know all you need to know at the appropriate stage. You can trust that It does what It does, not only efficiently but always in Its own way. As Gabriel said, what is often perceived as being a miracle is a miracle, not because it occurs but rather when and how it does.

All will be made clear in good 'time' and it is nearly earthly time. From my experience, with the way the Eternal One works, do not expect to understand Its motives or meaning. Its desire is to create solutions, but always in accordance with Its own agenda, while we may be busy focusing on something else. No doubt It will surprise us, as usual," explained the celestial messenger.

*"At least, I will be seeing Dana. I wonder how she will look. How will it be if she cannot see or hear me? Will I be able to communicate with her at all under these strange conditions?"* he wondered.

"Only their time will tell," repeated his guardian angel, again reading his thoughts.

*"What does it all really matter? I will be with my Dana and that is all I care about."*

"Good," said the celestial messenger. "When It is time to be ready, so will we be."

*"Oh yes, I will be ready. No doubt about it. You can bank on it. In fact, I am already. But what do you mean so will 'we' be? Why will you also be ready?"* he asked.

"I, too, do not know what is planned but I was informed that my loved ones are also to be healed. The love we both have is to be tested."

*"I do not understand, as usual,"* he said for the umpteenth time.

"Nor do I," said the celestial messenger. "But it appears that the wheels have already been set in motion for both of us. You will not be seeing me here for a while but do not be alarmed. We are both ready."

# Chapter 22

Everyone was kind and friendly when Guy returned to school. They related to him with consideration, plying him with questions and told him, in great detail, what had happened in class during his absence. Being back with his friends and with Ms Commins was a long-awaited pleasure for Guy.

But he did not quite feel himself. He was troubled by the incessant throb from the cut above his eye, which seemed to become more painful as time passed. His joints and legs were sore and he had no appetite. He was tired and dizzy most of the time and he was pleased when his father called for him two hours later to take him to see Dr Barnett, who had agreed to an appointment, although he was extremely busy.

Guy liked the doctor. He always produced lemon-drop candies from hidden pockets in his white, linen jacket. He would offer them to him with a sly wink and the secrecy of co-conspirators.

Dr Barnett welcomed Guy and Teddy and to put Guy at ease, first let him listen to his own heart-beat through his stethoscope. Then the doctor took over, moving the instrument over the boy's chest and back. It was cool and pleasant on his skin and Dr Barnett laughed when Guy gave a slight shiver. He did other tests, asked many questions and even examined the gash on his forehead, after carefully removing the dressing, which fortunately, had not adhered to the wound.

After a thorough examination, including checking the lymph nodes under his arms and in his throat as well as searching carefully for any other signs of swelling or bruising, he referred Guy to a nurse, who drew a blood sample. Guy recoiled and sucked in his breath as she inserted the needle. Teddy held him on his lap and consoled the cringing boy.

"We will send the specimen to the laboratory for an urgent analysis. We need a complete blood count of red and white cells and platelets, which carry oxygen through the blood stream to all parts of the body. They also counter disease and form clotting to prevent bleeding. At this stage, the information is crucial before an accurate diagnosis can be made by a specialist child-oncologist."

Teddy listened to the doctor's explanation in a daze. The terrifying word 'oncologist' resonated in his ears. He could not believe it was happening, again and he wanted to scream in rage and desperation.

"Oncologist! Was once not enough? Have we not paid a sufficiently heavy price? What sort of kind and loving Lord would allow this to happen, again?" he cursed under his breath.

Guy had calmed down but was still snivelling as he nestled in his father's comforting arms.

"Guy had a slight temperature when I measured it, earlier but I would prefer to reserve any diagnosis until we receive the results of the tests, especially, the blood count. I have flagged them as urgent and I expect them within a few hours." Dr Barnett continued.

"Is there anything you can tell me now?" he pleaded. "It is unbearable having to wait."

"I am sorry. I know how you must be feeling but please trust me. We will have the haematologist's report post-haste."

"First, Nurse Dunfort and now you, Dr Barnett. Why are you being so secretive? You will need to tell me later, anyway."

"We are not being secretive, Teddy. We are being professional. Only when we have all the relevant information are we able to give you accurate and precise information instead of guesswork. It will not take long, a few hours at most."

"I'm sorry, Dr Barnett. It is all too reminiscent of what happened with Mona so…"

"I understand, Teddy but I suggest that you go home so that Guy can rest. When I receive the information, I will be in touch and we can meet again to discuss the matter with the greater clarity."

In the car, Guy asked Teddy, "What is a haematologist."

"It is a doctor who specialises in anything connected with the blood. He will check your blood to see if everything is alright or whether they need any further tests."

Guy was perplexed. "Is there anything wrong with my blood?"

"I hope not." answered Teddy. "They just want to make sure that everything is as it should be, especially after the nasty accident you had. When Dr Barnett receives the report from the haematologist, he will call me, and we will come back to talk to him."

"If the haematologist is a lady, do they call her a 'hermatologist'?" asked Guy, seriously.

Teddy laughed. "The word 'haematologist' includes a lady specialist. It is a kind of doctor, who focuses on a specific type of medical knowledge, in this case connected to the blood. Then other doctors can refer to them, if they need something they do not know, which is in the haematologist's field of expertise."

Guy looked less puzzled than before and asked, "Is it a specialist blood-doctor?"

"Yes, it is," Teddy admitted, ruefully, wishing he had had the sense to explain it as simply as the lad had just done.

"Will I have any more injections, Dad? I don't like injections."

"I really don't know, Guy. I am sure they will try not to give you injections unless they are absolutely necessary. Anyway, they also make sure that they don't hurt much, just a small pin-prick. The last one wasn't so bad was it, son?"

"It did hurt, but not so much. Still, I don't like them."

Not convinced, he changed the subject. "When Mummy was sick was there something wrong with her blood, too, Dad?" He recognised the fear and concern behind Guy's innocent question and thought carefully before he replied.

"No, son," he answered, "She had an illness that only women sometimes have."

"Are there illnesses that only children have? Do children sometimes die from these sicknesses?"

He realised he was out of his depth. It was obviously not advisable to fob him off with inanities, but he had no idea how to answer Guy's question. He wished Edna or Dr Barnett had been present at that moment. They had the experience and wisdom to answer Guy.

While he was considering how to couch his response, he thought of Dana Weston. Out of sheer desperation, he decided that it was time to reconnect with her.

He knew Guy's latent fear of dying was caused by Mona's passing. It was essential that Dana intervene to prevent any further trauma due to his current medical condition, the seriousness of which was still unclear.

He was dreading what he was about to learn from the pending test-results and Guy's question was still hanging in the air, unanswered. Dana was the only therapist Guy was willing to see.

He collected his thoughts and eventually said, "Yes, even children could die from a sickness but most of the time, they do not. They get better even if it sometimes takes quite a long time. Usually, there is nothing to worry about even though the child, who is sick, does not feel very well."

The explanation seemed to have satisfied Guy as he never pursued the subject further although Teddy suspected that he was simply churning the matter over in his mind and in due course, he would resume cross-examining his hapless father.

"Are you going to take me back to school, now?"

"I don't think so. I want to get to the bottom of the problem so there is no point in going to class. Anyway, we will be going to see Dr Barnett as soon as he calls."

"OK, Daddy, I suppose you are right. I still don't feel well and I have lessons to do for Ms Commins."

"If you don't feel like school, I am sure Ms Commins will understand and excuse you."

"I know but I want to do my work and catch up. I have already missed so much" the boy said.

He immediately went to his room to do the lessons Ms Commins had set as homework, while Teddy procrastinated phoning Dana. He was not clear what to say to her. He dialled her telephone number several times but each time, he disconnected the call before he heard the ringing of her phone.

He was not sure why he was so hesitant to speak to her. She had won Guy over and he, too, had felt safe in her company. In the present circumstances, he was out of his depth with Guy and they both needed her support because he was incapable of facing the coming period, alone. But it was strange that he also looked forward to seeing the woman, who so easily managed to lift his spirits. His conscience was pricking him.

Suddenly, his phone rang. When he answered, Dr Barnett's secretary advised that the results from the haematologist were at hand. He bundled Guy into the car and drove to the doctor's surgery.

Although there were several people in the waiting-room, as soon as Dr Barnett discharged the patient he was treating, Teddy was ushered into his surgery, alone. The nurse entertained Guy by showing him the various medical instruments and explaining their different uses. It had all been prearranged, especially when he saw the solemn expression on Dr Barnett's face. His heart sank as the doctor began explaining the import of what had been discovered.

"I won't fob you off with platitudes and at the same time, although the news is not good, it might have been worse."

Teddy was as white as chalk and his head spun. Dr Barnett's voice reverberated in his ears.

"There is a very high incidence of white blood cells, known as immature lymphocytes and consequently Guy is suffering from serious anaemia, which requires a blood transfusion to rectify his extremely low haemoglobin. There is also a lack of sufficient protein in his low red cell blood count. This would account for his lethargy and loss of appetite, as well as the bruises and even the sores in his mouth."

He listened, stony-faced with disbelief and rising anger. Mona had succumbed to her illness. Would that be Guy's fate as well? Where was God, who allowed such injustice and pain to be wrought on living angels, when evil people flourished and often, were even rewarded despite their iniquities?

"Good God, it's not fair. And what about me?" he raged. "Am I expected to be a superman, again? I don't think I am strong enough to deal with this," he screamed in frustration and anger, thumping the desk with his fists.

Dr Barnett waited patiently until the storm abated.

As it ebbed away, so did Teddy's vulnerability. He needed to be strong, even invincible. He needed to seal off his heart. Nothing would be allowed to touch it again or he knew, he would not be capable of functioning. All that mattered was his precious son, who would have to live with the fear every day. Worst of all, in the end, it was Guy who might pay the supreme price as had happened with his precious Mona.

When he had regained some composure, he faced Dr Barnet and asked him directly, "Please, just tell me. It is leukaemia, isn't it?"

Dr Barnett nodded grimly. "Yes, it is although we are not yet sure which form of leukaemia it is."

"Isn't leukaemia, leukaemia?" Teddy asked with despair. "It could not be worse."

"No, Teddy, it could be worse, but fortunately we have caught it early," the doctor said.

"I pray you are right, Dr Barnett. But leukaemia is still cancer of the blood, isn't it?"

"Yes, Teddy, leukaemia is cancer of the blood. But I want to clarify. There are two main types of the disease and they make up for something like thirty percent of all cancers in children. They are what are known by their abbreviations, ALL or AML, Acute Lymphoblastic Leukaemia or Acute Myeloid Leukaemia. The blood stem cells are produced in the bone marrow. When too many irregular white blood cells are produced, there is no room in the bone marrow for healthy white or red cells or platelets."

Teddy stared at Dr Barnett in sheer disbelief. This could not be happening. He was talking about Guy, not about some faceless stranger. He was all that was left of his precious family. Was he going to lose him, too?

Dr Barnett continued explaining the situation with as much compassion as he was able to muster.

"Most importantly, in order to precisely identify the type of leukaemia, it is imperative that Guy undergoes a bone-marrow aspiration and biopsy, which necessitates attending hospital for a short time, so the doctors can extract the sample, on which the examination will be carried out. This is the only way to ascertain the nature of the disease."

Teddy sat, speechless, shivering with tension.

"Once we do know, Guy will be referred to an oncologist, specialising in this field and he or she will decide what treatment to prescribe."

Dr Barnett continued, "There have been great strides made in this field, Teddy and there is an excellent chance that all will be fine. The recovery rate is extremely high. However, I know you well and I can imagine how you must be feeling. I wish it was not so, but we must face the reality of the situation to prepare young Guy for what lies ahead of him."

"How do you prepare a child for something like this when he has already witnessed the effects of sickness on Mona and the terrible end result?"

"That, to a great extent, depends on you, Teddy. The appropriate treatment could be lengthy and complicated, with possible unpleasant side-effects."

"How do I prepare myself, let alone, Guy? I haven't gotten over Mona."

"As far as possible, it is very important that he witnesses a positive attitude from you. He should not be concerned with your welfare as he was before. I am sure you remember. He needs all his strength to overcome the illness. I know it is a huge responsibility and a great burden for you to carry. I sympathise with you but it is essential for his sake."

"It is going to be almost impossible for me to do so the way I am feeling right now but of course I will do everything in my power to adopt a positive attitude for Guy's sake."

"I know you will," Dr Barnett assured him. "And remember, I am always here for you."

"Thank you, doctor. I will never forget how you supported both of us when Mona…you know…" The doctor smiled and nodded sympathetically.

"How much should we tell him? I suppose his whole life is about to be turned upside-down, isn't it? Everything will suffer, his studies, his friendships and social life, even the way he looks, right?" he asked, miserably.

"Yes, although it affects people in different ways. There are very personal reactions. Naturally, for many, the physical changes are very distressing, the loss of one's hair, for instance. Fortunately, after treatment ends, all that returns to normal but the effects at the time can often be devastating for the individual. So great strength and support are vital."

Teddy looked at Dr Barnett with an expression of utter defeat. He was on the verge of total collapse.

"I suggest you tell Guy as much as he wants to know. He needs to be aware of what lies ahead of him. The less surprises, the better. At the same time, saying too much is not advisable, either.

He is still quite young. Let him lead you. He is a bright lad and anyway, he will meet other children with the same illness, while he is going through his treatment. He will learn a lot from them. Just hide nothing or you could lose his trust when he discovers more from other sources."

"Yes, Mona always used to say that trust was everything. The trouble is the way I am feeling at the moment. I am not sure I can manage, let alone be the strong example you suggest," he cried.

"I suppose it feels like déjà vu, Teddy but just as you were last time, I have no doubt you will be, now. To the best of my knowledge, you have never avoided responsibility and you will handle it, again."

"I hope so," he replied, hesitantly. "I will try but I feel so alone."

"Is there anybody you can turn to at a time like this?"

"I thought of Dana Weston. Guy took to her, before. I am going to speak to her. Hopefully, she will be available."

"Remember, any time you need me, I am at your disposal. Please know that."

"I do know," he said, wearily, with a degree of resignation that caused the doctor concern.

"Keep your spirits up, Teddy. It will help Guy to keep up his own."

Everything was spinning out of control. For the second time in his life, he was not sure he had the emotional fortitude to face such a monstrous challenge.

"I have arranged for Guy to have the bone-marrow test done tomorrow morning at nine o' clock," Dr Barnett said. "You should have him at the hospital by eight-thirty to attend to the registration and other procedures."

"Is it that urgent?" Teddy asked, fearful of the answer.

"We must start treatment immediately. There is no time to waste."

Teddy had no idea to whom to turn for support but his promise to Dr Barnett to contact Dana was clearly an obligation on his part. He knew he would never avoid carrying out such a promise. This would be his first step on a long and trying path.

# Chapter 23

Dana waited for Teddy to answer her call but the answer-phone clicked in.

"You have reached the home of Mona, Teddy and Guy Goodson. As there is no one available to answer, please leave a message and we will get back to you as soon as possible." After so much mental turmoil, she was disappointment but at the same time, a little relieved when there was no reply.

*Still 'Mona', after all this time*, she thought with surprise. He was not the only person who had refrained from deleting an old message from the voicemail. Mike's name was still on hers, too.

At the beep, she said, nervously, "This is Dana Weston, if you remember me. Sorry, I have been unavailable for so long. I spoke to Edna, Guy's nursery teacher. I would like to see you and Guy, if you still want to meet. Please ring me back." She left her telephone number.

"I wonder how long it will be before he returns my call. If he returns it at all," she wondered.

Within half an hour, her phone rang, and she saw the caller was Teddy Goodson. In a steady voice, so as not to betray how she was feeling, she said, "Hello Teddy, I am glad you called. It is nice to hear from you again."

"Hello, Dana, thank you for ringing. It has been a long time since we last talked."

There was silence for a few moments but before she was able to say anything, he spoke, choked with emotion. "When I heard your message, I was so relieved. You have no idea how much we need you now."

"I just heard from Edna. She suggested I phone you," she explained.

"I am pleased she did. I am not sure you know the latest situation. It could not be worse." He ceased talking, again. Once more, she was not sure whether he had finished or if he expected her to say something in reply.

She could hear him breathing heavily, so she chose to wait. Finally, he said, in a cracked voice, "Guy and I just came back from an appointment with Dr

Barnett, our family physician. Guy is in his room now, but he could walk in at any time and I do not want to say too much in front of him. But the position is terrible." Her heart went out to the distraught man.

"Edna told me that Guy had an accident at school. Is that the reason?"

"No, it's not that. The doctor just told me that Guy has leukaemia. They are going to do a bone-marrow examination and we need to be at the hospital early tomorrow morning."

She went cold at the import of what Teddy had just told her. How could something like this be happening to the Goodson family? Haven't they suffered enough? Why, oh why, do such terrible things take place? It is too much for anyone to bear.

"Oh! Teddy. That is awful. I am so sorry. Does Guy know? What have you told him?"

"I said to him that the tests have shown that he is sick but I have not found a way to let him know exactly what is wrong. I also have to tell him about the bone-marrow test tomorrow. I see his fear and confusion, poor child. I don't know how to deal with it. What should I do, Dana? How can I tell him so he won't be as shattered as I am?" he pleaded.

She was shocked. Since she could hear the panic and desperation in his voice, she recognised that he was on the verge of a breakdown.

"I will come over now, if you like. I am sure you could use some support. Perhaps we can talk to Guy together."

"That would be fantastic, Dana. I would be so grateful. We will both be overjoyed to see you."

"Fine, I'll be there in forty-five minutes."

She felt better at the relief in his voice as she disconnected the call.

Although she was anxious to leave as soon as possible, she was careful in choosing what to wear. She wanted to look professional but not austere, business-like yet feminine.

She selected a straight-fitting skirt that showed off her figure and matched it with a blouse with long sleeves and a Chinese collar. She stood in front of the mirror in her high heels, which accentuated her shapely legs, admiring herself, turning this way and that, checking her hair and make-up. She was pleased with the reflection she saw.

"Not bad," she said to herself. "I can't believe it, especially considering that this is the first time for so long since I have bothered to dress up or put on make-up."

She reached the Goodson home about thirty minutes later, not sure what she would find. Teddy had not said how Guy had reacted to the information or how much he did know.

She was no expert in the medical aspects of leukaemia, but she knew enough. It was often fatal. No matter how difficult it would be for Teddy, especially after his heart-wrenching experience with Mona, it would be far more so for young Guy. She feared for their mental as well as Guy's physical well-being.

Teddy greeted her warmly but with a detached formality. The moment she saw him framed in the doorway, she noted his deep despair. He looked haggard and drawn. His shoulders were slumped, and his body sagged. He had dark rings under his bloodshot and tear-stained eyes. He was close to collapse, much as he tried to conceal it.

She was so moved with compassion to see him in such a forlorn state that without thinking, she stepped forward to comfort him and put her arms around him in a motherly fashion. She could feel the tension in his body, his back, ram-rod stiff and his fists, tightly clenched against his sides.

She continued holding him until he began to relax, bit by bit. Nervously, he lifted his arms and returned her gesture with a light embrace, which they held for a few moments.

It struck her that during the past year or so, neither of them had been aware how much they had needed the physical contact and solace of another human being to help assuage their pain and ease their loneliness.

He was the first to step back.

Not able to maintain eye contact due to his embarrassment, he just said, "Thank you."

She blushed. "Thank you, too. I think both of us needed that," she said in a quiet voice, pleased that she had instinctively done what she did, even if it was not precisely professional. They were a bit awkward with each other, but it was obvious that he felt better.

While still in the small entrance hall, they heard soft foot-steps approaching. Suddenly, Guy appeared. When he saw them, he stopped, taken by surprise, as though he was seeing an apparition. He stared at her in disbelief.

"Hello Guy. I am so pleased to see you again," she said, warmly.

"Hello, have you come to see Daddy?"

"I came to see you, too. I have wanted to speak to you often and invite you to come to my house. The trouble is that we have all been very busy, haven't we?"

"Yes, we have. Daddy has been busy looking after me. Have you also been working very hard?"

"Well, not as hard as your daddy, but yes, I have been busy, too. I am sorry I was not able to see you for such a long time. Something happened, and it has taken all this time for me to be ready. I hope you forgive me."

Guy grinned from ear to ear. "Of course, I do." he said as though it was obvious to him that there was nothing to forgive.

"I am glad we will now be able to spend more time together and play as we planned."

"So am I," the boy said. She grinned at him.

"Wow, how you have grown since I last saw you, Guy! You are getting so tall. Soon, you will reach up to my shoulder," she said.

"Daddy measures me against the door in my room. He marks it each time. I can let you see, if you like," he said. proudly.

"I would love to see it when we have time," she answered.

"Great. Whenever you want, I can take you to my room to show you," Guy said with a smile.

"I really missed you, Guy. I enjoyed our talk very much. Do you remember the things we spoke about?"

"Yes, I do," he answered. "We talked a lot about books. I can read, now. I learnt at school and I learned a bit from Daddy while I was still at nursery-school. I love reading. You said you had many books for children at home."

"I do, and it is wonderful that you can read, already. I heard that you are doing very well with your lessons."

"Yes. I like school. My teacher is Ms Commins. She is nice."

He hesitated for a moment as though he was considering whether to say what he was thinking out loud. "I remember you said when children come to your house and play in your special room they often feel better. I am sorry I couldn't come to your house. Are you cross with me?"

"No. Of course, I am not cross with you," she reassured the boy.

"My Mummy died," he said, as though he needed to explain why he had not come to her house for such a long time.

"I could never be angry with you, Guy and I am also very sad about your mummy," Dana said.

He smiled at her, broadly. "I am glad you came to visit us today."

"Perhaps, now may be a good time for a visit to my house?" she said, looking at Teddy.

Guy waited for his approval and when he nodded, he whooped with joy.

Guy took a couple of paces towards her when he saw her warm smile. She knelt in front of him and he fell into her arms. She held him tightly as he nestled in her embrace with his arms around her neck and his head resting on her shoulder. He seemed reluctant to let her go. Teddy felt the stinging sensation of tears in his eyes as he witnessed the scene.

After a few moments, she released him. "Dana, will you come to my room? I want to show you my measurements on the back of the door and my lessons from school. I am in first grade. I told you I can already read and write, and I can do sums and I am learning to play the flute and I am going to be in the school orchestra, soon and I drew some special pictures, which I want to show you and…"

"Whoa, there!" she said. "Slow down a bit. I cannot keep up with you, young fellow. I want to see everything. Why don't we all go to your room and you can show your daddy and me, together. I am sure he would also like to see your work, right Teddy?"

"Definitely," he said.

"OK, then," chirped Guy. "Let's go," he said, taking her hand and leading the procession.

On the desk in Guy's room, Dana noticed some unfinished pictures, which he had been painting. She noted the signs of anguish in them. They were darkly-coloured, with streaks of the brush, forced across the paper, crisscrossing and intersecting, haphazardly.

"I started them today when we came home from Dr Barnett," he told them. "I haven't finished because when I thought I heard your voice, I wanted to see if it really was you."

"It looks like you were angry when you painted them," she said.

"Yes, I was. That is why these pictures are so funny. The doctor told Daddy that I have something wrong with my blood and I have to go to the hospital tomorrow for more tests. I don't like going to the doctor. They always want to give you injections and I do not like injections. I also do not want a blood transmission."

"They are called blood-transfusions, Guy," Dana laughed. "They will help you feel stronger, you will see. I know injections are not nice but sometimes they are necessary if we want to get better," she said.

"I don't know if they gave injections to my mummy. They probably did. Doctors always give them, but she never got better. She died and went to heaven."

"I see you are worried about people dying when they get sick," she said.

"Yes. I don't want to die and go to heaven. I want to stay here with Daddy. Are you going to stay with us, this time?" he asked.

"I will be here as much as you need me. I just hope you do not get tired of me," she said, looking quizzically at Teddy.

"Will you be able to come to the hospital tomorrow for my blood test? Is that alright, Daddy?"

"Guy, I am not sure if Dana has the time."

"I am not busy, so I can be with you if you like."

"That's great. I am really happy you are going to come with us tomorrow," Guy said.

"Alright then, I will see both of you tomorrow." Guy hugged her and hung onto her until, laughing, she managed to extricate herself. This time, Teddy initiated their embrace at the front door.

"He is so happy to see you, again. It is amazing," he said. "It is only the second time he has met you and as you can detect, he is infatuated by you. Your husband needs to be very careful, now that you have such an ardent suitor," he remarked, flippantly.

She recoiled in shock as though pierced by a razor-sharp stiletto. Even though Teddy's comment had been intended as a compliment, it sliced away the wafer-thin layer of scar-tissue covering her unhealed heart. Teddy saw the reaction, immediately.

"I hope I have not offended you." he said with a worried expression on his face.

She smiled at him, weakly. "No, you never offended me, Teddy. It is just that I lost my husband in a car accident some time ago. That is the reason I stopped seeing any children."

"Oh! Dana. I am so sorry. I had no idea. I apologise for my lack of tact."

"It is alright, but as you see, the wound is still raw. I am sorry but I don't think I am ready yet to give Guy the professionalism he deserves," she said, ruefully.

"Please know you have already made a huge difference to both of us," he said.

"So far, I have done nothing, Teddy. I do not intend abandoning you, though. I want to support you in any way I can. I will spend as much time as possible with you if you'd like."

"We will both be happy if you do."

"I am not working, yet so it is not a problem. Although it may not be formally defined as therapy, I am sure I can help ease Guy's burden…and perhaps yours, too."

"We really appreciate that, Dana. How can we compensate you for your trouble?"

"Firstly, it is no trouble. It is my pleasure. Secondly, I need to get back into work-mode, again. I have been licking my wounds for far too long. This is a perfect opportunity for me to start edging myself back into my career, which I have neglected. And, of course, I owe it to you after what happened last time."

She put out her hand. "Let's shake on it."

He took her hand with obvious relief. His shoulders, which had been poised tightly just below the level of his ear-lobes, seemed to fall a few centimetres and he smiled at her for the first time since they had met again.

# Chapter 24

That evening, Guy never stopped talking about Dana while he played with his toys in the bath while Teddy sat watching over him. He even ate a light supper although he still had little appetite. He stopped complaining about the pains in his legs and joints, as he had done constantly for the past few weeks. Her sudden appearance had acted as a magic potion.

Nonetheless, there was a simmering apprehensiveness lurking below the surface. He was worried about the bone-marrow aspiration and 'blood transmission' he was due to undergo the following day. Her visit had invigorated him but it had simply provided a temporary respite.

Teddy, too, was pleased at Dana's re-entry into their lives and found himself constantly thinking about her. Whenever she was around, his son relaxed and although he was still very frightened, her mere presence had a calming effect on the boy. He, too, also relied on her as an ally because of her ability to handle awkward situations with the aplomb he lacked. It made his own life easier and lightened what was already an excessively heavy burden for him to bear alone.

Guy spent a restless night, tossing and turning, unable to sleep. Finally, he got up, quietly and shuffled into Teddy's room, where he slipped into bed alongside his father. Teddy drew him very close and held him tightly, wondering how many more times he would be able to do so. The blood in his veins turned to ice at the thought.

"Are you awake, Daddy? I can't sleep. I keep thinking about tomorrow," Guy murmured.

Teddy stroked his head, gently. "It is quite understandable to be afraid. Even adults are scared, sometimes. Just know, I love you very, very much and I will always be here with you. Whatever happens, we will be together."

"Daddy, what happens when you die?" he asked as he snuggled closer. It was a question Teddy had dreaded. He wished Dana was present. She would have known how to explain it without unduly alarming the boy.

"Um! It is like when people get very old or have an accident. Then, sometimes they die," Teddy explained, facilely.

"Mummy wasn't old and she didn't have an accident?" Guy said, innocently. Teddy could see where the conversation was leading. He knew he had to be honest with the child.

"No, son, she never had an accident nor was she old. She was still young, but she was very sick."

"Will we ever see her again?"

"No, Guy but she will always be with us because we love her."

"I only remember her a bit. Whenever I see her picture, I think I remember her. She was very pretty, wasn't she?"

"Yes. She was beautiful."

"I think Dana is pretty, too, Daddy?"

"She is also kind and gentle and although she barely knows you, she already likes you very much," Teddy said.

"Is she going to look after me?"

"No Guy, I will always look after you. She just wants you to get better, like I do."

"I hope I do. I don't want to die. I want to stay here with you."

"That is why the doctors are going to start the treatment, now, so you will get better quickly," he said, to placate the boy.

Although Guy appeared to be satisfied with the explanation, Teddy was acutely aware of the mental upheaval engulfing the child as he wrestled with the issues he had raised.

To reassure him further, Teddy added, "And do not forget, Dana is going to be with us as well."

"Are you also pleased she will be with us?" said Guy.

For a moment, he was at a loss for words how he should answer his son's innocent question. He was surprised at his reaction to Guy's comment although he never fully understood why, and he tried to hide it.

"Are you, Daddy?" Guy persisted.

"Yes, I am. She knows what to say and do so you feel more…" he searched for the appropriate word that would accurately express what he meant and which Guy would understand.

"Do you know what the word, 'secure' means?" he asked.

"Does it mean 'safe'?" Guy said. "I feel safe when Dana is here. I think you do, also, don't you?"

"Yes. And it is time to go off to dreamland. We have an important day, tomorrow?"

Guy yawned, rubbed his eyes and fell asleep.

Teddy lay awake, thinking about the conversation with his son, who had exhibited signs of perspicacity and observation, which caused him a great deal of food for thought. His mind flitted from Guy's frightening condition and the upcoming examination, next day to Dana and the effect she was already having on Guy's and his life. Try as he might, he could not get either subject out of his thoughts until he too, fell asleep through sheer exhaustion.

Next morning, Dana was waiting for them at the entrance to the hospital. She had dressed simply but attractively, and her light application of make-up enhanced her natural beauty. Again, she had felt good about herself when she had examined herself in the mirror before leaving home.

She had already checked where the examination and transfusion procedures for children were performed. Holding Guy's hands, they hurried to the Haematology Department, where the staff welcomed them warmly.

Guy looked around at the strange environment. It had been designed to relax young patients by creating a friendly atmosphere instead of the 'clinical' one, normally found in a hospital. The trouble was that there was no possibility of disguising the fact that it was indeed, a hospital. The smell of disinfectant and medicines, the orderliness and quiet bustle of activity and the crisp, green or white uniforms of the staff were a constant reminder of where they were and more importantly, why.

After completing the registration and official formalities, Teddy accompanied an apprehensive Guy while he changed into hospital pyjamas. They remained with him in the ward while they waited for Doctor James Simpson, the surgeon, who was going to extract the bone-marrow sample.

When he arrived, he did his utmost to put Guy at ease. He advised them, in layman's language, what was going to happen. He was informal and friendly, occasionally, even joking with Guy.

"It will not be painful," he said. "Guy, we will give you a small injection, which you will hardly feel, just a tiny prick. I was told that you don't like injections, but you are a brave boy. Aren't you?"

"Not so brave," he said, when he heard the word, 'injection'.

"It seems to me you are the bravest person here today, even more than your parents." Dr Simpson said, giving Teddy and Dana a reassuring smile. But the child was very frightened. Although the ward was heated, he shivered as he clung to Teddy and Dana.

"Don't worry. You will see it will all be finished very quickly. If you want to know anything else, you can ask me, now, or if you like, afterwards should you think of something."

"I don't know what to ask," Guy replied.

"Well, if there are any questions you do want to ask later, just go ahead."

Dr Simpson then turned to Teddy and explained that Guy would be given a local anaesthetic in his lower back. As soon as it took effect, the procedure would commence.

"It only takes about twenty minutes and we do not anticipate any complications," he explained.

Guy gave them a smile, trying to be courageous but he was terrified at what was happening to him. Fortunately, he had been given a sedative, earlier and the effect was causing him to become drowsy.

They stayed with him until the last minute and walked alongside him, holding his hands as he was wheeled down the long corridors leading to the operating theatres. Neither of them was capable of hiding their own apprehension. They were still waving to him as he disappeared behind the sliding-doors at the entrance to the area with admission strictly reserved for authorised members of staff.

They sat in silence throughout the time Guy was undergoing the procedure. Dana considered taking Teddy's hand, as much for her own reassurance as for his but thought better of it.

Guy found himself surrounded by people in green clothing, wearing masks and funny caps, covering their hair. They were all friendly and fussed over him. He recognised Doctor Simpson, who greeted him and gave him a thumbs-up sign.

"Don't you worry about a thing, Guy, everything will be fine. Before you know it, you will be back with your parents."

Guy was laid on his stomach and the area of his lower back was sterilised with a cold solution, which caused him to shiver, partly from the cold but more from fear.

The doctor said, "You will feel a slight prick and then slowly, you will begin to lose feeling in the area." While the doctor was still explaining, Guy felt the stinging pierce of the needle, which caused him to gasp.

"Well done, Guy. That's it. It was not too bad now, was it?" said the doctor. "We will need to wait a few minutes for the anaesthetic to take effect and then we can start. We want to get you back to the ward, quickly."

Dr Simpson kept on checking periodically to ascertain when it would be ready for them to begin the aspiration. Guy's lower back began to lose feeling just as the doctor had explained. Having been given the sedative, earlier, he also felt a drowsiness descending over him, When the doctor was satisfied that the area was sufficiently numb, he commenced the procedure.

Sure enough, exactly as Dr Simpson had promised, the whole matter only took a short time and Guy was soon taken back to Teddy and Dana in the ward. They were overjoyed to see him, anxiously waiting for the effects of the operation to wear off. He opened his eyes as he began to come round and smiled at them, weakly. He could feel something in the numbed area, but it was more uncomfortable than painful.

"Welcome back, son. Just relax. It is all over. You were very brave. The doctors told us how well you behaved," said Teddy.

"We can't tell you how proud of you we are," added Dana.

The child was still under the influence of the anaesthetic and sedatives and for the next hour, he drifted in and out of his drowsy state and barely responded to them. Nonetheless, he was reassured by their presence and smiled, weakly, each time he opened his eyes and saw them, before dozing off again.

Dr Simpson came out to talk to them after he had changed from surgical into his regular clothes.

"Everything went according to plan, no problems. The specimen has gone to the laboratory for analysis and I expect the results, shortly. As you know, Guy also needs a blood transfusion, so it is advisable to keep him hospitalised for the day to monitor the situation. Sometimes, there is pain after the bone-marrow procedure. I hope not, but if it turns out to be so in Guy's case, it is preferable to have him on hand to attend to it. There is also the matter of his slight temperature, probably occasioned by the infection in the cut above his eye, that the staff wants to track and bring under control."

"We understand, Dr Simpson, we are entirely in your hands. Will we be able to stay with him?" Dana asked.

"Of course, you may."

"By the way, I am not Guy's mother. I am a therapist attending to him and I am a very close friend of the family."

"Oh! Sorry, my mistake. It is just that it is obvious how much you care about the boy and I just assumed...I apologise for the error" said the doctor.

"No problem and yes, they are both very special to me."

Guy was upset at having to spend the night in the hospital but Teddy pacified him.

"I promised you I would not leave you alone and Dr Simpson has given me permission to stay with you."

"I am not allowed to stay but I will be here with you until you fall asleep tonight, no matter how late it might be," Dana said. "Of course, I will be back, early tomorrow morning. ...very early! So, you will not be on your own for even one second," she added.

Guy, though, was extremely perturbed and fearful. It broke her heart to witness his and Teddy's distress.

For the next few hours, the boy lay on his bed in the ward, dozing on and off. The nurses called in to see him, giving him the blood transfusion, measuring his temperature and pulse or checking his blood pressure. On occasions, they just came to say hello or to give him a tablet or a drink of water.

Dr Simpson also visited to check on him. "Well done, young fellow. You were a real trooper. I hope you don't have any pain? If you do, the staff can give you a pill or something."

"No, I just want to go home," he said.

Even Dr Barnett called in to see his young patient. "Hello Guy. How are we? I heard you were a hero, this morning."

"I was not so brave, but I tried my best not to cry. I did a bit, though."

"No," said Teddy. "He was amazing, wasn't he, Dana?"

"He was fantastic, and he is also very modest, as you notice," she said, taking the doctor's hand, which he had extended to her.

"I am Dana Weston. I came to be with Guy and Teddy because we all thought it was a good idea. I am glad that they allowed me to be here."

"It is nice to meet you, at last, Dana. I have heard a lot of complimentary things about you. I have no doubt that you will make a significant difference to the Goodson family."

"I will try my best. I hope I don't disappoint them."

"You won't disappoint me," Guy piped up.

"Nor me," added Teddy.

Turning to the boy, Dr Barnett said, "I bought you a book by Roald Dahl, Charlie and the Chocolate Factory. I was told you read very well. And I brought you a portable compact-disc player, so you can listen to some of your favourite music while you are in the hospital."

"Thank you." Guy said, far from his customary self as he slipped back into his previous languor.

"I was told you enjoy classical music, which I love as well. I am really impressed. I am sure you father is proud of you," said Doctor Barnett. Teddy smiled and gave Guy a thumb's up sign.

"I believe you are learning to play the flute and are already quite good at it. Perhaps, I can hear you play, sometime?"

Teddy answered for Guy who was still a little groggy.

"He plays extremely well for somebody who has only been learning for such a short time."

"I look forward to hearing you play when you are better. Meanwhile, I also brought you a compact-disc which I think you will enjoy. Have you heard The Nutcracker Suite?"

"I went to a concert with my Daddy and they played some music from the Nutcracker Suite. Now I can hear other parts," he answered, sleepily.

"I hope you like it," said the doctor with a wink.

As he turned to leave, Dr Barnett nodded to Teddy, who followed him out of the ward into the corridor.

"The results of the biopsy will be available in the morning. Before Guy is discharged from hospital tomorrow, I will be back with Doctor Simpson to speak to you about the results and subsequent treatment. No doubt, I will find you at Guy's bedside."

Teddy nodded without taking his eyes off the doctor's serious face.

"I am very happy to have met Dana Weston," Dr Barnett said, as he was waiting for the elevator. "She is an outstanding young woman."

"I agree. She has made a big difference to Guy. He is much calmer when she is around," he said.

"I can see how fond of her Guy is and she is no less fond of him. No doubt, in the coming months, her expertise will be invaluable. I am sure she is also good for you, Teddy. You need someone on whom you can depend and a person with whom you are comfortable and able to lower your barriers a little. She seems the ideal woman. Hold on to her," he advised, with an impish grin, as he entered the elevator and the doors slid shut behind him.

Teddy slowly walked back to Guy's ward thinking about what Dr Barnett had said. He had been a pillar of strength for them throughout Mona's illness and even after she had passed away. It was no surprise to him that the doctor had recognised his loneliness and the extent to which he had closed himself off to the world around him. He had virtually become a recluse to protect himself from more hurt.

He knew he had slipped back to being the 'old' Teddy, no longer the man of whom Mona had been so proud to have as her life's partner. No doubt, she would have been disappointed in him. He was ashamed of himself. He had allowed himself to become the hesitant and impotent character he had been until his Mona had succeeded in getting him to recognise some of his outstanding qualities. She had instilled in him self-belief and confidence, but he had slipped right back.

When he reached the ward, Guy was lying on the bed, listening to music through headphones, which Dr Barnett had brought for him. The strains of the Nutcracker Suite soon lulled him to sleep and his eyes closed.

Dana smiled at Teddy, as she looked, lovingly at the pale, little boy. His heart filled with gratitude.

*She barely knows us and yet, here she is, sitting at Guy's bedside in the hospital, and providing me with company and succour in our hour of need*, he thought.

She whispered something to him, which he could not make out. As they did not want to disturb the sleeping boy, he leant across Guy's bed to hear what she was saying. She too, bent forward until they found their faces very close. Due to their extreme proximity, he could smell her perfume. It startled him and he drew back.

She assumed that he had not heard what she had said so she came around the bed until she was beside him, closer, in order for him to be better able to hear.

"I think it is time for me to go home," she whispered, softly, in his ear. When he felt her breath on his face, his head spun.

"I imagine you will spend the night here with Guy. Will you call me in the morning and let me know how he is and what the next phase in the treatment will be?"

He was still intoxicated by her scent and it took him a moment or two to recover.

"I suppose if Guy is well enough, he will be discharged, tomorrow. He has already had the blood transmission," Teddy said and Dana gave a quiet chuckle.

"Whatever the case, we will find out the results of the biopsy from Dr Simpson and Dr Barnett, tomorrow morning," he added.

"If you like, I can be with you as well when they speak to you. I am sure you could use the company," Dana suggested.

"Dana, you have been a lifesaver and heaven knows how much we need it. I do not want to impose on you any more than we already have done. I will talk to you tomorrow and then you can decide what to do."

"It is not an imposition," she said. "I want to be here for you and Guy. Somehow, I feel a special connection with you both and I can see how happy Guy has been simply to know I am with him. So, yes! I will be here if you want me to."

"I do want you," replied Teddy, who turned crimson when he realised what he had just said. Dana laughed heartily, clamping a hand over her mouth as she realised the noise might waken Guy.

After she left, he sat in the armchair next to Guy's bed, wondering what was going to happen to his young son.

He had been told what the treatment for leukaemia entailed. The procedures could be painful and the side-effects, extremely distressing. Guy was going to need his unconditional support and love for the coming months, perhaps, even years and he was not sure that he had the physical or emotional fibre to handle this second, monstrous challenge.

However, he knew that he was totally committed to his son and he accepted that he would need to draw on deep reserves to deal with this new and unexpected crisis. There was no room in his world for anything else except what would support him in his goal, to be there for Guy.

He would need to put everything else out of his mind, including the undeniable attraction he may have felt for Dana, the woman who, in such a short time, had found a way to infiltrate his heart, even if that was not her intention…nor his.

Suddenly, Guy awoke and looked around, for a moment, not sure where he was.

"Is Dana here?" he mumbled, still half-asleep. Teddy took his hand and stroked his forehead.

"She went home. It is very late. She sends you her love and asked me to tell you to have a good night's rest."

"Did you ask her to come back?"

"She told us that she would be here, tomorrow. Now, off to sleep. Good night, sleep tight, mind the bugs don't bite."

Guy never heard the last sentence as he had already dozed off, with an angelic smile on his little face.

Dana drove slowly through the empty streets, thinking about Guy and Teddy. She was aware of the frightened, young child's needs in facing the unknown. He was still not fully aware of the pain and discomfort lying ahead of him.

On a whim, she phoned Sally.

"Hello, Sal," she said when her friend answered. "I am on my way home from the hospital where I spent a trying day with Guy and Teddy Goodson." Sally was both shocked and pleased to hear from Dana. This was the first and sole occasion since Mike's death where Dana had taken the initiative to phone her or anybody else for that matter.

"Hello Dana, I am so happy to hear from you. What a surprise! And wow! You have really jumped in at the deep end, haven't you?"

"Well, that is just the way things turned out, but I can tell you it is not easy."

"I can well imagine," replied Sally.

"It is very upsetting to see the sword of Damocles suspended by the flimsiest of threads over the head of an innocent child. What he will only need to go through. He had a small sample of that in these last two days with the bone-marrow aspiration and the transfusion, probably the first of many."

"Poor child, how did he take to the hospital environment?"

"He was pretty good but he will become far more familiar with it in the coming months."

"I suppose Teddy was there with him throughout. What about you?"

"I stayed with them all day. I left only after Guy fell asleep."

"That is a huge responsibility, isn't it, Dan, so much time?"

"I chose to do it. It is clear what I must do. They both need me."

"It is amazing to see the old Dana back in action with all cylinders working," laughed Sally.

"Not all cylinders but I am on the way. Can I bounce something off you, Sal?"

"Of course, you can. That's what friends are for, as Peter says."

"As far as Teddy is concerned, I am completely confused. I can sense his interest in me as a woman, but it has been so long since I have been involved with the opposite sex in any way that I am not sure whether my suspicions are even reasonably well-founded."

"Why don't you trust your instincts?" Sally suggested.

"Because he is so worried about his son that he may just be clutching at any straw."

"You may be right but then it is also possible that your suspicions are well founded," Sally said.

"I doubt it. Guy makes no bones about his feelings He likes me and is happy when I am around. Perhaps Teddy is just reacting to that."

"It is all very confusing, isn't it?" said Sally, with a deep sigh and a trace of sarcasm.

"I may be imagining it all, both of us having been in such a fragile state for so long. He is so preoccupied with Guy that he cannot be interested in pursuing a relationship, even if that is what he thinks this might become."

Quite out of character, Sally listened, patiently until Dana stopped talking.

"I notice that you are always analysing Teddy's feelings, never your own."

"Yes and no because it is not clear what HIS emotions really are."

"Alright then, but what are your real feelings for him? Remember, I am your best friend. Speak to me, woman."

"My relationship with Mike was such that it never occurred to me that there would ever be another man in my life. There can never be another Mike."

"Dana, you are still a young woman and you have every right to be attracted to another man."

"Yes, but since his accident, I have been so immersed in mourning and self-pity that the thought of another man never crossed my mind. Is what I am feeling, an attraction to Teddy? I doubt it. And even if it is, how appropriate is it or rather, how inappropriate, in his present, vulnerable state and under the current circumstances? And me as a therapist for his son."

"Perhaps, at last, you are allowing yourself to begin to feel again. Don't you think that is a positive step after all this time?"

"I don't know, Sally. While I welcome the return of positive emotions, I also feel pangs of guilt. The only things I've felt since Mike's death are misery and gloom, which have pervaded my very existence."

"Come on, Dana, you have a life to live and a contribution to make. How long do you think is an appropriate length of time?"

"Mike was everything for me. How would it be if he saw me succumbing to instincts of passion, all right, not exactly passion, but interest in another man? No, I am not ready, yet."

"I don't agree at all but I understand your attitude. The decision is yours, Dan. Any time you want to discuss it with me further, you know I am available. And, I am so happy to see you back. What now, though?"

"I need to be the one to take a step back and make sure that he does not reach the wrong conclusion, especially in his present sensitive condition," Dana said, decisively. "I don't want to lead him on in any way."

"What else can I say that may make a difference in your decision?" asked Sally more in hope than conviction.

"Nothing, I will need to be very circumspect in the way I conduct myself with him in the future. He can be hurt so easily. I have already seen his patently exposed heart. He wears it openly on his sleeve. It is essential that he knows that he can rely on me, nothing more!"

"If that is your final decision, so be it," Sally said, ruefully.

"I will do anything I can to make his and Guy's lives easier. We have actually spent very little time together. We have only been in each other's company three times. That is nothing, time-wise. Both of us have endured a traumatic loss and what we are experiencing may just be the rebound syndrome."

With this clarity, she breathed a sigh of relief. She was not sure if it was because she truly believed it was a correct professional decision or whether it just let her off the hook and she would not need to risk the danger involved in a new relationship, should it transpire that this was potentially, what it was.

Sally shook her head in bewilderment and frustration.

# Chapter 25

After he woke up, Guy took a few seconds to orientate himself with his unfamiliar surroundings and remember where he was. He was feeling uncomfortable because the nurse had inserted a thermometer under his arm while he slept.

She grinned at him. "How are you feeling, this morning, Guy?"

"My back is sore, and I want to go to the toilet." She immediately went away and returned a few seconds later with a tablet and a glass of water.

"That should help," she told him, smiling, kindly. "I'll show you where your private washroom is, now," she said after he swallowed the pill.

She waited beside him until he had walked inside. He was relieved to see his father leaning over a sink washing his face. When Teddy looked up, he noticed Guy's reflection in the mirror and gave him a broad grin.

He knelt down and took him into his arms, lovingly stroking his hair as the boy nestled, his head on his father's shoulder.

He knew that Guy was at the start of a long road that would have many twists and turns, some possibly far more demanding than today. Again, in his heart of hearts, he berated and at the same time pleaded to the all-merciful God, in whom he had lost all faith.

"What else do you have in store for this child? Has he not experienced enough pain? So early in his life, you took away the person he loved and needed most. Please have some compassion for him. Why should this innocent boy have to suffer more than he has done?"

"Did you sleep well, Guy? How are you feeling this morning?" he asked, tenderly.

"I am feeling better, Dad. Are we going home today?"

He did not want to depress Guy. Dr Simpson had advised him the day before that the nursing staff still had to attend to reducing his temperature and deal with the infection in the gash above his eye.

More importantly, though, only when the results of the bone-marrow biopsy were received would they discover the exact nature of Guy's leukaemia. The doctors would then inform them of the treatment they envisaged and how long Guy needed to be detained in hospital.

"Dr Simpson and Dr Barnett will start their ward rounds soon, son," he said. "They want to make sure you are OK before they send us home. When they get here, we can ask them whatever we like. You remember, yesterday, Doctor Simpson told us he would answer all of our questions."

"I don't remember but I hope he says we can go home today," said Guy.

Fifteen minutes later, Dana walked into the ward and greeted them both with a warm embrace.

In Teddy's case, it lasted less time than those from the previous day. She noted that he released her first and she concluded that her reasoning the night before had been accurate.

Apparently, it appeared that he had chosen to maintain his connection with her on a more impersonal level, even if her assumption on his part, that there was a romantic interest in her had any basis. She felt both disappointed and, at the same time, relieved. It certainly made everything far less complicated.

Guy, though, was overjoyed to see her and made no effort to disguise the fact. He grabbed her and boisterously, danced her around, wincing every now and then when his back gave him a twinge. She revelled in the grip of the young boy.

"When we go home later, will you come to our house?" he asked her.

"As I told you yesterday, I will be with you as long as you want me. But I cannot wait for you to come to my home and see where I live" she answered.

"Please, can we go to Dana's house?" said Guy. "I feel fine. You told me that children, who go to her house, feel better afterwards. Maybe if I go to there, I will feel even better."

"Hoisted by my own petard," said Teddy with mock resignation. He looked at Dana for salvation.

She obliged by explaining the situation to the boy. "We will have to wait for the doctors before we decide anything. When they have checked you out, they will tell us if it is alright to go home. They know nobody likes staying in the hospital for even one second longer than necessary."

"OK," answered Guy, willing to agree with whatever she said. Dana smiled at the boy's instant acceptance.

"They should be here soon, anyway," she added so Guy would not feel that he had been left with no alternative other than to agree.

"That's OK, Dana, as long as you are here with us, we can wait," Guy said without any sign of having been forced to compromise.

She smiled with pleasure at the facility with which the boy had agreed.

"When you do visit me, we can play together in the playroom. I even have a music system. I know you love classical music. I do, too, so we can listen to some of my favourite pieces, together. There are many you would enjoy and I want to hear them with you."

She turned to Teddy. "I assume you are also a classical music lover?"

Before he had an opportunity to reply, Guy interjected, "Yes, Daddy loves classical music. We went to a concert, together. That is when I heard Peter and the Wolf."

"Wonderful. I have a lovely recording of it at home. Perhaps, when you feel well enough we can all listen to it, together."

In the middle of their conversation, a boy of Afro-Asian descent, roughly Guy's age, came into the ward accompanied by his parents. The nurse, who had been tending to Guy, informed them that they would be sharing the ward.

For the next few minutes, they all spoke in hushed tones, not wanting to disturb each other until Dana decided to take control of the situation Without further hesitation, she went over to them as the child was getting into bed.

"Hello. I am Dana. And this is Guy and Teddy Goodson," she said, warmly. They shook hands.

"Meet my wife, Sandra. I am Gary Weaver and this is our son, Bobby. Sometimes we call him by his nickname, Wee Bobby." The boy grinned and nodded.

"It is nice to meet you," said Dana. "Guy had to have some tests done yesterday. If the doctor is satisfied, we hope to go home later, so you may have the ward to yourselves."

The father was a big, burly man, with a stubbly beard and a gruff voice.

"Wee Bobby also has to have a special test and I hope he can go home soon, too if everything is alright."

Bobby looked at them shyly. He was small for his age and despite his coppery-coloured skin, he seemed sallow and wan.

He turned to Guy. "What kind of test did you have?"

Guy replied like a veteran addressing a freshman. "I had a bone-marrow examination because I have a blood disease. They want to find out what kind it is, so they know what they need to do to make me better."

"Hey! I also have a blood disease and I need to have a test like that," said Bobby, pleased to have discovered someone, who could give him the benefit of personal experience.

Bobby's father explained that the boy was scheduled to undergo a bone-marrow aspiration, similar to Guy's, although he did not use the term, 'aspiration' but said 'test' instead.

Wee Bobby turned to Guy. "Is it sore?" he asked.

"Yes, it is a bit," he replied. "But it is not so bad, really. You will be alright, you will see."

After a short pause, Guy could not contain his curiosity any longer. "How did you get the name Wee Bobby? You are not that small."

The boy's father answered. "No, it is not because of Bobby's size. Our surname is Weaver, Robert Weaver. Bobby is called Wee because at school the boys addressed him by his surname, Weaver. The Wea was just short for Weaver and when one of the boys decided to call him, Wee Bobby, as a joke, the nick-name stuck."

"Wow! That's cool, Bobby," Guy exclaimed with genuine admiration.

"Bobby also likes the name and now everybody calls him that. Even we do, sometimes, don't we, son?"

Wee Bobby nodded but he was more concerned with the pending procedure. He took the opportunity to ask Guy what they had done to him during the bone-marrow test. Guy described what he had experienced the day before in graphic detail.

"I wish there had been someone to tell me like I am telling you. I would not have been as scared as I was because in the end, it was not that bad." Guy said.

The two boys became involved in conversation around the subject of the blood test, which allowed the adults to talk amongst themselves.

Gary Weaver told them how they had observed symptoms, similar to those Teddy had seen with Guy and subsequent tests had produced the same sort of results. The two boys were following parallel paths.

"As parents, I suppose you were probably as shocked as we were when you got the news about Guy?" said Gary Weaver. Teddy looked very uncomfortable at Dana. She answered quietly, so that Guy would not hear.

"Yes, we were very distraught when the doctors told us what they suspected.

Of course, we are very worried about him even now. Teddy went through a very difficult period, recently. I am here to give him the support he needs. We are really close friends."

He breathed a sigh of relief, not having to correct the inaccurate assumption made by Gary Weaver. Again, he was struck by her ability to overcome awkward situations, which appeared to him insurmountable.

Their discussion was interrupted by the appearance of Dr Simpson, accompanied by Dr Barnett, who greeted Guy with a friendly smile.

"Good morning, young man. We have spoken to the night staff and the nurses told us you were a hero. They said it is a pity that not all the patients are as good as you are," said Doctor Simpson.

"I wasn't such a hero." Guy answered, modestly, and they all laughed.

"I see you have a room-mate," said Dr Barnett, "Are you friends, yet?"

Guy smiled with pleasure. "Yes. This is Bobby and he has the same as I do."

"So, you can tell him all about it then, can't you?" said Dr Barnett. "By the way, I brought you another disc. I think you will enjoy it. It is a compilation of music from different Ballets. When you get to know it, I am sure you will enjoy it." He handed the disc to Guy and turned to Teddy and Dana.

"Dana, would you stay here with young Guy while Dr Simpson and I take Teddy for a short walk? We need to talk over a few details."

They left the ward, deeply engaged in conversation.

Guy started telling Wee Bobby about his new compact-disc player and showed him the discs of classical music Dr Barnett had brought him.

"I was not a fan of classical music before I went to a concert with my father. I heard Peter and the Wolf and music by Tchaikovsky. That is when I began to like it. It makes me feel like I am floating in the air or riding on a roller-coaster."

"I have never ever heard classical music. I prefer popular music, like we have at home, sometimes, and West Indies music," Wee Bobby said.

Guy countered by saying, "I don't think I have heard West Indies music, yet but I am looking forward to it."

Guy extolled the merits of classics and Wee Bobby expounded on the advantages of the music to which he was accustomed.

"Maybe, we can hear each other's music and then we can make up our own minds," suggested Guy.

"Wouldn't it be cool if we find we like both kinds? As I said, I have never heard classical music. Hey! How about this?" said Wee Bobby. "When we are better, I can teach you about my music and you can let me hear yours."

"Great," said Guy. "As soon as we get out of here, we will ask our parents to bring us to each other's homes and we can start. You must hear Peter and the Wolf. Once you do, I am sure you will be like me. I am learning more and more all the time. I already have quite a few discs."

"You have to hear reggae and calypso, though. My parents are from the West Indies. That is why they love that kind of music. It reminds them of back home. But we don't have any discs."

Back and forth, they went, their dire situation forgotten, two young boys, whose lives were so precariously balanced, chatting and planning for the future.

Teddy returned to the ward twenty minutes later with good news. "OK, Guy, you have been temporarily discharged and we can go home."

"Fantastic!" Guy said. "I hope you can go home soon as well, Bobby."

"I hope so, too," said Wee Bobby, brightly. "Bye, Guy. great meeting you."

"So long, Bobby, see you. Hope the test goes well. Don't forget the music."

"Don't worry. I can't wait for us to get started," Wee Bobby said, excitedly.

# Chapter 26

Guy wanted Dana to come home with them but she suggested that instead, they visit her house.

"The doctors told you it was alright, Teddy. Guy can see where I live and spend some time in the playroom. He has looked forward to it for so long."

Teddy relented after Guy assured him he felt up to it and he promised to let his father know if he began to feel tired.

Before going inside, Guy noticed the mosaic plaque alongside Dana's front door, two apples, leaning on each other with the words, 'Dana and Mike's Home', inscribed above.

"Hey, Dana, it is lovely," Guy said, admiringly. "Who did such a nice sign for you?"

"I did," answered Dana, proudly. "One of my hobbies is mosaics, Guy. If you want to learn, I would enjoy teaching you," she explained.

"Why, thank you, Dana, what a lovely idea, Guy. You are very creative, and Dana's suggestion is right up your street," Teddy said. Guy agreed, enthusiastically.

"I love the 'musaic' outside Dana's house. Maybe I will be able to make one for our home, Daddy," Guy said, excitedly.

"That would be fantastic, Guy," said Dana, "but it is mosaic. I know it is an unusual word so it is easy to make a mistake if you have never heard it before."

"Thank you, Dana, I learn so much from you," Guy said, looking at her with an expression of idol-worship on his face.

Teddy, too, looked at her with incredulity, finding it hard to believe the extent and speed with which she had won his precious son over.

Guy was thrilled to be with Dana, in her house and about to see the fabled playroom, which had intrigued him for so long.

As she opened the door to the room, he stood with his mouth agape. He could not believe his eyes. Shelves of multi-coloured miniatures, toy figures of every description, naturally including famous super-heroes, covered one wall at a level accessible to children. In the corner stood an art table with paints and paint-brushes, crayons, pens and pencils, sheets of coloured paper, transfers, scissors, staplers, glue, play-dough and other paraphernalia, enough to exercise the most creative children's minds.

There were musical instruments, dolls' houses, tea sets, models of foods, such as hamburgers, French fries, pizza, etcetera, different types of fruit and vegetables, toy farms with an assortment of animals, barns, sheds, trees and fences, a fully equipped toy zoo and Lego building-blocks. Fancy-dress costumes of every description and different hats to enthral any child hung from a stand, shaped like a tree. And of course, the piece de' resistance, the famous sand-box took up a fair amount of space in the room. There was also a comprehensive library of children's books, an encyclopaedia for young people as well as a small music system and a neat stack of compact discs.

"Wow! Can I go in?"

"Of course, you may," she said.

"Will you come and play with me?"

"I will but first, I want to prepare some refreshments. Then, I need to speak to your father for a short while and afterwards, I will join you." She showed him where everything was and pointed out her shelves of books.

"Why don't you browse through them until I come back?" she suggested. "I will only be a few minutes. Meanwhile, you can get acquainted with the playroom." She went to the kitchen to talk to Teddy as Guy immediately took out some of the books.

While she prepared a light snack, Teddy elaborated on the information he had received from Dr Barnett and the specialist, Dr Simpson.

"I can't believe what is happening It is a recurring nightmare. Guy has leukaemia, as we feared."

"I suppose they explained to you what that actually means, didn't they?"

"They did. Guy has A.L.L. acute lymphoblastic leukaemia. Just the name is shocking."

"Did they give you any idea of the severity of Guy's condition, Teddy?"

"I never understood everything I was told because of the medical terminology," he admitted. "But the bottom line is that there can be no delay and treatment must commence immediately."

"How long should the treatment take?"

"They just said it might extend over a lengthy period, perhaps as much as two years."

"Poor Guy, two years is a lifetime for a child! Sometimes, it might be less time, though, right?" she enquired.

"Yes, but it all depends on how he responds to the combination of drugs prescribed by the specialists. Fortunately, the illness has been identified early. They say the recovery rate is high for the type of leukaemia which Guy has."

"That is really good news, isn't? Why do they say that? What do they mean, exactly?" she asked.

"They told me there are different stages. The first is to bombard the affected white blood-cells and bone marrow with massive doses to destroy these cells or at least inhibit them and prevent any metastasis, the spread of the disease to other parts of the body. That is called the 'Induction' phase, so, I was told," he elaborated.

"I suppose it will be very distressing for Guy, especially at the start," she said with a worried expression.

"That's right. Unfortunately, as with most chemotherapeutic drugs, there are often severe side-effects. There is usually hair loss, tiredness and weakness, anaemia and an increased risk of exposure to infection because the immune system is weakened by the destruction of not only leukaemia-affected, white blood-cells but healthy ones, as well."

"It sounds terrible," she said. "I suppose there will also be the need for constant blood tests to determine whether the drug recipe is having the desired effect."

"Yes, and you know how he hates injections," he said. "All the chemotherapy drugs are applied intravenously so it might be preferable to insert a central infusion device, through which, most of these functions can be carried out."

"Will that save him the trauma of all those injections?"

"Yes, to some extent, but the trouble is that the device is inserted under general anaesthetic, which means another one. He has had enough shots, already. Fortunately, though, it can remain in place for as long as necessary, even a full two years, provided the instrument and the area around it are kept clean and proper hygiene is always maintained."

"Thank heavens for small mercies," she said, caustically.

"There is much more, like other chemotherapy tablets or pills to counter the biliousness, steroids, bone-marrow or stem-cell transplants, if all does not go according to plan. Various other things are possible, but at this stage, it is pure conjecture until they ascertain how he responds to the combination of drugs."

"You sound as though you are a doctor yourself, Teddy. I don't know how you remember all those medical terms," Dana said, flippantly.

"I don't know either. It is just that I want to make sure I know as much as possible so I can take care of Guy, properly."

"Don't worry, Teddy. He is in safe hands. The doctors are very experienced, that is the main thing," Dana reassured him.

"Absolutely. You are right. Thank goodness for that but what is certain is that my little boy will go through hell in the coming months. I don't even want to think about the end result. Who knows what might be? I can't get what happened with Mona out of my mind."

"I can well understand that, Teddy. Just remember, though, they caught this early so they are more confident of a positive outcome. Just trust. It will also support Guy."

"I will try my best, Dana. I so appreciate your advice and your willingness to be with us at a time like this. Everything you say or do makes the world of difference to Guy…and me," he added.

"I already told you how important you both are to me even though we only met a short time ago. It seems as though the fates have conspired to bring us all together," she said.

Teddy gave her a smile of gratitude, which she acknowledged with a smile of her own in return.

She felt her face begin to flush with embarrassment so she decided to divert the focus back to Guy.

"How awful for the poor child. He hates injections and he is going to become a human pin cushion. I suppose that is the least of the troubles, though."

"You are right. There are far more serious things to worry about. That is why I am so afraid to build up my hopes in case…because of what happened when Mona was sick," he explained.

"Of course, Teddy, it is quite understandable but we will be here together to get him through it all. And remember, you need to put on a cheerful face even if you are not feeling cheerful. Please, it is essential, Teddy. We must keep our spirits up. Let's remember this in the coming months, OK?"

"OK, I'll try. The doctors said the same thing."

"Obviously, they would. The one who matters most is Guy."

"Sure, but God, it feels like a bad dream. When the doctors explain, they sound cold and clinical. But, remember, it is my son they are talking about," he said, bitterly.

"You are right, Teddy, although I am sure they do not mean to be impersonal," she said.

"Perhaps not. I suppose professional etiquette demands it of them. The burning question, now is how much should I tell him?" he asked, in despair. "It isn't fair to overburden such a young child."

"We will tell him, step by step. Not too much at once is the best way. We will not hide anything from him. There is also no need to overload him, beyond answering his questions and telling him the things he needs to know."

"In the meantime, just look at me! I can't allow him to see me like this. I am not sure I can hold it all together, Dana."

She took his hands and stood facing him.

"I was told that he would be supported by a team of people, aside from the medical staff responsible for his treatment. Psychologists, physiotherapists, even social workers are all on call. They are there to support you, too, Teddy."

"Of course, we appreciate them all but, in the end, without you, I do not think I would be able to deal with what lies ahead. I am not sure Guy can either. You have become our saviour even though you only came back into the picture a few days ago."

He was overcome with emotion. His concern for his son had loosened his tongue more than he had intended. She did not know whether, due to extreme distress, his choice of words had conveyed his true feelings. Was he just being emotional or was there something deeper?

Not wanting to overstep the mark, she reassured him, "As I said, Teddy, Guy is in safe hands and you can depend on me. I will not desert you. Let us just make sure that your beautiful little boy knows there are two people on whom he can rely, completely."

He looked at her, gratefully. She was taken aback by the intensity of his gaze and realised that it was necessary to defuse the potency of the moment.

"When do they intend starting chemotherapy?" she asked. He looked at her forlornly, the stuffing having been knocked out of him.

"Tomorrow!"

"Gosh! They want to begin that soon? I imagine they know what they are doing, though. There is really no reason to delay so treatment needs to start as soon as possible. If they are ready, we are, too. Let us keep our chins up for Guy's sake."

"Funny, but that is exactly what Dr Barnett said to me once, a long time ago when Mona…" he said, bitterly.

"This is a new time, Teddy. Now, let me go and see how Guy is doing."

"Okay, Dana, I will wait here until I am wanted," he said.

She joined Guy in the playroom.

At first, he had been disconcerted by the vast array of possibilities but eventually, he had settled down on the floor and started building an elaborate locomotive and carriages from Lego building blocks.

She watched him as he carefully selected the different colours and sizes of blocks. She saw his nimble fingers converting his mental image to physical reality as, slowly, the train took shape.

Guy carefully added block after block, until he was satisfied. He turned to her with a flamboyant gesture of pride and pointed to his creation.

She praised his dexterity and clarity of vision. "It is beautiful," she said. "You seemed able to picture what the train would look like before you began to build it. It was amazing watching the way you put it together. You have a lot of patience and imagination, Guy. You can use those same qualities for mosaic work when we start."

The boy swelled with pride and clapped his hands together.

"Shall we call your father, so he can see what you have made? I am certain he will be as proud of you as I am?"

"Yes, let's do that," cried Guy, excitedly.

When Teddy saw what Guy had built, he swept him off his feet, twirling him around. The boy laughed with pleasure, something he had seldom done in the past few weeks.

Then, Guy opened a small, plastic case. He stared at it for a few moments in shock. His face fell. The case contained a variety of toy medical instruments.

"When do I have to go back to the hospital?" he asked.

Dana realised immediately what was going through the boy's mind.

"The doctors want you to get well quickly so they think it is best to start the treatment tomorrow," she answered, knowing there was no easy way to tell Guy.

"What are they going to do to me?" he asked, fearfully.

"You can ask them any question you like at the hospital, tomorrow. That way, there will be no surprises," she said. "The nurses and doctors will do whatever possible to make things easy for you."

"Will you and Daddy be with me all the time while I am there?"

"Of course, I will be," said Teddy.

"And I will make sure that I am with you as much as the doctors permit," Dana promised.

"Will I miss school, then?"

"Don't worry. We will speak to Ms Commins and let her know you will not be coming to class, so she can prepare some lessons for you to do at the hospital," said Teddy.

"I have already fallen behind the other children and I do not want to fall behind further," he said, sulkily, as he went back to building his train.

"Dr Barnett asked me to bring you to the hospital first thing in the morning. It is already getting late, so we need to go home and pack a bag for you."

Suddenly, with a violent sweep of his hand, Guy scattered the blocks across the floor with a resounding clatter.

"You are very angry and upset, aren't you, Guy," Dana said immediately, employing techniques she knew well in order to empathise with the extremely distraught child.

"I don't want to go back to hospital," he wept.

"Nobody likes being in the hospital, Guy. I am sure you want to get better, though, don't you?" she said.

"I don't want to be sick anymore. It's not fair!"

"When people are ill, they need to trust the doctors will make them well again," said Teddy.

"They never made Mummy well."

"Yes, that is true, but I am certain that before long, you will be fine. We will be with you all the time," Teddy said, doing his utmost to encourage him.

"And it is also quite alright to be angry," said Dana.

"I want to go home. I am sorry, Dana," snivelled Guy.

"There is no need to apologise, Guy. You are tired. Whenever you are ready, you are welcome to come back."

"You may be there for a few days, so we need to bring quite a lot of things including some books and, of course, your compact-disc player and discs," said his father.

"Perhaps your friend, Bobby is still there. I am sure he will be happy to see you again," Dana said.

Guy was still very upset.

At the front-door, she held him, tenderly for a few moments, rocking him to and fro until he was calmer. Teddy was moved, seeing the boy melt in her embrace.

Out of the blue, Guy asked her, "Do you live in this big house alone?"

She grinned at him and said, "Yes, I live on my own. There is nobody else here. Why do you ask?"

He thought for a moment. "Who is Mike? I saw his name on the sign outside. Is it your dog?"

She laughed. "No. I don't have a dog. My husband was called Mike. We lived here together before he died."

"My mother also died and just Daddy and I live in our house. Couldn't we all live together? It will be easier."

"Firstly, let us get you better and then we will busy ourselves with things like that," said Teddy, looking at Dana, who giggled at Guy's facile solution to their accommodation and relationship arrangements.

"You will be at the hospital, again, tomorrow, won't you?" Guy reminded her.

"Of course, I will. Just like today and every day," she assured him. "I hope you enjoyed your time in the playroom."

"It was great," he answered, a little more brightly. "You were right. While I was there, I forgot about the hospital…mostly."

"That is terrific. Next time, you will have more time and I hope that, little by little, all your worries will disappear completely."

He came up to her. "Thank you, Dana. I love being in your house." Once more, he nestled in her arms and she held him, tenderly.

Recognising the adoration on Guy's face, Teddy said to her, quietly, "We hardly know each other and already you have made such a difference in Guy's…and my life. He loves you and so do I." He turned the colour of beetroot.

"Now, that is what I call a Freudian slip," she said with a giggle.

# Chapter 27

Teddy's face fell more and more until it could sink no lower. Although, Dr Barnett had warned him what to expect, the specialist, James Simpson explained things to him and Dana in greater detail when they met again before they began Guy's treatment. Teddy was shocked.

"As you know, during the induction stage of chemotherapy, the doses are normally massive. The specialist experiments to determine and monitor the efficacy of the chemotherapy-drug recipe. It is fairly certain that this phase of the treatment might be very difficult for Guy due to the concentration and toxicity of the drugs building up in his system."

Teddy sat stony faced as he listened to Dr Simpson. He knew it was important for him to know exactly what lay ahead. Dana, too, was quiet, concentrating on all the information the doctor was giving them.

"Each time, Guy may be in the hospital anywhere from two days to two weeks. Please bear in mind that after the drugs begin to take effect, the number of healthy white blood cells in his body are severely depleted and the possibility of infection is far greater. It will be necessary to accommodate him in a special section where he will be kept in isolation to limit such exposure to any virus."

"At least we will be with him all the time, won't we?" Teddy asked.

"Yes, that's true." answered Dr Simpson. "But each time, the number of visitors will be restricted until his white blood-cell count increases sufficiently. He may be disconcerted by this because visitors are required to dress appropriately, with sterile robes over street clothing, face-masks and hair covering. You even have to cover your shoes or wear surgeon's slippers."

As Teddy had no idea how to explain all this to the boy, Dana later told the child in language which he could understand.

"Thank heavens for your support, Dana," Teddy said. "I would have botched up the explanation and made matters worse. We have both grown to rely on you more than is fair."

"Stop being so apologetic, Teddy. I told you I intend to be there for you no matter what. If I can help, it is my wish to continue for as long as you want."

He never answered but Dana had the impression that he wanted to say something and had chosen not to speak.

They drove to the hospital in separate cars as Teddy intended staying with Guy at night while Dana would only remain until he fell asleep.

He was admitted to the children's oncology section where the staff members did their best to put him at ease, unfortunately not too successfully. He was on the verge of tears. Dana herself had great difficulty in maintaining her own equilibrium in the face of the pending ordeal. They were advised that the specialist team would examine Guy, shortly and then he would be allocated a ward.

He lay staring wide-eyed at the instruments around him. The strangeness of the surroundings was frightening for even the most stalwart adult let alone for a child not yet seven. Poor Guy clung to them in absolute terror.

The first treatment had the precise effects that all the prior briefings had predicted. Guy came back to the ward, unconscious, his body flopping like a rag-doll. Teddy and Dana were shattered. They held his hands while he slept.

After a short time, Dr Simpson came out to meet them. "Everything went according to plan," he assured them. "Guy will probably sleep for a good few hours. He did very well. I will call in on him during the day to check the situation. Meanwhile, I suggest you get something to eat. I will keep you up to date."

They were about to leave for the cafeteria when Dana saw Gary Weaver turning into a doorway in the corridor outside the ward. She called to him quietly.

When he heard his name, he looked round and walked back towards her bearing an expression of abysmal dejection. Her heart sank. He seemed to have shrunk in size. His eyes were bloodshot and his unshaven face was covered with greying stubble. She waited for him to speak. In a voice barely, a whisper he told her the shocking news.

"The results were far worse than expected. Wee Bobby's leukaemia is very aggressive and has already spread to other organs. The doctors said they still have to identify the violence and degree of the metastasis, but the prognosis is grim. Did I say those long words, right?" he asked.

"Yes, Gary, you did," she answered, kindly although she knew he meant 'virulence'. She was aghast. "I am so sorry. I know it may be pointless, but if there is anything we can do, please let us know."

"At the moment, there is not much anyone can do."

"Guy started his treatment today, too, so he might be in the hospital for a while. I am sure our paths will cross again, especially as the boys are confined to the same department," she said.

"Probably," he agreed. "I can tell you, Bobby was very impressed with Guy."

"And vice-versa! Guy loved meeting Bobby," she replied. "He thinks they will be close friends. They are good for one another."

He smiled, weakly. "Bobby kept on telling us about the new friend he made and how he was going to introduce him to classical music. Neither of us knows anything about that kind of music but Guy's enthusiasm really rubbed off on him."

"Guy is also looking forward to learning about reggae or Reggy, as he calls it," she said. They both laughed.

"Bobby never had many friends at school. He was always shy and kept to himself. He was bullied, too, but nobody knew because he never told anybody. Fortunately, it stopped after the teachers found out but by then, the damage was done. Now, this," he said, bitterly.

Dana was appalled by the unfairness of Wee Booby's fate. "That is why it was lovely to see the connection with Bobby and your Guy."

Dana unsuccessfully. tried to swallow the lump in her throat.

"I only pray that the two of them have a chance to develop their friendship," Gary Weaver said, vain hope ringing in his voice.

Just then, Teddy came up to them and joined in the conversation. "Guy mentioned that he will be very pleased if Bobby and he can spend time together. He would jump at the chance to visit his new friend."

Gary nodded. "I hope so."

"Depending on what the doctor says, he may be able to call in on Bobby some time. He just finished his first treatment. It was horrendous I can tell you. He is still asleep so he may be confined to bed for a while," said Teddy.

"The doctors told us to prepare ourselves for just such a thing," Gary whispered. "We are dreading the next few months."

"I know what you mean, Gary," said Teddy. "We are in the same boat."

As the nurses were fussing around the sleeping boy, checking the different instruments, monitors and infusions flowing into his arms, Teddy and Dana decided to leave for the cafeteria and tiptoed out of the ward.

Over a cup of coffee, she reported what Gary Weaver had told her before

Teddy had joined them and she saw his face drop at the news.

"Please, Teddy, there is no sense in overdramatising our situation. That is Wee Bobby's condition. Fortunately for us, although Guy's state of health is not good, it is not nearly as bad as poor Wee Bobby's, so let us keep things in perspective. We will need to show a brave face to him, as we agreed. He has enough to contend with without having to be concerned about us. You know very well how he worries when he sees you down."

"You are right, Dana," he said, apologetically, realising that her admonishment was for Guy's benefit and he was ashamed that once again, she needed to bring his shortcomings to his attention.

"I am sorry. Thank you for telling me the truth, even though sometimes, it is not nice to hear. I know it isn't easy for you, but I appreciate it when you call me on my failings. I keep on slipping back and all my good intentions go out the window."

"I know, Teddy. Please do not think I am criticising you. It is just that Guy is such a sensitive child. I do not think he should be put in a position where he expends time and energy worrying about you or anyone else, for that matter. He has so much on his plate, already. I am sure you understand."

He nodded sheepishly.

"Would you like me to be here with you, tomorrow? I know it is going to be a very difficult day for both of you," she asked.

He gave her a wry smile. "Yes, Dana, of course I do. I wish you could be with us, always."

Again, she wondered whether he meant what she thought he did. Whatever his true intention, she decided it was essential to establish their relationship on a more impersonal basis, immediately and not to postpone any further, what was already an unpleasant necessity.

When she had seen the expression on his face, she had realised that it was not advisable to postpone the confrontation any longer.

"Teddy, we need to talk," she said, with downcast eyes. "We have not communicated properly with each other, understandably so, in light of the current circumstances. We have only been in each other's company a few times but I think we need to establish a fitting professional framework for our relationship."

His confusion registered on his face as he reacted to her statement.

"What do you want to talk about, exactly?" he asked, with something of a puppy-dog expression on his face.

Due to his fragile mental state, she concluded that the time was inopportune to say more at this stage.

"I am leaving to go home, now, but I will see you and Guy tomorrow morning. We must find an opportunity for a heart to heart talk as soon as we can. Please give my love to Guy when he wakes up and let him know his greatest admirer will be back here, bright and early."

She hugged him and hurriedly fled the scene, leaving him completely confounded.

She could not wait to confide in Sally, who was thrilled to hear from her again when she phoned her from the car. "Sal, I need to speak to you urgently, again."

"Same subject, darling?" Sally inferred.

"Yes, except that the issue is more pressing than ever."

"Why don't we go to our old haunt, the coffee shop near the University? I can be there in about fifteen minutes," Sally said.

"OK, thanks, I need to be able to talk to you and clear my head."

"Is anything wrong, Dana?" she asked, worriedly.

"No, not really or maybe there is, I am not sure. And you are a good listener. That is what I need right now."

A few minutes later, they wedged themselves into a secluded booth in the coffee shop and ordered two cups of coffee latte. Sally rested her elbows on the table and cradled her chin on her hands, never taking her eyes off Dana for an instant.

"Is it man trouble, again?"

"We spoke about it once before, Sal. Just allow me to talk until I get it all out. I may sound a little confused because I am. Then, I really want to hear what you think. Ok?"

"I am all ears."

"Right, here goes. I more or less made a decision after our last chat and although I never said anything about it to Teddy, I have done my best to behave in accordance with that decision. So far, to some extent, it has been manageable, but it is becoming more complicated by the day. I know I have been delaying the moment when I would need to face up to the truth of my feelings for him. He is Guy's father. I sensed his interest in me as a woman, almost from the start.

Although I am not acting as a therapist, we have been together a lot in a short space of time, just a few days really. I have observed him as a man, a very shy man I can tell you, and not only the father of a child who I am treating.

In my heart of hearts, I realise that I am attracted to him. But, as you once pointed out, I always analyse how he might be feeling towards me instead. So, I use that logic as the excuse for not truly confronting what is happening for me. It is clear, though. I am not ready for an intimate relationship. I am not even certain that what I feel for him is an emotional attraction or just extreme sympathy and compassion for a very sensitive man, who is undergoing such heart-rending trauma for the second time.

Now, his behaviour and the things he says, especially after they came to my house, leave me in no doubt regarding the feelings he has towards me. What do you think, Sal? What should I do?"

"Well, my dear friend, to me you sound like a therapist in love. What would the therapist advise a patient? Why do you feel you are not ready yet for an intimate relationship? When will you be? There are so many questions, Dan."

"True, Mike has been gone a long time, but he is still an intrinsic part of me, like an arm or a leg. I am still his wife and there is no room to even entertain the idea of a love affair. My commitment and faithfulness to him demand that of me."

"Come on, Dana, stop acting like such a martyr and resisting any possibility for future happiness." Sally said, abruptly.

Dana shook her head, clearly not agreeing with her friend's assessment of her situation.

"If you truly feel something deeper for Teddy, why should you consider it a breach of commitment and faithfulness? You are a young woman and a sensitive and integrous one, what's more. Don't you deserve a full life, for God's sake," Sally said with a trace of anger in her voice.

Dana stared at her friend for a few moments before she replied.

"It is not only that. How can I be sure that Teddy is not simply reacting to the extreme pressure of his present circumstances? His son is ill with a potentially fatal disease and he is facing an impossibly difficult time with no assurance of Guy's survival at the end of it."

"Quite right, Dan and then what? Perhaps, he is also not sure of himself. You say he is shy and your attitude may be causing him to be even more diffident and uncertain."

"Perhaps so, but he is still mourning his beloved Mona. The combination of that coupled with my appearing on the scene at the exact moment that his son was diagnosed with leukaemia, has probably converted me into his 'life-saver'. He almost told me that in so many words. I think the stress he is experiencing has even turned me into his Mona."

"Why don't you just let things be and take it one step at a time? Or, what about talking to Teddy, openly? You are both adults and maybe if you bring everything out into the open, it may make it easier for you both to decide where you go from here."

"Because when the crisis passes, and things return to 'normal', he could wake up and discover I am not the vision he created in his vulnerable state. Maybe at that stage, if I permit this relationship to progress any further, it will be too late and the pain Teddy…or I might endure would be too great to bear. It may even affect my connection with Guy."

"Everything you say may be correct and maybe not. If you do not buy a ticket for the lottery, you have no chance of bagging the prize. Is it worth it?" Sally asked.

Dana shook her head as though she had reached a conclusion, for the second time.

"It is time for me to be the strong one and scotch the whole matter before it gets out of hand. You were right, neither of us is a teenager. We are mature adults, who have already been through the fire, each in our own way. To act irresponsibly, now is out of the question" she said with finality.

"So, it seems you are going to take the bull by the horns this time and tell him you are there for him and Guy but a relationship, other than a purely professional one or a platonic friendship, is not on, no matter how close you two become."

"Exactly," Dana confirmed. "But whether I have the will-power to do so is another question. At least, now, I know what I need to do. It is simply a case of finding the right moment and the appropriate way to do it, without breaking Teddy's spirit, which is so fragile at present. And it might adversely affect Guy."

"Even if Guy is trying his level best to engineer a relationship between you, are you saying it is still not realistic," Sally queried.

"Definitely, it is now or never, Sal."

"If that is your final decision, so be it. Personally, I am very sorry," said Sally. "From the little I know of him, he seems a special man. I think it would be worth the risk."

"You may be right, but I am not willing to take that risk. I need to ensure that it does not progress any further. And even if the conversation needs to be postponed for a while, we must have it. Integrity demands it."

Sally shook her head as she had done so often listening to Dana rationalising what was so obvious to her but apparently, not to Dana.

"It will be like walking a tight-rope without a safety net but I am positive my instincts will enable me to keep my balance. For how long will I be able to do it without falling is the only question."

"I don't agree with you at all but if that is really what you want, what right do I have to interfere?" conceded Sally.

"It is for the best, Sally. Guy and Teddy are too precious for me to abandon at this critical juncture, but I need to put a stop to this personal issue developing any further."

"I am not convinced it is for the best, but what the hell, there seems no point in trying to persuade you otherwise. You are being your usual stubborn self. Just remember, as I told you last time, I am there for you any time you want."

"Thanks, Sal, you always have been."

# Chapter 28

The side-effects of the chemotherapy drugs took a heavy toll on Guy, both physically and psychologically. Nonetheless, Teddy took Dana's recommendation to heart and made a super-human effort to show a sunny disposition, despite his depleted spirit.

As the weeks and months passed, Teddy was experiencing an ever-increasing loss of confidence and faith in the treatment. Although, sometimes, there were positive results, often there was either no improvement or even a slight regression in Guy's condition. The doctors reassured him that it was still too early in the process to determine future prognoses.

Watching Guy undergo all the suffering with such fortitude and acceptance of his lot moved him to tears, which he managed to hide from his son but not always from Dana, who had become his rock.

On several occasions, she determined to speak to him about the issue, which still bore so heavily on her. Each time, though, another crisis arose, which rendered it impossible for her to broach the subject.

He was so preoccupied with the boy that it seemed as if he had put his personal feelings aside and the only thing that concerned him was Guy's condition. Yet, to her, it was clear that he harboured what she imagined were romantic notions and she was uncomfortable at not being able to be her natural self for fear of providing him with additional fuel for his fire.

She had no qualms that he would not continue to be the perfect gentleman or that he would ever take advantage of her. It was precisely the opposite. She believed he was waiting for her to express what he imagined were her true feelings for him. She thought his most ardent hope was that those feelings were a reciprocation of those he felt for her.

He was so shy and reserved that she knew he would never declare his feelings unless she initiated the subject, which she had no intention of doing. She was aware that on occasions, she might have shown more than a soft spot for the unhappy man, who had already faced tragedy and was now reliving his worst nightmare. This may have produced the precise opposite result from that which she was trying to create.

Sometimes, she even entertained the idea that she was postponing the confrontation with him, not only because she did not want to hurt him but perhaps she did 'love' him more than she was willing to acknowledge to herself. Perhaps her own fear of being hurt was stifling her willingness to open her heart to him.

Meanwhile, time was passing and before they knew it, Guy was nearing the end of the first phase of his treatment. After a short respite, he would resume the next stage of chemotherapy. Perhaps, then would be the appropriate time to speak to him, she reasoned.

For weeks, while Guy had been hospitalised she had constantly been at his bedside. She and Teddy had spent hours together and an unspoken understanding had developed between them. They fitted together, perfectly and complemented each other in attending to Guy's needs.

In interactions with the doctors or medical staff, her presence was already taken for granted and often, when Teddy was not available, they would approach her. She spent almost all her time at the hospital to allow Teddy an opportunity to deal with things that needed his attention at home and at work or to bring clothes or books for Guy.

Even during the very brief interludes when Guy was allowed to go home between the sessions of the infusion of the chemotherapy drugs, which necessitated his internment in hospital, she was with them all the time. It was as though she had become an intrinsic part of the Goodson family.

Nonetheless, it was an accepted arrangement and taken for granted that she would go back to her own home every night to take care of her personal affairs only after Guy had fallen asleep.

They often met Gary and Sandra Weaver, who, like them, spent most of the time in the hospital with their son, whose condition had shown a sharp decline.

"He has not responded well to the chemotherapy and radiation has also been given to counter the advance of the cancer," Gary told them.

"They are considering a bone-marrow and a stem cell transplant, but Bobby's condition is not strong enough for him to undergo these procedures at the present moment. We were told that the doctors think it is too risky to expose the child to surgery or any further, aggressive therapy if there is no reasonable prospect of success."

"How terrible for you and Sandra and of course, for Bobby," said Dana. "Our thoughts and prayers are with you all."

"Thank you, we appreciate that. Bobby talks about his friend, Guy, all the time. We were hoping he is doing well enough for him to be able to visit Bobby. He always perks up around his new friend," said Sandra.

"Guy is due to go home before he begins the next stage of his treatment. I am certain he would love to see Bobby. As soon as we know exactly what the timetable is for the coming days, we will make a plan for the two boys to get together," Teddy said to her.

"That would be great. Give our warmest regards to Guy."

"Will do. Same to Bobby. Bye, Sandra, bye, Gary," Dana said. "Cheerio, take care," Teddy added.

# Chapter 29

Mike waited, impatiently for the moment when he would be summoned and given instructions regarding his return. Although she would not even be aware of his presence, presumably, he would be able to see Dana, again. To him, that was all that mattered, almost.

*If she doesn't know I am there, how will I be able to communicate with her? She will not see me or hear me, I was told, categorically. Will anyone else know I am present so we can communicate, perhaps a medium or someone with a more highly developed sense of spirituality?* he wondered.

The enigma was completely baffling but as he had been assured, often enough, the Eternal One's agenda was not always obvious, not even to Its heavenly minions, who were far closer to It than other mere ex-mortals.

Without warning, Gabriel appeared, out of the blue. One minute he was not there and the next, he invaded Mike's consciousness in a blinding flash.

*"Where is my celestial messenger?"* he asked. *"Why have I not seen it for some time?"*

"It too, has a mission linked to yours. The Eternal One has already sent it on its way. Fortunately, it is not as argumentative as you are," said Gabriel with a chuckle and then, became more business-like.

"Firstly, do not interrupt me. I have much to tell you and I suggest you focus on the information I provide and desist from employing your customary legal wrangling." Mike was tempted to say something but wisely, kept 'his tongue'.

"You will be leaving soon. You are familiar with the term, reincarnation. Many mortals believe fervently in the concept. Even in religions, which man has concocted to assuage his fear of the 'unknown' after death, some of their so-called holy men expound on the idea of reincarnation to explain the eternal cycle of life.

In truth, occasionally, the Source does send certain spirits back to earth, but never in their own bodies or with their own identity. It is not for the reason so many humans believe, just to continue the cycle of physical or even spiritual life. It is done as a tool to affect the All Knowing One's will, whenever It deems appropriate.

In most cases, therefore, whenever It chooses to employ this mechanism, the memory of the returning 'departed' spirit is erased in whole or in part, according to the needs of the occasion."

Mike listened intently, concerned he might miss something that Gabriel was communicating and he would not know what to do when the time arrived for his return to the world.

"I am sure that during your life on earth, you heard of mediums or fortune tellers, people with apparently, 'supernatural' powers," Gabriel continued. "In truth, they did not have supernatural powers but rather theirs' were very natural abilities. The Source simply chose not to limit the extent to which It normally erased past-memories or the accumulated knowledge of that particular individual. Traces of the past were deliberately retained, not details or vivid recollections, but rather vague shadows of long-forgotten occurrences. That is all. That is what accounts for their seeming uniqueness.

When you examine humankind in general, you will recognise that the Heavenly One has ensured that every individual is as unique as he or she or it should be. Man though, with his inflated ego and gross arrogance, has convinced himself of the unfounded belief that the humans are the chosen people or the chosen creation, the favourite of the Eternal One, whom they call their God.

To complicate matters even further, each human believes that his own God is the true or real God and in typical inhuman fashion, man is even willing to kill to prove this claim.

They have even established a list of what they consider is permitted or forbidden, right or wrong, good or bad, even supernatural or prosaic. Man has set the boundaries and made the rules and then claims that that is what their 'God' ordains or desires. Man's opinion of his own opinion is that it is more valid than his own God's opinion. How vain! How typically human!" He never dared question Gabriel's monologue although he was brim-full of questions.

"The Heavenly One has deliberated long and hard to decide to what extent your recollection of the past is to be eliminated and, not only which parts are to be deleted, but more importantly, which parts are to be retained," Gabriel said.

"Some time ago, It initiated the process of bringing about the realisation of Its intention as far as Dana is concerned. It has waited to see how events would unfold because It gave man the gift of free will in areas where the outcome is in his own hands. The die is now cast because the situation has reached a point where the Source's intervention is necessary to ensure that what must be, will be."

Mike was completely baffled by Gabriel's monologue but he refrained from commenting as he sensed this was now a crucial moment.

Like a bombshell, Gabriel continued his thesis. "You are soon to begin your journey. You too, will have free choice as you will see. It is rare for a phenomenon like this to occur. The Eternal One has decided you are to be the vehicle to give expression to Its will. You will have an opportunity to do a final act of charity on a pain-wracked world and prove that your love for Dana is such that her happiness is more important than your own. You are very fortunate."

Mike was elated and at the same time, nervous of the responsibility on his spiritual shoulders. Gabriel, sensing his hesitation and uncertainty, assured him, "You would never have been selected and empowered to undertake such an obligation if there was any doubt of your capability."

*"Thank you for the faith the Eternal one has in me but how will I know what to do? How will I get there? How can I communicate if Dana does not know I am there? I have a million questions. Is this the extent of my briefing before departure?"* he cried with frustration.

"Michael! Michael! When will you learn to trust? Do you need to undergo several reincarnations before you learn to accept that only what is required by the Source is what will ever be and it is all for a purpose, far too complex for us to fathom or decipher?" With that final barb, Gabriel disappeared and left him mulling over the explanation he had received.

*Good God, oops, here we go again*, he thought. *I will just have to wait and see although this time I doubt if it will be as long a wait as before.*

# Chapter 30

Guy was ecstatic to be home. He was still weak and a little embarrassed at his smooth, bald head but just to be surrounded by familiar things was wonderful. He was able to read and build things with his Lego blocks. He could listen to the music he loved and above all, there was no nurse or doctor to check his temperature, feed him pills or stick needles into him, wherever they could find a place without punctures from previous jabs.

But being with his father was one of his greatest pleasure. He held on to him as though he might disappear at any second unless he paid undivided attention to him. But, for Guy, Dana was the cherry on the top.

She spent countless hours at their home and Guy even managed to visit her house, once and went to the playroom with her, where she was able to help him to begin restoring trust in his body and in the future by using techniques she had almost forgotten that she knew.

He was also very excited to be going back to school since he missed his friends and Ms Commins. She had ensured that he receive all the material they had covered during his various stays in the hospital, but, not surprisingly, he had fallen way behind.

Most of the time, during his absence, he had not been in any condition to attend to class-work. His treatment had wrought havoc on the young boy, rendering him weak and incapable of concentrating. But at least, he had managed to read, which became his passion. He devoured everything, from children's books to magazines and even to the text on the sleeves of music discs.

Although he may not have fully understood some of the terminology, he would check with Dana or Teddy to find the meaning of any unfamiliar nomenclature.

His reading skill was far above average, and Ms Commins heaped well-deserved praise on him for his accomplishments.

On his first day back at school, the children in his class welcomed him warmly yet treated him with the utmost care. They had been warned of his illness and were strongly advised not to act roughly with him to avoid the danger of him bruising or suffering any kind of injury. Their curiosity knew no bounds. With typical, youthful disregard for polite convention, they asked many questions.

"Did you cry when they put needles into you? Was it sore? Will you have to go back to the hospital, again? Can we catch what you have? Are you completely better?" There was no limit to their inquisitiveness and no reserve to their frankness. He would have preferred not to be reminded of the hospital, especially as he was aware that he still had to go back for one final cession to complete his treatment. Nonetheless, he answered their queries like a warrior returning home after fighting a lengthy war in a distant land.

The bell signalling the end of the school day rang and Guy was pleased to be going home. Time in class tired him out and he just wanted to relax in his room for a while. Half an hour later, Dana arrived.

She gave Teddy a brief hug. "How is Guy, today?" she asked. "The first day back at school must have exhausted him."

"It did. He handled it well, but it tired him out a little. He is resting. You can be sure he will be thrilled to see you when he gets up."

She had become a permanent fixture in Guy's life and he in hers. He loved her as a mother and, to her surprise, she knew she loved him, too, if not quite as a son, then as a very special child. She realised that she could not bear the idea of them being separated. He had surreptitiously crept into her heart and was lodged there. He had become the child that she and Mike never had. The thought of him dying had filled her with dread.

She fully identified with Teddy, who was so involved with Guy that, to her great relief, the intensity of the relationship between them had cooled, certainly on his part. She was relieved but missed Guy and could not wait for him to come out of his room.

An hour later, he got up and walked into the sitting room, rubbing his eyes, sleepily. When he saw her, their reunion was the customary celebration of the special relationship that normally exists between a young son and his mother. There was total devotion on her part and Guy flew into her arms and cuddled there with no self-consciousness. It was as natural an arrangement as any young child would have with his mother.

The fact did not escape Teddy's notice and, again, he was filled with gratitude to this amazing woman, who had become such an essential element in both their lives.

A few days later, Teddy received a phone call from Gary Weaver, who informed him that Bobby had also been given permission to return home for a brief stay. Guy whooped with joy when Teddy gave him the news.

"Bobby's father told me that he has to go back to hospital in a couple of days because his condition is still very serious. He said he hoped you would visit him because Bobby is too weak to travel. We have arranged that we go to their home tomorrow afternoon after school if that is that alright?"

"Wow! Of course, Dad, that is fantastic. I can take some discs and my C.D. player, so Bobby can listen to classical music. I will also take my Lego-blocks. I am sure he will enjoy building things with them and I can teach him."

On the way home from school next day, Teddy reminded him of the arrangement.

"Our plan is to visit Wee Bobby, today. I think a nap and a few hours of relaxation will do you the world of good. Then, if you still feel like going, we can drive to Wee Bobby's home."

"I will be fine, Dad. I don't want to disappoint him. I don't need to rest today. It is very important that he does not have to wait. You know how sick he is," he said with an air of professional assurance.

Dana was already waiting for them at their home because of her impatience to see both Guy and to her consternation, also Teddy, difficult as it was to acknowledge the fact. She could not quite understand why, lately, she had begun to accept what might be her true feelings for him. Mona, though, knew why.

When Guy saw her, he threw his arms around her neck but to her disappointment, Teddy was more circumspect and only gave her a brief hug.

"Bobby came back from the hospital for a very short stay at home and we are going to visit him, today," he told her.

"I am taking my Lego-bricks with me," Guy chimed in. "Maybe, Wee Bobby will want to build something. I don't think he has many toys. I am also taking my compact-disc player and some discs. Will you come in our car, Dana?"

"That takes care of that, doesn't it?" she laughed.

Teddy smiled, relieved, because she would be going with them after all. He knew her presence would obviate the responsibility of his having to converse with Gary and Sandra, on his own. Even though he knew how sick Wee Bobby was, he was never able to say the appropriate things whereas she always had the knack of handling such situations with ease.

The Weavers lived in an apartment block, in a poorer part of the city. Most buildings were in need of painting and there were few gardens or green areas. The streets were littered, and graffiti covered many walls. However, the entrance to their building was clean and tidy.

Their apartment was small, the furniture, worn, the carpet, threadbare and the few ornaments scattered around, adding a touch of colour, were mostly cheap baubles or photographs of the Weavers in happier times.

In one of the pictures, the family was smiling, proudly. A small girl, a year or two older than Bobby was standing next to them. Bobby, wearing a T shirt with 'Man of the House' emblazoned on the front, sat on Sandra's lap.

They were warmly welcomed and served tea and light refreshments in plastic cups. Sandra had specially baked an apple tart for the occasion. Guy and Wee Bobby gave each other the usual greeting, a high five and immediately disappeared into Bobby's room and shut the door.

"How is Guy's treatment progressing?" asked Sandra. Dana deliberately held back to give Teddy an opportunity to answer.

When he realised this, he replied, "It is too early to say. The doctors have told us that it will take a good few weeks, perhaps even months, before we have a real indication but thank heavens, the prognosis is fairly positive."

"We are both very happy for you," said Gary, doing his utmost to hide a trace of jealousy in his voice.

"Of course, the side effects such as the biliousness, the tiredness and of course, losing his hair, have all distressed him. I am sure you know how it is because you are going through the same thing with Bobby. It is cruel, seeing what they have to endure. Sometimes, I wonder if there is a God in heaven, to inflict such suffering on innocents," Teddy said.

Sandra answered him with firm resignation. "We are believers and know that God's purpose is beyond our understanding. Our faith allows us to deal with this crisis, as it was when Jemima was knocked over and killed nearly two years ago. He took our daughter. Of course, we miss her and mourn that her life was cut short but our belief helps us get through, day by day."

"A truck-driver failed to stop at a pedestrian crossing and she and her best friend were killed. But, if that is his will, so be it. We must accept it," added Gary, looking at Sandra meaningfully.

"I know Gary does not feel as strongly as I do but we have been able to overcome our grief using our faith as a balm against the pain. We have forgiven the driver and we pray for Bobby's deliverance but whatever will be, we accept it in the same way. These events were sent by Him to test our faith."

Dana was shocked and concerned for Teddy, whom she noticed had recoiled when he heard that they had already lost a child. She kept her eyes on him until he glanced at her and she gave him a loving smile to encourage and reassure him.

"I wish I had been able to draw comfort from such deep belief in my own hour of need," she reflected as she saw his tense expression ease and she was pleased she had done what she did. Having witnessed the unshakable foundation of Sandra's belief, she envied the woman and at the same time pitied her in this dual catastrophe. To those without faith, it may have sounded callous. She could not comprehend how even such faith could seal the heart of a mother to the loss of a child, let alone both children.

"What is the latest position with Bobby? I am so sorry. When I spoke to Gary last, he told me that the tests showed a spread of the disease. What are the doctors recommending?" she asked.

Gary answered, without waiting for his wife to reply. "It is just as I told you when I saw you at the hospital. There is metastasis to the brain and it is quite far gone. The doctors are considering different treatments, but they have told us not to have too much hope as Bobby's condition is fairly advanced and very grave."

Sandra continued as Gary found it difficult to speak. "They told us that if there is not an improvement in Bobby's health soon, it won't take very long," she said, impassively. Tears welled up in Gary's eyes and his body shook with emotion, while Sandra sat motionless, looking stoically at her husband.

"Of course, we have not told Bobby. He is nearly eight. He is slightly younger than Guy, I think. A few months, correct? We were advised that there is no benefit in saying anything to him," explained Gary.

"What is there to say to a seven-year-old who is dying?" asked Sandra. "Seven years, and few of them have been really happy. He was bullied and humiliated because of his colour. His parents have not been able to give him much of what other children have in life. And then his sister is killed and his parents are ripped apart by that," Gary added.

"Fortunately, we can accept it if that is God's will," Sandra added.

"Poor Bobby has paid the heaviest price of all. It is not fair and truthfully, I find it almost impossible to maintain faith in a merciful, heavenly father who brings such suffering to his flock here on earth," Gary said, looking at his wife, who, throughout his outburst, sat without a flicker of emotion.

An awkward silence followed the obvious disagreement between Wee Bobby's parents.

Suddenly, Guy appeared at the entrance to the sitting room. "Please Dana, can you come and tell us one of your stories. I told Bobby you have lovely stories for children. He wants you to come and tell us one, but he is too shy to ask himself. Will you, please?"

She agreed to his request, immediately, wanting to get away from an uncomfortable situation, with the clear difference of opinion between Gary and Sandra. She knew how important it was for parents to be aligned in the eyes of their children. Here there was conflict and she was concerned that it could cause damage to young Bobby without it being his parents' intention or even of them being aware of the fact.

Guy casually took her hand, as he would take the hand of his own mother. The gesture filled her with love and pride in the boy.

"Is it alright if we all come to hear the story?" Teddy asked.

Guy nodded. "That would be nice. I think Wee Bobby would like that, too."

They settled down, cramped in Bobby's small room while she considered which story to tell them. Her reputation was at stake, as was Guy's, because as her sponsor, it was his recommendation that had put her on the firing-line. She sat on the floor between the two boys. Teddy perched on the sole, rickety chair while Sandra and Gary sat on Bobby's small bed.

"Now, let's see," she mused, although she had already decided on the story she was going to tell them.

"All right, here goes. Once, a small Pekinese gave birth to a litter of six puppies, five healthy, strong pups and one small pug. The little tyke was always bullied, not only by other pups she met, but even by her older brothers and sisters. When it was time to suckle from their mother, they would leave no space for her. They would push her aside as she tried to get close to her mother to feed. She was never included in their games while they frolicked, together. They mocked her and made fun of her because she was so small and puny."

"You are just a weak, little runt. You don't even look like us. We are all light-brown with dark patches and you are different, dark-brown with some light ones." The sad, little pup was very lonely and felt unloved. The boys listened intently, every emotion registering on their faces.

"One day, after their mistress had filled the feeding bowls with tasty food, a huge black Doberman Pinscher came into their yard. He was an uninvited guest.

He strolled around as though he owned the yard. He could see that he was not welcome by the pups so bared his sharp fangs to scare them. Grrr!" growled Dana, with a vicious expression on her face.

"He was very menacing and the pups did not know what to do." The children sat wide-eyed.

"All the pups cowered in a corner of the yard, as far away from the trespasser as possible. They were shivering in fear because he looked so cruel. Suddenly, the black dog noticed the food-bowls, which had just been filled. They looked very appetising. Nonchalantly, he trotted over to them and gave the food a sniff to see if it was to his liking. He was quite satisfied and began gobbling down the food.

When the pug saw the big Doberman devouring their food, actually stealing it, she was enraged. Without thinking, she charged at it, yapping loudly. With that, the huge, black dog turned and snarled at her, threateningly. The pug was very frightened, but she never let the big dog see that. Giving the loudest bark she could and yelping all the time, she leapt at the intruder. It was shocked and surprised. It could not believe that such a small pup was not afraid of him.

The Doberman tried to bite the pug but she managed to evade him and barked even louder. The black dog forgot the food and began to chase the pug. She ran as fast as she could and crawled under some planks, piled up in the yard. The Doberman could not reach her because he was too big and in his anger, he began scratching and digging at the earth in front of her hiding-place so he would be able to get closer to her.

He was so busy that he never noticed her crawl out of the pile of planks at the back. She circled around and sneaked up behind him. She leapt up as high as she could and bit the trespasser's back leg and hung on for dear life. He yelped in pain and tried to shake her off but she would not let go. He whirled round in circles, trying to reach her but the more he turned the harder she bit. Finally, she let go and stood in front of him, defiantly, barking even louder. It knew that the little pup would never give up and like all bullies, the Doberman caught such a fright that it turned tail and fled."

Dana's audience clapped. She took a deep breath and continued. "When the other pups saw what happened and how brave their small sister was they rushed over and began nuzzling and licking her. From that day on, they kept a place for her at feeding time and always made sure to include her in all their games."

"Just because someone is big does not mean he is strong and just because you are small does not mean you are weak," they said to the tyke. "You have taught us that courage does not depend on size. Being different, too, is not a reason to leave others out or to think there is something wrong with them. We are all different, really, aren't we?"

From that day on, the little pup was always included in all their games and they even allowed her to feed, first.

Wee Bobby's face glowed. He identified with the pug and was basking in vicarious pride because he knew how brave he was. Guy was looking at Dana, adoringly. She recognised the same expression on his face, as that, which she often saw when Teddy looked at her.

All the decisions she had made with cold logic were thrown into disarray. Something was nagging at her, questioning her resolve although she was still of the firm opinion that the most sensible course of action was to adhere to her original commitment. Teddy was still extremely vulnerable. It was the only right thing to do. She prayed that she would succeed in honouring her commitment to tell him, whenever the appropriate time arrived.

# Chapter 31

On the way home, Guy was quiet. Teddy and Dana exchanged concerned glances and waited for him to say something. Finally, when nothing was forthcoming, she asked, "How was it seeing Bobby, again, Guy?" Clearly, he was very emotional. It took some time before the storm had passed and he was able to talk.

"Wee Bobby told me he knows he is very, very sick, much worse than I am," he admitted, eventually. "He also told me the doctors always talk to the nurses when they come around in the morning. They give them instructions about each patient.

Once, they thought he was asleep, but he wasn't. He just had his eyes closed. He heard one of them speaking to the nurses. The doctor said, 'There is no chance this boy is going to recover. It is just a matter of time.' He heard the doctors tell the nurses to pay special attention to any changes in his behaviour. Bobby did not know why they said that."

Dana and Teddy were horrified because they knew the reason. The cancer, which had metastasised into his brain, was likely to produce fits or outbursts of uncontrollably strong emotion and perhaps ultimately, unconsciousness and frequently, coma.

"Wee Bobby never understood everything the doctor said because he used words he didn't know. He knows he is going to die but he told me he does not want to tell his parents."

"He is a very brave boy but I don't think it is a good idea to hide it from his parents," said Dana.

"He can see that his father is already very miserable, and his mother just prays more. Wee Bobby feels guilty because he says he is to blame for causing them so much unhappiness, especially after all they have done for him. He just wishes it would all end soon."

They looked at each other, bewildered, not sure whether or not to explain the doctors' comment to Guy. In light of his still fragile state, they were concerned it may set him back.

Before they could say anything, Guy continued, "He is not afraid of dying. Then, he can go to heaven and see his sister, Jemima and the angels. His mother taught him that. I wish there was something I could do for him. What else can I do, Dana?"

"There is nothing anyone can do except for the doctors, young fellow. You just need to show Wee Bobby how much you care about him and make sure he knows that his friend is always there for him," she said.

"They didn't help my mother, either, did they?" said Guy. Teddy glanced at Dana.

"Even the doctors cannot do much, sometimes, I am afraid," she said.

"At least, I let him hear some of my discs. He liked them, especially Peter and the Wolf and the Nutcracker Suite."

"Incredible! So you have already started teaching him about classical music as you promised," said Teddy.

"I decided to leave him my compact-disc player and the discs I took with me. He needs to get used to the music."

"What do you mean? Did you give Bobby your compact-disc player and the discs, you love?"

"Yes. He has no way of listening to any music, not even the music he likes because they only have an old radio. Poor Bobby, it is not fair. He can't even play with the Lego-blocks I gave him."

"Why Guy, your Lego-set, too? That is very unselfish and amazing. We are so proud of you, aren't we, Teddy? We don't have words," she said.

"We certainly are but how are you going to be able to hear your music now that you don't have a compact-disc player?" Teddy asked.

"I saved up money from my birthdays and I can buy another one."

"I am sure Bobby will love the music you left," said Dana.

"I hope so, but I have to find a way for Wee Bobby to hear Peter and the Wolf at a concert. It is much better than hearing it on a compact disc. I promised him that I would. He is such a good boy. Why does he have to die?" Guy started weeping.

They were amazed. Guy had never shed a tear for himself but was beside himself for his friend.

And the fact that Bobby was protecting his parents and the unjustified guilt he was carrying, worried Dana, immensely. Nor did Teddy miss the similarity to

Guy's concern for his wellbeing, often putting his father's feelings before his own. Dana felt it was essential that she intervene at this point.

"Bobby has not done anything wrong. He is ill but he is not to blame. His parents love him very much. They know how sick he is so he doesn't need to hide anything from them. I am sure the doctors have always told them exactly what the position is. It would be easier if they would all talk openly instead of bottling up their feelings," she said.

"Then why do you and Daddy hide your feelings?" asked Guy. "Wouldn't it be better if you talked about it, too?"

Dana looked at Teddy, who was staring straight ahead at the road. She reached out behind her seat and took Guy's hand.

"Yes, Guy, you are right. It is best we speak about things instead of avoiding what needs to be brought out into the open."

At home, she went with Guy to his room while Teddy prepared a light supper. Guy was still engulfed in a whirlwind of emotion.

"You are really upset over Bobby, aren't you?"

"Yes, but it is not only that. I know he is very frightened, even if he says he is not. He told me. He feels all alone because his father is so sad and he has to protect him." Guy paused, and she waited for him to continue.

"You must be very unhappy that your friend feels so alone because his parents are not there to take care of him the way they should."

"No," he said. "They do look after him but it is hard for Wee Bobby. He worries about his mum and dad. He can't tell them how he is feeling. It is hard when he has to worry about his parents and he can't be open."

"I see," she said. "You think that Wee Bobby worries about his parents more than they do about him."

"He told me that his mother is not worried because she thinks the Lord will decide what happens to him. He says she cares for God, who she does not even know, more than she cares about him. His mum and dad do not agree about God. He is disappointed with his father because he hasn't told his mother that their son is more important than God is. She should be there for him instead of sitting and waiting to see what God is going to do."

Her heart went out to the Weavers, who were trapped by the situation in which they found themselves. She could imagine the pain of a parent, who had to watch a child, fading away before their very eyes, too sick to recover from the scourge of this disease and on the other hand, their religious beliefs decreeing that they accept their God's decision, stoically and without question. Yet, she could not accept Wee Bobby enduring the horror of his fatal condition, alone.

Before she had a chance to say anything, Guy said, "Bobby loves his mum and dad so he does not say anything in case he hurts them."

Dana knew there was a subtext to Guy's outburst.

"Have you ever felt like Wee Bobby does, Guy?" she asked, softly.

Guy was relieved to be able to speak, at last. "For a while I did. When my mummy was sick, I felt the same as Wee Bobby. Daddy was always with her because he loved her very much. But, he forgot about me, even though he still did a lot for me. I knew he loved me but I still felt bad. There was nobody else to look after me and when he did, he could not be with Mummy.

Now, it is better because you are here. I can see how much Daddy likes you and I think you like him. I wish you would talk to each other and not be like Mr and Mrs Weaver. I want to stop worrying about Daddy. When he is with you I see how happy he is. Me too, Dana. I wish I still had my mother. We love you."

"I love you too, Guy, very much. You are special, everything a young man should be. Your father also adores you. We are so impressed with the way you have dealt with the treatment, with everything, really. The doctors told us you have responded well, and you only have one more session to go. Things are looking very good. If all the tests are positive, then, that's it for now. It is already well over a year. Isn't that wonderful?"

"Yes, but what about poor Wee Bobby?" he replied. "I promised him a classical concert. The trouble is that he is so sick I may not have a chance to keep my promise. We have to keep our promises, don't we?"

"Yes, but you already gave him the Lego-blocks and all those discs and even your mobile-player. What more can you do?"

"It is not the same as going to a real concert, Dana. I remember how I felt when I went to that concert and saw the players and watched the conductor. It was so exciting. Wee Bobby deserves to hear music at a concert. It will make such a difference to him. I think it will also help his parents when they see how happy he will be."

"Do you know what I am going to do? I am going see if I can find a live symphony concert somewhere. If so, perhaps we can get special permission to take Bobby out and you can keep your promise."

"Can you, Dana? That would be great. You always find a way. It will make Wee Bobby so happy."

"You also deserve to be happy, Guy. You care so much for others," she said, almost moved to tears.

"Dana, can I ask you for something?"

"Of course, you may, anything. What would you like?"

"Can Wee Bobby come to the playroom before he has to go back to the hospital?"

"What a wonderful idea, that is, Guy? I will phone his parents and invite them for tea tomorrow afternoon. Then, you can spend as much time as you like in the playroom, especially now, that you know where everything is."

After he had fallen asleep, she decided that it was as appropriate a moment as any for the delayed discussion concerning their relationship. She found Teddy in the living room poring over a crossword puzzle.

"Just like an old married couple," she said but regretted her comment when she saw, by the expression on his face, that she had stung him.

"Sorry," she mumbled apologetically. "Not exactly getting off on the right foot at the start of a very difficult conversation, is it?"

Teddy had no idea what she meant and said nothing.

Nonetheless, wanting to get it over with as quickly as possible, she rushed on. "Teddy, you know for a long time I have wanted to speak about us but I never felt the time was right."

"I am pleased you finally feel the time is appropriate, Dana. Even Guy said we should not hide our feelings as the Weavers do," Teddy said with a smile. He looked at her, expectantly.

"I do not think we should postpone it any further," she said, forgetting everything she had rehearsed in advance and planned to say due to the tension she was feeling. She stumbled on. "Guy is beginning to take for granted the fact that we are his father…and mother, a couple." Shocked, Teddy averted his gaze and looked at his crossword puzzle, afraid to face her, not having anticipated such a turn of events.

"He is doing his level best to engineer such a situation even though he may not be doing it, deliberately. We need to be careful not to disappoint him by doing something, which he might later, perceive as a betrayal," she rattled on and waited for a response.

When none was forthcoming she continued, "We should not permit him to maintain this incorrect impression. I suppose I sound a bit obtuse but bottom line, what I mean is that we need to make sure Guy does not continue to believe that there is a romantic relationship between us."

She was startled by the look of disappointment, even pain, which flashed in Teddy's eyes for a brief second before he succeeded in stifling it and hiding the emotion. It was as though she had given him a violent slap across the face. He was desolate, having waited patiently for Dana to acknowledge that she felt the same way about him that he did about her, despite his never having spoken of it to her or to anybody else.

"Yes, maybe it is best to tell him now instead of possibly disillusioning him later," Teddy said with a marked lack of conviction to cover his shock and harrowing disappointment.

Hoping to ease the distraught man and due to her own very awkward situation, she said in a voice, tense and overly formal, "True, we have become very close friends in addition to our semi-professional contact, but that is all," she said.

She immediately, regretted the way she had expressed herself and how much pain it had caused. She had been anxious to avoid such hurt but it was done. In retrospect, she knew she had not been entirely truthful, nor had she expressed herself as she had frequently rehearsed in her mind. She sensed him shutting down and withdrawing from her, but it was too late to repair the damage. She had failed completely in her intended aim and her rejection was devastating to him.

He did his utmost to pass the matter off, blithely, but the pain he had suffered was patent. He had sincerely believed that one day, she would surrender to the truth of her feelings for him and she would accept what she had been reluctant to acknowledge. Now, hearing what she had said so bluntly, left him bereft, speechless. He wilted before her eyes.

She decided that it was best to get away from the very uncomfortable atmosphere her diatribe had created and picked up her purse and car keys to leave.

Teddy sat without saying another word. He looked desolate. He could not bring himself to respond to her outburst.

Trying to cover her embarrassment, she rambled on, "Please, Teddy, don't look so crestfallen. The news with Guy is encouraging. At last, we can see light at the end of the tunnel. Hopefully, after this last stage of chemotherapy, we can breathe a sigh of relief and start afresh." He smiled, weakly.

"By the way, Guy asked me to invite the Weavers to my house so Bobby can see the playroom before he goes back to hospital. Isn't he amazing, that Guy of ours?" He never answered, utterly destroyed.

"Come on, Teddy, I have no intention of abandoning Guy…or you," she said. "Give me a hug before I go."

The hug Teddy gave her was cold and distant.

She had lost him. Mona was distraught.

# Chapter 32

Guy could not stop thinking about the final stage he was about to undergo in a few days. With each session, the dosage was strengthened, causing him to feel worse since the after-effects became more debilitating and longer-lasting. In vain, he tried his best not to think about the treatment but it insidiously kept on creeping back into his thoughts. True, he was relieved that it was nearly over it but he was still very apprehensive. He was hopeful that after the eighteen-month nightmare was behind him, all would be well and he would be able to put the fear of any forthcoming treatments out of his mind.

He was also fixated on the seriousness of the condition of his new-found friend. Bobby had confided in him about what he overheard the doctor telling the nurses, 'he was never going to get better, ever'. As a result, his confidence in the success of his own treatment was compromised.

Suddenly, without warning, having been confronted by of the lethal potential of their commonly-shared disease, Guy wondered whether he, too, might have any future. He was not yet out of the woods and here he was, on the verge of another dreaded chemotherapy session. His churning thoughts prevented him from falling asleep.

He was fully aware how worried his father was and he recognised how hard Teddy tried not to show it. During Mona's illness, Guy did his utmost to ensure that he never added to Teddy's burden. It was patently clear to him, now, how pleased his father was because Dana had suddenly come back into their lives Her presence buoyed his spirits and he became more and more reliant on her.

Guy, personally was overjoyed to have Dana close by. Instinctively, she seemed to know how he was feeling or what he was thinking. With her, there was no need to put on a brave face or do anything just to please her. She accepted him exactly as he was, so he could be Guy, a small boy, bearing a very heavy cross on his young, vulnerable shoulders.

It still worried him that he could not picture his mother clearly, any more. He was almost five years old when she died. Yet, there were things he did vaguely recall, the sweet smell of her skin and the softness of her hands when she caressed him after his bath. He still recalled the songs she crooned to him in her gentle voice and he loved the way she would play 'this little piggy went to market' on his chubby fingers, finally tickling him on his tummy while he giggled, helplessly.

As a small child, the stories she told him with such drama and creativity were always the highlight of his days and he had always looked forward to them with childish impatience.

In the last few months, for some unaccountable reason, he had thought about his mother more. Dana's arrival had been perfectly timed. His father, too, obviously admired her. Guy detected a spring in his step and a lilt in his voice that had been missing for as long as he could remember. He knew, in his heart of hearts that Teddy loved Dana. If only she could be his mother. It was the thing he wanted more than anything else in the world…and to be healthy, so they could all live together happily ever after like in a fairy-tale.

He had tried his best to fall asleep but he knew it was a waste of time. His mind was spinning, flitting from subject to subject. Again, the thought of Wee Bobby sneaked back into his head.

He heard sounds coming from the living-room. People were talking but he could not make out what was being said. He decided to get up and speak to Teddy and Dana, whose voices he assumed were those he could hear.

In the lounge, he found his father alone, slumped forward on the settee, resting his head in his hands. He looked up immediately with a guilty expression. "Where is Dana?" Guy asked.

"She had to go home but she promised she would see us again tomorrow."

"What were you talking about? You seem sad. Is Dana cross with us?"

"Of course, she isn't. She just needed to take care of things at home and she left because she thought you were already asleep."

Guy was not convinced and pressed his father further.

"Why are you so sad, then?" he demanded. "Wouldn't you like her to be with us, Daddy? Did you ask her?"

"No, I never asked her," he stated, defensively and a little more aggressively than he intended.

"Can I ask her, then? I think she would like to but she may be shy."

Teddy realised he was venturing into uncharted territory and with Guy's innocent persistence, the conversation was becoming too confrontational for his liking.

"Let's go, young man. Tomorrow is a big day and you need to get some sleep. Dana told me that she was going to invite Wee Bobby and his parents to her house before he, and afterwards you return to the hospital. You need to be fresh when we go there."

Guy rubbed his eyes. "I can't sleep, Daddy. I was going to ask Dana something, but she is not here and I may not be able to talk to her about it because I will be in the hospital. Can we speak about it now? I don't want to put it off, again."

"Of course, what is it?" He was taken by surprise when Guy began to talk about Bobby.

"I spoke to Dana and told her I have to keep my promise to Wee Bobby."

"Do you mean the promise you made about a concert?"

"Yes, Dad, I said I would take him to a live concert. But when he told me he heard the doctor say how sick he is, perhaps I won't have time to do it."

Teddy shrugged. "It is unlikely that we will find a concert with Peter and the Wolf. But I promise you we will check and find out what is available."

"That is what Dana told me but it has to have Peter and the Wolf. Would you remind her about it? I know you can arrange it because you always work things out when you are together."

He gathered the young child in his arms.

"Why are you smiling, Daddy?"

"Don't worry, son," he answered, dabbing his eyes. "I am so proud of you for the person you are. On the brink of having to go back to hospital and all you think about is Bobby. I am so lucky to have you as my son. Of course, I will speak to Dana when we see her but I am sure she will not forget, just like she never forgot to invite Bobby and his family to her home."

"I know she won't forget. She never does. But, together, it will be easier for you, both."

As he was carrying Guy to his room, the child asked, "Can I sleep with you in your bed, Dad?"

Teddy, immediately did an about turn, tucked Guy into bed, switched off the light, kissed him lightly on the forehead and whispered, "Good night, sleep tight, mind the bugs don't bite."

# Chapter 33

Guy had spoken to Wee Bobby endlessly about the special playroom. After Dana's invitation, Bobby counted the minutes until he and his parents would visit her house. At long last, the time arrived. They came with a cake, which Sandra had specially baked for the occasion. Wee Bobby presented it to Dana with great ceremony.

He was very proud of his mother, who had acquired a reputation as an outstanding cook, excelling in traditional West Indian fare. The cake she had baked was eminent proof of her expertise.

The Weavers were overawed by her house, which could quite easily have accommodated their small apartment at least three times over. At first, they were a little uneasy, not accustomed to such 'august' company.

Dana noticed it, immediately and put them at their ease. First she offered them refreshments and said, "I cannot tell you how honoured and pleased I am that you agreed to visit us. Just relax in the sitting-room with Teddy while I take the boys and show them the playroom." She noticed Teddy's panic-stricken look. "I will be back in a flash."

"We appreciate your invitation, Dana. Bobby has not stopped talking about it. It is a dream come true for him," Gary said very deferentially.

"Of course, I love having you in my home but don't thank me, Gary. It was Guy's idea. He is very fond of Bobby and their blossoming friendship is beautiful to see."

"Pity it may turn out to be just a short friendship," Gary said, bitterly. "They get on so well, together, though, don't they?"

Dana glanced at Teddy but he sat, poker-faced, holding back the flood of emotion Gary's comment had elicited in him. Sandra, too, was more reserved than her husband but neither Dana nor Teddy could ascertain whether she felt inadequate or whether it was just her stoicism and lack of emotion. Guy had told them of Wee Bobby's regret at his mother's impassive attitude because of her religion. Dana appreciated the boy's despair when she observed Sandra's seeming detachment.

Dana sensed the tension in the air and to break the ice, she said. "It will be interesting to see how the time Guy and Bobby spend together in the playroom will affect them." Except for Sandra, they all nodded their acquiescence.

The adults could vaguely make out the sounds of the children in the playroom. Occasionally they heard the boys laughing and the four of them would smile, appreciatively whenever the boys did so.

"There has been a dearth of opportunities for laughter in the past months, hasn't there?" said Teddy to exhibit identification with the Weavers' distress.

"I told you Bobby loves being with Guy, didn't I? Just listen to the two of them, as though there is nothing in the world to worry about," said Gary, shaking his head.

"Yes, you did. I think Bobby is good for Guy, too," Dana said.

"I wonder why they are laughing?" Sandra ventured.

"Yes, I wonder, too," said Dana. "I will go and see what they are up to and make sure they are alright. If they agree, I might even spend time with them. I hope you don't mind."

"Of course not," both Gary and Sandra assured her in unison although Teddy appeared to be uneasy at her suggestion. Dana noticed it and realised his nervousness at being left alone in Gary and Sandra's company but it was too late to backtrack.

She excused herself. "I will be back in a while. Please make yourselves completely at home."

The boys were pleased to see her. Guy had been the doctor and had finished treating Bobby, the patient.

"Bobby needed to have an injection after I checked him with all my instruments. I took his blood-pressure, measured his temperature and listened to his heart and lungs through my stethoscope. I think he will get better."

Bobby smiled, happily.

"I also advised him to tell his parents what I have said in case they don't know. It is important to tell your parents whatever the doctor says, isn't it, Dana?"

"Most definitely, Doctor Goodson, you are quite right. I hope the patient listens to his doctor's advice."

They had just reversed roles after Bobby had first examined Guy. Their diagnoses were the same. Now, they needed the nurse to begin the treatment, starting with the injections and then progressing to infusions. Her arrival was perfectly timed. She joined in, not noticing how much time had elapsed. Eventually, Teddy knocked on the door, quietly and came into the room to let her know that the Weaver family was ready to go home.

Reluctantly, Guy and Wee Bobby ended their game.

"Don't forget to take the pictures you have painted and drawn," Dana reminded them. "I think it would be a good idea to show them to your parents. I am sure they would like to see them."

Wee Bobby scooped up a batch of pages and they accompanied her back to the living room where their parents were waiting.

"Tell us about the pictures before you leave," suggested Dana.

With great seriousness, they explained their artwork to the adults.

"This is me in the hospital and that is Guy," explained Wee Bobby, brandishing two sheets of paper.

The boys had drawn themselves lying in a hospital bed with different medical instruments surrounding them. Each was attached to an infusion device. In his picture, Guy had decorated the tubes with ribbons, small pictures and flags and had chosen to draw everything in bright colours. He was smiling in his bed. He had even drawn Teddy and Dana, sitting alongside him. There was a lightness and optimism in the drawing.

On the other hand, Wee Bobby had used dark hues and thick, black lines in his drawing. The sombre atmosphere and gloom were glaringly obvious. His picture was filled with foreboding. He had sketched his mouth in a scowl and there even appeared to be tear-drops falling from his eyes.

Besides himself, there were only nurses and a doctor in the picture. They were all very large and loomed over the tiny figure lying in the bed. It was clear that the small child felt very alone and fragile. Their drawings spoke volumes, not only to Dana but to all the adults. No professional training was required to be able to interpret the pictures.

Guy smiled as a bashful Wee Bobby handed Dana another sheet of paper.

"This is for you, Dana. We had a great time in your playroom. Guy was right. We do feel better."

The boys had drawn a thank-you picture for her. In the centre of the page, they had sketched a large, red heart surrounded with colourful flowers, reds, greens, pinks, oranges, yellows and many others. Animals gambolled about and a bright, golden sun blazed in one corner. Two birds were soaring, high in an azure sky. The boys had written their names, Bobby and Guy, with an arrow pointing to each of the birds. "Thank you, Dana. We love you" was written in their childish handwriting in the middle of the heart.

She was overwhelmed. She knelt and took the two boys into her arms. "Thank you, too," she whispered, her heart filled with love and admiration for two young heroes.

# Chapter 34

Mike had reflected long and hard on what Gabriel had told him about the concept of reincarnation and he had considered the implications of his situation. He had no idea how it would be to see Dana again but he was impatient at having to wait, now that he knew he had been given permission to return. For him, the most worrying factor, the one he thought would present the biggest complication was how to speak to her.

*This is really ridiculous. If nobody else knows of my presence and if Dana doesn't, how am I supposed to communicate with her or anyone else, for that matter?* he thought, as usual, forgetting Gabriel's injunction.

Fortunately, it did not take long before he recalled more of what Gabriel had said to him in his briefing. He had warned him that because the Source did things according to Its own agenda everything had a reason and everything had been prepared, taking even the tiniest detail into consideration. He had not understood what Gabriel had meant when he had told him that his personal celestial messenger had already been dispatched on its mission, one tied to his. Gabriel had not expounded further with the result he was more confused than ever.

Mike found himself lying in a soft bed in a pleasant room, the dim light, reminiscent of early morning. The quietness enveloped him like a warm blanket, comfortable and reassuring.

It had always been his favourite time of day. He loved the stillness of the early hours before the world awoke and the daily rush began. He always enjoyed preparing a steaming cup of coffee for himself and Dana, she, still asleep in bed. He would sit in the kitchen, watching the news on TV, poring over a crossword puzzle before the day swept him up in the relentless hustle and bustle of everyday life.

Without warning though, everything was no longer ephemeral. There was substance to things, solid form, content, physicality. Even sounds and smells were not like before.

*How peculiar*, Mike thought, *What on earth is happening? My body is not weightless. I see that I actually have a body.* He patted his legs and chest to make sure his mind was not playing tricks on him but sure enough, he heard and felt the physical slapping of his mortal hands on his mortal body.

"Where can I be?"

He threw off the covers and climbed out of bed. On the floor, next to the bed were his slippers. He slid his feet into them. They were a perfect fit.

He slowly shuffled into a short passage leading to the living area. Ahead of him, he noticed an entrance hall and a kitchen, adjoining the lounge. The house was well-furnished although in his opinion, it lacked the warmth of a woman's touch. There were only a few pictures on the walls. Due to his aesthetic taste and his love of nature, the absence of house-plants or flowers was striking. It was a functional abode without the beautifying features of a home.

As he walked the length of the passage, his footsteps were muffled by the thick pile of carpeting. On his left he saw a door, slightly ajar. He peeked through the opening, but the room was too dim for him to see much. He pushed the door open and softly tiptoed into the darkened room. Against one wall was a child's bed and when he got closer, he saw a sleeping boy. The child had noticeably pale skin and his head was smooth, devoid of any hair although the shadow of a fresh growth was just beginning. The boy's eyes were closed but Mike noticed his beautiful features in repose, as he slept.

"What am I doing here?" he wondered.

Unlike the coldness in the rest of the house, in the child's room, posters of Disney characters adorned the walls, which had been specially painted to portray a country scene. Trees and flowers grew in profusion in the idyllic picture, with fat turtle-doves, nesting on the branches. On the banks of a rippling brook, a little boy sat holding a short fishing pole, while smiling fish leapt out of the water and cavorted in the air. The lad in the picture bore a striking resemblance to the sleeping child. It was a typical boy's room.

As his eyes grew accustomed to the gloom, he saw his reflection in a mirror standing against the wall. It had to be him. He could see everything else around him in the mirror. And yet, it was not him. He was tall with black eyes and wavy hair, the same colour as the shadow of the boy's new growth. He had broad shoulders and a narrow waist and looked athletic and fit. *Quite handsome*, he thought, although, as his gaze moved from his reflection in the mirror to the slumbering child and back, he perceived a deep sadness pervading the image of his host. He knew he had never been in the room before. Everything was unfamiliar but, to his incredulity, he knew where everything belonged.

He was stunned. *I must be back in the world. Wow, just like that, with a click of Gabriel's fingers. It is unbelievable*, he thought. "Obviously, I am in someone else's body, but whose? And where is Dana? I wonder if she is here. And then, there is this child. Who is he?"

His mind was racing, thoughts cascading into his head in a frantic jumble. Automatically, he leaned down and gently stroked the sleeping boy, who suddenly stirred and opened his eyes. The child stretched like a kitten and smiled when he saw him. His eyes resembled those he had seen in his reflection in the mirror.

"Morning, Dad" he said and reached out to Mike, who, without thinking, sat down on the edge of the bed and bent forward to kiss the child's forehead.

"One for you, one for me and one for us," he laughed as he planted a light peck on each of the boy's eyes and the last on the tip of his nose. Guy giggled with pleasure, but Mike was shocked, as it was not his voice, just his words. Also, his actions shocked him. It was as though he was operating on automatic pilot. Whatever behaviour was appropriate at that moment came to him without thinking.

"It is clear that the body in which I am, belongs to my host and I just do whatever he decides. I am like a passenger in a car. Where the car goes, so do I. Gabriel! You are a wily scamp. What a system you have come up with. I suppose it will take some time until I get the hang of things."

The little boy sat up and put his arms around his neck as he snuggled up to his father.

"Would you like to get up yet?" he asked, as he stroked the boy's fuzz.

"In a minute, Dad, let's stay like this for a bit," said the young child.

He remained sitting, holding the boy who was clearly his son, overwhelmed by emotion at the intimacy and tenderness of the moment.

*Is this how it would have been if we had had a child of our own*, he thought.

He was a tad surprised at the familiarity of his host's actions. He never had to think what to do. It was all natural, as though what he was doing was what he had done often enough so that both he and the child were completely at ease with each other.

Teddy had always marvelled at the deft touch Dana had in building trust and establishing a bond with children. He had never been certain whether he, too had that ability. He had longed for them to have their own children but the accident had taken care of that. Now, as he sat lovingly caressing the child in his arms, any doubts he may have harboured began to evaporate.

"OK trooper, rise and shine, time to brush your teeth and wash your face. Then, get dressed, while I make breakfast. It will be on the table by the time you are ready. OK? We need to leave for the hospital early. You remember who is going to be meeting us there, don't you?" said Teddy.

"Yippee! Dana," yelled Guy and he ran off. Mike felt a tremor of excitement.

They were going to meet Dana at the hospital. He was not surprised that Guy was so excited at the prospect of seeing her and even more surprisingly, that he had known without being aware that he knew. He thought he had comprehended what the Eternal One had engineered. He would have to wait and let things develop.

It was clear that his 'host' was unaware of his presence. He, on the other hand, was conscious of his dual existence and was beginning to get used to letting his host do whatever he was supposed to do. He simply had to reside in his host's body and just go along with him as he had done, earlier when he had kissed Guy after the boy awoke. He could take actions that were his but he was not sure how many of his wishes and intentions it would be possible to effect unless he could find a method to influence his host.

"It is not my life I am living at the moment but rather that of this other man, whom the Source has decreed is to be the vessel for my existence for as long as I want to remain here. Also, it seems It has chosen not to erase my memory, too much. Smart move. That is the last thing I expected. I am still curious to know why, though. Knowing how the Eternal One works and plans things, I imagine it won't take too long to find out."

He was intrigued that the boy was thrilled that Dana was going to be meeting them at the hospital although he never knew why.

"She must be working with him. That must be why she is meeting them at the hospital. I am glad that she is working again. She probably mourned for too long after the accident. Hmm! I wonder if that could be the change in circumstances Gabriel referred to."

When they were ready, dressed and fed, his host picked up a small bag packed with everything Guy would need, hopefully, for his last sojourn in the hospital. Guy took Mike's hand and they got into the car. Although the environment was unfamiliar to Mike, he sat behind the steering-wheel and drove the short distance to the hospital, relying on his host to take the appropriate actions for them to reach their destination, safely.

Again, he recognised the good sense in simply allowing Guy's father to take the lead and do what was required without his interference unless there was something he wanted to achieve. In such a case, he needed to find a way to insinuate his ideas into the mind of this man. Mike was already aware enough to realise that, in fact, his host was only doing what he always did, naturally and therefore it was possible for him to rely on his host to continue doing whatever he decided to do without question.

The journey did not take very long. After parking the car, they walked to the entrance of the building, where Dana was waiting for them.

"A very good morning to you, Guy, I have missed you," she said.

He ran to her and she knelt and held him closely, as he showered her with kisses.

She looked over his shoulder at Mike staring at her and she smiled, sweetly. His heart skipped a beat as she stood up and came up to him to embrace him. He was giddy with emotion. He felt her body against his, every curve and contour, so familiar. He could smell the intoxicating fragrance of her subtle perfume and it brought back powerful memories.

He had bought the very scent for her many years before. He remembered how he had visited a store to choose a gift for her birthday and the sales assistant had recommended this particular brand. She had loved it and from that moment on, it had become 'their fragrance'.

He did not want to let her go and held her in his arms for a few more seconds, savouring the moment, until she stepped away from him. "Hello Teddy, how are you today?" she asked, looking at him, coyly, surprised by the persistence of his embrace.

"Fine and glad to see you," he replied with uncharacteristic forwardness, which surprised her. Confusion registered on her face as she tried to analyse the unexpected warmth in the tone of his voice and the way he had just embraced her.

Teddy was also surprised at his reaction. He was still smarting from her recent, outright rejection of him, much as he tried to hide it. The expression on her face and her tone of voice were completely incongruent with their earlier conversation. He could not understand what had occurred since then to elicit this change in attitude by Dana.

As usual, holding Guy's hands, they entered the building and hurried along the winding corridors to the Oncology Department.

*Aha! So, the boy's name is Guy and his father is Teddy. Where have I heard their names before?* he thought. *Could these be the father and son Dana mentioned on our way to the railway-station? They seem completely familiar with the lay-out of the hospital, so they must have been here often.*

He was captivated by the ease with which she connected with the boy, who was clearly infatuated with her. Teddy also appeared to have a special relationship with her, but not like the parent of a child, who was undergoing therapy. It was more like one where she was a member of their family or a close friend, who was accompanying them to the hospital. It appeared to him that they had placed their trust in her and she had become their 'guardian angel'. He laughed to himself at the irony of the expression.

"Guy told me that he had spoken to you about finding a concert for Wee Bobby so he will be able to hear Peter and the Wolf. I know it will not be easy, but I assured him that we would do our best to make sure that he keeps his promise to Wee Bobby," he said to her as they strode along the corridor.

"I have not forgotten," she replied. "In fact, I telephoned Mr Horne at school and I have arranged to meet him as soon as possible. He was very excited." Guy smiled at her and squeezed her hand.

"I already checked the concerts in the coming weeks but, as expected, there are none with Peter and the Wolf," she said. "There are quite a few other possibilities, though. In the meantime, what is most important is that you finish your treatment and be well so we can relax and enjoy our time together. In a few weeks, we can meet Mr Horne and discuss it with him. After all, it is your idea. You deserve the credit."

"But what about Wee Bobby?" he asked, anxiously. "You know how sick he is. I can't disappoint him. Time is of the incense."

"Where on earth did you learn that expression? Many adults wouldn't know it," Teddy said, with obvious pride. "By the way, we don't say 'time is of the incense? It's' essence, son. Time is of the essence. Incense is something else."

"I read it in one of the books Ms Commins gave me. She said I am so advanced in reading that I should read books for older children. She lent me some from our school library."

"I saw the books you have at home," said Dana. "Very impressive, I may add. Perhaps next time you come to my house with your dad, you can choose books you like from my collection and take them with you to read at home."

"That would be great. Right, Dad?"

"Sure, Guy, it will be great but, in the meantime, here we are and we need to start the preparation for your last treatment."

"Soon, it will all be behind you and then we can start doing the things you like, again," she reminded him.

"Will you do them with us, Dana? If you like, we can sometimes do things you want as well, can't we, Dad?"

"If Dana wants to, of course, we will. But we will see when the time comes."

Mike knew that Teddy's reply had been directed at Dana rather than at Guy. He did not need to rely on human faculties to ascertain what Teddy was thinking or really meant as people did during their earthly lives. He had spent sufficient time in 'heaven' to dispense with such a need. It was patently clear to him that Teddy was in love with Dana but was too shy to express his feelings. What he felt was clear to Mike as his spirit was living in Teddy's body and mind and so Teddy's thoughts were his, too.

"Is she even aware of his true feelings for her, I wonder? Perhaps not! As far as I can detect, she only expresses friendship to him, no more."

Suddenly, a germ of doubt crept into Mike's consciousness. He began to consider what she thought about Teddy. He was disconcerted for the first time since he had come back to the corporeal world.

She was 'his' Dana. It was impossible that she had established a relationship with someone new. How could it be? At first, he felt hurt, pangs of jealousy and, to some extent, betrayal. Perhaps he had been sent back to remind her of their special, eternal love for each other. Surely, she could not have forgotten him, already.

But, he realised that she was entitled, no, not just entitled, rather obliged, to live her own life and most certainly, not his death. He accepted that the interest she may have in Teddy was not betrayal or a sign of her having forgotten or not loving him any longer. He had been apprised of the intense grief she had suffered after his 'death'. That had formed the basis of his appeal to the Source. Could it be that It had decided to allow him to return to earth to encourage her to let go of the past and seize an opportunity for a new love? Was this, perhaps, such an opportunity?

"Carpe diem!" said Mike with determination. "I wonder what is required for her to open her heart, again, if it is indeed love that she may be feeling."

He remembered Gabriel's injunction against trying to work out the All Knowing One's will. Was this a test of his love for Dana? In any case, he was powerless to influence either Dana or Teddy. He had not yet worked out a system to get his host to express his true feelings and she seemed completely oblivious to his own existence and according to Gabriel, always would be.

Like a flash, he had an important realisation. It struck him that if his host's thoughts were his own, then his thoughts were his host's, too. Therefore, to a certain extent, it was possible for him to express his will through him. That way, Dana would be able to hear his ideas, if not his voice.

He needed to get to know Teddy better before he could intervene. It may take time but that was one commodity he had in abundance. Whenever he had discovered enough about his host, he would be ready to start influencing him, should he decide to do anything. As he learnt the art of inculcating his own ideas into Teddy's mind and finding ways for him to express them more openly, then and only then, would his true mission on earth be attainable, despite what the Source intended.

How typically, Mike!

# Chapter 35

The following weeks passed in a flurry of frantic activity for everyone. In addition to their regular responsibilities, Teddy and Dana spent most of the time at the hospital, as did Sandra and Gary Weaver.

The boys had reached different stages of treatment. In Guy's case, hopefully it was almost all over. But as far as Wee Bobby was concerned, there was a possibility that he might never leave the hospital. The doctors had prepared the Weaver family for the worst. Reluctantly, they were at their wits end and were not able to offer any further solutions with regard to Bobby's deteriorating condition. They forewarned the Weavers that they needed to gird themselves for the end.

Mike was distressed when he saw how Guy suffered the procedures. He was appalled at the side-effects, often having to carry the lad back to his bed after chemotherapy. The semi-conscious boy was like a rag doll. His limbs hung down, loosely and his head flopped on his shoulders. He could not believe the All-Knowing had an ulterior motive, which Sandra continued to expound as her balm against the agony of having to confront the ghastly reality of their personal situation.

*A merciful and loving Supreme Being would not punish an innocent child with such cruelty*, Mike thought. Guy though, never complained and was far less concerned about his own condition and more so about Wee Bobby's, which was steadily getting worse. He constantly reminded Teddy and Dana about his promise to him.

"Have you been able to find out if there is anything," he pleaded.

She, as usual, took the initiative in consoling him. "I met Mr Horne, again. I will make another appointment as soon as you leave the hospital and are strong enough to accompany us. So far, there is not much to report. But Mr Horne is exploring other possibilities and hopefully, by the time we all meet next, he will have some encouraging news. We have not allowed the idea of the concert to become less important, or less urgent I promise you."

Her reassurance had the combined effect of easing his concern and of giving him inspiration to get through the treatment with more positivity. Nevertheless, his major concern remained his promise to his friend.

"It has to be, soon. I can't let him down," he insisted.

Dana spoke to Mr Horne and begged him to find a way to put the idea of the concert into effect as expeditiously as possible because of Wee Bobby's dire state.

"I am exploring every possibility and should there be any chance of finding a solution, I will let you know, immediately. I am afraid it won't be easy but I will leave no stone unturned to make sure Guy's concert happens."

I know you will, Mr Horne. By the way, it is Bobby Weaver's concert, not Guy's."

Even when they received the long-awaited, positive update about his health, all that Guy could think about was his promise to Wee Bobby.

"Although there is still a long road ahead and it will be necessary to monitor Guy's condition very carefully, especially in the coming months, the good news is that he will probably make a complete recovery" the specialist, Dr Simpson, informed them.

"He has shown the hoped-for response to the therapy during the past year and a half. I know how upset you were at the fluctuations in his condition during the entire period but I can assure you, soon he will be able to resume his normal routine and begin life where he left off."

When they told Guy, he was thrilled but the fate of his friend weighed heavily on him. He was heartbroken that Wee Bobby had not overcome the disease as he had done and was nearing the tragic end of his short life.

On occasions, they would see Gary and Sandra Weaver. Gary always displayed great emotion and extreme distress but Sandra, with her customary cold indifference and unshakeable faith in her God's will, behaved much like a zombie.

"Bobby is spending nearly all the time in the hospital, now," said Gary, who was at the end of his tether. "He is being kept sedated most of the time because he is having these violent attacks more often. The combination of drugs is very strong, but they have had little effect on containing, let alone destroying, the leukaemia." Dana looked at Teddy meaningfully.

"We are so sorry, Gary, Sandra, what can we even say? We have no words.

Bobby and you are in our prayers," Teddy said.

Sandra said nothing, just nodded. Suddenly, a tear began to trickle down her cheek. Gary was startled. He took her into his arms as her body began to tremble. Then, the flood gates opened. She broke down and wept, uncontrollably, the ocean of tears released. Gary guided her out of the corridor into an empty ward.

"Please, excuse us," he mumbled. "I will be back as soon as I can."

When they were out of earshot, Dana whispered to Teddy, who was clearly shattered by the news about Wee Bobby, "It is soul-destroying to witness Bobby withering away like this. We are so lucky. I don't know how anyone could bear such a thing, Teddy, losing someone we love?"

He stood stock still, frozen, with an expression of agony on his face. She, herself, was also shocked at her comment. It was as though momentarily, she had forgotten her own calamity, the loss of her beloved Mike. Perhaps, for the first time, she had experienced and given voice to her subconscious acceptance of her affection, nay love for Teddy. Her pain had been eased by her feelings for Teddy so that the longing for Mike was not the predominant emotion in her consciousness.

"Oh! Teddy, I am so sorry. It was thoughtless of me," she said.

At that instant, she understood to what extent the trauma of his beloved Mona's illness underpinned the reason for his reticence in opening himself up to her, or anyone, for that matter.

Her heart was filled with pity and caring for the distraught man. She moved up to him and took him in her arms, gently stroking his neck. As had been the case once before, his trembling body was ramrod stiff. He struggled to suppress the emotions engulfing him, which the events of the last few minutes had evoked. Little by little, though, the shaking subsided. Slowly, Teddy's arms enfolded her and for the first time, she surrendered herself to him. They stood holding each other until Gary Weaver reappeared.

"I hope I am not interrupting anything," he said with a shy grin. "Sorry for that." Mona too, was grinning.

"No, of course not," said Dana, with the shadow of a smile.

"Sandra has recovered but it has been very difficult for us, impossible, actually. After the tragedy with our Jemima, she has kept it all bottled up inside and now..." he explained, bitterly. "What caused her breakdown was the specialist telling us that he is not sure Bobby will ever leave hospital. It was bound to happen sooner or later. Thank God it has at last. Her breakdown, that is," he explained, unnecessarily.

An aghast Teddy asked. "Is there anything we can do?"

"Not really, but it would make such a difference if Guy could drop in to see Bobby even though he is kept sedated most of the time. He often asks about his special friend when he is conscious."

"Guychick is going home, later," said Dana. "I know he will want to say goodbye to his friend before he leaves. So, we will probably see you in a while." Teddy gaped in disbelief—Guychick?

"What is it?" she said, coyly. "You are standing there, looking at me like a teddy-bear."

Teddy's jaw dropped even further. Apparently, Mona was more adept at influencing Dana than Mike was in affecting Teddy.

"And give our love to Sandra and Bobby, please," she added.

Before he left the hospital, without any prompting from Teddy or Dana, Guy insisted on calling on Wee Bobby.

Fortunately, the lad was conscious and able to receive visitors. The reunion between the two boys was very moving. There was no formality or artificiality on the part of either of them. Bobby was overjoyed to see his friend. Guy had brought some coloured ribbons, which he attached to the infusions leading in to Wee Bobby's frail arm.

"Just like in your drawing," said Wee Bobby, giving Guy a weak 'high five' and laughing out loud for one of the few occasions on which he had laughed, recently.

"Now, at least, you can see some bright colours. I know how much it helps to make you feel better," Guy said.

"I listened to some of the discs you gave me, too. You were right, Guy. The music does make you feel good. Sorry, I haven't had a chance to let you hear some reggae or calypso."

"Don't worry, man. When you get out of here, we can start properly."

"Thanks for the Lego, too. I haven't used it very much, yet. Guy, mostly, thank you for being my friend."

"I will always be your friend," he promised.

The adults left the two boys alone and went into the corridor outside Bobby's ward.

"I am sorry for my fit of emotion, earlier, but I have kept it all inside for much too long," Sandra confessed.

"No need to apologise. It is quite understandable, Sandra. You and Gary are bearing an impossible load and you have been very brave," said Teddy. "If there is anybody who can identify with you, it is us. We admire you more than you can imagine."

"Thank you, Teddy," said Sandra. "We know what you went through before. If there is anyone who can appreciate that, it is Gary and me. May God shine his light on Guy and both of you."

"How gracious of you. We will do anything we can to support you," Teddy retorted.

"Yes, Sandra, anything at all," Dana accentuated. "What is the latest prognosis?"

"Very discouraging," answered Gary. "They have tried everything possible to halt the 'metastasis'," a new word that Gary had learnt through tragic circumstances and now used, frequently, "but it seems the disease has spread too far. How ironic that I have learned words like metastasis, etcetera at this stage of my life." He shrugged, sadly.

"Although he has had radiation as well as a much stronger drug regime, there was no improvement. He even had a bone marrow transplant to try and bring the cancer under control, but without success," Sandra added.

"We are girding ourselves, getting ready for the end," Gary whispered. All they could do was to give Sandra and Gary a hug for the first time, something they had never dared to do, before. Sandra and Gary both accepted it with shy smiles of gratitude.

On the way to the car-park, Guy said, "Do you think Wee Bobby's mother cares about him like you care about me?"

"I am sure she does although sometimes, it may not seem like it," Dana replied.

"I told you that Wee Bobby thinks she does not really love him although she is his mother. He thinks that maybe she is even angry at him for getting sick."

"She is not angry, Guy, just very upset and worried," she said.

"He is not to blame, is he? He has not done anything wrong. I know you are not my real mother, Dana but you are like my mother. I wish Bobby's mother loved him and showed him like you do with me."

She never answered but his comment caused her to acknowledge to herself the truth of her feelings for the young boy. Indeed, she had grown to love him as her own son.

They had spent hours together and the love she felt for the child had blossomed like a flower, whose petals had opened after having been nurtured by life-giving rain and kissed by warm sunlight.

She accepted that it was Guy, who had brought her out of her misery and back to life and she was flooded with gratitude. This innocent boy was able to grasp the principles of goodness, naturally and disentangled the complications of life with such simple logic.

She knew that Teddy had inculcated these values in the child he had raised on his own. She recognised many of Teddy's finer characteristics in his son. For the first time, she acknowledged to herself that she did feel an attraction to him, not as Guy's father but rather, as a man she admired and respected.

He had always intrigued her. At first, his shyness had confused her. She had interpreted it as haughtiness, when it turned out to be precisely the opposite, a deep sensitivity. Mona was only too familiar with that characteristic and had succeeded in insinuating the realisation into Dana's consciousness.

He was highly intelligent and well-read and had a broad knowledge on a wide range of subjects, which he put to good use in his favourite hobby, solving cryptic crossword puzzles. Surreptitiously, she loved watching him, struggling to find a word, like a dog, gnawing at a bone. Sometimes, he would consult her but she seldom came up with the answer. This only aroused in her a greater admiration for the man, who, on the one hand, was extremely sensitive and on the other, canny enough to analyse the clues with such mental agility. He reminded her of Mike, who had also been addicted to crosswords.

Yet, unlike Mike, Teddy lacked confidence and finesse in social situations. As a result, she had found herself taking the lead and dealing with issues, such as talking to the medical staff or strangers like Gary and Sandra Weaver. This had only endeared him to her even more.

She giggled when she admitted to herself that she had often dressed as a woman to impress Teddy, the man.

*Was it that soon? I can't believe I resisted it so stubbornly*, she thought. "Apparently, even at such an early stage, I could not take the man out of the equation. He is so different from Mike and at the same time, he has so many similar qualities. I just hope I have not scared him off, completely?" she worried. "It's funny, I feel very different about us, today. It is as though I have just woken up and I have no idea why," To her amazement, she suspected she might even love him.

Guy's comparison between Sandra Weaver and her had opened the valve. The question now was what to do about it. She had no time to consider the matter further because they had reached their cars. She said goodbye to Teddy and Guy, who beseeched her to come home with them.

"You need to get some proper rest, Guy. You go back to school tomorrow to meet all your friends and Ms Commins. I am sure they will be very happy to see you. Anyway, I must take care of a few chores. I want to phone Mr Horne, who is expecting my call. After I talk to him, I will let you know what he says. OK?"

Guy reluctantly accepted her explanation but he held on to her for a long time. Teddy gave her a cursory hug but this time, she held the embrace for a few moments longer. When he tried to step back, he realised that she had not released him, quite as quickly as she had been doing for a long time. He was not sure how to interpret her actions. But Mike did with absolute clarity and in that moment, he knew what he had to do. With his customary hubris, he thought he knew exactly how to go about it.

Gabriel looked on, appalled but with an impish smile on his spirit-face.

# Chapter 36

When she persisted in their embrace for those extra few seconds, she knew it had not gone unnoticed by Teddy. As a result, she could imagine his quandary. She tried to analyse the ideas racing through her head.

"He will never take the first step, especially after I disillusioned him so badly. Stupid me. Since then, he has been typically Teddy, correct and formal. He has taken pains not to overstep the mark in case he offends me…and risk further rejection. Stupid Teddy," she laughed. "Now that Guy is on the road to recovery, there will be far less opportunity for us to meet. Of course, Guy will still come to my home and spend time with me in the play-room. I will probably visit the Goodson household too, on occasions. But a change, there is. The ball is firmly in my court. What should I do?" The ringing of her telephone roused her from her musings.

"Hello Dana. Remember me, Sally, your once best friend?" cooed Sally.

"Oh Sal, you are still my very best friend and always will be."

"Thank heavens for that," she replied with an over-dramatic sigh of relief.

"We have not spoken for ages. I am happy you rang. There is so much to tell you," Dana said, brightly.

"Well, well," said Sally. "I can't wait to hear the latest news."

"I won't make excuses. I should have been in touch, but you would not believe what has been happening these last few months. Do you have the time…?"

"I am dying to hear," interjected Sally. "You have always been in our thoughts, Dan. I just wanted to give you space without getting under your feet. I have been keeping tabs on you, anyway so I have a vague idea. I know you are involved with young Guy and you have given more than your all."

"Yes, Sally, I have been. And whom may I ask is the source of your information?"

"I am sworn to confidentiality, Dana Weston but more importantly, I see you are back to your old self. I can't wait to see you again and have a chance for us to talk. We have not seen each other since that time you asked my opinion about your indecision with Teddy Goodson. Are there any developments?"

"Yes, there certainly are. I decided that as Guy is now out of the woods, I can allow myself the liberty of exploring my feelings for Teddy. I intend to test the water."

"Wonderful. It makes sense as you were obviously attracted to him when we spoke. I am glad you have come to your senses."

"I haven't said anything to him, yet. I need to go about it carefully because I may have scared him off."

"I don't know how you managed to do that, but I actually rang to invite you to a barbecue in our garden the week-end after next. Maybe you can bring Teddy and Guy with you. That may help."

"Yes, it might. He is so shy. I hope he will agree. Meeting new people always scares him. You are right, though, it may encourage him to recognise where I am coming from in our relationship at the moment."

"I agree. Is Sunday mid-day or thereabouts, alright? I hope it suits you."

"I need to check with Teddy, first."

"You have to come, Dan. Peter just bought a top-of-the-range grill and he has all the utensils to go with it, including the chef's hat. It is a trial run for him to experiment. We don't want to poison all our friends, not all at once and not just yet. It would be lovely if you came. I won't take no for an answer this time."

"Oh. I see. So, you think it is alright if your dear husband poisons me, instead. I thought you said I was your best friend. I would hate to be your worst enemy. But yes, I would love to come."

"Good. I am so excited," said Sally. "I hear on the grapevine that you have seen a lot of Guy…and not only the young man, the older one, too. If they come with you, I can check him out. And you know how barbecues are. There is always too much food."

"I am sure Peter will excel at barbecuing as he does with everything else," said Dana.

"He will probably do a small test run before the big day but the main thing is that after all I have heard about them, I want to meet Teddy Goodson and young Guy. I see Dr Barnett from time to time. You know how it is with two children. There is always something. I spend as much time with them at Dr Barnett's surgery as I do at home."

"Aha!" said Dana. "You are not very good at hiding the identity of your informant."

"All right, then. So you caught me out. Anyway, he told me how impressed he was with you He also said that the little boy was smitten with you after five minutes and the father was not far behind. Now, I need to give the final approval." Her knowing chuckle left Dana in no doubt that she was up to her old tricks.

# Chapter 37

Mike was overwhelmed by the connection he saw between father and son. The tenderness Teddy exhibited towards Guy and his infinite patience made a deep impression on him. There was nothing that was too much for him. He always made sure that the boy was conscious of his support and protection without stifling him. Wherever necessary, he left him to his own devices and no doubt, this attitude had contributed significantly to the rebuilding of Guy's confidence and his ability to think and act of his own volition.

He would answer his never-ending flow of questions with great truthfulness. He never patronised him, ensuring that he knew he was interested in and respected his opinions. He complimented the boy where necessary but never used platitudes. It was clear that they were completely at ease and comfortable with each other. Mike was learning more from him than he had expected. He was also very impressed by Guy's determination and resolve. The subject of Wee Bobby came up again and again.

"Dana said we might see Mr Horne today, Dad? Will Wee Bobby be able to hear Peter and the Wolf in time?"

"Sorry, son, there are no concerts with Peter and the Wolf in the programme in the near future." Guy's face fell.

"Please, don't worry, though. We are going to ask Mr Horne whether it is possible to arrange for the school orchestra to put on a special performance of Peter and the Wolf, even if it is only on a limited scale."

Guy looked sceptical. "I have not been to music practice with Mr Horne for a long time, but I don't think we have enough children, who are good enough to play the whole thing, Dad. We will probably have to find a different way."

"Well, if you, Dana, Mr Horne and I sit down together, we may be able to find a solution. We know how important it is to you and Bobby. We will make sure Bobby has his concert."

Guy was upset when he heard what his father had told him but there was no way he would ever throw in the towel. His friend was in dire need and come hell or high water, a concert there would be.

"We cannot take too long, Dad."

"Trust us. We will move heaven and earth to make sure Bobby gets his concert and knows that his friend never let him down," he said, hoping to pacify Guy, despite his own doubts.

Mike was fascinated by the conversation Teddy was having with his son. He was impressed with the ease with which he fielded Guy's questions and succeeded in inspiring the boy to keep faith.

He wanted to make comments of his own, which he felt would give a degree of comfort to Guy but the Source's decree that his voice not be heard prevented him from doing so. He wanted to reassure Guy that dying was not an unpleasant experience. Although it was the end of life, it was not the end of living. It was both liberating and enlightening, but he acknowledged that at this stage of man's evolution and with humanity's limited knowledge and superficial awareness, much of what he wanted to say would fall on deaf ears. They might regard him as a false prophet and even today, were it permitted, they would burn him at the stake as an heretic.

*Man lives on earth and not in heaven*, he thought. "They are not yet ready for the insights I could provide. To them, they would appear to be the words of a charlatan, anathema.

Organised religions have too much to lose by surrendering their hegemony on man's spiritual well-being or questioning their concepts of good and evil, with the attendant assurance of a reward for good deeds in heaven or eternal damnation in hell, for bad ones."

Mike's spirit had discovered during his sojourn in the afterlife when he had abandoned his earthly body that there were no good or bad people, only good or bad deeds. In addition, Gabriel had succeeded in persuading him that anyway, people were purely instruments utilised by the Eternal One to give expression to Its will.

*All man's attempts to interpret and unravel the mystery of life are a waste of time. Those unhappy souls, who seek salvation through the people, who profess to know, simply feather the nest of so-called religious experts, who trade on man's fear of the unknown after death. The All Knowing is really wily.* he thought. *It has allowed man to fall into the trap It laid for him right at the beginning. By hiding from mankind the truth about life after death, the Source is able to test man's faith.*

He laughed at himself. *Here I am, still using terminology, like 'angel', 'good', 'bad' when I already know there are no such things. What chance do humans have, when I, who has had personal experience, still think this way and should know better? It is unbelievable how deeply ingrained these beliefs are*, he tut-tutted.

Guy's return to school was memorable, especially for Mike, who had not known Guy, previously. The enthusiasm with which he was greeted by his friends and the warmth and obvious pleasure of Ms Commins, when he walked into her classroom was unequivocal evidence of the esteem in which Guy was held by everybody…even loved.

The children gathered round him to welcome him back. In the classroom, Ms Commins allowed the noise and excitement to continue for a long time.

She approached him at his desk. "I am very pleased to see you with us, again, Guy. We have all missed you so much, haven't we, girls and boys?"

"Yes, yes," screamed the pupils.

"May I give you a hug, Guy?" she asked.

"Of course, Ms Commins, I like hugs."

After she stepped back, she found the children lined up behind her. She was thrilled at the chain reaction her embrace had initiated. The children, patiently waited their turn to hug Guy although some of the more macho-like boys preferred to give him 'high-fives'.

When the school-bell rang at the end of the day, Dana and Teddy came to his classroom to accompany him to the appointment she had made with Mr Horne. She wore a flared skirt and a short-sleeved, floral blouse and on her feet, a pair of summer sandals. She had put her hair up in a stylish chignon and the attractive contrast of casual and elegant, drew much attention from onlookers, including Teddy. When Guy saw her, he rushed over and took her hand and led the procession to the music-department, where Mr Horne was waiting for them.

With an unruly goatee beard and thick horn-rimmed glasses, Mr Horne appeared somewhat formal but in fact, he was open and friendly.

"I am very happy to see you, Guy. Welcome back," he bellowed. "You would have enjoyed being a part of the progress we have made in the youth orchestra. I sincerely hope you will pick up where you left off. You were doing very nicely."

"Thank you, Mr Horne," said Guy. "As soon as I catch up with my schoolwork, I will start again."

"We have all looked forward to your return," said the jovial Mr Horne. "The children have learnt a great deal about music while you were away. You would have enjoyed it."

"While I was sick, most of the time I listened to classical music so I also learnt a lot. I can't wait to join the orchestra, again."

"Well done. Anyway, Dana has told me about the promise you gave. Most impressive, I might add. I had considered the idea of organising a concert with the school-orchestra but unfortunately, it will not be possible because, although there are some excellent youngsters, there are not enough proficient, youthful musicians who are able to master the requirements of an entire concert."

"I told my father that I also thought so."

"And with all the practicing and rehearsals needed, it would take too long, anyway," said Mr Horne.

Guy's expression darkened.

"So, what can we do?" he asked.

"I believe the solution lies in a different direction. I have been in contact with the music-masters in other schools to explore the possibility of arranging for a combined orchestra, with children from different schools. I am very excited at the idea. It has never been done before and if successful, it will open up possibilities for musical development in schools on a far broader scale."

"That is a brilliant idea," Dana exclaimed. "I imagine with all the schools involved, it is far more likely that we will find enough children of a suitable level."

"I am quite optimistic, since the teachers to whom I have spoken have all been as pleased at the innovative idea as I was. They promised to get back to me by next week. If there is any likelihood of success, a meeting will be arranged, immediately. Of course, you are cordially invited to attend," said Mr Horne, turning to Guy. "After all, you are the inspiration for the whole idea and at present, you are the one driving us on with your determination," he added, patting Guy gently on the back.

Dana was very excited by Mr Horne's interest in the project and at the amount of thought and work he had already invested.

"I hope you will accept any support I can offer," she volunteered. "It will be my pleasure. I think your idea of involving other schools is a brainwave."

"I am quite proud of the idea, I must say," said the music-master, modestly.

Dana nodded to him as a token of agreement. "We are not going to disappoint these two boys, either. It is vital that we succeed. And time is of the essence," she said, winking at Guy. He smiled at her, angelically.

"Thank you," Mr Horne said, beaming at her. "I welcome your support. Let us maintain close communication and exchange email addresses and telephone numbers. It will be easier to keep in touch."

Once again, Teddy was impressed by Dana's ability to captivate her audience. Mike noticed Teddy's fascination with her and a plan began to formulate in his mind. Everything was falling into place. He was beginning to see the course he believed the Source intended events should follow and, with a trace of human arrogance, he began planning to make sure it happened as predetermined. He completely forgot the warning he had been given by Gabriel, never to do what he was doing, second guessing the Source's intention.

Gabriel shook his head in disbelief at his lapse of memory but realised it was only natural to be human and Mike was being just that, human.

*There is still much to be done before this chapter is over*, thought Gabriel.

# Chapter 38

Teddy was nervous, not sure what reaction he might receive. He had intended telephoning Dana to invite her to accompany them on an outing he was planning He vacillated, endlessly, before finally making up his mind to do so, encouraged to some degree by the change he had detected in her attitude towards him of late. He was not entirely convinced. He may have been imagining it, but he sensed that there was something different. Both Mike and Mona had been busy.

"Hello Dana. I am planning to take Guy for a drive in the country this weekend and he suggested I invite you to join us."

"Oh! So, you don't want to speak to me unless Guy tells you to," she teased.

"No, No," he said, defensively, "I would have called you. It is just that we have been so busy since we came home that there has been no time for anything."

"I am only joking, Teddy," she said to relieve his stress. "I would love to come with you. I miss you both even though it has only been a short time since I last saw you. Where are you planning to go?"

"I don't want to go too far away at this early stage. It will be Guy's first outing for a very long time."

"I agree with you, Teddy. What are you planning?"

"I thought we would go to a place I found when I was paging through a guide-book. My eye just fell on this venue. It is not very far, apparently only about a ninety-minute drive. It seems ideal."

"Yes, I think that is the perfect start for getting Guy out into nature after having been cooped up in the city for such a long time."

"You are right. He needs the fresh air and I read that there is a forest in the vicinity with a small stream flowing through it. It looks very beautiful. If we feel like it, we can take a dip in the water as the weather is so beautiful. I can't imagine a more suitable spot."

"It seems like it. I used to go on short trips with Mike, quite often, you know. It was one of our favourite pastimes. I would love to go with you."

He smiled with satisfaction at her response. There had certainly been a change in the way she was towards him, more open, and, dare he even think so, more loving.

"I hope the weather holds. It has been sunny and warm for over three weeks. The gods need to favour us a bit at last. We have earned it," she said.

"You are right. They haven't done enough up to now. They owe us."

"We will see on the day," she laughed. "I think you said it takes about ninety minutes to get there, didn't you?"

"Normally, it takes about an hour and a quarter, but we can take the drive slowly and enjoy the scenery which is very beautiful and pastoral, once we are out of the city."

She smiled at his terminology, especially the word 'pastoral'.

So did Mike. *I am getting better at this.* he thought.

"Leave the catering to me. I will prepare a picnic hamper. By now, I know what foods you like. I have all the cool-boxes and other stuff. As I said, I used to go on excursions like this often. I am an experienced picnic-buff."

"It all sounds great then, Dana."

"I am sure Guy will love it. I imagine he cannot wait to spread his wings and get some sunshine and a bit of freedom."

"Yes, he is looking forward to it and now, it is even better because you are coming with us. We will call for you at about nine o' clock on Sunday. Does that suit you?"

"It suits me to a T, perfect."

"Wonderful, Guy will be thrilled to see his Dana, again and so will I."

"OK, see you at nine on Sunday. By the way, my very good friends, Sally and Peter Broome invited us all to a barbecue at their home the following weekend. Will you come? They are lovely people and there will only be them and us. Guy will have a chance to meet their two sons, Julian and Peter. The older boy is roughly his age."

Due to his customary reticence at meeting new people, he hesitated for a moment before he decided to accept the invitation. Mike, though, was more excited than anyone else at the prospect of seeing his friend, Peter, again. Without having given it a second's thought, he had influenced Teddy to accept. He was amazed at the facility with which he had succeeded in having Teddy express his ideas out loud.

*Perhaps, I should stop trying so hard*, he thought, mulling over the realisation.

"Lovely! I know we will have a fantastic time, together. Give my love to Guy," she added. Teddy was not quite sure what she meant by the word, 'together'.

The Gods did smile on them and the day was fine. As they drove out of the city, they sang songs and played I Spy and other games. By the time they reached the open countryside, Guy was ecstatic, being outdoors for the first time. With a little coaxing, he even entertained them by playing some songs on his flute.

"I promise I will practice more." he said, when he suspected that they were relieved after he finished his recital.

"Don't you worry. You are doing fine, Guychick. We love hearing you play," she said.

Teddy gave her a sideways glance. *That's the second time she called him Guychick!* he thought.

"It's a pity I won't be ready in time to play at the concert," Guy said.

"You are amazing, young man. You have already played an essential part by being so determined to make certain that the concert takes place. Without you, there would be no concert. Do you realise that?" she said. "You are so modest."

"And also dedicated," Teddy added.

"It will definitely happen, though, right?"

"You can count on it," she assured him.

"I trust you and Dad."

"I am pleased you do. Trust is very important, Guychick. I always said so. I remember when we first met. You were still a young child. I am sorry I was not there to watch you grow up and go to school," said Dana.

"That makes three times," Teddy calculated. Also, he never understood what Dana meant but Mona knew exactly why she had said precisely what they had heard. She was already more adept at influencing Dana than Mike was in getting Teddy to do his bidding.

"Where are we going, exactly?" she asked.

"I don't know, exactly, as I told you," he answered. "It seemed perfect and completely off the beaten track. We will probably have the area to ourselves."

"The terrain looks familiar. It would be amazing if it is the place I think it is. We should be at the turn-off to a sand-road leading there in the next twenty minutes or so," she said.

"What a coincidence if it turns out to be a spot you know," he said with surprise.

As she had said, they soon reached a dirt-track leading off the highway. They turned onto it and drove for ten minutes, until they reached a clearing at the edge of a forest, where they parked the car. She was quiet as they got out. Teddy noticed a strange look on her face.

"What is it, Dana? Is everything alright?" he asked.

She put her arm around Guy. "I know this spot, well. I used to come here with Mike. It was our favourite place. I can't believe that this is the same one you chose. It brings back such happy memories for me. I am overwhelmed to be back again, especially now, sharing it with the two of you."

He could not understand why he felt happy for both Dana and himself and, at the same time, a little melancholy with nostalgia. He had never been here before but Mike had and the melancholy was his.

Guy immediately rushed into the shady bower and began to scale one of the sturdy oaks. Teddy wanted to call him back and warned him to be careful, but she touched his arm, lightly.

"Let him be. He has a guardian angel watching over him. He will be alright," she said. Mona watched her son, nimbly perched on a branch, high up in the tree, knowing that Dana's observation was spot-on.

He called them and excitedly pointed out the sun-beams, dancing and shimmering in columns of light, penetrating the umbrella of foliage created by the towering trees. Dana took Teddy's hand and together, they ran towards Guy, who was yelling with glee.

"There it is, a stream. I can see it from up here. Let's go for a swim," he said, excitedly. He pointed in the direction of the stream.

They ran to the bank of the stream and marvelled at the beauty. The meandering water sparkled in the morning sun and gurgled as it flowed over smooth, white river-stones or tumbled over low gradients, forming shallow pools on its leisurely way to the sea.

They went back to the car and changed into their bathing-suits. Shivering, they tiptoed, cautiously into the cool water. Guy began to splash them, mercilessly despite their entreaties for him to desist.

"Stop, Guy, please," begged Teddy in vain.

"Guy, how can you be so cruel to us?" said Dana and he ceased, immediately.

"Oh! I see. Only when Dana asks, do you listen?" Teddy said, laughing.

At that moment, he slipped on the muddy river-bank and came up, spluttering, shaking the water off his face and hair like a wet puppy. Guy and Dana shook with mirth and he joined in when he realised how funny he must have looked.

They frolicked in the water and dried off in the warm sunshine, lying on the soft grass, coating the meadow.

The physical exertion had brought on their appetites. They went back to the car and carried the cool boxes and food baskets into the shade, where Dana spread out a large, colourful table-cloth and unpacked the hampers. Then she laid out the feast she had prepared.

They devoured the delicious lunch before them, taking turns to compliment Dana on the different salads, boiled eggs, smoked salmon beigels, cold cuts, barbecued chicken wings, sandwiches, fruit and the various desserts she had chosen, including vanilla ice cream and jelly and custard.

"Yummy, yummy, I love vanilla ice cream," crowed Guy.

"How did you know?" asked Teddy.

"Just a wild guess," she said, with a sly grin. Except for the vanilla ice-cream, the menu was almost identical to the one she remembered from the last time she and Mike had come to their special hideaway. Both Teddy and Mike enjoyed the food immensely. Guy, too, ate heartily, overjoyed to be able to feast on Dana's excellent choices.

"Thanks Dana, I am bloated. It was delicious, outstanding," Teddy said.

"Dana always does outstanding things, Dad. We know that." Teddy smiled, shyly when Dana took his hand and gave it a gentle squeeze.

They revelled in the warm sunshine and filled their lungs with the embracing, fresh air. Guy was ecstatic as he sat in the shade and read a book or listened to some music through the headphones of the new compact disc player, which Dana had given him as a gift on his completing his treatment. He chased butterflies in the meadow, paddled in the stream, climbed more trees and explored the forest trails, burning up energy at an incredible rate.

Wherever the boy went, the adults tried to follow. He was always accompanied by Dana and Teddy, who walked hand-in-hand, at her initiative.

But they were no match for Guy, though, who, despite his recent health-trauma, was invigorated by his new-found freedom. He seemed to have tireless energy and showed no sign of slowing down his frenetic activity. His father watched him carefully all the time, doing his best to make sure that Guy never noticed so he would not feel inhibited in any way.

Afterwards, leisurely relaxing on the soft grass, Dana lay on her back, with eyes closed.

"You can rest your head on my lap if you like," Teddy offered, shyly.

"Thank you, kind sir," she said. She moved closer to him as she accepted his invitation and dozed off. He sat watching her sleeping, gently stroking her hair, with an expression of wonder on his face. Every so often, when he thought they were not looking, Guy would peek at them and smile to himself with satisfaction.

*They are in paradise and I should know*, thought Mike.

The day was perfect. When it was time to leave, they packed away everything and ensured they left no litter.

As she got out of the car when they reached her home, Guy would not let her go. He hugged her, tightly. With a laugh, she struggled to break free. "Come on, young man, give me a chance to hug your father. Look how lonely he is."

"No, he looks fine, but I am sure he wants to give you a hug, too. You made us such a lovely lunch."

"It was more than just the lunch, Guy," Teddy said. "Not only did Dana teach us those new games, she made the day extra-enjoyable for us. We are lucky she agreed to come with us."

"I had a wonderful time, too," she said to Guy but really directed to Teddy. "Thank you for inviting me. And of all the places in the world, you chose one so special to me."

Mona and Mike had enjoyed the day as well.

# Chapter 39

Teddy arranged to pick up Dana on the way to Sally and Peter's barbecue.

Guy was hyper with excitement, thrilled to be seeing her. He had quickly reverted to being the child he was before the illness had struck him down. He regained all his old energy and caught up with his studies with no problem. As they drove to Dana's home, Guy kept his hapless father busy, plying him with questions, some of which, as before when Guy was much younger, he found difficult to answer. This time though, Teddy happily accepted the challenge. He intended being a worthy contender to his renascent young son.

"Why does God let poor Wee Bobby get so sick when he has never done anything wrong?" Guy asked. "He has had a hard life. Now, he may even die. Why does God not make him better? Do you think God is fair, Daddy? I don't think he is."

It was a question Teddy had often thought about when Mona was first diagnosed with cancer and again, when Guy become ill. He was familiar with the platitudes fed to the masses but to accept them demanded a degree of faith of the sort held by Sandra Weaver.

He never had such faith. However, he was wary of saying anything, which might be interpreted as pontificating.

Mike, too, was pleased with his increasing ability to influence Teddy's thinking. It had already resulted in a significant advancement of his plans for Teddy and Dana, such as his choice of the picnic venue the previous week. He thought this was an appropriate moment for him to intervene and comment. Again, he forgot Gabriel's injunction.

"It is really impossible to answer your question, Guy," Teddy explained "Just think about it objectively. Do you understand what the word 'objectively' means?"

"Please, Dad. I read a lot. Of course I know what it means," he answered, dismissively.

Teddy smiled. "Sorry, I apologise. Sometimes, it is hard to remember that you are eight years old and not eighteen."

"No, Dad, I think I act my age."

"OK, but just look at our situation. Here you are, well and healthy, thank goodness. One could ask why you and not Wee Bobby. We are happy but for the Weaver family, it is very hard. They are pleased for us but I am sure they wish Bobby was the one to get better even though they prayed that you would both be well."

"I also think so, Dad."

"So, there are millions of inexplicable occurrences happening every moment. How can we ever really understand why? It is best just to be grateful for everything we receive and try to be better people," he said.

He was taken aback by the way he had responded. The words had come to him as he was speaking.

Although Teddy had spoken, Mike knew it was precisely what he would have said. Perhaps the Source intended to teach him a lesson for being so arrogant and this was Its way of doing so, by preventing him from being heard.

On the other hand, he had just witnessed an instance when, with no effort on his part, his host had expressly stated his opinion, exactly as he would have done, even using the same words. It dawned on him that perhaps that was the solution to his dilemma.

He had tried to influence Teddy's thinking or actions, when, in fact, there was no need to do so because he was a natural part of his host and not an intruder, separate from him.

His thoughts were Teddy's and vice versa. If he surrendered and let his host make his decisions, they would turn out to be his own. Since they were one and the same person, Teddy could be relied upon. It was certainly not necessary to struggle to achieve this, quite the contrary. His resistance got in the way. That was the obstruction. He needed to trust Teddy and not oppose or resist him.

Teddy thought of Mona at that moment and how she had always spoken about trust being everything. *What an incredible coincidence*, he thought.

Mike. though, was happy because he was learning to influence his host with greater ease. He continued his philosophising about humankind's inverted awareness. He was also pleasantly surprised that he, himself, was growing from his experience of being back in the 'real' world. Guy's question and Teddy's response had elicited in him a questioning of accepted human concepts.

"Man is born with an innate knowing of the truths of life. This awareness is inherent in everyone, but it is gradually lost through the passage of time, due to so called 'education' and conditioning.

Instead of relying on this ability, man has been led to doubt the veracity of his own knowing and instead relies on the so-called wisdom of his teachers who, generation after generation have herded him further and further from these truths."

He inhaled deeply as he digested these ideas.

"When individuals allow this God-given talent to simply be present without interfering with it, they are able to function in any situation. Invariably, they discover that people are their best when they are themselves rather than being the person they may think that they or others expect them to be.

Perhaps the purpose of life is to return to this basic knowing. Everything is pre-ordained, and nothing can be changed, anyway. We are each capable of greatness, as we carry the spirit of our God in us and the All-Knowing wants only the best both for and of us."

Once more, he thought, arrogantly, *That's it. I think I have the key.*

Guy was not completely convinced by Teddy's explanation but they had reached Dana's home. He bounded out of the car and rushed to the entrance. Teddy followed, wondering how it would be seeing her after the short break, almost a whole week, the longest interval since she had come back into their lives. He tried his utmost to ignore his excitement, but he felt tremors of anticipation running up and down his spine.

Although he was not yet completely convinced of the change in her attitude, he was pleased and flattered when she had telephoned. He accepted the invitation although, as usual, the demons sprung up immediately. He realised he would be obliged to deal with the frightening prospect of meeting new people. His hesitation before accepting her invitation had been short-lived. Mike had done his work well as he became more adept at the task at hand.

As they entered the house, Mike immediately felt a strong sense of déjà vu. Dana had made few changes. Familiar sights and smells assailed him and the nostalgia was bitter-sweet. He was at 'home'.

Guy gave her a warm hug and ran straight to the play-room. She turned to Teddy and allowed herself to dissolve in his arms in an embrace unlike any they had shared before. It was patently clear to him that something had indeed changed in her attitude. Teddy could feel her body pressed firmly against his and she was holding him more tightly than ever before. Her perfume overwhelmed him.

Mike too, remembered past occasions when he had relished the scent of her. They embraced for several seconds before they separated. Still holding hands, they looked deeply into each other eyes. There was a softness Teddy had never seen. His head spun.

"I am so sorry for all the heartache my doubts have caused you, Teddy. I promise I will make it up to you from now on. I feel blessed to have met you," she whispered in his ear.

"You need never apologise for anything, Dani, not after all you have done for us."

It took a few moments before Dana realised the way that Teddy had addressed her and this time it was she, who was shocked at his use of Mike's nick-name for her. Without his realising how shocked Dana was, he continued, "You saved Guy's and my life. We owe you so much. I can never thank you enough for all the love you have shown us. Now, it is our turn to give it back to you."

In the intimacy of the moment, a flood of emotions, love, gratitude, passion, fear, all registered on his face. She could read them, clearly, as if she had been looking at an open book. Their hearts were locked in an embrace as powerful as any physical connection they had ever experienced.

Mike was overjoyed because he had initiated the reaction in Teddy in the same way as he had done in the car when Guy had confronted him about God's lack of compassion.

Mike knew of Teddy's love for Dana, but he had also recognised her love for him because he had had personal experience of it during their lives, together. Her gestures, facial expressions, even her tone of voice were patent signs, but patent only to someone who had known her as intimately as Mike had.

*Perhaps the All Knowing's true intention was not about Dana. She has already come back to herself.* he thought. "Teddy though has endured years of pain but never allowed his despair to dull his sensitivity. His dedication and love for his wife and son and then, secretly for Dana are examples of the huge capacity of the man's ability to love.

Maybe, he was chosen to be rewarded for his years of self-sacrifice by my being sent here to spur him on. Could it be that It intended that I be the catalyst for him to accept the gift of this extraordinary woman?

They have both suffered and this way, two people who have known more than their fair share of grief can be together to bring one another happiness."

He looked lovingly at his Dana. To him, she was as beautiful as ever. The years had added a maturity and softness to her. The charm and warmth she always exuded was now tempered by wisdom and experience. Teddy was a lucky man to have found a woman as special as Dana and she would enjoy the love of a man who adored her. She would also have the family she had missed with him. He was contented. He knew Dana was safe and he was at peace.

"I think it may nearly be time for me to go home."

# Chapter 40

Sally and Peter lived in a double-storied, face-brick house with a large well-manicured front garden. Behind the house was a small swimming pool surrounded by a large expanse of lawn. Snap dragons, red, lilac and pink rose bushes and a profusion of yellow daisies added a blaze of colour. A lush weeping willow tree provided shade in one corner of the secluded garden and a blazing orange-coloured bougainvillea in another. Parasols and deck-chairs were scattered around the pool. The new state-of-the-art, jet-black barbecue took pride of place, glistening under a large awning designed to protect the chef from the glare of the sun. Suspended from the metal frame of the canvas canopy, an array of pots with variegated, green ferns swayed gently in the breeze.

Peter shook Teddy's hand and slapped him on the back when Dana introduced them.

"It is so nice to meet you at last, Teddy and you, too, Guy," he said, turning to the boy. "We have heard so many good things about you."

Guy looked embarrassed but Dana saved the day. "Yes, Peter, this is Guy, who is a very brave young man. We have become close friends, actually even more than that, almost mother and son," she said, turning to Guy and putting her arms around the beaming child.

"So we understand," Peter said, tousling Guy's hair.

Sally gushed with her customary exuberance as she shook Teddy's hand.

"I am very happy to meet you, Teddy. Dana is my closest friend and she has told us so much about you, all good, I assure you," she laughed.

"Hello Guy, I want you to meet my sons," she said, looking around for the boys. When she saw them, she called them over.

"Guy, meet Julian and young, Peter. Boys, this is Guy. Why don't you show Guy some of your video games until Dad has lunch ready?" Needing no further bidding, the children ran off.

"You can give me a hand with the barbecue, if you like, Teddy. I hate to admit it but I am still not totally au fait with the new gadget. If Sally finds out, she will kill me," said Peter with a wry smile.

"I must admit, I haven't done much grilling for a long time, myself so I am not sure I will be much help," said Teddy "But at least it will give the girls an opportunity to catch up a little."

"You are absolutely right. Just look at them. They can't wait," Peter agreed.

Holding her hand, Sally steered Dana to a secluded nook in the garden.

"He is adorable, Dan," was the first thing she said when they were seated.

"Do you mean the father or the son?" Dana asked, innocently.

"Both, silly," Sally said.

Before Dana could ask why she had said 'he' rather than 'they', Sally continued to bombard her with questions.

Their intimate tete-a-tete continued, uninterrupted, while Peter and Teddy each took a cold beer and walked over to the ultra-modern appliance, which was already lit. On the front of Peter's apron was written 'MasterChef' and with his chef's hat, he looked the part, fully.

To christen the brand-new device, he covered the grill with steaks, chops, hamburgers, chicken-wings and spicy sausages. He reserved space on the side of the barbecue for skewers of tomatoes, onions, mushrooms and red and green sweet-peppers. As Sally had warned Dana, there was enough food to feed an army. Apparently, quite surprisingly, she had not exaggerated.

Mike was pleased to see Peter so happy. He appeared to be successful in his career and he and Sally were happily married. They had built a good life together.

The memories came flooding back as he stood in the company of his old friend. He noticed Peter staring as though he was comparing Teddy to him. There was no resemblance, physically or otherwise, and yet, it was eerie the way that Peter was examining him.

"I was told that Guy was very ill, although I believe he is well now. I can imagine how difficult it must have been for you. You must be relieved," Peter said.

"We all are, I assure you," Teddy replied.

"I don't know how you did it. Where did you get the emotional as well as the physical strength?"

Teddy laughed, bitterly. "As you may know, unfortunately, I have already had a lot of practice."

"Sally mentioned to me about your loss. It must have been terrible for you."

"It certainly was, beyond description, Pete. I never believed I could live through another tragedy like that one."

"I am really glad for you and Guy that he is well on the mend, now."

"Yes, it has been a long haul but at last, the worst is behind us."

"It seems Dana came into the picture just in time."

"Thank goodness for her. I don't think I could have done it on my own."

"She is an incredible woman isn't she, that Dana?" Peter said.

"She certainly is. She was a pillar of strength throughout the ordeal. Even when the situation was at its darkest, she never lost faith. She was the one who kept our spirits up."

"That is typical Dana. Are you aware of the number of children she has saved in her career?"

"Although she has not spoken about it much, I know enough, I assure you. It is as though she was sent from heaven." It was Mike's turn to smile. Dana had indeed been sent, if not from, then certainly through heaven.

"Guy has really taken to her, hasn't he?" Peter said.

"Yes, he most definitely has. He is besotted with her."

"It looks like the feeling's mutual," said Peter, as he started clearing the grill, removing some of the meat that was ready.

"We are both very fond of her…and grateful."

Peter turned to him. "It seems that it is not simply that Guy is fond of Dana, besotted as you said. That is plain to see. She loves him too, from what I gather from Sally, who has been Dana's best friend almost since childhood. They speak to each other frequently so Sally is in the know about her life more than anybody else."

"Yes, Dana told me that. She also mentioned that her late husband, Mike was a good friend of yours." Teddy said.

"Mike was my oldest and closest friend and I miss him a lot. Do you know that she met him through Sally and me?"

"I believe so. What luck?" said Teddy.

"Yes, it was touch and go that they even met at all. Neither of them was too keen on the blind date we arranged," Peter chuckled.

"Isn't it incredible, even miraculous, sometimes, how things pan out?" said Teddy, although it was Mike who was playing with his new-found talent. "I understand they were very much in love, the perfect couple."

"That is the reason Sally and I were worried about her. She took Mike's death very badly."

"I believe she fell apart, completely," Teddy said. The Goodson family had first-hand experience of the fact.

"Yes, she stopped working altogether she was so devastated. She withdrew from all her friends and buried herself at home. All she wanted was to mourn Mike's passing. She missed him so much."

"I am happy to see that she has come back to herself," Teddy said.

"I think Guy and you have given her the inspiration to return to the world of the living."

"I assure you, it was all Guy. He was also the key to my own recovery from the dual tragedies which almost destroyed me."

"We are sorry for your loss, Teddy, but Sally and I are now concerned that she not be exposed to any more upset, which might set her back. We all want to see her happy, don't we?"

"No need to worry, Pete, so do I. I assure you, Dani will be fine, and no harm will come to her if I have anything to do with it."

Peter stared at him, his eye-brows raised in surprise.

"Do you always call her that?" he asked in amazement.

"Call her what?" asked Teddy, feigning innocence.

"Never mind," said Peter, rattled. "The main thing is that no harm comes to her. She is very special for us and Sally thinks she may still be a bit fragile. I am glad you are watching over her."

"Don't mention it. That's what friends are for. And I don't think she is at all fragile, just the opposite, superwoman with a halo."

Peter just shook his head and went back to his grilling.

"By the way, I prefer to be called Peter."

"I will try, but Pete just seems to come to me, automatically. Maybe when we grow up a little it will be easier," Teddy said, smiling.

Peter almost burned the meat still on the barbecue.

The chatter flowed freely, as they sat around the long garden table enjoying the sumptuous meal. Peter noticed that Teddy was very attentive to the needs of young Guy. Although he never crowded him, he was constantly on the alert for any signs of discomfort from the boy. Guy, though, had blended perfectly with the other two youngsters. They were already like old friends.

Dana spent a lot of time with the children. Guy was very proud to be her 'patron' and laid claim to her as his own special adult-friend. The children were extremely impressed by her, which brought great relief to Sally. She had not been sure to what extent Dana had returned to being her old self but the way the children accepted her dispelled any lingering doubts.

"How did you like the video games?" Sally asked Guy.

"I am not too good at them because I've never played them before," he replied. "I could improve if Julian and Peter are willing to teach me."

"I am sure they would be glad to. You can visit us more often if you like, now, that you have met each other. You are always welcome, you and your dad."

"Dana told us that you love reading and you enjoy classical music," said Peter. "That is quite unusual for children your age."

"When I was sick, I couldn't go to school. So, I read or listened to classical music all the time, instead."

"What is your favourite piece of music?" asked Sally.

"I love Peter and the Wolf. That was one of the first pieces I heard when I was little. My dad took me to a concert and they played it. Since then, I have collected quite a lot of compact-discs. Now, my dad is teaching me about Beethoven. He says Beethoven is his favourite composer and his favourite piece of music is the Pastural Symphony."

"Guy, I am sure you know Beethoven wrote nine symphonies and the Pastoral is Beethoven's Sixth. And do you know what? It is also my favourite," Dana said.

"Dani, isn't it amazing that you and I love the Pastoral as our favourite piece of music." Teddy commented.

Peter's eye-brows rose again in shock. He could not believe it. It was way beyond coincidence. He stared at Teddy. Since they had arrived, he had had the weird feeling that he knew him although they had never met. He could not shake off the feeling that he knew Teddy, who showed no signs of recognition in return.

Seeing Dana had also brought up memories of Mike. Hearing Teddy use Mike's nick-name for her was uncanny and then the Pastoral Symphony. *Well! There are too many inexplicable coincidences*, Peter thought.

The conversation around the lunch table continued. "My friend, Bobby Weaver is very sick. We met at the hospital. He never heard classical music in his life but after he listened to some of my compact-discs, he began to like it, too. So I promised him that I would arrange for him to hear Peter and the Wolf at a live concert," explained Guy.

"Why Guy, that is a fantastic gesture. What a wonderful thing to do, to introduce a child to classical music," Peter said.

"I just want him to feel better. He deserves it."

Dana looked at Teddy with the shadow of a smile which said, "Can you believe this boy?" Teddy grinned back at her, each bursting with pride.

"Would you like to come to the concert?" Guy asked Peter and Julian, who nodded enthusiastically. With that, the three boys dashed off, again.

"Guy seems to have great determination, as well as a heart of gold," said Peter.

"It is that determination that pulled him through his illness," Teddy told the others. "He endured the pain and discomfort with great courage. He was an example to everyone. What's more, I think he was more concerned about me than he was about his own situation."

"He is an amazing boy. In some ways he is so mature and wise and yet, he has not lost his childlike innocence. I think Teddy has done a wonderful job of raising such a balanced human being," Dana added.

"I am not sure of that," Teddy retorted. "I made many mistakes en route, I assure you."

"Don't be so modest, Teddy. With all the difficulties you had to deal with, just look at the end product," Dana insisted.

"Thank you, all the same, Dani. Anyway, he has another examination in a couple of months and hopefully, all will be well," said Teddy. "I want to take him on a short holiday, three or four days, so he does not miss any more school. He has caught up, but it would not be fair to have him slip back again after all his hard work."

"That seems a good idea," agreed Sally. "Where are you planning to go?"

"I was thinking of taking him to Barcelona," he replied. "I believe it is a city, where you can just walk around. There is so much to see and do. I think Guy would enjoy it. Of course, there is also the soccer."

"Do you know that Mike took Dana to Barcelona as a surprise?" Peter said. "Why don't you talk to her about it? She knows the city quite well."

"Perhaps, she will also tell you about Mike's surprise," Sally giggled.

Teddy turned to her. "Will you, Dani? There is always a benefit in talking to somebody, who has first-hand knowledge."

She smiled. "It will be my pleasure. It is a beautiful city."

"I am sure the break will be good for all of you, whenever you decide to go," said Sally.

"We recently had a lovely outing with Guy at a place Teddy discovered," said Dana. "It was so relaxing."

"Where was it?" Peter asked.

"I read a description of the site in a guide book. What a coincidence that it turned out to be a spot that Dana knows well," Teddy said.

"It certainly surprised me, I can tell you," said Dana. "You know the place, Peter. I used to go there with Mike. The whole time, it felt as though he was stage-managing everything."

She laughed but Peter just gaped, again. He had the same feeling about today.

"Well, we need to make sure that the concert is arranged first, before we do anything else or Guy will never forgive us," Teddy said. "Once that is behind us, we can start making plans to visit Barcelona. I know he would be overjoyed if his Dana would come with us…and so would I," he said, with uncharacteristic forwardness.

Dana showed no sign of embarrassment at his comment, quite the contrary.

"That is sweet of you. I would love to come," she said.

Then, she quietly whispered to him. "Now, where did that come from, being as brash as you just were? I like it,"

Teddy beamed although he, himself, was surprised at his making such a remark. It had just slipped out or had it, with Mike in the background.

As they were taking their leave, Sally hugged her friend and whispered in her ear, "Teddy is a very special man. He reminds us of Mike. So much so, that Peter said to me, twice that he feels as though Mike is here today. He obviously adores you and Guy is an angel. You have captured both their hearts, Dan. Take good care of them and I am sure they will take good care of you."

She squeezed Sally tightly. "I don't know what happened but the feelings I have for Teddy have surfaced today even more than ever. He has been constant in his attitude towards me, very gentlemanly and he has done everything to avoid offending me. I just hope I have not frightened him off."

"You definitely need not worry about that. From what I see, it is quite the opposite."

"It feels as though the chains that bound me have fallen away and I have been set free," confided Dana to her bosom friend.

"Of course, I still love Mike but I know that I must let him go and allow him to rest in peace. I learnt that through Guy.

He still loves and misses his precious mother. Yet he is willing to let her be and accept me. He showed me there is always room in your heart for love, much more than we adults can ever imagine." Mona smiled with satisfaction.

"It took an innocent child to teach that to the teacher," said Dana.

"He is a special child, that is obvious and don't forget, the teacher is special, too," Sally reminded her.

"Thank you, Sal. I have grown to care so much about both of them. Teddy is totally different from Mike but I really admire his many qualities."

"Yes, of course, they are different, but both Peter and I felt the same thing about him. To us, he seems very much like Mike."

"I suppose because Mike was super-confident whereas Teddy is more reserved, they create such a different impression."

"Agreed," said Sally.

"He is very sensitive and loving and his devotion to Guy is an inspiration. He has the courage of a lion although, occasionally, he tends to underestimate that....as well as some of his other qualities," Dana said.

"Perhaps so, but you complement each other perfectly, much as it was with you and Mike."

"Funny, but I never thought about that until you mentioned it, Sal. You are so right. He is the best thing that has happened to me since Mike died and that young son of his has been the catalyst for us both to open our hearts. I am so grateful that I met them."

"So are we, Dan." They embraced.

"Now, we just have to make sure Guy gets his concert for Wee Bobby and then everything will be perfect," Dana said.

"By the way, Peter mentioned that he wants to help with the concert, but he does not want to say anything more, yet."

"How lovely," said Dana, "he always has such bright ideas."

"He will tell us what he has in mind when he is ready. And you know Peter. He thinks of things no one else does. Some of them come to nothing but those that do are pearls. He is really excited about this but he wants to keep it to himself for the time being."

"I won't say a word, Sal. Thank you for a lovely day. I know both Teddy and Guy really enjoyed it, too."

On the way home, Guy dozed off in the car. Teddy and Dana sat quietly, wrapped up in their own thoughts. Mike was pleased at the day's events. He had discovered how to communicate through Teddy.

Mona, too, was pleased. She felt it had not been as easy for her to pry open Dana's heart as it had been for Mike to do with Teddy's. Mike, naturally, felt the opposite.

# Chapter 41

Mr Horne rang Dana to report on his progress with the project.

"I have received replies from the heads of the music departments at most of the other schools."

"How exciting!" said Dana. "And...?" She waited with bated breath.

"It appears that there are approximately thirty pupils, who, in the opinion of the particular masters, are of a suitable calibre to perform in an orchestra of the sort that we have in mind. Unfortunately, this is an insufficient number, especially in the string section. Unless we find a way to bolster the orchestra with other players in order to achieve an adequate standard for the satisfactory delivery of any classical piece of music, it is not going to be possible to put on the concert, I am afraid," explained an obviously disappointed Mr Horne, somewhat bumptiously.

Her face fell. "We can't just give up, now that we are so close," she cried.

"We have given the problem endless consideration and checked every possible avenue but unfortunately, we have not managed to unearth any more children to make up for the lack of numbers for a full orchestra. I am at my wits end and have no idea how to proceed further."

"Are there no children, who are almost ready and with intensive rehearsals might make the grade?" she asked.

Mr Horne sighed. "I am truly sorry. Although the basis already exists for the formation of a viable youth orchestra, the obstacle is the urgency because of Bobby's condition. There is just not enough time to bring additional children up to scratch."

"I understand that this is a major hurdle. However, we cannot disappoint Guy...or Bobby," she replied.

"My colleagues and I are very enthusiastic at the prospects for the future, so we intend developing the project. It opens up countless new horizons for music at schools throughout the country. But for now, we have no idea what to do."

"You know Guy. He will never take no for an answer. There has to be a way," Dana insisted.

"It is only because of Guy that the project ever came to light in the first place," replied Mr Horne. "Whatever happens, Guy deserves all the credit."

"Guy is not interested in any acknowledgement for himself. All he cares about is that Bobby gets his concert."

"We admire his persistence but unless a solution can be found for the current dearth of capable musicians, it will be impossible to organise the concert. I will wait a few more days, before informing the other masters that the idea has to be been shelved for the time being. Hopefully, something will come up although I must admit the prospects do not look too good."

Dana reported a summary of her conversation with Mr Horne to Teddy. He never had the heart to be the bearer of such bad tidings to Guy.

"We cannot abandon the idea or just give up. It will break Guy's heart. We have to find a solution. There must be a way."

"I agree but what else can we do?" she asked, her forehead furrowed in concentration.

"Maybe they can find some recently matriculated ex-pupils who play musical instruments," Teddy proposed.

"The problem is the urgency because of Wee Bobby's condition," Dana said. "That is exactly what Mr Horne mentioned. We are trapped by the time complication."

"You are right. Dani. If so, it looks like we are at a dead-end."

"It can't be, Teddy. There has to be a way."

They were desperate, willing to clasp at any straw that might prove helpful, but nothing came to mind. She was so preoccupied with the seemingly insurmountable obstacle facing them regarding to the proposed concert that she missed Teddy's use of Mike's appellation for her.

Suddenly, she remembered Sally confiding in her about Peter's potential involvement. She decided to speak to her.

"I just pray he comes up with one of his brainwaves," she said to Teddy with a tinge of vain-hope.

She dialled Sally's cell phone but was diverted to her voicemail. She left a brief message explaining the bare bones of the outcome of Mr Horne's enquiries and requested Sally call her as soon as possible. They were reluctant to give the bad news to Guy.

Meanwhile, at Guy's behest, Teddy had ascertained that Wee Bobby was still in the hospital. He was anxious to visit his friend and prevailed upon Teddy to drive him there, so he could see him. Dana offered to join them.

"I know you are uncomfortable when you are left alone with Wee Bobby's parents. While Guy spends time with Bobby, I can relieve the pressure on you," Dana offered.

"At least, it will also be an opportunity for us to see each other again. Admittedly, not exactly the most ideal circumstances but it is better than nothing," Teddy said. "You know how I dread conversations like that, talking to Gary and Sandra Weaver on my own. I never know what to say."

"Well, I do, Mr Goodson. Together we make a good combination. We have proven it over and over," said Dana.

"Yes, we are a good combination, Dani. You manage to bring out the best in me. You are the only person besides Mona who could do that. You understand me and I am so grateful."

"My pleasure, Teddy bear," said Dana, to his amazement.


In the lobby of the hospital, Guy was the first to receive a hug from Dana and, as usual, he responded by showering her with kisses.

She turned to Teddy, coming close to him, again pressing her body firmly against him. Her fingers stroked the back of his neck and she lingered in his arms. When they stepped back, a soft smile played on her lips. Teddy's eyes shone with a light, which had been missing for a long time. His body tingled. Dana was also breathing deeply.

They each took one of Guy's hands and, without exchanging a word, floated along the corridors to Bobby's ward, those same corridors, which, until recently, had symbolised for them the nightmare of Guy's illness.

When they reached the Children's Oncology Department, Gary and Sandra Weaver were sitting on a bench opposite Wee Bobby's room. Teddy led Dana and Guy up to them and greeted them. They looked up without answering. Gary was sobbing while Sandra was trying to console him, without any appreciable success. "What is the matter?" asked Dana, softly.

"It is Bobby," Sandra replied, also with a tear-streaked face. "He has gone into a coma and the doctors have told us that there is nothing further they can do, other than to alleviate any pain. They recommend discontinuing further treatment and they have warned us to prepare for the worst."

"They requested our written consent and we were discussing it when you arrived. We don't know what to do," said Gary, his voice choked with emotion. "I do not want him to suffer any further. I say we should respect the doctor's opinion and sign the release."

"And I want him to have the benefit of even the slightest chance of survival and pray that the Lord will still intervene and in His mercy heal Bobby," Sandra said.

"It is like signing Bobby's death warrant. He has had to bear too much already. Enough is enough," said Gary.

Guy began shaking and Dana took him into her arms.

"It is not fair," he cried. "Bobby deserves to live. Why can't they help him? They helped me. And what about the music?" he wailed. "He has not heard it, yet. We need to talk to Mr Horne. We have to go, now," he beseeched them. "Please, let's go and see Mr Horne."

"Just a moment, Guychick, let's finish talking to Bobby's parents."

"Have the medical people provided you with any specific prognosis?" Teddy asked.

"They say it could be days or weeks, perhaps. They are not sure. But they do not think it will take very long, no matter what they do," said Gary, swallowing the words.

They spent a few minutes more with Gary and Sandra before they left. Guy kept insisting they speak to Mr Horne. Eventually, Teddy consented and Dana rang Mr Horne, who agreed to meet them in his music-room at school.

The moment they arrived, although he was in the middle of a choir lesson, he excused the pupils, immediately. Teddy explained the extreme urgency due to Wee Bobby's dire condition.

"I know you told us that there were only about thirty children who were good enough and the trouble is there is no time to find more children."

"That's right. Mr Goodson. I have been racking my brains to think of other ways to overcome the problem but up to now, nothing positive to report, I am afraid."

"We must have the concert at the hospital, anyway because Wee Bobby cannot be moved. I am sure there are also other children in the same predicament, who would like to hear the music. Do you think it is possible for a small orchestra to come to the hospital and play there? Then, Wee Bobby will be able to hear the music even if he is unconscious…sleeping," he corrected.

Mr Horne rubbed his bearded chin, considering the idea.

Finally, he said, "I looked at the list. It seems there are enough children who can play the different instruments, so we could put on a very limited version. Fortunately, I think we may have discovered some more young musicians, all ex-pupils, so we almost have the full string section and the tympani. We are still a bit thin in the woodwind and brass departments, yet we could scrape by, only by the skin of our teeth, I must add."

"Why, that is an amazing achievement, Mr Horne. Funny, Teddy suggested we explore that avenue less than an hour ago," said Dana. "Congratulations, sir."

"Thank you, Dana. Either, I or one of the other masters, could conduct and we could probably manage with three or four rehearsals. All we really need then is to find a narrator and that is probably the most difficult part. The narrator can make or break the performance, naturally, as long as the musicians do not make any glaring mistakes, that is.

Now, it is just the narrator. Hmmm! It is actually very exciting isn't it?" he said, stroking his beard as he tended to do when he was thinking.

Dana turned to Guy. "You could be the narrator, couldn't you? What do you think, Teddy? Don't you agree that our boy would be ideal?"

"What a great idea!" Teddy said with enthusiasm. "He knows the music, perfectly. And as far as the narrator's text is concerned, his reading skills are excellent. He knows it all off by heart, anyway. I do not think there is anyone better equipped to do the job, so, yes, definitely, yes!"

Guy never hesitated. "I will do it for Wee Bobby. I know he would do it for me and I do know it off by heart. The thing is we need to start practicing soon or it might be too late."

"Give me twenty-four hours and I will arrange everything. I will let you know by this time tomorrow and we can start rehearsals, immediately," boomed Mr Horne with excitement.

"We need to talk to the hospital authorities, immediately, to make sure that everything is acceptable to them and that they have a hall big enough to accommodate a thirty-five to forty-piece orchestra with all the instruments and an audience of who knows how many, some of them confined to their beds." Dana, as usual was the responsible adult and had just highlighted a serious obstacle.

"Don't worry. I will take care of that," said Teddy. "Fortunately, or unfortunately, I know the powers that be in the hospital, so I am sure I will be able to organise the logistical requirements. I will go to the hospital tomorrow morning and talk to them."

"Well, that is that, then. We will speak tomorrow and, as they say in the entertainment business, let's get the show on the road," said Mr Horne.

Guy could barely contain his excitement. His friend's condition had never been as serious as it was but he was thrilled and relieved that Wee Bobby might be able to hear Peter and the Wolf, especially now, with him as the narrator.

He did not want to become too confident, yet, since he knew there were still many hurdles to overcome before Bobby would have his concert. At last, though, it seemed there was a reasonable possibility of it taking place.

# Chapter 42

So much had happened in such a short time that Dana found it difficult to fully digest recent events.

Guy's clean bill of health; surprisingly, her willingness to acknowledge and share her feelings for Teddy; being overjoyed at his response and now the possibility of the concert taking place was all too much.

However, Wee Bobby's critical condition dampened her excitement.

She had seen Guy's reaction in the hospital and it had alarmed her. She suspected there had been a degree of guilt in Guy, a syndrome often affecting people, who had undergone extreme trauma and who had come through it, only to see others in a similar plight, who were not quite so fortunate.

The syndrome was prevalent with holocaust survivors from Nazi extermination camps during the Second World War and often, even with their children. Guy witnessing his friend succumbing to and he having been cured of the same disease was a typical example.

She resolved to take some action in that regard as soon as possible and start therapy with Guy to alleviate the syndrome before the situation became more acute, possibly, even irreversible, aggravated by the extremely grim prognosis for Wee Bobby. Although she had not practiced professionally since the accident, she was excited at the possibility of starting, again.

She felt confident enough and psychologically, ready to do so. She smiled to herself when she compared her present attitude to her fragile state, which had persisted until the crisis with Guy's health was brought to her attention. Her reaction to Mike's death those long months ago had seemed a natural response and thus, she had backed out of her commitment. Now, she was raring to go.

Suddenly, Dana's cell-phone rang. She was relieved to see it was Sally as she might have good news regarding Peter's idea. She answered, immediately, as it would also be an opportunity to share with her best friend how she was feeling. Before Dana had a chance to say a word, though, Sally, could barely contain herself. She was delirious with joy.

"Dana, you won't believe it," she screamed with excitement. "Here is Peter. He has the most wonderful news. I will give him the phone, so he can tell you himself."

Peter came on the line. He, too could barely speak because he was laughing uncontrollably.

When he had managed to calm down, sufficiently, he said with difficulty because he was still overwhelmed, "Hello, Dana. No doubt you remember the concert the four of us went to many moons ago when you met Michael?"

"Of course, I do. How could I ever forget it? Why?"

"Because, young lady, coincidently, Miguel Santos is in town to lead the annual series of Christmas concerts at the Arturo Toscanini Auditorium as he does every year. If you recall, he was the conductor of the concert on that famous night."

"Yes, I remember. We were all very impressed with him," she said. "Maybe Sally a bit less than us but even she came round in the end. So...?"

"Well, I happened to see the advertisement for the current series in the local press and I remembered what the self-same Miguel Santos said at the party after that memorable event. Do you, by any chance?"

"Yes, I do, vaguely. We all thought he was very genuine and sincere and..." Suddenly, the penny dropped, and the realisation hit her like a bolt of lightning.

"Peter, you are incredible. What a stroke of genius. I can't believe it" she yelled.

"Why not, you just said I was a genius."

"No, Mr Swollen Head, I said it was a stroke of genius. There is a big difference."

"OK, there is no need to split hairs, woman. Anyway, I called him and spoke to him today and, believe it or not, he remembered us. He is willing to meet to see how he can support us in this venture. I made an arrangement to see him at the concert hall tomorrow morning before rehearsals begin at nine o' clock. I told him we would be there, and I was going to bring three guests, perhaps four, if Mr Horne can accompany us."

"Incredible, Peter. OK, you are a genius. Satisfied?" she said and turned to Teddy and Guy.

"Boys, you are not going to believe this but Peter had the most unbelievable idea. He followed it up and now it looks like a miracle has happened."

"I have never seen you like this before, Dana," Teddy said. "It must be something very special."

"Isn't it lovely to see Dana so happy, Dad?" Guy said.

"Yes, Guychick, thank goodness for her and you. Luckily, you both make me feel happy when I am still a wet blanket, sometimes." Mona grinned at his use of her nickname for their son.

She gave Teddy and Guy a brief summary of what Peter had told her and they all began speaking at once. It took a while for them all to settle down at the sudden turn of events.

"That Pete, he never fails to come up with some idea nobody else could ever have thought of," said Teddy.

Dana looked at him with an expression of surprise. *How strange*, she thought, "He doesn't really know Peter very well and yet he just made a comment about him as though he knew he had this particular characteristic. And he called him, Pete, again, for God's sake."

"We need to talk to Mr Horne. No doubt, he will be over the moon at the prospect of meeting such a famous conductor. If anyone can make this concert happen, it is Miguel Santos," Teddy said.

"Will I still be the narrator?" Guy asked, quietly.

"We will make it one of our conditions when we speak to the maestro," Teddy and Dana agreed.

"Who is going to tell Mr Horne the good news?" asked Teddy.

"I will phone him," Dana said. "He has invested so much time and thought into the project. I have no doubt he will want to meet Miguel Santos. I can't imagine his reaction when he hears the news."

Mr Horne was overjoyed at the fact that Miguel Santos had offered his support and that the much-vaunted concert was going to happen.

"Isn't it exciting? Things seem to be falling into place. It is like an Act of God," he said, almost swooning with joy. "And I will be at the concert hall tomorrow at the appointed time to meet Maestro Miguel Santos with you. It is a great honour. I would never miss such an opportunity, no matter what."

"It is amazing! Together, we have pulled off a miracle," Teddy said, not realising how close to the truth it was.

Unaware of each other's presence, Mike and Mona nodded in unison.

"I will also advise Ms Commins that Guy will be late for school. No doubt, she will approve. It appears that someone up there likes us," M. Horne quoted dramatically, pointing skywards.

The security guard at the entrance to the concert hall found their names on his roster and admitted them without further delay.

Accompanied by Peter, who had been waiting for them in the foyer, they were ushered into the empty auditorium, where the orchestra was tuning up for the rehearsal.

As the conductor entered, the members of the orchestra stood and applauded. He bowed and was about to commence the rehearsal, when he noticed the small party, which had come to the front of the hall. He greeted them and invited them to come up onto the stage.

"It is my pleasure to meet you all," said the Maestro after Peter had introduced them one by one. When he reached Guy, Miguel Santos shook his hand.

"Hello, Guy. I understand that you are the inspiration for the idea of the concert for your friend. It is very rare for a child as young as you to love classical music and then pass on that gift to another young person. You must be a very special boy."

Guy saw that the entire orchestra was watching them and listening to their conversation. He blushed.

"When I was small, my dad took me to a concert for children. That is when I heard classical music for the first time. I liked it very much. Now, the more I hear, the more I love it. You played Peter and the Wolf at that concert and that is why I want Bobby to be able to hear it before he..." He never finished the sentence. He was close to tears and the Maestro was clearly moved.

"And that famous concert was an unforgettable event," said Teddy.

"So you must have been present at that concert when we played Peter and the Wolf. Were you one of the children who conducted the orchestra together with me at the concert?" Miguel Santos asked, incredulously.

"Guy was actually the child who started the whole thing," said Teddy, proudly. "He was so thrilled that I could not keep him in his seat. He jumped up and began imitating you. It never took long to ignite the chain reaction you saw when you turned to face the audience."

"Unbelievable! I can't believe it and now, after all this time, to meet the instigator of that event! It is incredible..." he chortled.

The small group of visitors beamed at Miguel, who was obviously overwhelmed.

"It was one of the most moving moments of my entire career," said Miguel. "I am so pleased we are going to be doing something together again, young fellow."

"I was lucky my father took me to the concert when I was small. Dr Barnett gave me a compact-disc player and some discs when I was in hospital. It helped me when I was feeling bad. I think Bobby and other children will also feel better when they hear Peter and the Wolf."

"I wish there were more children like you," the conductor said. "You deserve to have your concert, Guy and you will. I will make sure of that."

The conductor turned to the orchestra members who had been listening to their conversation.

"Ladies and gentlemen, friends, many of you played in the orchestra on the night of that concert not that long ago. I am sure you remember when the children conducted 'The Nutcracker Suite' for us. I have never forgotten it and probably, nor have you." Many of the musicians smiled and nodded and applauded.

"At last, I am honoured to meet the person who led the phenomenon. And today, I am humbled by the stature of this outstanding young human being. We are going to enjoy playing with him at his concert. I am certain you all agree with me."

The orchestra members began to clap and stamp their feet until one of the trumpets started playing 'For he's a jolly good fellow' and the rest of the orchestra joined in, either playing their instruments or singing.

Teddy, Dana and Mr Horne also sang, lustily, while Miguel Santos conducted, deliberately, in his most outrageously, melodramatic style. Guy beamed with pleasure, although he was beetroot-red with embarrassment.

"We are due to start rehearsing in five minutes. You are welcome to stay and listen to the rehearsal and then afterwards, we can talk. Tell me what you need and leave it to me to make sure you get everything you want. A person with your passion cannot be denied," Miguel said to Guy.

"Can we stay, Daddy?"

"Of course, we can. We wouldn't miss this for the world, would we, folks?" Teddy and Mike exclaimed, together.

"Alright then, take your seats in the auditorium and enjoy the rehearsal. Afterwards we will get down to business."

They spent the following two hours, entranced, listening to the maestro at work, as he put the orchestra through its paces. Guy was fascinated more than anybody.

After the rehearsal, the conductor invited them to his dressing room and they sat talking, while refreshments were served. Mr Horne described their predicament due to the dearth of proficient, young musicians. Miguel listened attentively until Mr Horne was finished.

"I am willing to do anything you like. We can have the limited concert you envisage, and I would be honoured to serve in any capacity you wish. We could supplement your smaller orchestra with some of our members and perform in the hospital."

They all started speaking at the same time and clapping hands, excitedly.

"Or…" he said, tantalisingly slowly, looking from one to the other. "I am sure I can persuade the owners of this concert hall and the members of the orchestra to provide a programme for the children, free of charge.

As you know, there are several thousand seats in the auditorium and we could sell them to the general public as a premier charity-event. The proceeds can be donated to any fund of your choosing. I imagine that musically, we could be ready in about ten days.

That is a short time to make the other preparations and sell all the tickets but when the media get wind of the idea, I believe they will promote it extensively and the public will snap them up."

Again, they all started speaking at once.

"I think I am more excited than you are," said Miguel Santos and laughed. "All that is left, then, is to choose a suitable programme and find a narrator for Peter and the Wolf." They could hardly believe what was happening.

"From the short time I have known him, I believe there is someone who would ideally fit the bill as narrator," said Miguel Santos. Guy's face fell, which Dana noticed but before she had a chance to say anything, Miguel Santos turned to Guy.

"Young fellow, I have never been as inspired by anyone as you have inspired me. Your love for your friend is an example to us all. I would be honoured if you would agree to be the narrator. We can call the concert, The Guy Goodson Charity Concert."

"No" said Guy. "It has to be the Bobby Weaver Charity Concert."

The maestro grabbed Guy in a bear hug while Teddy took Dana's hand and a broad smile lit up Peter's face. Mr Horne watched the unfolding drama in sheer disbelief.

They were unanimous that the concert be held in the Arturo Toscanini concert hall with the full orchestra under the baton of the Maestro and with Guy Goodson as the narrator.

Afterwards, in the parking area, they huddled together, congratulating one another. They discussed tactics and formulated a plan of action. It was decided who would do what and by when to ensure that the momentum be maintained.

"I think Mr Santos is very kind but I think we should include the children good enough to play in the orchestra, too," said Guy.

"I agree," said Peter. "I will ask Miguel Santos if it is possible. There are some obvious complications, but I will talk to him."

"Don't you think that for the sake of the children, it would be best to hold the concert on a Saturday or Sunday, during the day, rather than in the evening?" asked Dana.

They agreed to have all the relevant information within twenty-four hours so that their recommendations could be offered to their new ally, 'Miguel', as he had become familiarly known since their meeting.

Finally, Guy introduced an important rider. "We can only do it this way if Bobby is able to come to the concert. Otherwise, it has to be at the hospital."

Teddy shook Peter's hand warmly and embraced him before they parted. "I just want to say thank you for all you have done to make this happen." he said. "Had you not remembered Miguel and his comment, when we were at the concert all those years ago, nothing like this could ever have transpired."

"I was surprised when I saw the advertisements for the concerts in the daily press a few days ago." said Peter. "It was pure chance. I seldom read advertisements in the paper. It was almost a miracle. Thank you anyway. I appreciate your comments."

"Well," Teddy said, with a knowing smile, "that's what friends are for."

As he drove away, Peter had the same uncanny feeling he had experienced often in the few weeks since meeting Teddy. When he thought about it, he could have sworn Teddy had said, "When WE were at the concert."

The last pieces of the puzzle had fallen into place. Fate was working its magic.

# Chapter 43

The events of the following two weeks were a blur with the multitude of tasks assigned to each person. In the end, the concert hall was provided free of charge, as were the services of the orchestra. Miguel Santos took care of that. Sick children would be driven by private transport, if their condition permitted or by ambulances, which would ferry them from and back to the different hospitals.

Although Wee Bobby was still in a coma, the doctors agreed that, with proper medical supervision, he could be present. Indeed, Bobby was the guest of honour. Without him, there was no point in having any concert.

Approximately two thousand five hundred people were expected to attend the concert, mostly from the public. At Guy's suggestion, a block of several hundred seats was set aside for school children.

As Miguel Santos had expected, radio, television and the press adopted the project as a moving, personal interest story, especially during the festive season of goodwill.

Guy's surname, Goodson, was very apt and the media had a field day with it. Their coverage ensured the overwhelming financial success of the concert as all the available tickets were eagerly snapped up. Naturally, Guy and Miguel Santos were the focal point of interviews in the pre-event publicity.

Guy attended five rehearsals with the orchestra. Miguel Santos nurtured him and made certain that he would be ready for the big moment. The musicians too, adopted him as one of their own. They were inspired by the child who, despite fame and attention, continued to be the same modest and compassionate young boy. All that really mattered to him was that Wee Bobby would have his concert.

His friend's condition had not improved and he was gradually sinking deeper into his coma. Gary and Sandra prayed together but they had given up hope and were girding themselves for the end. They included in their prayers a plea that at least Bobby live to hear his concert.

Dana and Teddy found themselves thrown together more than ever and quite the contrary to how they had been previously, they were not embarrassed to openly exhibit their love for one another.

They walked everywhere, hand in hand. At the dress rehearsal the night before the concert, they sat close to one another, Dana resting her head on Teddy's shoulder, his arm around her shoulders as he beamed with pride and happiness.

Mona and Teddy, too, were happy. They had accomplished their mission.

Finally, everything was ready.

The musicians were seated at their places, practicing solo snatches of music they would be playing or simply tuning their instruments.

Just a few minutes remained before 'curtain' and they were all gathered in the dressing room. Guy was the one least affected by 'opening-night' nerves.

He kept peeking through the curtains, searching for Bobby in the audience as he watched the people filing into the hall. He was worried because the ambulance, which was to deliver Bobby, had not yet arrived. He would not relax until he knew his friend was present.

The ten-minute curtain call was announced just as an usher brought them news of Bobby's arrival. "He is still unconscious but the medical team asked me to inform you that he is comfortable."

Guy immediately went to Miguel Santos. "Bobby is here. I must go and see him before we start. Is it alright?"

"This is your big day, Guy," Miguel said. "You do as you think fit. I am sure Bobby will appreciate that his friend knows he is here and cares about him."

Miguel patted him on the back and steered him in the direction of the stairs leading from the stage into the hall.

Accompanied by Dana and Teddy, he made his way down the stairs until he reached the auditorium, which was buzzing with the sound of the audience chatting, prior to the commencement of the performance.

As he entered the hall, people saw him and began applauding. He paid no attention and made a beeline for the stretcher on which Bobby was lying at the front of the hall.

Row by row, people stood and began applauding. Teddy explained to him why the people were cheering but he ignored the ovation. He hurried straight up to Bobby and leaned over the unconscious child, who seemed to be sleeping, peacefully.

He was dismayed to see how much his friend's condition had deteriorated since they had last seen each other. Bobby had shrunk in size. The paper-thin flaps of skin covering the features of his face were taut, giving the impression of a skull. His normally copper-coloured skin was almost ebon and although he was unconscious, his eye-sockets looked like two pieces of black charcoal, sunken deep in his shrunken face. Guy stared at his friend with tears stinging his eyes.

Then, he took one of Wee Bobby's hands in his and for several seconds, stood looking down at him.

Suddenly, Guy bent forward and kissed Wee Bobby on the forehead and whispered into his ear. "Enjoy the concert, Bobby. This is especially for you. I promised you."

Heartbroken, he turned to go back to the dressing room, in preparation for his final call. He never noticed the faint smile on Wee Bobby's lips nor did he see that his eyes were open.

One of the orchestra musicians stood and played the note known as A440 on his oboe. This was the note according to which, the rest of the musicians began tuning their instruments. The familiar cacophony was a warning to the audience that the concert was about to start.

When silence descended, Miguel Santos walked up to the podium to wild applause. The orchestra members tapped their music stands, acknowledging the youthful conductor. He bowed to the standing audience, which continued applauding.

When the crowd had settled down Miguel Santos turned to the musicians and raised his baton, in preparation for the first item on the programme, the lively Overture to the Thieving Magpie by Rossini.

His method of conducting was even more flamboyant than before, and the audience was entertained, not only by the music, but also by his dramatic style on the podium. At the end of the overture, the audience applauded, wildly.

The second item was the popular and melodic Nutcracker Suite by Tchaikovsky, which had been included for the sake of the children in the audience, who might not yet have acquired a more sophisticated appreciation of classical music.

For Miguel, it had a special meaning too, as he reflected on that never-to-be-forgotten concert, which had been the inspiration for the young visionary of this event to fall in love with classical music. The audience swayed in time to the familiar music and clapped, loudly as the last notes faded away and the musicians lowered their instruments.

Dana turned to Teddy. "That was lovely, wasn't it? You remember I told you that I met Mike at a concert? I can't tell you how right it is for us to be together, today. To be at a concert with people you love is really something special."

"It is special for Guy and me as well, Dana," Teddy replied.

"That is what I meant, Teddy. I love you both very much." He looked at her, baffled but Mona had spoken.

Miguel Santos left the podium for a brief interval. The rafters rang with the thunderous applause of the crowd. There was excited anticipation as the audience waited for the highlight of the concert, Peter and the Wolf.

The orchestra members resumed their places and prepared for the final item on the programme. There was a hum from the audience when thirty-five children entered the hall from the wings and took their places amongst the orchestra members.

When everybody was settled, Mr Horne appeared on the stage and walked up to a microphone, which had been set up. He coughed and silence descended in the hall.

"Ladies and gentlemen, it is my honour and it gives me great pleasure to welcome you, a little belatedly, to this very special event, the Bobby Weaver Charity Concert, so named at the insistence of young Guy Goodson.

No doubt, you are familiar with his name by now. He is about to participate in a musical endeavour, the likes of which, I dare say, has never been witnessed before. I am proud to tell you that I am his music master, but instead of my teaching him, he has taught me one of the greatest lessons it will ever be my privilege to learn.

I, and many others, have observed his determination, commitment and love during the past few months and today are witness to the proof of what those qualities can achieve by turning the impossible into reality.

Guy, at a very early age developed a deep love of classical music. He promised his friend, Bobby, who he met during his treatment for a near fatal disease, that he would take him to a live, classical concert to hear Prokofiev's Peter and the Wolf, which was the catalyst for Guy's own initiation into the magical world of classical music.

He has been an example to us all.

Fortunately, Maestro, Miguel Santos was also inspired by Guy and he has been instrumental in bringing this event to fruition. We deeply appreciate, and we are indebted to this wonderful man and musical genius.

You must have noticed a group of young musicians, invited by Maestro Santos to join the orchestra for an out of the ordinary rendition of Peter and the Wolf. We welcome them and compliment them on their hard work in preparing themselves for this special occasion.

However, without question, the man of the moment is young Guy Goodson. This concert is a tribute to his personal vision. I ask you, therefore, to join me in welcoming to the platform, both these outstanding people, Maestro Miguel Santos and Guy Goodson, the youngest narrator in the history of classical music."

Miguel Santos and Guy came from the wings, hand in hand as the audience and orchestra, to a man, rose to their feet. There was an explosion of sound. The audience began applauding, clapping, whistling, yelling, even stamping their feet, behaviour, totally out of character at a classical concert. But this was no regular concert. The cheering continued, unabated for at least five minutes, growing in volume all the time.

Only after Miguel had signalled many times for an end to the acclaim, did the audience pay any attention to his request and start to calm down.

People settled in their seats, the theatre lights were dimmed, and Miguel Santos took up his position on the conductor's podium. The diminutive figure of Guy climbed onto the small stand, alongside, which had been especially prepared for him.

Miguel raised his baton and Guy glanced for the first and only time at the script, which rested on a lectern in front of him. He was about to narrate a story of courage and loyalty, of the triumph of good over evil and of the fact that strength was not based on size or power, but on love and commitment.

It was the story of Guy's personal struggle, his indomitable bravery and his unflinching will to make sure he kept his word to his friend. There was nobody more fitting to narrate the story.

That day, the audience experienced an unforgettable rendition of Peter and the Wolf. Miguel Santos and Guy were connected by an almost spiritual bond.

Miguel conducted the orchestra with a passion that emanated from his soul and Guy, uplifted by the miracle of his achievement, narrated the adventure with no signs of stress. He drew on the memory and creativity of his mother, by using different voices and accents for each of the characters in the tale, just as she had once done. Now, swelling with pride, she witnessed the rapturous reaction of the audience to her precious son.

They listened, enthralled. The music and the story wove an entrancing web around them. The fairy tale atmosphere was intoxicating even for those who were familiar with the fate of the various characters in the tale, represented by the different musical instruments, until they reached the happy ending.

The hunters arrived in time, the wolf was captured, the duck was saved, alive, albeit inside the wolf and brave Peter, his grandfather and their animal friends marched out of the woods, accompanied by the brave hunters and lived happily ever after.

Before the last notes faded, the audience erupted and began applauding and cheering till their hands hurt and their voices were hoarse.

The orchestra members also got to their feet to acknowledge Guy and the conductor.

After a while, Miguel Santos moved aside, leaving the boy, the true hero of the day in centre-stage, alone, accepting the rapturous applause of the delirious crowd. Miguel Santos too, joined in and smiled at the young boy's success.

Guy was beaming with pleasure. Not only was he basking in satisfaction at his personal achievement and at the success of the project but he had kept his promise to his friend. That was his overriding consideration and he was in heaven knowing that Bobby had been present at the concert and heard a live rendition of Peter and the Wolf.

Suddenly, he noticed that Wee Bobby's eyes were open. Without a moment's hesitation, he bounded down the steps leading into the auditorium. He ran up to him and threw his arms around his friend's frail body, tears of joy flowing down his cheeks. When he drew back, though, he saw that Bobby's eyes had closed again.

Guy's body shook with grief but Dana had reached him. She took him in her arms and spoke to him, as only she knew how, gently soothing him. Teddy came up to them and, protectively, put his arms around both while the audience looked on, stunned. The medical staff wheeled Bobby out to the waiting ambulance, accompanied by a heartbroken Gary and Sandra Weaver.

Meanwhile, the audience again began its applause, which continued to grow in volume, uninterrupted for three or four minutes. Miguel Santos beckoned to Guy to return to the stage as the concert was not yet over.

"The audience is demanding an encore and I think they deserve one, don't you?"

"Yes," said Guy, "but what are you going to play?"

"I have an idea," Miguel said.

A choir of approximately sixty men, women and children walked on to the stage and ranged themselves in rows on low platforms, behind the orchestra.

"Guy, you get onto the conductor's podium," Miguel said. The young boy did so, hesitantly, looking questioningly at the Maestro.

Miguel handed him his baton and then he took up his position on Guy's low stand. With a broad grin, he announced to the audience that Guy was going to conduct the final piece of music, the Hallelujah Chorus from Handel's Oratorio, the Messiah.

When Guy had recovered from his surprise, he flourished his baton, melodramatically, as he had so often seen Miguel Santos do. At his signal, the famous music began, Miguel Santos and Guy conducting the orchestra together, the way they had done once before with Miguel again, facing the audience throughout.

As is the custom, during the piece of music, the entire audience stood in homage. The atmosphere was reminiscent of the famous Promenade Concerts in London.

At the same time, dozens of children and teachers from Guy's school, including Ms Commins, Nurse Dunfort and Edna entered from the rear of the auditorium and began moving down the aisles carrying baskets of small candles, which they distributed by passing them on along the rows.

They then lit the candles of those sitting on the aisle seats at the ends of the rows. They, in turn, lit the candles of the people alongside them and the process continued until all the candles in the auditorium were burning.

As the music ended, Maestro Santos smiled and indicated to Guy to turn and face the audience. To his amazement, he saw over two thousand people, each, silently, holding a lighted candle. Guy stood stock still, watching the flickering flames.

There was not a sound. The lights in the auditorium had all been extinguished but the flickering candles cast a magical aura, throwing shimmering silhouettes and shadows onto the walls and ceiling of the concert hall, an acknowledgement to a hero. Guy stood staring at the awesome scene in wonder, tears of joy trickling down his cheeks.

After a minute, the lights were switched back on and people blew out their candles.

"Guy, would you like to say something to all these people? I think they want to hear from you," Miguel said.

He handed a microphone to Guy, who took a deep breath and, after a slight hesitation, spoke in a quiet voice.

"Thank you for coming to the concert. It was very important for Bobby. I don't know how much he heard but at least, now, his parents know how many people care about them. I hope Bobby is happy. I also want to tell my father and Dana that I always trusted them, so I could keep my promise. Together, they have made me so happy."

Turning to Miguel Santos, he said, "Thank you for teaching me about classical music and making Bobby's concert happen."

The audience exploded with thunderous applause, once more, roaring and whistling, yelling their approval and love for the modest child.

Guy and the Maestro left the stage many times. The audience, however, refused to allow them to leave, continuing the never-ending acclaim. Miguel had to lead Guy back, time after time, for another curtain call.

Eventually, Miguel whispered to Guy. "Go to the front of the stage, Guy. The people want you. They will not stop until you do." Guy hesitated but a gentle nudge by Miguel Santos sent him on his way. The small boy wended his way through the phalanx of standing musicians until he reached the front of the stage, where he stood, smiling, shyly.

After a few minutes of continuous applause, Miguel beckoned to Dana and Teddy to join them on the platform, which they reluctantly did after some coaxing by Peter and Sally, who also encouraged Mr Horne to go up onto the stage.

They bowed to the thousands of people, who were acknowledging them for an incredible experience. Bouquets of flowers were presented to Guy and Miguel Santos by two children, who were undergoing treatment for leukaemia.

At last, the ecstatic audience began filing out of the auditorium, each receiving a flower at the exit.

Miguel Santos invited them to a celebration he had organised with the orchestra members in the staff cafeteria. At the party, Teddy and Dana held hands like star-struck teenagers. Guy was overjoyed to see the two people he loved most in the world, together. He was besieged by well-wishers, showering him with praise which he accepted, modestly.

Miguel Santos wanted to say a few words and took a microphone. He blew into it once or twice until there was quiet.

"Friends, I am not going to make a long speech but I do want to say a few words. I wanted Guy to have a memento of his incredible achievement and I requested a video-recording of the entire evening from the television-station, which broadcast the concert, live. I was just handed the internet link and I want to give it to Guy with our thanks and appreciation.

Now, he will always be able to relive his moment of triumph. On a more personal note, I would also like to present him with my personal baton, the same baton with which he conducted an orchestra, officially, today, for the first time. May he stand on the conductor's podium with it, himself, as a maestro one day in the future and use it to bring pleasure to thousands of people who come to hear him conduct the music he loves so much."

An hour later, when all the festivities were done, it was time to go home. They thanked everybody and took their leave of Miguel Santos and the orchestra members, who cheered Guy until he left the cafeteria.

Standing next to the car, Guy turned to Dana. "Could you come and live with us now if Daddy asks you to?"

"He has not asked me, yet," she said. "You might want to live in my house, instead."

"Then, have you asked Daddy?"

"Again, not yet, but now that the concert is behind us and you are well again, we will talk about it. Right, Teddy?"

"I agree, Dani, the sooner, the better."

"Dana, I already have many friends but after my mother died, I never had a mother like other children until you came along. I am so happy you did. I can see you are too, Dad. I hope from now on, you will be with us all the time, Dana."

She looked at Teddy. "We will have to see if we can do something about that too, won't we."

He grinned at her, embarrassed. Suddenly, he cupped her face in his hands and kissed her on the eyes, the tip of her nose and lips and whispered, "One for you, one for me and one for us."

Dana looked startled for a second but recovered quickly and kissed Teddy back, as Guy watched with embarrassment, amusement and happiness.

Peter and Sally also came to say their farewells before leaving.

"It looks to me like I can finally stop worrying about you," Sally said, with a warning glance at Teddy, who smiled, innocently.

Teddy threw his arms around Peter. "Thank you for introducing Dana to

Mike all those years ago and for looking after her till now. You have been a true friend, Peter. And don't say, 'That's what friends are for.'" Peter stared at him, eyebrows raised in shock. It was also the first time Teddy had called him Peter.

Peter embraced Dana, warmly. "I don't know about you but I have had the strangest sensation that today, Mike was watching everything that happened and he gave us his blessing."

"You may be right, Peter," she said. "So have I."

On the way home, Teddy's cell-phone rang. The caller was Gary Weaver. Teddy decided not to accept the call as he had an uneasy premonition. It was Guy's day of triumph and nothing was going to ruin it. Whatever the news, it would keep until morning.

# Epilogue

## Eternity

There was no reason to delay any further. It was time to leave. Once again, he felt the vortex sucking him in, ever deeper. His celestial messenger was waiting for him.

"Welcome home. It is good to be back, is it not?"

"Yes, I am pleased to be here."

"Gabriel advised me that The Eternal One is satisfied with us. We have done well. We no longer need to be concerned about their lives."

True, the worry he had felt had disappeared. He knew he was home.

"WE have done well?" he questioned.

"Absolutely, both of us. Your work here, though, is just beginning. The Source has decided that you are ready. You have been summoned. Come."

He followed the light, floating through the ether. Suddenly, as before, he was dazzled by the brilliance of Gabriel's aura.

"Greetings, you have both proved yourself. You have succeeded in showing that your love for Dana and Teddy is true and enduring. Their happiness was all important, above yours, and you were willing to let them go. Now, Teddy, you are to be assigned your new role."

He said nothing nor did he ask any questions. It was not that he knew what he was supposed to do. He did not even know if he would be able to do it. Rather, he had reached the stage where he trusted himself and the Source, implicitly.

"Thank you. I am honoured," he said, simply.

Gabriel nodded and vanished as suddenly as it had appeared.

His celestial messenger again beckoned him to follow.

The light guiding him wafted effortlessly through the emptiness, gradually growing dimmer, until it too, disappeared. He saw a small boy of African descent sitting all alone.

"Hello, Bobby. Welcome to forever. I am your celestial messenger."

*"Hello. What do you mean? What is a celestial messenger?"*

"It is a sort of Guardian Angel."

*"Oh! Are you going to look after me, then?"*

"No, I am not. You are quite safe, here. You do not need looking after. There is no need to worry about anything."

*"I am not worried. I am pleased to be here. I knew I was coming home, so I was ready. Anyway, I wanted to be an angel like Jemima. Will I be able to see her?"*

"She is already here, looking forward to being with you again. She knows how much you miss her."

*"Great! I can't wait to see her. There is classical music here too, isn't there? I loved Peter and the Wolf. I want Jemima to hear it. Now, I want to hear The Messiah. I missed it."*

"Everything is present, all the time. All you need to do is to look and listen. You just have to remember how to do that."

*"I was not with them long enough to forget. Children know that their way, the old way, is not the best way. I have not forgotten the right way."*

The new celestial messenger 'nodded' and disappeared. Clearly, his presence was not necessary. And anyway, the newcomer appeared not to know him. The boy had not even asked his name.

## FOREVER

Ingram Content Group UK Ltd.
Milton Keynes UK
UKHW020114300523
422450UK00005B/51